PROMISED

THE EQUINOX PACT BOOK 2: A YOUNG ADULT PARANORMAL ROMANCE

LEIGH WALKER

YOU AGAIN

"DAD, I told you—I'll be back as soon as I can." I paced the front porch, the sun warming my bare feet. "Eden's doing better, but she still needs more time."

Eden was my best friend. My dad, Big Kyle, thought she was upset because her boyfriend, Brian, had died recently. The situation was more complicated than that. Actually, it was a *lot* more complicated: Brian was dead because my stepmother, Becky, had shoved him down an abandoned well.

That same night, James had turned Eden into a vampire.

But my dad didn't know any of that. He didn't even know that vampires existed...

"Taylor honey, I understand she's been through a lot. It's terrible what happened with Brian. But you have to come home. You're supposed to start classes next week." Big Kyle sounded frustrated. "You can't skip your senior year of high school. No matter what's going on."

He wasn't just talking about Eden, and I knew it. "I have to go. I'll call you tomorrow, okay?" Before he could argue, or worse—before he could mention James —I hung up.

James Champlain was my boyfriend. At least he *had* been. Back before all this happened, back before he'd turned Eden into a vampire and banished us to one of his estates while she healed...

I stared at my phone. No text messages, no missed calls, no nothing. I opened my photos and flicked to the last one I had of me and James, the night of the gala, the lavish fundraiser he'd hosted at his home. James looked insanely handsome in his suit, his arm thrown casually over my shoulders. His smile made my heart stop. Then there was me, nestled against him, wearing the blush-pink gown he'd bought me just for the party.

There was something funny about me in the picture —I looked different, and it had nothing to do with the dress. I was smiling in the photo, which was rare but not impossible. I stared at the image, searching, but then I realized what it was: the smile reached all the way to my eyes. That was the difference. I looked genuinely happy.

But now my boyfriend, if that's what he still was,

hardly returned my calls.

"Hey," a familiar voice said.

I stuffed my phone into my pocket as Patrick lumbered out and crouched down next to me, his dark skin glistening in the morning sun. He wore his usual uniform of mesh basketball shorts and a plain white T-shirt. He'd taken his cornrows out and cut his hair shorter, which showcased his high cheekbones and handsome face.

"Eden's all set for now," Patrick said.

Eden became a vampire six weeks ago, and Patrick and I had been taking turns babysitting her. Her transformation had been difficult. It pissed her off that we'd strapped her to her bed—she wanted to hunt. She wanted to drink. She wanted to feast on...*humans*.

"You want to go for a walk, or something?" He squinted out at the yard. "I need to get out of here."

I grabbed my flip-flops, and we trekked across the lawn to the beach path. I always felt small standing next to Patrick; at six-foot-two and two hundred pounds, he had that effect on people.

Two vampire guards waited at the path's entrance, dressed identically in dark suits and sunglasses. All the guards who patrolled the property wore the same uniform.

"Let's get through Vampire Secret Service." Patrick

smiled at them. "Morning. Taylor and I are just going down to the beach. Is that okay?"

The female guard nodded almost imperceptibly.

"T-Thanks," I said, but she didn't respond.

The guards worked for the James's family, the Champlains, who were wealthy vampire aristocracy. At first, I'd been uncomfortable being surrounded by strange vampires, but I'd gotten used to their constant, silent presence. If nothing else, they reminded me of James.

Patrick and I headed down the path, the dunes rising on either side. "So how is she today?" I asked.

"Good. She's drinking a *lot*. She just guzzled another whole pint of blood."

"Is that normal—for her to drink that much?"

Patrick nodded. "My mom said that's common with newbies. They have to build their strength."

"We're lucky your mother can help." Mrs. Cavill, Patrick's mom, was also a vampire.

Patrick shrugged. "Yeah well, there are perks to having an overprotective parent."

"Does Eden remember anything new today?" I asked. In the weeks since her transformation, Eden had been confused. She remembered the accident that ended her human life, but she didn't recall becoming a vampire.

"Not really, but she seems more like herself this morning." Patrick shrugged. "It's going to take some time, you know? We're six weeks in. My mom says she'll get better after this—she's at a turning point."

My heart lifted a little. Poor Eden had been through a lot. "That's good."

We reached Lucy Vincent beach. Even though it was early, lots of families had dragged their belongings down the dunes and arranged their chairs and enormous coolers. Children were already in the water, boogie-boarding, shrieking as the gigantic waves crashed. August was the busiest month on Martha's Vineyard, or so I'd read. I hadn't really paid much attention to the island we'd been hiding out on.

"So…" Patrick peered at me. "How're *you* holding up?"

"I'm fine." I sighed. "But I just talked to my dad, and he wants me to come home."

"Don't classes start next week?" he asked gently.

"Yeah, but it's not as if twelfth grade is as important as my best friend. I can't leave her like this."

We walked down to the water's edge and dipped our feet in. It was so much warmer than home. The water back on Dawnhaven, the island we lived on in Maine, was perpetually freezing, guaranteed to turn your toes numb in under a minute.

"You're not leaving her alone. I already told you, I'll stay with her as long as it takes. I'm taking the semester off." Patrick scratched his neck. "She's getting better every day. And like I said, with my mom and all, I know what I'm doing."

"I appreciate that, I do. But I can't go back to the island and face Mrs. Lambert unless I know Eden's one-hundred percent okay." But would that ever happen? Could a new vampire *be* okay?

Eden was supposed to be a sophomore at Bowdoin College this fall, but she'd asked for a leave of absence. The school had granted the request immediately, but Eden's family was more difficult to navigate. They wanted her home. They wanted to see her. They wanted to know why she was, in Mrs. Lambert's words, "hiding from everyone."

There were excellent reasons, but we couldn't tell them the truth: new vampires had a hard time controlling themselves. We locked Eden up so she wouldn't attack us or try and escape to feed from other humans. We'd kept her hidden at James's private estate on the Vineyard, surrounded by a fleet of vampire guards, and fed her a constant supply of donated blood.

I spoke to Mrs. Lambert regularly. I assured her that Eden was getting better and would come home. I hoped it would be soon; I couldn't wait to get back to the island for my own selfish reasons...

"Taylor? Did you hear me?" Patrick asked.

"Uh, sorry, I spaced out for a second."

"I know. You had that look. What I was saying was, I talked to him last night." Patrick raised his shorts up a fraction and waded out deeper into the water. "He called to check in."

Him. He called to check in. Like everything to do with *him*, the mention of James hit me hard, almost knocking the wind out of me. It took a moment for me to get the question out: "You talked to James?"

Patrick nodded. He looked as though he felt sorry for me.

"What did he say? How is he? Did he sound any better?" Once unleashed, the questions crowded out of my mouth.

"Woah, woah, easy. He sounded fine. Not good, you know, but fine."

I waited while Patrick stared out at the water. Any tidbit of information about James was something I could take back with me, to dissect at my leisure, to hold on to and think about in the lonely hours of my day. "Please tell me what he said—tell me everything." I didn't even try to mask the eagerness in my voice.

He sighed. "James said your dad's been calling him twice a day. Mrs. Lambert even went out to the Tower and brought him some food. She said she's worried about him."

"That was nice." Mrs. Lambert was a skilled cook. She hadn't been happy that James had lent Eden his Vineyard house, abetting her escape. That she'd put her issues aside long enough to bring him food was a good sign.

"Yeah, James said she stayed out there a while, talking about Brian and what happened. She wants Eden to come home." Patrick frowned. "She thinks the longer she stays away, the harder it's going to be."

"So...what did he tell her?" Eden wasn't exactly preoccupied with her ex-boyfriend's death. She barely mentioned it. She was too busy craving human blood every second of the day.

Patrick shrugged. "He said that he hoped she'd be able to come back to the island soon."

"What else?" I licked my lips. "Did he mention anything else?"

"He said Josie and Dylan drove home to the city. They left yesterday."

"Yeah, I know. Dylan's classes start next week." Dylan Khatri and Josie Banks were two of James's closest friends. They'd stayed on Dawnhaven for the summer but were returning to Manhattan so Dylan could finish her engineering degree. "Josie said they didn't want to leave him, but they needed to get back."

"Yeah." Patrick dragged his foot through the water.

"The thing is, I don't think James should be alone."

"Are you... Are you worried about him?"

He shrugged. "I think you should go home to the island, Taylor. He won't ask you to. But I know he misses you."

My mouth went dry. "I don't know if that's true."

Patrick gave me a long look. "Just because he's upset doesn't mean he's upset with *you*."

"Of course he's upset with me." I crossed my arms against my chest. "He's not talking to me. He's not texting, and he's not calling. And when I *do* talk to him, he speaks in one-word grunts. Every time I ask him how he is, he says 'fine.' If I ask him how things are going with the police investigation, he says 'okay.' If I ask him if he's mad at me, he says 'no.' And then he says he has to go."

Patrick looked past me, up the beach path, and raised his eyebrows.

"What?" I asked. "You don't believe me?"

Patrick's eyes got wide. "Um, it's not that..."

"I'm telling you," I said, warming to my topic, "it's been terrible. He won't talk to me—he's *impossible*. Literally impossible. I tell him I'm sorry, I cry, I tell him I miss him, and I get a one-word grunt. He barely calls me, and when he does, he just sits there and mouth-breathes."

My chest heaved as my long-dormant volcano of frustration erupted, words spewing. "I don't know what to do anymore. He hates me. I love him, and he *hates* me. He's never going to forgive me, and I don't blame him, but the least he could do is *talk* to me—"

"Um." Patrick winced. He looked as though he was in pain or might get sick. "Ah…"

"Patrick, *what* is your problem?"

Suddenly—like a mirage appearing—James waded into the water. He got closer, then stopped.

I took a stumble-step back. *I must be dreaming.* Six-foot-two, broad shoulders, steel-gray hair, dark-blue eyes, square chin. Pale skin. Absofreakinglutely gorgeous.

He—*the mirage?*—stared at me.

"What the…?" I gaped at him.

But James, if it was James, said nothing. He just kept staring. *Is he real?* I wondered if I'd finally snapped and was hallucinating his handsome form…

Patrick shifted on his feet, looking between us, obviously uncomfortable. "Oh boy."

I couldn't believe my eyes; I didn't. Tall, pale, and agonizingly attractive, James's muscles rippled in the sun. The dark tattoo on his bicep peeked out from beneath his close-fitting tee. I stared at the outline of his broad chest—I'd been starved for the sight of him.

His gaze burned into mine.

A mirage. A dream. A beautiful, painful hallucination.

"Are you...?" But I couldn't get the words out. *Are you real?*

James didn't smile, but his shoulders dropped, as if maybe he was relieved. "Hey," he said.

"Hey?" My voice was shrill.

I hadn't seen him in six weeks, and it was like someone had wrenched my heart out of my chest and stomped on it daily. I hadn't been able to eat. I hadn't been able to sleep. All I did was pace, berating myself, going over all the wrong I'd done.

He still stared at me, those blue-gray eyes mesmerizing. As if I'd been in the desert for weeks and he was a pool of fresh water, I drank him in, mirage or not. The thick, dark eyelashes I loved, the square chin, the way his hair blew back from his face...

My feelings battled inside me. I wanted to smack him, to kiss him, to cry while he held me, and to simultaneously beat my fists against his chest.

My emotions bubbled over, hot lava. *"Hey?* That's it—that's all you have to say?"

James shrugged a big shoulder. "You're the one who said it: I'm speaking in one-word grunts. So...yeah. Hey."

"Hey yourself," I said, then promptly burst into tears.

2

FACE TO FACE

I TURNED on my heel and ran from them. Tears streaked my view as I tore through the dunes, desperate for the safety of the house.

I flew past the guards, rushing up the stairs to my room. I couldn't believe James was here. I'd wanted, more than anything, to see him, to be near him again. But when he'd appeared like a ghost out of nowhere, all I'd felt was…pissed.

Because pissed was easier than heartbroken. It was easier than afraid, afraid that he didn't feel the same way about me anymore…

"Taylor." James had followed me. He knocked on the door. "Let me in."

I paced, running my hands through my hair. My

insides wrenched as he rapped on the door again. I glanced in the mirror. My eyes were puffy and red.

"You know I can just come in through the window." His voice was hoarse.

His words tugged at me, but I was still angry, raw. "Wait—*wow*. Was that a complete sentence?"

"Ha." Something pressed against the other side of the door, and I sensed it was his forehead.

"Fine," he said, after a minute. "You don't have to let me in if you don't want to. I probably shouldn't have come down here, anyway."

That did it—I couldn't bear the thought of him leaving again. I threw the door open, and James almost toppled inside.

"Well." He recovered himself and shook his head. "This isn't exactly going how I pictured."

I stared at him some more, overwhelmed by pure emotion. I'd been craving this. I couldn't get enough of the sight of him. James stood in a patch of sunlight in my room, so close—it seemed impossible.

That was partly because he'd been so distant, physically and emotionally, and partly because he was so beautiful, he looked as though he might not be real. With his broad shoulders and thickly muscled chest, he took up a lot of space. I drank in his handsome face, the blue-gray eyes, his square jaw. His thick hair was still windblown, pushed up off his face. With the sun outlining him, he appeared every inch an angel, too spectacular for this earth.

"How did you picture it?" I wanted to sound angry, but my voice cracked.

"I don't know. I have no idea. Maybe not tripping over myself, or making you cry in the first five minutes." He raked a hand through his hair. "How are you doing?"

I shook my head, tears threatening again. "Not good."

James winced. "I'm sorry."

"It's not your fault, remember? It's mine." My shame, always lurking, overwhelmed me. "I asked you to do the one thing you *swore* you'd never do again. I'm the one who begged you to turn Eden. You didn't want to—and I knew it—but I asked you to, anyway."

"What happened was my fault." His expression turned sour, a storm cloud gathering. "She was too young to die."

"You *saved* her."

"No, Taylor. I *ended* her." He shook his head, his eyes darkening. "I brought trouble to the island. If I'd stayed away—if I'd left you alone in the first place—none of this would've happened."

"That's not true." I yearned to go to him, to put my arms around him and take his pain away, his guilt. But since I was the source, I didn't know if he would ever want me to touch him again.

I'd asked him to turn Eden, and I was pretty sure he hated me for it. Or he hated himself. Most likely, he hated us both.

He glanced above me. "It's not true, Taylor." His voice was hoarse. "I could never hate you."

My traitorous aura, the swirling color above my head that only James could see, revealed everything to him. "That's not how it feels."

"Please." He took a step toward me, then stopped. "You have to understand—I broke a promise to myself. It's not something I can get over easily." James had vowed to never drink from a human again, a vow he'd kept for over a hundred years.

Until I'd begged him to save Eden by turning her.

"I'm not asking you to get over it," I said quickly. "I'm asking you to stop pushing me away. Or if you're done with me, to let me know. The waiting is killing me." Since we'd been apart, I'd felt a pressure on my chest, as heavy as a boulder, crushing me.

"I'm not done with you." James shook his head. "I couldn't ever be done with you, even if I should be."

Tears pricked my eyes again as I sank onto the bed. "That's not how it feels."

He stood rooted to the floor, clenching and

unclenching his fists. "Do you understand that the reason all of this happened—Brian, Eden, even *Becky*—is me? I'm the reason."

I shook my head. "That's not true. You didn't make Becky what she is."

His lips puckered. "You don't know that."

"I know you were trying to save Brian and Eden from Becky. What happened at the well was her fault, not yours." I wished more than anything that I could forget that terrible night. But those last moments before Brian died were seared into my memory: *Becky went to throw Brian at Eden, but James hit her with a burst of light. It shot Becky forward—Brian flew from her arms directly into Eden's chest, and they tumbled backwards into the well. Eden screamed as they sailed down into the darkness.*

I often heard Eden's screams in my nightmares.

"You see?" James's gaze flicked above my head again. "Your aura isn't trying to protect my feelings. I know it was the most terrible night of your life. And that's because of me—because you were involved with *me*."

"Can you please stop using the past tense?"

He cursed and rocked back on his heels. "You came to the island to be safe with your father, to start a new life. Then you met me, and all the craziness began."

"It's not like Becky needed a lot of encouragement to go off the deep end." The fact was, my stepmother had always hated me. When my mom died, I'd been forced to move in with my dad, Becky, and my half-sister, Amelia. Becky had made it clear that she didn't approve. Then she'd started exhibiting strange symptoms, and she'd completely unraveled the night of the gala...

"You know what happened with Becky wasn't within the realm of 'normal.'" James's voice was low, with an edge to it. "I brought these things to you. *I* brought supernatural danger into your life and into your *house*."

He scrubbed a hand across his face. Immortals didn't need to sleep, but his expression was tight. His shoulders sagged. He seemed exhausted.

"Hey. C'mere." I patted the bed next to me, even though I was petrified that he would say no. That the answer from then on would be no.

When he didn't move, I took a deep breath, gathering my courage. *"Please."*

He finally came and sat on the edge of the bed, closer to me than he'd been for weeks. I tentatively reached out and put my hand over his, and as soon as our skin touched, I sighed. Relief flooded me. Touching him made it seem like something had been returned to me, something I needed to feel whole.

"Taylor." James closed his eyes. "I missed you so much."

"Why don't you sound happy about it?" In fact, he sounded miserable.

He opened his eyes and looked at our hands. "Because I don't want to ruin your life."

Then he turned to me, and I saw it on his face: the devastation.

I gripped his hand. "Please don't do this. Please don't say goodbye to me."

James looked up at the ceiling, as if searching for divine intervention. "I don't want to destroy you."

"You won't. You *saved* me."

He leveled his gaze with mine. An edge of blue tinted the steel-gray of his eyes, which in the bright cheeriness of my room, made him look even more sad. "I don't really think either one of us believes that anymore."

3

WANTS

"*I* DON'T REALLY THINK *either one of us believes that anymore.*"

The dead certainty in his voice undid me.

"*Please.* You haven't ruined it—you *made* my life." I didn't want to sound desperate, but I was crap at hiding my actual feelings. Hysteria bubbled inside me. "Just because bad things happened, that doesn't make *us* bad."

"It's nothing to do with you." He sighed. "I'm the one that's bad. And I've tried so hard, for so long, to be good. But I've turned."

"James, *no*. That's not true. I asked you to do something—to save my friend—and that doesn't make you a monster. It makes you a hero."

His lips were so pale, they were almost white. "I'm not who I thought I was."

My heart thundered inside my chest. "What are you saying? That our relationship…what…ruined you?"

"No. *No.*" He threw his head back. "I am screwing this up."

I swallowed hard, waiting for him to continue.

"I promised myself I'd never drink from another human again. And I'm not just talking about Eden, here. When I met you, I… I wanted something from you. I *craved* you." James hesitated. "You got to me in a way that no other human ever has—especially not since I gave up drinking blood and began my new life."

"I've never felt afraid of you." That was the truth.

He ran his thumb along the back of my hand. "But maybe you should. Look at what's happened."

I raised my eyebrows. "I think you're being a little dramatic. You've never once made me feel scared, like you were going to hurt me. I've always known I was safe with you."

James sighed. "I know myself well enough to trust I'd never bite you."

"I do, too."

"Good." He leaned closer, his expression intent. "But I still changed when I started having serious feelings for you. My self-control evaporated when it came to others. I *wanted* to fight Drunk Guy that night."

Drunk Guy was an island visitor who'd come to

James's solstice party. He'd attacked me at Becky's house a few nights later, but James had come to my rescue.

James shook his head. "If you hadn't told me to let him go, I might've really hurt him."

"But you didn't—"

"And when Becky went after you the first time? I started thinking about plans to take her down. And it made me happy to lie in bed with you and watch over you, imagining all the ways I could undo her. It gave me...pleasure."

The muscle in his jaw went taut. "I started plotting excuses. I wanted to hurt her just for looking at you wrong. Just for disrespecting you. Just for touching one hair on your precious head."

"Okay..." I hesitated. "So what are you saying? That you hate yourself for caring about me? That having feelings for me made you a bad..." What? *Person? Ex-vampire? Angel?*

"My feelings made me want to take revenge. *Savage* revenge, Taylor. I thought I'd put those types of desires away—I didn't even think I was capable of them anymore. But the night that Brian died? If Becky had come near you... I could've done anything to her."

James stared down at our hands. "I would've snapped her in half. I would've been happy to do it," he whispered. "And these past few weeks on the island, I keep watching her. If she ever tried to hurt you again, I don't know what I'd do."

I took a deep breath. "James?"

He looked up at me.

"That doesn't make you bad," I said. "It makes you *human*. If someone tried to hurt you, I'd feel the same way. I'd go after them, too. When you love somebody, you'll do anything to protect them."

I swallowed hard—it felt risky, using the l-word. I didn't know where he stood.

"But you can't do what I can do." His voice was hoarse.

"No, but people do all sorts of things. Just because you're supernatural, it doesn't make you any better or any worse than anybody else. I understand you took a vow to stop drinking from humans. I'm sorry that I made you break it when I asked you to turn Eden. But you did nothing wrong—you were helping our friend. And if you'd hurt Becky that night, it would've been because you were protecting us, which makes you *good*."

James shook his head. "I don't know about that."

"That's because you've been beating the crap out of yourself these last few weeks. Maybe you've talked yourself into believing some things that aren't true."

He shrugged. "And you've been doing anything

different? You don't look like you've been sleeping too well, Taylor."

I nodded. "My protector hasn't been here to watch over me at night. It's been a little lonely."

"Did you miss sleeping with me?" The faintest glimmer of hope lit his face. "I thought you didn't like it, because I'm always watching your mouth hang open..."

"My mouth does not hang open," I said quickly. "And of course I missed you."

"You did?" His gaze searched mine, then tracked above my head.

"Really, James? You have to double-check?"

"I just wasn't sure how you felt after everything that happened." He frowned. "I didn't think you'd want to be with me after... After."

"Of course I want to be with you." The words tumbled out in a rush. Even if he didn't feel the same way, I had to tell the truth. Otherwise, I'd never forgive myself. "I don't blame you—I blame myself for asking you to turn Eden. I hate myself for it, but I didn't want her to die. I was selfish. I'm sorry that it's been so hard for you."

"You were trying to protect your friend. It wasn't selfish." He squeezed my hand. "I would do anything for you."

"So why won't you talk to me? Why have you been staying away?" My voice was thick.

He hesitated. "Because I want what's best for you."

"Being with you is what's best for me."

James gave me a long look. "Even if it gets your best friend turned into a vampire? Even if it might be dangerous for you to go home, because you don't know what sort of monster Becky is—or what she'll do next?"

"So...what? What are you saying?" Panic rose inside me.

"I don't know."

I refused to believe that being with James had caused bad things to happen. "Are you saying we should stay away from each other? Is that what you want?"

"No, it isn't." His eyes darkened. "But I need you to be the voice of reason, Taylor. I only want what's best for you. Tell me it's the right thing to do, and I'll stay away from you." He sat, rigid, as if waiting to be sentenced.

"N-No." I shook my head, my hair flying. "No, I won't."

"You're going to make me be the bad guy?" he asked, softly.

"Yeah, I am. I'm going to make you say it: you don't want to be with me anymore. Because I won't be the one who walks away."

I refused to be even more desperate and tell him

the truth: he was what I cared about most in the world. If being with James meant that I invited danger into my life, I could live with that. I could live with any risk —with all the risk. What I couldn't live without was *him*.

He blew out a deep breath. "I can't do that. Maybe I should—I know I'm being selfish. But I…can't."

Hope bubbled inside my chest. "I can't, either."

James moved a fraction closer, then stopped.

We stared at each other for a beat.

"Can I… Can I hold you?" He reached for me.

I didn't hesitate—I threw myself against him. Tears brushed my cheeks as he wrapped his arms around me and kissed the top of my head.

"Taylor. Babe, don't cry." But James's own voice was thick with emotion as he crushed me against him. "I didn't know if I'd ever be this close to you again."

"I couldn't stand it. I couldn't stand being away from you." Just inhaling his scent made my heart soar. "Please don't ever do that again."

"What?" His voice was husky.

"Leave me." My feelings, unleashed, actually scared me. I knew that I loved James more than I'd ever loved anyone or anything. How could I bear that? How could I stand it, when we could be torn apart?

He kissed my hair again. "If you don't want me to, I

won't. It was the worst six weeks of my existence, and that's saying something."

"I need to know that you mean it."

He put his big hands on my cheeks and raised my face, staring into my eyes. "Taylor Hale, I vow to you: I'll never leave you again, not unless you ask me to. It was hell on earth. I love you so much. I'm so sorry."

"I-I love you too." Then I started really crying. I tried to stop—I didn't enjoy feeling vulnerable, exposed. But the tears kept coming.

"Babe, please." James kissed my forehead.

"Since when did you call me 'babe?'" I asked, and we both laughed. It felt so good, even mixed with my tears.

"Since I couldn't stop thinking about you twenty-four-seven and finally got you back in my arms." He pulled me closer against his chest, his breath in my ear. "I'll stop if you want me to."

"Don't stop." I ran my hands over the muscles in his back, so familiar and dear.

"I'm sorry about everything." He kissed my hair again. "I love you. I love you so much."

"I love you, too." I pressed my face against his broad chest.

He held me close. "Good."

I peered up at him. "Good?"

He grinned at me, his beloved dimple deepening. "If I can describe it in a one-word grunt, I will. It's *good*."

"It is good," I agreed.

WE STAYED like that for a while, just holding each other. I felt my equilibrium come back—the rollercoaster of my emotions stilled, returning to normal, restored by his touch. That scared me, but it was okay.

As long as he didn't leave me again.

After a while, I kissed his cheek and slid off his lap. There was so much we needed to talk about. "What's the latest with the police?"

The night of the gala, James had rescued both Brian and Eden from the well. But Brian hadn't survived the fall. James had returned him to the bottom and told the authorities that, distraught over breaking up with his girlfriend, Brian had ended his own life.

"They've been out to the property a few times, taking pictures and asking some more questions. I know they interviewed the Lamberts. They told me they're required to do a full investigation, but it's not being handled as a suspicious incident. I guess Brian's parents told the police they'd been worried about him. He wasn't dealing with the breakup well."

Eden had told Brian, her college boyfriend, that she'd started dating someone else—Patrick.

"How's Eden doing?" James asked.

"Patrick said she's better today. The first couple of weeks were scary—"

James winced, so I skipped the part where Eden had threatened to guzzle my blood if I didn't take off her wrist restraints and let her go hunt the locals. "Anyway, we should probably check on her. I know she'd like to see you."

While he hadn't been talking much to me these past few weeks, James had faithfully texted or called Eden every day. "And maybe we can bring her some more blood. Patrick said she's already gone through a bunch this morning."

James nodded. "It's good that I have a stockpile back at the Tower—we're ready for her. She's going to need it."

I stopped short. "When's she going to the Tower?"

"Today." James grimaced. "Taylor, I have to tell you something."

I stared at him. "What?" If he said he was leaving me behind, I would scream.

"There's something I need to do back on the island. And I need you with me."

My heart lifted a little at that, but I still shook my head. "Okay, but what's going on?"

James took both my hands and looked into my eyes. "My parents are coming to Dawnhaven."

"Huh?" My mind raced to catch up to what he'd said. "I thought they couldn't come back to the island. Won't everyone notice they haven't aged in twenty years?"

He shook his head. "They aren't going to see anyone but us."

I swallowed hard. *"Us?"*

"Yes. I told you before, my father wants to meet you. He needs to talk to us about something—a favor."

I gaped at him. What could James's father, Nelson Champlain, possibly want? He was an ancient, powerful, gazillionaire (Eden's word, not mine) vampire. I was petrified to meet him, let alone James's mother. He'd told me he and his mom weren't close. What else had he said…? Something about her being a vampire *supremacist*?

"A favor?"

The muscle in his jaw jumped. "It's sort of a vampire thing. I have to take it seriously."

"Can you explain?"

James sighed. "I will. Later, okay?"

"Um… When are they coming?"

"This afternoon."

"*What?*"

He started from the room. "We should go and see Eden. I'll have your things packed."

Still reeling from the news, I hustled after him before he could leave my sight—something I intended to never let happen again.

4

LAUGH OR CRY

WE REACHED Eden's room before I could ask more about his parents.

The master bedroom was large and bright, with a spectacular view of the ocean beyond. But my best friend couldn't enjoy the scenery—all she could focus on was her thirst. She lay on the king-sized bed, her wrists restrained at her sides. A captive for the previous six weeks, she was *not* happy about it.

"Hey Eden." I kept my tone upbeat. "How's it going?"

"Fine, I guess—except for the fact that I'm a prisoner." She peered past me as she managed a tiny wave from her wrist restraints. "Oh, we've got company, huh? The ultimate warden, James Champlain himself."

"Hey Eden." James's tone was gentle.

"Hey yourself." She frowned at him from the bed.

Eden's deep-red curls spread around her, their fiery, vibrant color striking against the white pillowcases. She'd always been pretty, but since her transformation, her beauty had sharpened, becoming more dramatic. Her creamy complexion was brighter, more luminescent. Her eyes had changed, too. Once a sparkling light blue, they'd darkened toward James's hue, a combination of blue and steel gray. Her lashes were dark and thick, and her lips had become fuller and were a rich pink.

Eden sat up a little. "It's nice to see you, even if the circumstances are weird. You're, like, my vampire daddy."

"Ha. Something like that." James went closer, his gaze raking over her, inspecting every detail. "It's nice to see you, too. You look well. How are you feeling?"

"I'm good. Hungry though, *starving*. But good." Eden's gaze skipped back and forth between us. "Did you two kiss and make up?"

"Taylor has a heart of hearts, so yes. She's giving me another chance." James reached for my hand and squeezed it. "Listen, I'm sorry I haven't been down to see you."

Eden's eyes were bright. "I know you needed some time. I appreciate you calling and texting, though. It really helped with...everything. Patrick's been great too, he's super knowledgeable. Who knew that his mom was a vampire?" She laughed.

James sat down on the edge of her bed. "How are the cravings?"

Eden's gaze flicked to me again, then quickly away. "Pretty bad."

James nodded. "I can help you with that. Patrick said you've been drinking a lot, that's good."

"I wish he'd give me everything we've got. I'd drink it all right now. Or maybe you could let me loose for just two minutes?" she asked hopefully. "I heard the gardeners outside. I just want a *taste*. I'd stop, you know. I wouldn't hurt anybody. I could totally stop."

James smiled at her tightly. "No, you couldn't. You'd kill them in under a minute, and then you'd find someone else and drain them, too. And you'd still be starving."

She gave him a nasty look. "I'm freaking starving right *now*. A blood bag's not going to do it for much longer!"

"I know it's hard, but you *can* do it." He motioned toward me. "Remember the people you care about. Human life is valuable. You don't want to hurt anyone. You'd feel terrible."

"Oh, I think I could live with myself." She fought against her restraints. "What I *can't* live with is the cravings. Blood, blood, blood." She flopped back against the bed. "I want to guzzle an ocean of it."

James grimaced. "I know."

"Do you?" Eden suspiciously peered at his face. "You said you don't drink it anymore—why?"

"Because I don't need it."

"What?" She frowned. "How's that possible? You can smell Taylor, right?"

I shifted uncomfortably as James sighed. "Of course I can. But I'm not… I'm not exactly a vampire anymore."

"You know, that story still doesn't make sense to me." Eden's brow furrowed.

"I don't think our existence is something you can necessarily make sense of," James said.

Eden stared at the ceiling. "I don't want to live like this for much longer. I want to go outside. I want to see the sun. I want to *eat* something. I want to eat *all the things.*"

"You're in luck, at least in part. You get to see the sun soon." James patted her hand. "We're going home today."

"Home?" Eden's curls flew as she whipped her head at him. "Can I see my family?"

"Not yet." James took a deep breath. "When it's time, we'll tell your parents you're staying with me for a while. We'll just tell them you still need a break. You can see them, at least on a limited basis, but not yet."

"Because it's not safe." Eden frowned again. "Patrick's been drilling this into me. He said I would hurt them—that I wouldn't be able to help myself."

James nodded. "That's right. I'm so sorry, but that's right."

"It's okay." Eden's eyes brightened. "But can I see *anyone*? Maybe, like, a person convicted of a horrible crime? I don't want to suck blood out of a plastic bag for the rest of my existence. I want something with a *pulse*."

"You can't eat anyone." James was firm. "Not even your worst enemy."

"That sucks!" Eden roared, an unearthly sound that rattled the windows. "This whole thing *sucks*. Why did you turn me? Why'd you do it? *Why?*"

I stepped forward, even though I was afraid to be near when she got like this. "Eden, we've already talked about this. I asked James to turn you. You were about to die, and I didn't want that."

"Gee, thanks. Because this is such an improvement." Eden jerked against her restraints. Over the past few weeks her mood had careened between normal and friendly, to vindictive and aggressive. She'd seemed better recently, but apparently not with the subject of blood...

"I'm going to give you a *ton* to drink before we go," James promised her. "And I have so much stock at the

Tower, you aren't even going to believe it. You'll never be able to consume it all."

"That sounds great, but I *want* a *pulse*." Eden's eyes had a hard glint. "A pulse, James. I want to hold someone down and feel their heartbeat while I suck every last drop of blood out of them. I want them to fight me. I want to fight *them*. I want thrashing. And fear. And panic! I want to hear their blood freaking *rush*. Do you hear me? *I WANT A FREAKING PULSE!*"

"You don't have to worry—I heard you." James coughed. "I'll bring you some more to drink while Taylor and Patrick get ready. Then we'll go to the airport."

"Airport?" Eden perked up. "Will there be a pilot?"

"A vampire one." James smiled and Eden cursed.

"You're a buzzkill," she said.

"Get used to it, roomie."

He closed the door behind us, but I could hear Eden curse some more as she wrestled with her restraints.

"She seems good." James nodded.

"Seriously?" I glanced back at her room. She was still thrashing around, grumbling to herself.

"Seriously. A lot of time, newly transitioned vampires are absolutely out of their minds. Even though she's starving, Eden is still Eden. She's going to be fine."

My heart lifted. "You think so?"

"I know so. The fact that she has a semblance of a sense of humor means everything. She might even end up being...*okay.*" He looked both surprised and pleased. "Let's go find Patrick—you guys need to pack. We have to get going. My parents don't wait for anyone."

I followed him back down the hallway, not sure whether I should laugh or cry.

To avoid the curious stares of the locals, they'd agreed to take the wrist restraints off of Eden for the trip home. We took a practice walk around the enormous yard. Patrick and James stayed close to her side, trapping her in a burly sandwich of male muscle.

Several black SUVS pulled down the drive. Half a dozen men and women, dressed in dark suits identical to the guards, poured out of them. Some went into the house, some started speaking in low tones with the other guards, and a couple tapped things into their cellphones.

"James," I said, careful to keep my voice low, "who the heck are all these people?"

He cleared his throat. "Employees of my father's corporation. I told him we had plenty of guards down here already, but he deployed them for our trip home."

"Deployed?"

Patrick leaned close to me and whispered, "Like I said: Vampire secret service."

I wrapped my arms against my chest as the additional guards swarmed the house. "What are they doing?"

"Shutting down the house, wiping it for prints—that sort of thing." James's tone was casual.

"Wiping it for prints?" Even though I'd been living at one of his many estates these last few weeks, I'd forgotten what it was like to be a part of his world. I felt like Alice in Wonderland, going down the rabbit hole again.

He shrugged a big shoulder. "We like to keep our properties as anonymous as possible. It's no big deal. Our guards do it all the time."

"Do you think maybe your family could hire some *human* guards? These guys smell like deodorant sticks, and I *don't want to eat deodorant sticks.*" Eden glowered at each of us. "This sucks. You all suck. The only thing that doesn't suck is *me*—because there's nothing to suck from!"

"Easy, easy." Patrick linked his arm through hers and led her toward the SUV. "Let's not cause any trouble, okay?"

"Trouble sounds fun." Eden narrowed her eyes at him. "What have you got against fun?"

"Nothing." Patrick and James exchanged a look. "Let's get you in the car, and you can have some more blood. The bar's stocked."

"I want someone *in* stocks. Not a stocked bar."

Patrick rolled his eyes. "Just get in the car, Eden."

The SUV packed, the house closed down, our entourage headed toward West Tisbury. The Martha's Vineyard airport consisted of a single gray building with one lone runway. We parked, and then James brought us to three brand-new, small planes. The side of them read: *Champlain Enterprises.*

"This is us." James sounded as if his three private planes were no big deal.

I blinked as the guards started packing them with our things. The captains consulted with one another. It shouldn't surprise me, but still—I was *not* used to this world.

We buckled in and James held my hand as the plane taxied down the runway. "Are you glad to be going home?"

I squeezed his hand. "Yes. And..."

"And?"

"Um..." My stomach dipped. "Did I tell you I've

never flown before?" I asked, inadvertently changing the subject.

"What?" James looked shocked.

"Vacations weren't exactly in the budget." I giggled nervously and somewhat inappropriately as the island disappeared beneath us and we rose into the sky.

He leaned closer, his familiar scent washing over me. "Are you frightened?"

I blinked at him, momentarily dazed. "Huh?"

He smiled patiently, and his dimple peeped out. "Are you afraid?"

I stared into the depths of his eyes, the steel color so dear to me.

"Taylor?" The dimple deepened. "You okay?"

"Y-Yeah." I giggled again. "I think the take-off made me nervous, but then I got distracted by your face. So I'm good."

"Ha." He leaned over and kissed my cheek. "But what else? I know there's something on your mind."

I looked around. Patrick and Eden were talking to each other in low tones, and the two guards who'd joined us were each looking out the windows. I took a deep breath, my giddiness seeping away.

"I'm nervous," I admitted, careful to keep my voice low. "I still don't understand what your parents want.

What's the favor about? Also, I'm nervous for other reasons…"

He squeezed my hand. "Becky's not coming anywhere near you. I've been watching her these last few weeks, and there have been no signs of what happened before. She's been normal, as much as Becky *can* be normal."

"But that's exactly what I'm worried about. What if I'm the reason she went crazy?"

"She won't know that you're back, at least not for a couple of days. I'm going to keep you all to myself." The undercurrent in his voice made my stomach do a somersault.

The prospect was tantalizing, but there were other pressing issues. I winced, thinking of Big Kyle. "I can't hide from my dad. He's been calling me every day."

"He's been calling me, too." James chucked me under the chin. "And I don't want to hide from him, either. It's just for a day or two… Just enough time to see my parents and get Eden settled."

My nerves started grinding again. "What *about* your parents? Will you please tell me what's going on?"

"I honestly don't know what they want. Whatever the 'favor' is—my father won't tell me unless it's in person." He leaned closer, lowering his voice. "The term 'favor' means something specific to vampires. It's a pact, a formal promise that we have to honor. Whatever they're asking for, I can't say no. And it's probably important."

His eyes darkened. "But we have to go home to find out what it is."

I licked my lips. "Why do they need *me* there?"

James sighed. "I've made it clear to my father that you're in my life for as long as you want to be there."

"Even though you've avoided me the past few weeks?"

"Yes." He sighed. "I was hoping we could find a way...forward."

"I'm glad we did."

"Me too." He kissed my hand. "He said if that's the case, he needs to meet you. He said you should hear what he's asking for—that's why I came today. They didn't give me much notice."

"And what about your mother?"

His expression immediately turned grim. "My mother's opinion doesn't matter to me."

"Her opinion about what—*me*?"

James shook his head. "You, me...anything. She's not someone I take counsel from."

I wanted to ask what he meant, but I could tell from his face that he didn't want to discuss it further. So I focused on the sensation of flying, instead. Now that the plane had leveled off, it felt normal, almost as if we were driving.

I clutched his hand and stared out the window as the islands became tiny specks below us. It was strange, being so far up in the air. "It's beautiful, isn't it?" I gestured outside to the vast ocean below.

"Yes." He stroked my hair tenderly, his eyes never leaving my face. "It's the most beautiful thing in the whole world."

5

THE RETURN

I CLOSED my eyes as we landed on the tiny grass air strip at Bar Harbor airport. The plane bumped up and down —I clutched James's hand until it was over. But once we got outside, and I inhaled the scent of the clean Maine air, I grinned.

Home. I was finally home.

I smiled up at the blue sky. The fir trees rose all around us, swaying in the gentle breeze.

James read a text on his phone. "We should get going. My parents are on their way."

I swallowed hard, my relief evaporating. The guards unpacked the planes as James led me through the airport to the parking lot. His big black Yukon waited. Patrick kept his arm firmly around Eden—she sniffed the air and eyed the thankfully deserted area. No other passengers were arriving in Bar Harbor at that random hour on a Tuesday. Eden looked disappointed, but Patrick seemed relieved. As soon as he got her inside the Yukon, he locked the doors.

The guards followed, stowing our luggage in the SUVs that flanked ours on either side. Then we drove off, caravan-style, to Route 102, which would bring us to Pine Harbor. It was a vampire entourage. I briefly wondered how I'd ended up in such company, but a glance at James's profile was all I needed to remind me.

"How are we going to keep this a secret from my family and Taylor's?" Eden asked. "Everybody on the island knows everything. You know that. You can't even go get your mail without people talking about it. Comings and goings are a big deal on Dawnhaven."

James nodded. "We won't use the dock in Pine Harbor. I parked my boat down at the Everly's—they're out of town. I'll drop you guys over there, park the truck and come back."

Eden frowned. "Someone will notice us on Hart Sound. We'll probably see ten of my cousins going across."

"Don't worry about it," James said. "By the way, I talked to your mother yesterday. I told her you'd be back next week, in time for Taylor to start school. No one's expecting you today."

"Hopefully we can visit our families soon." I turned to smile at Eden. "I know your mom will be happy to have you home."

Her pretty face twisted into a scowl. "I don't know about that. I'm not exactly her little girl anymore."

James glanced at her in the rearview mirror. "You're still the same person, Eden. I told Taylor this morning—you've transitioned amazingly well. You're going to keep your family in your life. You haven't changed who you are inside."

She narrowed her eyes at him. "What if I want to *eat* them? What about that, huh?"

Patrick patted her shoulder. "We'll help you with that. James and my mom have all sorts of tricks that they've developed over the years, tactics for dealing with humans. You'll get through this."

"We'll see." Eden turned away from us and stared out the window, lost in her thoughts.

James brought us at the Everly's compound, which fronted Pine Harbor. We followed a pristine path down to their private dock. The vampire guards carried our bags down and stacked them neatly on James's boat, the *Norumbega.*

The lead guard nodded to James. "I've just received word—your parents will land soon. We'll stay on the mainland. I expect orders from your father," he said.

James thanked him and turned to us. His eyes were suddenly dark, the muscle in his jaw tense. "I'll go park the car—be right back." He jogged to the SUV, his shoulders rigid.

"What did he mean, they'll be landing soon?" I asked Patrick as he helped Eden onto the boat. "Are they flying into Bar Harbor, too?"

"Ha, no." Patrick chuckled. "They have a helicopter. They'll land on the Tower's front lawn."

"Aren't people going to notice it?"

"Of course they'll will," Eden snapped.

Patrick dug through the cooler and poured something. A second later, he handed Eden a silver tumbler with a lid and a straw. "Drink this. You're getting cranky."

She rolled her eyes but did as she was told.

"I'm sure James has a story worked out." Patrick shrugged. "My mom takes a helicopter over sometimes. People on the island are used to it."

"Everybody will still be talking." Eden clutched her cup. "All they do is talk."

"We're safe here." Patrick sat down next to Eden. "It's nice that we could use this spot."

I nodded. The Everly's berth was in a little cove protected by pine trees; at least ten locals would have seen us if we'd used the town dock. To get to Dawnhaven, people either rode the mailboat, booked a water taxi, or drove their own private boats. They'd leave the bay at Pine Harbor, cross Hart Sound and head to Dawnhaven or one of the other two nearby islands, Spruce and Crescent.

James hustled down the dock a minute later, frowning. "Eden, Taylor—you're going to need to stay down during the ride over. Elias was just pulling into the parking lot. He's taking the mailboat." Elias was our friend from the Portside, the only restaurant on Dawnhaven. Eden and I had both waitressed at the Portside before... Before.

James started untying the boat. "And Eden—two of your cousins were at the dock." The Lamberts were the largest family on the island. Including Eden's mother, there were five brothers and three sisters, all married, all commercial fishermen, with at least three children apiece.

She snorted. "Of course they were. Got nothing better to do than go back and forth all day. I told you so."

James handed blankets to us. I hunkered down on one couch, and Eden took the other. Patrick untied the bumpers and James pulled away from the dock. We emerged into the harbor slowly, navigating through the boats moored nearby. The process was welcome and familiar—except for the fact that Eden was a vampire and had to hide under a blanket.

That changed the tenor of things.

We reached open water and picked up speed, then drove through another boat's wake. The *Norumbega* bumped up and down, and Eden peered out at me. "Good thing this is a cushy yacht. There are no fancy couches on my mom's boat."

"What do you think about coming home?" I asked over the noise of the motor and the whipping wind.

"I don't know. It's better than being chained to that bed, but I feel weird. I feel a little wild, like I might do anything." She leaned closer and Patrick sat down on her couch, boxing her in. She glowered at him. "I didn't mean 'anything' like *eat Taylor.*"

He raised an eyebrow. "Whatever. I'm here to protect you from yourself."

In answer, she pulled the blanket back over her face.

With the wind, the ride was bumpy, but I didn't mind. The way the ocean smelled as we crossed from Pine Harbor to Dawnhaven was my favorite scent in all the world. Patrick kept waving to other boats that we passed, and I was glad I couldn't tell who else was on the water. I missed my dad a lot, but I wasn't ready to be anywhere near Becky or Amelia, not yet. Maybe not ever.

Eventually, we turned in a wide circle; we were making our way to James's private dock at the Tower. The Champlain estate was on the island's isolated western beach. James slowed the boat and announced to us, "It's safe—we're here. You can come out now."

I sat up and yanked the blanket off. The immense house loomed above me. The Tower, as we called it, directly abutted the ocean. It looked just as I remembered—enormous, white and sprawling, its lookout jutting into the sky. It sat atop a seawall comprised of massive pink and gray stones. The tide was low, lapping gently against the stone slabs that rose from the water.

My heart soared as we approached: I hadn't known when, or if, I'd see it again.

James pulled alongside the dock and parked the boat. Patrick hopped out and tied the *Norumbega* up. James turned and caught me staring. "What?"

"I'm so happy to be back. I... I love you." I went closer and threw my arms around him. "I missed you so much."

"I love you too, Taylor." He laughed and held me tight, nuzzling his face in my hair. "I'm so glad to have you home—I missed you more than I can say."

Eden stood up and glared at us. "Barf." She sniffed the air. "But even worse than you two—is there literally *no one* to eat around here? All I smell are seagulls and squirrels. I'd like to order a fresh Homo sapiens, please."

"Ha. C'mon." Patrick grabbed her hand and brought her up to the dock. "There's a huge stockpile of blood inside. I know you're hungry. We'll get you set up before the Champlains arrive."

Eden wrinkled her nose. "Ugh, that's right. For a second, I forgot they were coming. Hide me."

I wanted to hide, too. Instead, James and I took the bags off the boat and wheeled them up the landing. The grounds greeted us, the thick green grass rolling in the breeze, pine trees swaying at the lawn's edge. I tried not to think about the abandoned well hidden inside the trees beyond. An image of Eden and Brian tumbling backwards flashed in my mind, making me wince. But then a familiar caw echoed down from the pines, interrupting the ugly memories.

"Edgar?"

A set of large, black wings flapped. The crow dropped from his perch onto the grass, then hopped toward us twice. Edgar, the crow who lived in the Tower's forest, tilted his head, cawing again.

I grinned at the bird. "I missed you too, buddy."

James laughed. "You speak crow now?"

"Ha. I'm just guessing." But I focused on Edgar. "It's good to see you."

Seemingly satisfied, the crow hopped back toward the woods.

"We should get going." James picked up his bag, heading for the deck. But before we'd even made it up the stairs, a thunderous *whoosh* emanated from above. James tensed as an enormous, sleek-looking black helicopter appeared in the sky. The copter was fast—it quickly reached Moss Head, the tiny island across from the Tower, crossed the channel and hovered above the lawn. James put the luggage down and gripped my hand as the propeller's wings blew both our hair. Before I was ready, the chopper landed, its whirring rotor blades winding down to a standstill.

A guard hopped out of the cockpit and opened the passenger doors. James squeezed my hand almost painfully. "I just want you to know something." His tone was urgent. "I'm sorry about my family—Nelson and Marietta can be a lot to handle."

I shook my head. "You remember Becky and Amelia, right? Your parents can't be any worse than that."

He gave me a dark look. "Wait till you meet my mom."

My stomach plummeted as I caught the first sight of James's mother and father. *Here goes nothing.*

I had no idea what I was in for.

6

THE FAVOR

I SWALLOWED hard as two figures emerged from the shiny copter. First was an elegant-looking man—Nelson Champlain. He was tall and strapping, and wore an immaculate white polo shirt, blue linen trousers and flip-flops. His hairline receded slightly, and his steel-colored hair was slicked back from his face. Athletic, handsome, and wealthy, Nelson would fit in easily with the other rich islanders. He looked as though he'd invented the lifestyle. As he was hundreds of years old, he probably *had* invented it. Still, he appeared to be in his early fifties, healthy and vigorous.

Nelson held his hand out and helped down the second figure, a stunning woman—Marietta Champlain. Nothing prepared me for her striking physical appearance. She was almost as tall as her husband and looked younger than him, maybe forty. It was difficult to tell because her pale, smooth skin had few lines. Her thick, strawberry-blond hair tumbled over her shoulders and she held herself the way I imagined a former model would: with perfect posture, shoulders back, chest thrust out.

She surveyed the yard, with no expression on her face, until she reached James and me. Then she frowned.

Unlike her husband, Marietta would *not* fit in on Dawnhaven. The local women typically wore athletic shorts and T-shirts, and the occasional pair of white jeans for a night out. James's mother inexplicably wore a floor-length floral gown, with a pattern of pink and yellow petals, the green tendrils of vines snaking around her curvaceous figure. Her full skirt swept the grass. Both her hair and her magnificent chest bounced as she took her husband's hand and strode across the lawn toward us, still frowning.

Crap.

I quickly scanned myself. Five-dollar Old Navy flip flops, chipped blue toenail polish, running shorts and my favorite *Worcester Polytechnic Institute* T-shirt. Maybe nothing could prepare you for meeting your boyfriend's gazillionaire vampire parents, but a shower and a cute outfit probably would've helped. I plastered a smile to my face. "H-Here goes nothing."

James's only response was a groan.

His parents crossed the grounds, and Nelson smiled at us with warmth. Once he was closer, I could see that he also had few wrinkles. His pale skin glowed with good health, and his teeth were straight and perfect, a blinding white. "You must be Taylor. I'm Nelson Champlain, James's father. It's a pleasure to finally meet you."

"Y-You too, Mr. Champlain."

He turned to his son. They were each about six-foot-two. Close together, I could see that their eyes were the same color, and their smiles had a similar curve. "It's good to see you, son." Nelson embraced James and patted him hard on the back.

When they broke apart, James nodded at his mom. "Hello, Mother. This is Taylor Hale, my girlfriend."

"Girlfriend?" Her well-groomed eyebrows rose a fraction. "How plebeian of you, using a term like that."

"Marietta." Nelson grimaced. "Didn't we talk about this?"

She tossed her shiny hair. "You said I had to be civil, not a sycophant."

Nelson leveled his gaze with hers. "I brought you because you asked to come. We had a deal, remember? Now please behave."

I ignored the mounting awkwardness and smiled at Marietta. Up close, she was so beautiful, she seemed almost unnatural—a construct of someone's careful, worshipful computer generation. "I-It's nice to meet you, Mrs. Champlain." My palms were sweating and apparently, I'd developed a stutter.

Marietta looked vaguely in my direction, then back to James. "You know how mixing with the humans usually ends, James. We can't trust them—even the ones who are our little pets. I thought you were brighter than this, but I suppose a mother always overestimates her children…"

"Marietta, *enough*. James has assured me that Taylor has sworn to keep our secret because it's *his* secret. Anyway Taylor, the pleasure is ours. Really." Nelson smiled. "Shall we go inside? We have a lot to discuss."

"Sure, but first—Mother?" James's voice was strangled.

She turned her attention to her son. "Yes, dear?"

"You're not coming in the house unless you treat Taylor with respect."

"Really?" Marietta narrowed her eyes. "Because you might remember that this is *my* house."

He took a deep breath. "You *will* treat Taylor with respect. Understand?"

"First of all, treat your *mother* with some respect," she said, not missing a beat. "Second of all, it's fine if you expect me to be civil. But *I* expected that you would settle down with a nice vampire girl. So perhaps we both have some adjustments to make."

She eyed me up and down. "In any event, I'm failing to see what all the fuss is about."

"Marietta, that's enough. Get in the house. *Now.*" Nelson looked an awful lot like James when the muscle in his jaw bulged out.

Marietta didn't appear the least bit sorry as she shrugged, picked up her skirt, and climbed the stairs, the queen ascending to her throne. Even though she clearly despised me, I couldn't help but stare. She was the most beautiful woman I'd ever seen.

"You must forgive my wife," Nelson said, keeping his voice low. "She's wildly protective of her children."

"Really, Dad?" James kept his voice down, too. "That's how you're going to play it?" He grabbed my hand and led me up the stairs. "C'mon—let's get this over with."

I longingly glanced back toward the copter. I'd take a bumpy landing over a meeting with James's parents any day. Maybe the pilot would take me somewhere? Anywhere? Or maybe I could jump the seawall and swim away? But James brought me to the house before I could run. I inhaled deeply, but it did nothing to settle my nerves.

Marietta had already situated herself on the couch.

Her posture was regal; her mere presence somehow made the room appear more grandiose. I'd forgotten that James had bought new, more casual furniture right before he'd hosted the gala. The living room would have appeared softer, more comfortable, but for Marietta's imposing and expensive-looking figure.

She didn't look at me, but her gaze registered my hand entwined with her son's. I swallowed hard, then chose a spot on the far-opposite end of the L-shaped couch. James sat close by my side. I had the sense he was trying to shield me from his mother.

Nelson sat in the middle, an ambassador between his wife and son. "Let's get right down to business. We're concerned about what's been happening on the island, and we'd like you to stay on, son. Stay here though the winter and monitor things."

James squeezed my hand. "I was planning on staying, anyway. Taylor has one year of school left. I won't leave her."

Marietta snorted. When both James and Nelson whipped their heads at her, she blinked at them innocently. "What? Can't I cough?"

Nelson turned back to his son. "I think staying is the right thing to do. Based on what you've told me, I agree that there's an uptick in unusual activity. We have a responsibility to see that through. I want you to document everything, to assimilate a report I can present to the council. I don't want to involve them unless it's necessary, but we need to be prepared. And I know you're capable of handling yourself."

When James nodded, Nelson continued, "Speaking of responsibility. As you know, we have a favor to ask. You must understand that we don't take this lightly. It's something only you can do, son. You're the only one who can handle it, and the island is the perfect place, the *only* place, I feel we can accomplish this."

James sat forward, waiting.

"Even though it's an unusual step, we wanted Taylor to be here."

Marietta glared. "Speak for yourself, Nelson."

He continued as though his wife hadn't spoken. "She needs to understand that by choosing to continue in a relationship with you, she's going to bear some responsibility for this obligation."

James shook his head. "She doesn't need to be involved."

"I disagree. You're choosing to be with a human. You're also helping your mother and me. Taylor has to understand the risks." Nelson's intense gaze tracked to my face.

I nodded. "I don't know what you're going to ask, but I'm staying. No matter what." I held onto James's hand for dear life. "James has helped me—he's saved me more than once. I want to help him, too. You can trust me."

Nelson nodded. Marietta looked as though she wanted to whack me with a fly swatter and be done with it.

"I assumed as much." Nelson smiled, but the smile disappeared as he returned his focus to James. "There's been some trouble. Your mother and I need you to keep an eye on someone for a few months."

"Who?" James's expression darkened. "And what sort of trouble?"

"There was an incident at a bar." Marietta pulled a cellphone from the depths of her skirt and quickly texted something. "It involved a witch, a shifter, and a certain vampire."

James gaped at her. "That sounds like a bad joke—and the punchline involves someone you know I *hate*."

Marietta tucked the cellphone away and faced him. "Don't say 'hate' when you're talking about family."

"Now I know why you came." James looked as though he might leap across the couch and throttle her. "And the answer is *no*."

Marietta *tsked*. "You can't say no to a favor, dear: you know the rules. Ah, here we are." A guard appeared at the glass door that opened to the deck. Marietta nodded, and he motioned for someone in the yard to join him.

"Dad, *no*." James's face turned ashen. "You can't ask me to do this!"

"I'm sorry, son. But I don't have another choice."

I looked between James and his father, then to the door.

James's face was white. "I will never forgive you for this."

"I expect not." Nelson sighed, then signaled the guard. "Bring him in, please."

I held my breath as another figure appeared on the deck.

As soon as James saw who it was, he cursed.

7

NEVER REALLY DONE

"WHAT'S WRONG?" I whispered, but James didn't have time to answer. The guard marched a handsome young man, who looked a few years older than James, into the living room. He wore tight black jeans ripped in all the right places, a distressed crewneck sweater, and immaculate white sneakers. I'd been around enough wealthy people that summer to recognize the expense of his casual outfit: he'd paid a lot of money to have someone make his designer clothes look lived in.

He was a little taller than James, but with a thinner, more sinewy build. His hair was thick, wavy and on the long side, brushing his chin and framing his chiseled, smirking face. His hair was dark, the same color as both James and Nelson's. But the young man's eyes were turquoise, just like Marietta's. He was the type of person who, unable to stop yourself, you'd openly stare at. I wondered if I'd seen him before, on some Netflix show.

"*No.*" James shot to his feet. "Dad—how can you do this to me? You cast him out!"

The young man smiled at James, flashing perfect, even teeth. "Glad to see you haven't changed much. *'Dad! No fair!'*" He mimicked James. "Still whining—that's my baby brother, all right."

"Shut up, Luke." James bit the words out.

"Boys." Marietta's voice was scolding, but she smiled at them as if pleased. "That's enough."

"Dad?" James's expression was desperate.

Nelson sighed. "He's in trouble, James, a lot of it. And yes I cast him out, but he's still my son."

"No way." James shook his head. "I will not watch this fucker for you two. He's your responsibility, not mine."

"You don't have to watch me." Luke shrugged. "You just have to let me stay."

"*No.*"

"C'mon. I won't cause any trouble—there's nothing to do up here, anyway. Maybe I'll take up cow-tipping." He peered past James and looked me up and down. "So this is how *you've* been keeping busy, eh? She's cute. A little rough around the edges. But I guess that makes it easier for you to swoop in and be the big hero, right?"

He tilted his head and impersonated James: "'Let me rescue you! I used to be a fun vampire, but now I'm a white knight! I've got so much money, so much *angst*, so much light to zap the bad guys, please love me for me—'"

James's fist collided with his brother's face. Luke took a stagger-step back, clutching his jaw, then gaped at Marietta and Nelson. "You two weren't kidding. He's got it bad, huh?"

"Shut up." James got in his face. "Never look at her again. *Never.*"

"All right, all right. She's not my type, anyway." Luke rubbed his jaw. "Your witchy friend Josie, though, *mmm.* She's got that nice, tight, little package—"

James raised his fist again and Luke held up his hands, as if in surrender. "Fine, fine. *Geez.* You can't even take a joke anymore, huh? Too much white light, not enough fun."

When James took another step closer, Luke waved him off. "*Relax*—enough with the guardian angel act. I'm sure you want to keep her all to yourself, but don't you think you should at least introduce me? Your human plaything seems confused. Not that I'm looking at her," Luke added, "it's just her vibe."

James didn't lower his fist. "Taylor's not my plaything. Don't look at her, don't talk about her. Also, you can forget about Josie. She's certainly forgotten about you."

Luke raised his eyebrows. "I'm not sure how she could forget about my—"

"Enough, you two." Nelson's voice was firm. "James, step back. Luke, stop being an ass, if that's physically possible."

When they broke apart, Nelson sighed. "Taylor, this is our oldest son, Luke. Luke, this is Taylor Hale, James's girlfriend."

"'Girlfriend.' You've got a title, huh? That's adorable." Luke's aqua eyes sparkled as he looked me over. "It's a pleasure to meet you, Taylor."

"N-Nice to meet you." I gave him a small wave.

Luke's face split into a grin, and James stepped in between us. "Don't freaking smile at her like that," he snarled.

Luke chuckled. "Wow. I didn't know you had it in you. It's only taken a century for you to grow a pair."

James turned to his parents. "He's not staying here. I don't care about the favor—I won't put Taylor and everyone else on the island at risk."

Nelson sighed. "He's taken a vow to only drink donations, son. He won't cause any trouble. This is the safest place for him right now."

"I'm supposed to care about what's safe for him?" James glared at his father.

"He's your brother." Marietta's voice was ice. "It would be nice if you cared about him for once."

"I've already bailed him out more times than I can count." James's eyes blazed. "I'm done with him!"

"Enough everyone," Nelson snapped. "Marietta and I have to go. We have a council meeting." His gaze tracked to Luke, who looked back at his father impassively.

"You can't leave him here with me." James shook his head. "We have too much going on already. There's no way I can keep Taylor safe and babysit him—and don't tell me he's only going to drink donations. That's a lie and we both know it."

"He can help you," Nelson said. "He'll be another watchdog. Luke's promised me he won't get into more trouble, and I believe him. He hasn't got any chances left —this was the last straw. If the council receives another complaint, he's going to prison. And you know His Highness can't handle that."

For the first time, the smirk disappeared from Luke's face. He crossed his arms against his chest and scowled at his father.

James raised his eyebrows. "Seriously? What'd he do?"

"It was a misunderstanding," Marietta said quickly.

"You know your brother and his jokes. People blow these things out of proportion."

James shook his head. "You'll make any excuse for him. Nothing's changed."

His mother regarded him. "And you won't give him a chance. So you're right—nothing *has* changed."

"It's just for a few months," Nelson said smoothly. "In the scheme of things, it's just a blip. You'll both be fine. Maybe it will be good for you."

"I can't believe you're doing this." James stared at his parents.

Nelson ignored him, smiling at me. "We're happy to meet you, Taylor. I apologize for the extreme circumstances. I have to reiterate, though, that if you're staying in a relationship with James, by extension, watching out for Luke becomes partly your responsibility. Are you willing to accept that?"

"Don't answer him," James warned.

"Of course I will," the words tumbled out of my mouth. I kept my eyes on Nelson, not daring to look at Luke or Marietta. "I'd do anything for James. I'm happy to help your family if I can."

James cursed, which made Luke cackle. Marietta rose, skirts swishing, and gave me side-eye. "You're pandering, but I suppose it's better than nothing. Try to live up to it. Did you know that if you break a promise to a vampire, they'll drain you dry? Might want to keep that front and center of your inferior brain." She turned her nose up at me, then faced her sons.

She went to kiss James's cheek, but he pulled back. "I told you not to talk to her like that."

"And I told *you* to remember who and what you are." She gave him an appraising look. "How obedient have *you* been?"

She kissed Luke on both cheeks. "Behave, darling." Then she swept outside without another word.

Nelson went to James and took his face in between his hands. "Son, I know what you're going through up here. I understand this is a lot to ask."

"Then why are you asking it?" James jerked his head away. "I've been talking to you all summer, seeking your advice, because I'm worried about what's happening on the island. And now you do *this*? All Luke does is screw up. Everywhere he goes, everyone he touches—it's always a mess for our family to clean up. I thought we were done!"

Nelson glanced at Luke, then back at James. "It turns out with family, you're never exactly done."

"Well, I am," James said. "I have been for years."

"I can't keep him with us right now. Because he's gotten into trouble again, your mother and I have council obligations that prevent us from watching him."

Nelson shook his head. "And I won't exile him to one of the other estates alone. The guards won't go near him—he's gotten too many of them killed over the years. I can't ask them to take that risk anymore."

"But you can ask *me*?"

"That's because I know you can handle it." Nelson squeezed James's shoulder. "I trust you more than anyone in the world. You can handle the supernatural activity up here, you'll keep Taylor safe, and you can monitor your brother. You're special—I've known that since the day you were born, even before you were transformed. *Please.* I've never asked you for anything, but this is something I can't trust anyone else with."

James stared at his father. "What if I say no?"

"It's a *favor*." Nelson patted his shoulder. "You can't refuse, and you know it. Plus, I know you won't disappoint me. You never have."

He released James and pointed at his other son. "You, on the other hand, have one final opportunity to prove your worth to me. This is the last chance you don't deserve, Luke. Fuck it up this time, I'll call the council myself. And then it'll be supernatural prison for the rest of eternity, or at least until they starve you for one-hundred years and you die from the hunger pangs."

Nelson shook his head. "You cross me again, even

your mother won't be able to persuade me to protect you. Are we clear?"

Luke gave his father a tight smile. "Crystal."

Nelson nodded, then turned to me. "I enjoyed meeting you, Taylor. I appreciate your discretion. I hope to see you again someday." Without another word, he strode out.

The brothers looked at each other for a beat as the sound of the helicopter's rotor blades fired up, filling the room. From the window, we watched the copter rise into the air. Nelson and Marietta weren't wasting any time. I wondered if they worried James would drag Luke out of the house and try to stuff him inside… The noise subsided, and the chopper flew over Moss Head, back toward the south.

"That was some stump speech Dad gave." Luke tucked a lock of thick hair behind his ear, his bright eyes on James. "Must be nice to be his favorite."

"Must be nice to be Mom's."

Luke shrugged. "It doesn't have the same perks."

"You're alive, aren't you?" James asked. "You're being babysat in the comfort of my home. They seem like pretty good perks to me."

"We'll see." Luke flopped down into an armchair. "But six months of drinking donated blood, cow-tipping, and watching you and the human make goo-

goo eyes at each other? I might ask you to stake me yourself."

"Feel free." James's smile was savage. "I won't hesitate to help you out."

"Ah." Luke sprawled back in the chair and crossed his legs. "It's been too long."

"It'll never be long enough. Eternity isn't long enough." James grabbed my hand. "We're going outside. Don't touch anything, don't talk to anybody, don't be a total fuck-up for once in your life."

"Yes, Master." Luke's grin turned huge. "Your wish is my command."

"I wish you could drop dead," James muttered. White in the face, he pulled me out to the deck, away from his smirking big brother.

8

UNFORTUNATE

"ARE YOU OKAY?"

James slumped over the railing of the deck, watching the tide come in. "Not exactly."

"Is it… Is he that bad?"

"Yes. He's the worst." James glanced at me. "Stay away from him."

"Don't worry." From my brief encounter with his brother, I could tell that he was nothing like James— meaning he was nothing but trouble. "I just want to help."

"Yeah, about that." James grimaced. "It was nice that you told my father you would watch out for Luke, but never make promises to a vampire, okay? As my mother said, they take these things seriously."

I nodded. "I'm sorry."

James straightened up and gathered me into his arms. "Don't be sorry. I love you for it. You're brave, meeting my parents like that."

I buried my face in the muscles of his chest. "Your dad was nice. Your mom…"

He kissed the top of my head. "She makes Becky look good. Difficult to do."

The sound of a vehicle bombing down the long gravel drive interrupted us. My dad's truck flew into view.

James quickly released me.

My shoulders slumped. "Oh, *crap*." I watched as Big Kyle parked and leapt out of the driver's seat. "How'd he find out I was here?"

"It's like Eden said—everybody on the island knows everything." James's expression was grim. "He doesn't look happy."

In fact, my usually good-natured father—aka Big Kyle—looked downright pissed. He scowled at us. He was a large man, over six-foot-three-inches tall, and built like a linebacker. I didn't know much about football, but wasn't a linebacker one of the positions that tackled? If the answer was yes, James and I appeared to be in trouble as he stalked across the lawn toward us.

"Hi, Dad!" I called fake-brightly.

"*Taylor?*" He climbed the stairs and stopped a couple

of feet away from us. Up close, I could see that the skin around his eyes was a little red, as if he'd rubbed it roughly. "Are you all right?"

"Yes, of course!"

"Why haven't you texted me?"

"I just got back." I went and hugged him; he just stood there, immobile. Hugging my dad always felt like hugging a meat-locker, and although I'd never thought that in a mean way, he seemed particularly stiff and cold. "Dad... Is everything okay?"

He pulled away, then rubbed his eyes again. To my horror, I realized he'd been crying. "Donnie told me he saw a copter over here, and I didn't know if something was wrong. I was just worried, is all."

"Dad." I hugged him again, awkward or not. "I'm sorry I didn't tell you I was coming home. It all happened fast. I was just about to call you."

He relaxed a bit, squeezing me once before he released me. He still hadn't looked at James. "All right. You ready to come back to the house? We've got some things we need to talk about."

"O-Okay? Just let me get my bag."

"James can drop it for you later, if he doesn't mind." Big Kyle's voice was firm.

"Sure, Dad." I quickly kissed James on the cheek. Our plans for a precious few days of privacy abruptly went up in smoke. I didn't want to leave for a lot of reasons—not the least of which was the fact I was abandoning him with both Eden and his brother.

"Come over later?" I kept my voice low.

James nodded, gripping my hand. "I'm glad you're here, Taylor."

"Me too."

"Thanks, James." But my dad still refused to look at him. "Thanks for bringing her home."

"Sure thing, Mr. Hale." James smiled politely.

My dad waited to speak until we were in the truck, James and the Tower disappearing behind us. "I talked to you this morning, Taylor." His voice, so familiar and dear, sounded strained, laden with accusation and hurt. "You didn't mention one word about coming home."

"I didn't know, I swear. James just showed up. He mentioned that you were upset. He offered to bring us back." I was twisting things a bit, but it was going to be some work to get James anywhere near my father's good graces.

"Is Eden home, too?" Kyle asked.

Against my better judgment, I nodded.

"How is she? Her parents are a wreck."

"She's improving—but Dad, she needs more time. She's not ready to see anyone yet. She doesn't want them to know she's home." My guilt increased as we drove past the Lamberts' property, the lobster traps stacked neatly outside the green-shuttered house.

Mrs. Lambert would be gutted if she knew her daughter was back on the island and hadn't told her. Although that wasn't as bad as what could happen if Eden saw her family before she was ready…

I twisted my hands together. "Dad—can I ask you something? Can we not tell the Lamberts she's home yet? I think it should come from Eden."

He glanced at me, the corners of his mouth turned down. "As soon as they see you, they're going to be asking questions. You want to lie to them about their own daughter?"

"No, of course not." I chose my next words carefully. "But it could be a mistake, a big one, to push Eden before she's ready. You know how much she loves her family—she won't shut them out forever. She went through something awful."

The guilt crept up again, threatening to overtake me. "Can you understand that this needs to be on her terms?"

Big Kyle sighed. He pulled into Becky's driveway and parked next to the pristine, sparkling, abandoned pool. "Can *you* understand that lying to my friends about their daughter—who they're worried sick about—makes me feel like a jerk?"

"Yes." I nodded. "I totally can. But will you do it for me, anyway?"

Dad turned off the truck and inspected me. "You seem different, Taylor. You've always seemed mature for your age, but this is next level."

"W-What do you mean?"

"Not only are you asking me to lie, you're hiding something. I can tell." His face was a lined mask. "You're pretending everything's okay, but I know it's not. This isn't like you. You went through enough with your mother. I'm here for you now—you're safe. All I want to do is help. Tell me what's going on."

"It's not like that." I sighed. Sometimes my dad was too perceptive. "I'm sorry I took off, but I had to get Eden out of here. We were lucky that James could offer us his house."

My dad grunted. "Yeah. We're so damn *lucky* to have James."

"What—you don't like him anymore?" It surprised me how much that hurt.

"Oh, he's great. I love the kid. First, he throws a party and my fourteen-year-old daughter drinks so much she pukes her guts out."

"Um, that party was for *Becky*." My cheeks grew hot. "And wasn't the drinking Amelia's own fault? I'm not sure why you're blaming James."

"*Next*, at the same party," my dad continued, ignoring me, "my seventeen-year-old daughter's best friend and her boyfriend get into a drunken shouting match, and then the poor kid goes and throws himself down a well. So James whisks you and Eden off to one of his many secret mansions, and I don't see you for six weeks."

"Dad—"

"*Then* he flies you home by helicopter and lands you on his front lawn, the sneaky sonofabitch, and doesn't even tell me." He eyed me angrily. "Course I like James. James is my favorite."

I pressed myself against the seat. "You're not being fair—the only reason he had that party was for Becky. He didn't make Amelia drink her face off. She was partying with those kids down on the beach. And Eden and Brian... What happened was *terrible*, Dad. But it wasn't James's fault."

"Of course it was terrible. But you disappearing like that..." Even though the truck was off, he gripped the steering wheel. "I just need to know if there's something else going on."

I shook my head. "Like what, Dad?" *Like James turning Eden into a vampire?*

"Is it drugs?"

"No! I can't believe you'd even say that—"

"Is Eden pregnant?"

"No. Absolutely not."

"Are you?"

"Dad." I wished I could disappear into the seat. "No, I am not pregnant. It's not like that."

He said nothing for a few moments. He stared out at the pool. "I just want you to know that I love you, Taylor. You can trust me. You can trust me with anything."

"I appreciate that. I promise, I'm not hiding anything about anybody being pregnant or drugs. I swear." *Just vampires. And angels. And...Becky.*

"I guess I have to accept that for now. But I'm telling you, I know something's off."

"I promise you that everything's fine. I'm home, I'm starting school next week." I glanced at him quickly. "Okay?"

He grunted a reluctant assent. "Listen, I have to get back to work. But I wanted you to know, Becky told me what happened at the party."

I froze. "S-She did?"

I'd caught Becky with another man's hand on her ass as she ground herself against him. When she'd turned around to face me, her lipstick had been smeared.

"Uh-huh," Dad said. "She admitted that she'd had way too much to drink and was dancing with some guy from off-island. She said you interrupted them, and that you were upset that they were so close together. I'm sorry you had to see her acting like that. She's not exactly setting a good example."

That's a massive understatement. I kept my mouth shut.

My dad frowned. "You know, I probably don't pay enough attention to her."

I longed to say what I really thought, which was *she's literally crazy, and possibly possessed, not to mention a total bitch who doesn't deserve you*, but instead I cleared my throat. "I don't know about that—you're a good husband, and a great dad."

He stared out at the pool. It winked like an aquamarine in the middle of Becky's green, green grass. "She promised me she's going to cut back on the drinking. She's been better these last few weeks."

"That's because I haven't been here." My insides twisted. "She won't be happy I'm home."

"That's not true." But he sighed. "I know it was rough with her and Amelia once you got up here. It was an adjustment, for sure."

I stared straight ahead. I didn't really feel like there'd been many adjustments made on their behalf. Maybe they'd stooped a little lower, all the better to insult me at my level.

"I've talked to them a lot while you were away," he continued. "They're not going to treat you like that anymore. I told them if they did, things wouldn't work out."

"With me living here?"

Big Kyle shook his head. "No, with *me* living here."

I winced. "Dad—no. I don't want you to blow up your life just because of me. I get it. They never signed up for me to come and live here full-time. That wasn't the deal."

"You're my *daughter*. This has nothing to do with any 'deal,' it has to do with family. Your place is home with us." Kyle's shoulders sagged. "Becky has some problems, I know. But she's started going to therapy and she's working on it. Amelia's your sister. You two are blood. I think she missed you, actually. She's been sulking ever since you left."

I wanted to remind him that, since the day she'd been born, all Amelia had done was sulk. "That's nice," I said instead.

I peered past him to the house—it was gorgeous, perfect, straight from the pages of a magazine. I hated it. "Are they inside?"

"Amelia is. Becky's off island, seeing her therapist and going to an exercise class." He pulled me in for a quick hug. "I'm glad you're home. I'll be back in a couple hours. I'll grill some steaks tonight, does that sound okay?"

I nodded. I wanted to ask if James could come over, but I guessed that wouldn't be welcome. "Sure, Dad. Thanks." I climbed from the truck, smiling and waving as he drove away.

I frowned as I started toward the farmhouse-style home. It was lovely, with cedar shingles and tasteful white trim—a shining, perfect exterior. Immaculate. Luxurious. Enviable.

It was just another lie, masking what really lurked inside.

I took a deep breath, then went to see the half-sister from hell.

9

SPOTTED

AMELIA WAS SPRAWLED across the couch, her face buried in her cell phone. My half-sister had the perfect end-of-summer look. Her long legs had a golden tan, and her blond hair had lightened even more. She wore a tank top, athletic shorts, and her usual scowl—as if she smelled something fetid.

"Hey, Amelia." I forced myself to sound friendly.

She looked up from her screen, surprised. "You're home?"

"Yep, just got back." I warily sank down into the chair across from her. "How are you? You ready for school to start?"

She tossed her phone down on the couch. "No way. School sucks. MDI High is, like, a cesspool for mainland trash." A flash of guilt crossed her face: she remembered she was talking to mainland trash.

"What about private school?" I secretly hoped that Amelia would attend boarding school, preferably overseas, and take her mother with her.

"There aren't any good ones up here. All the rich people leave in the winter, so." Amelia shrugged. "What about you? Are you ready for the first day?"

"Not exactly. I'm trying not to think about it." Going to classes every day seemed like a prison sentence. I'd be stuck at MDI High, while James would be home coaching my best friend on how to be a vampire, not to mention babysitting his outlaw supernatural brother. Being apart from him would be hell.

"At least you're a senior. I have four more freaking years." Her scowl deepened.

"Do we really take the mailboat to school?" I couldn't imagine riding a boat every morning in the dead of Maine winter.

"Yep. Then we get the bus in Pine Harbor." She perked up slightly. "Unless Dad's gonna let you drive us. Ooh, or maybe James will lend you a car?"

"Let's not mention it to him." Knowing James, he'd *buy* me a car, and possibly hire a driver who doubled as a bodyguard. "How's your mom doing?"

"She's a total pain. She had the nerve to ground me after the gala. Can you believe that? She was drunker than I was!" Amelia snorted. "She said I made our family look bad. Like *she's* got any room to talk."

"Dad said she's doing better..." I wondered how safe it was to talk to my half-sister about this. "She's seeing a therapist?"

"Ha!" Amelia rolled her eyes. "Mom's the biggest *liar*. She's got an apartment off-island, that's where she's been going."

I shook my head, confused. "What do you mean?"

"I overheard Marybeth mention it one night when they were drinking." Amelia's eyes widened. "Don't tell Dad, okay? They were fighting a *lot* after you left. The last thing I need is him freaking out right now and leaving. It'll totally mess up my life if I have to go stay with him at some gross rental every other weekend."

"I won't say anything." I filed the information away to think about later. "Listen, I know we got off to kind of a bad start this summer..."

"Don't worry about it." Amelia picked up her phone again, dismissing me. "See if you can get us a ride to school, okay? If I can avoid that skank-ass bus, I'll owe you for life."

"Okay...?" I stared as she brushed the hair back from

her face and took a selfie. What was I waiting for, some sort of apology? "I'm gonna go sit by the pool."

Amelia grunted, not looking up from her phone.

Once I was back outside, I inhaled a deep, calming breath. Amelia was only out for herself, and Becky was still lying to my dad.

What's she doing with an apartment off-island? I didn't know the answer to that, but I knew that not much had changed.

I settled on one of the loungers and closed my eyes, wanting some peace for a few minutes, needing to sift through the strange events of the day. But car wheels sounded on the gravel drive, and an old truck pulled in.

It wasn't my dad, and unfortunately, it wasn't James.

Mrs. Lambert's bright red-curls showed through the windshield. *Oh, crap.* But of course Eden's mother was in my driveway, even though I'd only been home for a few minutes… Eden was right. Everybody on the island knew everything.

Mrs. Lambert was a commercial fisherman. She must've finished for the day and come straight from the co-op, because she still wore her knee-high rubber boots. Her cheeks were flushed, and her eyes darted around the yard as though she was looking for something—or more precisely, someone.

"Hey Taylor. I heard you were back." Her tone, normally friendly, was brittle. "Where's Eden?"

"Um… She's not here, Mrs. Taylor." My face heated. I was the worst liar ever. "She's still down on the Vineyard—James is going to fly her home next week."

Her brow furrowed. "Why didn't she come back with you?"

"She wasn't ready," I said lamely.

"Oh. I got my hopes up…" Mrs. Lambert, fit and strong from her years working outdoors, suddenly looked frail. Her shoulders sagged. Her creamy skin had a healthy glow, but in the weeks since I'd last seen her, she'd developed dark circles beneath her eyes. They were purplish, like twin bruises.

"What's wrong with her, Taylor?" Tears crept into her voice. "Why won't she come home?"

I'd always liked Mrs. Lambert. She was kind, and she loved her daughter fiercely. "She's okay, I promise. She just wasn't ready. I had to come back because of school." I jumped up and hugged her.

She hugged me back tightly. "I smell like chum. Sorry about that."

"I can't smell it," I lied. I shook my head. "I'm sorry she's not home yet, but she's doing better."

Mrs. Lambert sighed. Her bright green eyes searched my face. "Why don't I believe you, huh?"

What was it with these parents? "I know you miss her."

"It's not just that—every time I talk to her, I worry more. She doesn't sound the same. I want to understand what's going on."

I took a deep breath. I wanted to reassure Mrs. Lambert, but I needed to buy Eden as much time as possible. "The isolation's been good for her—it's given her some space to deal with everything."

"What happened with Brian was terrible, and I know she feels partly responsible—but..." Mrs. Lambert frowned as she stared off at the trees. "It's not like my daughter to forget about school. Eden's always had a good head on her shoulders. I just can't believe she's not going back to Bowdoin. *And* I can't get a straight answer out of her. She's being evasive—that's not like my daughter."

"You know her better than anyone," I said. "But she's never been through something like this before, right? Maybe she's still in shock. It can take a while to get back to normal."

She sighed. "You're a good friend, Taylor. You've been through a lot yourself. I appreciate you looking out for her these last few weeks."

"Thanks, Mrs. Lambert." But guilt zipped through me. I could never escape the fact that Eden's transformation into a vampire was my fault. Becky had been after *me*. Eden had been caught in the crossfire, and then I'd begged James to turn her…

"Let me know if you hear anything, okay?" Mrs. Lambert's eyes were watery.

I felt so guilty as she drove off, I could barely wave.

My phone buzzed. It was a text from James: *You ok?*

I should be asking you that, I texted back. *How's Luke?*

He sent a poop emoji, followed by a red devil.

I quickly texted back. *Can you come down later?* Now that we were on the island together, it was absolute torture to be separated from him.

I have to babysit, he wrote.

I sighed. *Ok. Going for a walk. I'll call you soon. xx*

I reluctantly put my phone away. I longed to march right down to the Tower, and directly into James's arms, but I had a feeling my dad would come and drag me home. I had to at least appease him the first night I was back. After that, he needed to understand that I was going to be spending as much time with James as possible.

James and Eden...and Luke, I reminded myself. I still hadn't wrapped my brain around the current situation. I kicked a rock as I left the driveway, heading away from Amelia, away from Becky's house. I headed down toward the beach. The local island signposts cheered me

—the makeshift mini-golf course erected by the local children, the grassy field where the summer residents played their nightly game of wiffle-ball.

There were several people down on the town dock, probably waiting for the mailboat. I spotted a familiar form—someone tall, with dark skin and a shaved head, a huge duffel hoisted over his shoulder.

"Elias!" I called, and the figure turned around.

I ran across the field to my friend. By the time I reached him, he'd dropped the duffel onto the ground. He wrapped his big arms around me and squeezed me in for a hug.

"Hey, New Girl."

"Hey." My eyes filled with tears. I hadn't seen my line-cook friend since the night of the accident, and I hadn't exactly been great about returning his text messages.

"Since when did you come home, huh?" His voice held no accusation in it, only kindness.

That made my tears well up further. "T-today. Sorry I haven't called you. It's been sort of crazy…"

"Hey now, it's okay. You've been through a lot." He eyed me, making sure I was calm enough for us to keep talking. "How's she doing? How's Eden?"

I shook my head. "She's not really the same."

He nodded. "I wouldn't expect her to be."

I motioned toward his large bag. "Are you going somewhere?"

He smiled gently. "It's the end of the season. This is the last of my things—I'm heading down to Portland to take classes and work at my uncle's fancy bistro."

My lower lip wobbled. "Will you be back?"

He winked at me. "You think I'd miss harassing my favorite waitress next summer? No way. How's James?"

"He's good." At least that was true.

"I'm glad to hear it. I always did like Daddy Warbucks—make sure he takes care of you."

I laughed. "He will."

Elias glanced over his shoulder; the mailboat was coming. "That's me. Listen, it upset Jenny that you guys both disappeared right before the rush, but she's over it. She'll hire you back. They're only open on weekends till Christmas, then I don't know." Jenny owned the restaurant we worked at, The Portside. "Go and see her—she was worried about Eden. We all were."

"I know." I ducked my head. I was ashamed that I'd been so withdrawn from my new friends.

"Hey." His voice was gentle as he nudged me. "Nobody's judging. It was a terrible thing, that night. And you've already been through a lot."

"T-thank you." I raised my gaze to meet his.

"Anything else you want to tell me, New Girl? I'm here for you." He looked right into my eyes.

In that moment, it felt like Elias was looking *through* me, as if he knew that my circumstances were not in any way, shape or form normal. I wanted to tell him everything—about Eden, about James, about Becky. I wanted to beg him to stay on the island just so I could see his handsome, friendly face.

"I'm going to miss you a lot," I answered, my voice thick with tears.

He briefly hugged me again. "Me too."

I watched as he hustled down and joined the others on the dock. When the mailboat pulled away, he waved and waved.

I trudged back across the field and headed toward the shore, heart heavy.

The island seemed unusually quiet. The road to the town beach was empty, save for a few bikes parked off to the side. Despite the gorgeous weather, the beach was mostly deserted. There were only two families, blankets spread on opposite sides of the tawny sand.

The wind picked up and I wrapped my arms around myself; there was a hint of real coolness in the air. My father said that the end of August always made him a little sad. The summer people headed home, readying their kids for school. Most of the locals moved off to their properties on the mainland, because it was easier to manage their family's hectic schedules from the shore.

The Hales were one of the few non-fishing families that stayed on Dawnhaven year-round—Becky didn't like to leave. I'd never asked her why, but then again, we didn't exactly talk much.

I walked past the beach, heading for James's boathouse, which was really more of a boat-mansion. If I couldn't be with James himself, I could at least hang out on his property. Just being near something of his, something familiar, would make me feel better.

Brand-new, the boathouse was enormous, shingled, with a metal roof and solar panels. I peered inside, glimpsing the *Mia*, the Champlain's sailboat. Then I headed down the side path to the private dock.

We'd had some intense conversations at the boathouse. It was there I'd discovered James could read my aura; later, once we'd started dating, he'd told me the story of his past. It seemed like a lifetime ago that I'd heard the tale of his staking, and that James had shown me the power of his light.

I ached with missing him. The phrase *so close, but yet so far* had never been so on point.

I went and sat at the edge of the dock, feet dangling over the freezing-cold water. The tide had come in, and the blue-green waves rocked gently beneath me, crystalline and clear. A small jellyfish pulsed by, its tendrils trailing.

It felt good to be near the ocean, to think. Meeting James's parents had been overwhelming. Then there was my dad, and Mrs. Lambert... One thing was for sure: the fact that Eden was back on the island wouldn't be a secret for long. Mrs. Lambert had known I was at Becky's before I'd even unpacked.

In that same vein, I wondered what we were going to do about Luke. We couldn't keep him hidden forever. Would James introduce him to people? Would Luke be able to go out in public? What sort of vampire was he— the kind you could trust around humans, like James and Patrick's mother, Mrs. Cavill, or the kind you absolutely could *not*? He was older than James, so he'd had lots of practice being in society. But if he was on the verge of going to supernatural prison for the rest of eternity, maybe conforming to societal norms wasn't really his thing.

I remembered, suddenly, what Josie had said about him: *His brother's crazy. I knew Luke for years before he tried to turn me—I should've known better and stayed away from him, crazy-ass vampire.*

I whipped out my phone, planning to call Josie. I wanted to ask more about Luke. But a boat coming into the harbor caught my eye, along with a flash of familiar white-blond hair. My stomach plummeted before I even knew for sure what I was seeing.

But there she was—Becky, laughing and talking to another passenger. They were on board the *Breathless*, the private water taxi that served the island. Normally the *Breathless* let off passengers at the town landing, but Bud, the captain, was heading toward the private dock to my right.

As the boat turned, I finally saw the other passenger: it was the same handsome man I'd caught Becky with at the gala.

My mind flashed back to that night. I'd found Becky and the man in the darkest corner of the party tent. *Becky turned around, lipstick smeared, chest heaving... My gaze traveled past her, to the handsome man she'd been making out with.*

There he was again, the same guy. Right by her side.

Shit.

I ran for the boathouse, praying they hadn't seen me. I flattened myself against the far part of the building. After the motor cut out, I peered around the corner.

Becky had climbed from the boat and stood on the dock. She wore a white sundress and a jean jacket, her aviators up on top of her head. Her back was to me as she spoke to the man who'd stayed on the *Breathless*.

After a minute, they waved goodbye and Bud started the engine again. Becky was still smiling as she turned and headed up the ramp. I sighed in relief—she hadn't seen me.

But as I glanced back, my stomach plummeted.

The man was staring at me as the boat pulled away.

10

DEPTHS

As PROMISED, Dad grilled steaks. It was our first family dinner since Brian had died, the first time I'd been back around Becky since the gala.

I held my breath as I set the table, nervous to be near her.

But she was the perfect hostess. In what seemed like an effort to placate my dad, she included me in the conversation. "How are you, Taylor?" she asked politely.

I blinked at her. "G-Good." *Fucking petrified of you.*

"Great. I'm glad you're back in time to get ready for school. We have a lot to plan." Becky discussed what supplies Amelia and I needed, our schedules, the expectations surrounding grades and curfews. The questions and answers flowed easily.

It was the Twilight Zone of a family meal.

To watch my stepmother eat her salad, to watch her ignore the fat slices of buttered, rustic bread that my father had grilled to accompany the steaks, was to almost be lulled into forgetting everything she'd done that summer. It made me feel crazy. *There's Becky, forgoing carbs. There's Becky, harassing Amelia about having seconds.* Could she be the same person who'd shaken so crazily, I'd thought she was having a massive seizure? Was this really the same woman who'd thrown Eden and Brian to their deaths right in front of me?

I watched as she poured herself more water. Becky's light tan showed off her bright blue eyes and summer-streaked hair; the smattering of freckles across her nose made her look friendly and accessible, which she most certainly was not.

Becky didn't blink when she asked me about Eden. "Is she coming home soon?" There was no irony in her question, only genuine curiosity.

My mouth full of bread, I only nodded. *Does she seriously not remember what she did?*

"Well, that's good." Becky speared a cucumber with her fork. "It's too bad about Bowdoin, though."

I nodded again, glad my mouth was full so I couldn't gape. If Becky was an actress, she deserved a Golden Globe.

"Taylor, I was wondering if you'd like to try out for

one of the sports teams once school starts." My dad passed me more bread. "MDI has soccer, cross-country, crew, volleyball, and—"

"Dad. *No.*" I quickly swallowed. "I've never done a sport in my life."

"Field hockey?" He looked hopeful. "I bet you could swing one of those sticks."

"I've never even seen a field hockey game." I shook my head. "I'd hurt myself."

"I think it's important for you to have some outside interests." He gave me a meaningful look. "You don't need to be hanging around the island all day after school. There's nothing to do."

I frowned. He meant there was nothing to do but spend time with James.

"I saw Elias today," I said quickly. "He mentioned Jenny was looking for staff down at the Portside. I could ask for my job back." Waitressing wasn't my favorite, but it would be better than trying to whack a ball with a stick while *running.* Plus, I'd be on the island...

"Great. You can work the Sunday brunch—it shouldn't interfere with your other commitments." Dad smiled. He looked pleased that he'd added another item to my agenda, all the better to keep me away from James.

He leaned back in his seat. "Besides, sports look good

for your college transcript. That's why Amelia here is doing golf."

"What?" Amelia almost spit out her water. "There is no way in hell I'm—"

"Amelia, watch your mouth." Becky's tone was firm. "Your father and I have discussed it, and we feel like it would be good for you to try something new. Learn some new skills. Make some new friends."

"I am not wearing a freaking *skort* and hanging out with nerds on a golf course. No way." Amelia crossed her arms against her chest. "You can't make me."

"If you just *try* it this semester, and if you make honor-roll, I'm thinking Fiji for February vacation," Becky announced. "Maybe the same resort that Sylvie stayed at last year. She said it was super-posh."

Sylvie was one of Becky's best friends. She was wealthy and had traveled the world. Amelia blinked at her mother. "Are you serious?"

Kyle stared at Becky, too. "Don't you think that's a little overboard?"

"Nah—Mimi and Pop-pop have been wanting to give us a trip as a Christmas gift forever. They'll be happy to book it." She smiled at them broadly. "It will be nice for us to take a family vacation. You haven't been out of the country before, have you, Taylor?"

"N-No." I was included in the family vacation plans? *Since when?*

"We need to get you a passport," Becky said, as if it were no big deal.

"I heard Fiji's gorgeous—I'm sure you'll love it." Dad smiled at me, pleased. "But probably not as much as you're going to love field hockey. Or crew. Or cross-country."

I groaned, but Amelia kicked me under the table. She didn't have to say it. The kick said it all: *Fiji*. I grabbed another piece of bread, but my appetite had dissipated. Fiji, waitressing and team sports only meant one thing to me: less time with James.

"I'll look into it, okay?" Becky smiled at us—all of us —and I wondered what she was up to. "So, Kyle, I just wanted to let you know—I took the *Breathless* over today with Bryant Pierce. I'd already booked it, but Bryant was heading over to Spruce, so I offered him a ride."

Ding ding ding.

"Bryant Pierce, huh?" My father stopped chewing. He was watching her.

"It's not a big deal. I just wanted to tell you. You know how it is around here—people talk about every-thing, including who shared a water taxi with whom. He was going across at the same time as me. That's all." She shrugged, indicating the matter was closed. "Amelia, let's look at my catalogs after dinner. We'll find you the perfect golf outfit."

"Great. *Yay.*" Amelia wrinkled her nose, as though she smelled something foul. "This better be some freakin' resort. I'm talking five stars, with butler service."

"We'll see, honey." Becky smiled indulgently at her daughter. "You just keep those grades up."

My dad stuffed another piece of bread into his mouth and said nothing. I did the same.

James came over after dinner. He said a quick hello to my dad, Becky, and Amelia—they'd all seen each other over the past few weeks while I'd been gone. Although James was still unfailingly polite, Becky still smiled, Amelia still ogled, and Dad still glared, they all seemed more comfortable with each other than when we'd started dating at the beginning of the summer. It was an odd feeling that my family had been around James when I hadn't.

"Hey James." Becky sounded friendly but casual. With the gala behind them, she probably didn't need to full-court-press suck up to him. "Nice to see you."

"You too, Mrs. Hale." He smiled at her automatically.

I knew him well enough to recognize that it wasn't sincere. But when he turned to me, his smile widened, reaching his eyes. "Hey Taylor."

Even under my dad's watchful glare, I headed straight to James's side and quickly linked my hand through his.

"Hey." I grinned. "I missed you."

His dimple peeped out. "Me too."

I wasn't sure, but I thought Big Kyle rolled his eyes.

"Wanna go outside?" I asked.

When James nodded, I happily pulled him away from the others. We went and sat by the pool. It was a beautiful night, the stars already winking above us. I could really feel a difference in temperature without the sun; the weather had turned cooler. For some reason, that made me sad.

I wrapped my arms around myself, wishing I could snuggle next to James, but knowing that my dad could watch us from the living room. *Ugh.*

"I can't stay long." James looked miserable.

"Why not?" The question sounded half-hysterical.

"My brother, and Eden…" He raked a hand through his thick hair, and I yearned to reach out and touch it. "I can't ask Patrick to watch them both. It's too much."

"Does that mean you can't sleep over?" Usually, James snuck through my window every night and stayed with me. It was one of the many things I'd longed for, and wept over, while I'd been away.

"I can't leave them. But I was thinking…" James leaned closer, and despite the cool weather, the familiar heat kicked up between us. "What if I came down and snuck you out instead?"

"Um." I glanced at the house. "How are we going to do that? I don't have your same…talents." James could silently jump up to my roof; he ran fast, so fast that he could leave his side of the island and reach mine within moments.

He smirked. "I'll drive and hide the truck out on the road. And I'll bring a ladder."

"Okay." I said it before I even let myself think it through. If we got caught, I'd be grounded for my entire senior year. I stared into James's steel-blue eyes. *Whatever.* I didn't care about anything, except being back in his arms.

"Great." James reached out and took my hands. "I can't handle being away from you another night. The last couple of hours have been torture, knowing that you're down here, and that I can't be with you."

"I know. I feel the same."

He leaned closer and brushed his lips against my cheek. He put his mouth to my ear. "I'm so glad you're home it hurts."

His whisper gave me chills. "Me too."

I gripped his hands. No matter what happened, I would never let myself be separated from him again.

James pulled back a little. "Your father's watching us."

I blew out a deep breath and glanced at the house. "That's too bad."

He chuckled. "He's not exactly my biggest fan these days."

"He'll come around." *I hope.* "And then I need to work on winning your mother over."

James shook his head. "Hopefully we won't be seeing her again for a while—for a *long* while. Unless she's picking up Luke."

"It's been a day, huh?" I wanted to ask more about his parents, this *vampire council* they'd mentioned, his brother... I wanted to tell him about Becky, about Fiji, about Mrs. Lambert's visit, about Elias's departure, about Bryant Pierce and the unfortunate requirement that I play a fall sport, but he fidgeted. He should get back to Eden and Luke.

As usual, James could read me. He squeezed my hands. "We'll talk tonight, okay? You can catch me up on everything, and vice versa. But you have to promise me you'll sleep. That's the only way this can work. I need you healthy and *alert*. Not only do we have Becky to deal with, my brother is a piece of work."

"I promise." I'd promise him anything. "Do you have to leave right now?"

He nodded, rising to his feet. "I need to make sure they're not tearing the house apart."

"Is it—is Luke—that bad?"

He arched his eyebrows. "You have no idea."

I groaned. There was a lot to take in, and a lot to consider, but my predominant feeling was still somehow *annoyance*. The babysitting of Luke, the impending beginning of school, of sports, even poor Eden's needs—all of these things were obstacles to what I wanted: James. All James, all the time.

"I'll be here a little before midnight." He kissed the top of my head. "It is going to kill me to wait that long. Good thing I'm immortal."

"Ha." I looked up at him, drinking in his tall form, the big shoulders, the iron-colored hair.

"Bye, Taylor." The dimple flashed one final time as he headed for his truck. "Love you."

"I love you, too."

I sighed as he drove away. We were finally close to each other again, but somehow, that made watching him leave even more difficult.

11

ARRANGEMENTS

MIDNIGHT COULDN'T COME SOON ENOUGH. I paced, waiting for James. A few minutes before twelve, something rustled outside—then his handsome face appeared outside my room, his pale skin bathed in the moonlight. "Hey." He grinned.

My stomach did a somersault. "Hi." I opened the window. He kissed me quickly, then scooted over to show me the ladder.

"Do you think you can climb down okay?" he whispered.

"Yeah, sure." I'd survived flying in his tiny plane and meeting his parents—this couldn't be much worse. I wriggled out of the small opening and carefully started down the rungs. James made certain that I had a solid grip and then dropped noiselessly from the roof. By the time I reached the bottom, he was already holding the ladder in place for me.

"That's pretty annoying." I shook my head.

He leaned close to me. "What?"

"How perfect you are at everything. How fast."

"Ha." He kissed my cheek. "I just don't want anything bad to happen to my girlfriend. I've put her through enough."

I rubbed his arm to reassure him and to simultaneously feel the hard lines of his tricep. "As long as we're okay, so am I."

"Good." He ducked closer, his face next to mine. "But there's still a lot of sucking up to do. I ruined the end of our summer—I need to grovel."

He kissed my cheek, his lips lingering for a moment. "We should go."

I secretly hoped groveling included lots of kissing. I couldn't wait to go to the Tower to find out, but first we had to get away undetected from Becky's. James took the ladder down, somehow staying silent. We snuck around the house in the moonlight, staying on the grass to avoid the crunch of gravel under our feet. It was quiet except for the peepers, the tiny frogs that lived in the ponds tucked inside the island's woods. I winced as he placed the ladder in the truck bed, metal clanging against metal. The last thing I wanted was to wake my dad—or far worse, Becky.

But the lights at the house stayed off. We'd done it.

We drove down the road with the headlights off, Becky's house disappearing behind us. Once we passed the mini-golf course, the school and the run-down store, James turned the headlights on, and we picked up a little speed. He put his hand over mine. "Tell me everything. How did it go with Becky? How did she behave today?"

"She almost seemed...normal. She acted like nothing ever happened this summer." I shook my head.

"I've been getting a very calm vibe from her." James frowned. "I don't exactly trust it."

"Me either. *Something's* going on," I said. "She was down at the Thompson's private dock this afternoon. Bud let her off there. She took the boat with the same guy I saw her with at the gala—she said his name... Bryant something. Bryant Pierce?" That sounded right.

James nodded. "I don't know him—I didn't see her with anyone these last few weeks. Did you talk to her about it?"

"No—she didn't see me. I was sitting down on your dock, but I ran around the corner and hid when they pulled up. *He* saw me, though."

"The guy?"

I shook my head. "Yeah. He gave me sort of a funny look."

James grimaced. "I'll zap him."

It was just like James to threaten to use his white light on somebody just for looking at me funny. "C'mon —it was only a look. He didn't do anything."

"I'm still going to zap him," James said under his breath. "But never mind. What happened after that?"

"Let's see… Becky told my dad about it. And oh wait, I forgot to mention. My dad said Becky was doing better, that she'd been going to therapy and stuff, but Amelia told me that was a lie. She said that Becky rented an apartment off-island, and that's where she's been going."

James listened intently but didn't say a word.

"At dinner, Becky told my dad about taking the boat with Bryant. But that was *after* she said she was bringing us all to Fiji for February vacation. She even included *me*. I think she was doing a bait and switch, you know? To distract my father?"

He nodded. "That wouldn't surprise me. But wait— you're going to Fiji?"

"If Amelia plays golf. And makes honor roll. Oh, and my dad told me I have to play a sport, too."

"Good." James grinned as we pulled up to the Tower.

"I'll be your biggest fan. I'll bring an air horn. And a cowbell."

"Nooo, no, no. That's not going to happen. My dad said something about field hockey." I shuddered as an image of me tripping and falling on my face in front of James flashed in my mind. "You keep saying you want to keep me safe, right? You don't want me playing a sport that involves sticks."

"Maybe cross-country, then." His smile widened. "You just run for miles; I hear it's very soothing."

I groaned. James knew full well I could barely jog down the street without getting a cramp.

"What else?" He didn't bother to glance above my head. "I get the sense you've been kind of busy."

I nodded, relieved to finally talk to him. "I saw Elias. We said goodbye. He's going down to Portland for the off-season. He said I could get my job back, if I wanted."

"That's good." James smiled.

I shrugged. I needed the money, but I'd hate to commit to yet another thing that would keep me away from him.

"Also, Eden's mom stopped by. She was almost in tears. She wanted to know why Eden hadn't come home with me." I winced at the memory of Mrs. Lambert's strained expression.

He sighed. "Eden needs more time. I'll have her call her mother tomorrow."

I nodded, even though I knew a phone call wouldn't be good enough for Mrs. Lambert.

He brushed the hair back from my face. "You had quite the afternoon, huh?"

"I guess I did. I missed you, though." I went to open the passenger door, but he stopped me.

"A couple of quick things." James eyed the house, and his mouth tightened. "Luke's a *complete* disaster. Patrick already looks like he's ready to move out. I haven't restrained Eden, but she's pacing in her room as if she's a prisoner plotting a breakout."

"Did she meet Luke yet?"

James shook his head. "No way. I'm going to keep them completely separate—my brother's a terrible influence. I don't want him near her."

He took a deep breath. "We should get in there. I can't leave poor Patrick alone for much longer."

"Okay." I had a million more questions—about Luke, about his history—but selfish considerations won out. "So... How are we going to do this tonight? Will we sleep in your room?" My heart rate kicked up.

"I hope so." His voice was husky. "I've been thinking about having you in my bed for weeks."

My stomach did another somersault. Just as he

leaned closer, Patrick shouted from the deck, "James? Get the *hell* in here!"

"Crap." James hopped out of the truck. "Stay here?"

"I'm all in," I reminded him. "I'm not staying behind anymore."

He cursed but grabbed my hand as we ran across the lawn. "What happened?"

Patrick glared as he pointed at the house. "Do not *ever* leave me alone with him again. He busted Eden out of her room. They're insane. They already got into the wine."

James cursed again and ran inside, leaving me and Patrick behind.

"Seriously?" Patrick shook his head. "I've met a lot of vampires, but I've never seen shit like this."

"I WAS ONLY GONE FOR TEN GODDAMNED MINUTES!" James roared from the house.

I went to follow him, but Patrick grabbed my arm. "You need to be careful. Luke's dangerous, but I don't think he'll bite you. Eden's another story."

"Did she try to bite *you*?" I asked, horrified.

"No—like I told you, my half-blood doesn't appeal to them. But she sniffed me tonight. She's desperate. If you go in there, do exactly what James says."

I nodded shakily. "Okay. Thanks, Patrick."

"Good luck. I'm staying out here. I'll take the mosquitos any day."

The mosquitos were terrible, so what awaited inside was probably pretty rough. I grimaced as I followed James. Music blared from upstairs, and I heard him yell again. "Turn it *off*, Luke! Eden, get the hell off there!"

I flew up the stairs to find Luke, Eden and James in one of the guest bedrooms. Some eighties rock song was blasting from a Bluetooth speaker. Eden was on top of the bed, dancing wildly, curls flying. Several empty bottles of wine littered the nightstand. James and Luke were in each other's faces, glowering.

Nervous, and eager to break up an impending brawl, I raised my voice up over the music. "Hey guys!"

"Taylor!" Before I knew it, Eden had jumped off the bed and landed directly beside me. Her eyes glittered as she leaned in close. "How's my bestie?"

I might've imagined it, but the closer she got, the more her nostrils seemed to flare.

"Get the hell away from her!" James roared over the pounding music. In an instant, he had her in a headlock.

Luke laughed until James decided to multi-task—he kicked the speaker to the ground and stomped on it, turning it to dust. "I told you to turn it down." His voice was icy calm, even as Eden struggled beneath his bicep.

Luke blinked at his brother. "That speaker cost five thousand dollars."

"Whatever." James leaned his face next to Eden's ear, and she clawed at his muscled forearm. "You go near Taylor again, and we're going to have a real problem. Do you understand?"

Eden's eyes were bulging in her head. "Y-yes."

James released her. She rubbed her neck and glared at him. "Your brother's right—you need to chill. I wouldn't hurt her. She's my best friend!"

"There's a reason you're supposed to stay in your room," James said quietly. "You're not in control yet. The people who care about you understand that—my brother isn't one of them. Now please go back inside."

Eden's gaze flicked from James to Luke.

"Go," Luke told her. "I'll come hang with you later. I'll bring the wine." He waggled his eyebrows.

Still rubbing her throat, Eden rolled her eyes at me on the way out.

"What the hell do you think you're doing?" James asked his brother.

"What?" Luke shrugged. He'd changed out of the distressed sweater into a tight-fitting black T-shirt. It clung to his sinewy chest and narrow hips. "She's *bored*. You think locking her up's the right thing to do? I thought you were some sort of humanitarian, not a zoo-keeper."

James flew toward Luke, resuming what appeared to be his new favorite position—getting in his big brother's face. "Do you understand that she could hurt someone? That she could hurt *Taylor*? Or escape and go pillage the island?"

"At least somebody would be getting some action around here." Luke shrugged.

Though his brother was slightly taller, James had the advantage of a thicker build. His bicep flexed as he jabbed a finger at Luke. "You are staying in *my* home because Dad asked *me* for a favor."

Luke frowned. "Don't remind me."

"I would *absolutely* throw you out if I could."

"Trust me, if there was anywhere else I could go, I'd do it," Luke said. "Dad stuck me with you to add insult to injury. Not only does my life suck, but now the Golden Boy gets to babysit me and boss me around. Just *perfect.*"

"I didn't ask for this." James practically spit the words out.

Luke shrugged. "So you know, I don't plan on getting into trouble. He meant it when he said he'd let me rot."

"Mom would come to your rescue. She always does."

"Not this time." Luke shook his head. "Dad said it

himself: he'd be happy to have me out of his hair once and for all."

"So don't give him anymore ammo, idiot. This can be as easy as we make it." James relaxed little, his hunched shoulders dropping. "Remember: it's my house, my rules. Eden has to stay in her room, unless I'm here and say it's okay for her to come out. You shouldn't be feeding her alcohol and cranking music—"

"She's *bored*. Can you blame her?" Luke narrowed his eyes. "You need to loosen up a little, otherwise you're going to have a mutiny on your hands. When was the last time you were around a newbie, anyway? Did you forget what they're like?"

"I know Eden. I understand what she needs. I've been looking out for her."

"That's not what she said." Luke crossed his arms against his chest. "She told me she's been down on the Vineyard on literal house arrest for the past six weeks. She said half-blood and blondie over there were the only ones who took care of her."

"That's because she needed to be isolated, and I needed to be here," James said. "I had to handle the police and deal with her family."

"Really?" Luke's eyebrow shot up a fraction. "Eden said you were having an emotional breakdown because you turned her."

"Did she?" James's tone became guardedly casual.

Luke watched his brother carefully. "What really happened? Dad didn't tell me anything, and Eden didn't understand much. What made you bite her? It's not like you. You've always been so…determined."

"I didn't feel that I had a choice. She's Taylor's best friend. The circumstances of her death were unfortunate." James's face darkened. "It was something I felt responsible for."

"James." I took a step closer. "It wasn't your fault. It was mine."

"By the way, Taylor—*hi*." Luke smirked when James tensed. "I know I'm not supposed to talk to you, but I don't want to be rude."

"Hey." I went and stood by James, linking my hand through his. James relaxed a little, then leaned in to kiss my cheek.

Luke watched, his eyebrow arching higher. "Woah— you two are something. You've got it bad, bro. Good thing there's a stocked wine cellar. It's gonna be a long couple of months."

"Get used to it." James squeezed my hand.

"Fine—whatever." Luke shrugged. "But can you please tell me what's been going on around here? I'm light on details."

"There's been some activity on the island." James frowned. "Something I've never seen before."

"Dad mentioned it was funky up here." Luke's face lit up. "If this island's got a nasty paranormal, I'm *in*. Dad said he wanted me to help you—maybe if I do, he'll let me off this rock and back to civilization. Preferably with a harem. I haven't had one of those in a while…"

James shook his head. "Can you please not talk like that in front of Taylor?"

"Only if you tell me everything. You want me out of here just as bad as I want to go. So help a brother out— explain what's happened." Luke grabbed an unopened bottle of wine off the table and started out of the room. "C'mon, it's not like we don't have the time."

James sighed as he turned to me. "You should go to bed. I'm sorry. But he's right—Dad wants him involved. I'd never say it to his face, but he has some talents."

"You don't have to say it to my face for me to hear it," Luke called from the stairs. "But thanks, even though it's a pretty limp description of my throbbing geyser of aptitudes."

James grimaced. "If he helps us, maybe we can get rid of him sooner."

"Lucky for you, I have thick skin!" Luke hollered.

James squeezed my hand. "I'm sorry."

I smiled at him. "You don't have to keep saying that."

119

He put his hands on my hips and pulled me closer. "I'm feeling sorry for myself. I wanted to spend every second of tonight by your side."

I threw my arms around his neck. "I'm not going anywhere. We have time."

He gazed down at me. "There isn't enough time. Not with you." He kissed me, and I clung to him.

And then once again, before I was ready, he was gone.

12

READY OR NOT

FOR THE NEXT FEW NIGHTS, I met James at my window. He brought me to the Tower, laid me down in his bed, then kissed me goodnight. He always left before I was ready. He'd updated the house rules: Eden was allowed out of her room under the direct supervision of James or Patrick—not Luke—but she was not to leave the grounds.

Luke made the best of Eden's newfound freedom by introducing her to the wine cellar. At any hour of the night, it sounded like a frat party out on the deck. Good thing there were no neighbors for miles.

In the early hours of the morning, while it was still dark, James gently woke me. He carried me out to the truck and drove me home, making sure I got into my bedroom undetected.

The last precious few days of summer slipped away quickly, without major event. Dawnhaven was quiet, too quiet.

It almost felt like...

It almost felt like the island was holding its breath.

I kept waiting for the other shoe to drop—for Becky to attack me again, for Eden to break loose and go wild, for something, *anything.* But an eerie calm settled like the heavy dew on the grass. Was starting senior year at a brand-new high school the worst thing I had to fear?

That felt like a truly rhetorical question on the morning of August 31st, the first day of classes. Amelia and I stumbled into the kitchen, grunting greetings at each other. I made myself a coffee in the Keurig, yawning while it poured. Amelia glared with puffy eyes, only perking up when she spotted the enormous cinnamon rolls my father had brought home the day before. She'd already popped one into the microwave when Becky appeared.

My stepmother grinned at us. "Happy first day of school!" Her hair was drawn up into a high ponytail; expensive workout clothes encased her lithe body. She wore no makeup, but with her Botox-plumped skin, eyelash extensions and light tan, she looked flawless. "Are you girls ready?"

Amelia snorted. I shrugged.

"You need to wake up. Time for a healthy breakfast." Becky pulled the fresh-squeezed orange juice out of the refrigerator but stopped dead in her tracks when she saw Amelia's cinnamon roll. "You have *got* to be kidding me. That is nothing but sugar and carbs."

Amelia stuffed a huge, gooey bite into her mouth. She gave her mother an innocent look as she chewed.

"Don't you dare finish that! It probably has thirty-eight grams of sugar—as much as a soda." Becky snatched the plate from her daughter's hands. "That's no way to start your day. You'll have a sugar crash, not to mention the bloating."

Amelia gave her mother the finger behind her back. I couldn't blame her—Becky constantly picked on her diet.

I grabbed a banana and slipped up the rear staircase as Becky chattered at her daughter. "Scrambled egg whites with spinach is a much healthier option. That way, you get your protein first thing. It helps you feel full."

She must've noticed my escape because she called, "Taylor? Aren't you going to eat?"

"I already did," I lied. "I'm going to take a shower."

"Don't make us late," Becky snapped. "I'm not paying Bud to take you across if you miss the mailboat!"

I yearned to remind her I had my own money from

waitressing tips, or that James would be happy to take me in his boat. But I kept my mouth shut. It was safer to stay in my room, away from her. I showered, washing my hair quickly, and then blew it dry in record time. I threw on an outfit that I hoped would be acceptable school attire: jean shorts, a hoodie, and my flip-flops. I vowed to buy some new clothes later that week once I figured out what everyone else was wearing. I wanted to fit in at MDI High, not so much to make friends but to glide by under the radar, unnoticed.

Becky frowned when I made it downstairs. "That's what you're wearing?"

"Um…"

Amelia came around the corner in a cute pale-yellow sundress. Her lips curled down when she saw me. "I'm changing. I knew it—I'm way too dressed up!" she wailed, then flew back to her room.

Becky threw up her hands. "You're the one who picked that dress out!" But the only response was Amelia's footsteps pounding up the stairs. My step-mother narrowed her eyes at me. "Thanks a lot."

Ah, there she was. The real Becky. "I'm sorry. I didn't ask her what she was wearing. This is kind of all I have." I motioned to my shorts and T-shirt.

"Then you should go shopping." Becky sounded exasperated.

"Hey pumpkin." My dad came in from the front door —he'd already been at work for an hour. "You ready for your first day?"

"Sort of?"

His handsome face split into a grin. "You're going to do just fine. Do you have everything you need?"

I nodded. Dad had bought me a new backpack, and we'd ordered all my school supplies online.

"What about your sneakers and stuff for practice?" Dad asked.

"Practice?" I tucked my hair behind my ear and blinked at him, as if I didn't understand the meaning of the word. "I thought I told you—fall sports started last week. I already missed tryouts." I tried to sound displeased instead of what I actually was: elated.

"Right, but did *I* tell *you*?" Big Kyle smiled. "I talked to the cross-country coach. She said they'd be happy to take you as a walk-on. The more the merrier, that's what she said."

My stomach plummeted. "Really?"

"Really. Go on and pack some workout clothes and your sneakers. Practice is right after school." Dad seemed cheered. "Amelia's got golf, so you two can take the late bus to Pine Harbor and grab the four-thirty mailboat home."

"Great," I said through gritted teeth. I loved my dad

more than anything, but I still cursed him as I went to get my stuff for practice.

The four of us awkwardly headed to the town dock together. Becky was proud as a peacock, ushering her daughter down the ramp to join the other island families sending their kids off to school. Amelia had changed into a more casual outfit, hot-pink athletic shorts and a white tank top that showed off her tan. She was silent, probably stewing that she had to stay after for golf. My dad seemed oblivious and happy: this was the first time he'd ever taken me to school, I realized.

I reached over and patted his arm. "Thank you for getting me my calculator and the rest of my stuff."

"Thank you for saying thank you, and also for going to cross-country practice." He grinned at me.

"Ugh."

"You'll be all right." But Dad's face darkened as he walked down the ramp to the deck. "Looks like I'm not the only one here to see you off."

"Huh?" But I immediately saw who he was talking about. James stood off to the side, his hoodie pulled up, his hands stuffed into his pockets. If he was trying to fade into the background, he was doing a terrible job. His handsome face drew all eyes. All the women on the dock were stealing glances in his direction—as were Becky and Amelia.

"Hi James!" Becky waved, motioning for him to join us. "Come on over." As always, she was unfailingly nice to him. Probably because he was gorgeous and rich.

The other families parted for him. "Hey." He linked his hand through mine as soon as he reached my side.

Cross-country or not, my heart lifted.

"Hey." I beamed at him. I'm pretty sure my dad snorted.

"Good morning, Mrs. Hale, Mr. Hale," James said. "Hey Amelia. You ready for school?"

"No." Amelia scowled. "First, we have to take this stupid mailboat, then the bus, then school—I heard ninth grade blows—*then* we have to go to practice. And then we have to take the late bus and the boat again. It totally sucks!"

"Gee Amelia, tell us how you really feel." My dad frowned at her. "You'll be fine. I know it's a new school, but you don't need to be nervous. You have a bunch of friends, and you're going to have a great day."

"I'm not *nervous*." She sounded every inch the disgusted teenager that she was.

James's turned to me, smirking. "So. You're staying after for practice, too?"

"Cross country." I said it under my breath, like a curse word.

"You're going to love it." James chuckled. "Hey—you

should take the Yukon to school. It's in the lot at Pine Harbor, just sitting there."

"We don't need to take your car. That's really nice of you to offer, though," I said.

Amelia pounced immediately. "Taylor, come *on*! Of course we'll take the Yukon!"

She smiled at James. "That's so nice of you—the bus *totally* blows. This way, we won't have to sit next to all the losers!"

"Watch your mouth," my father hissed. He eyed the other kids around us, some of whom were most certainly the losers Amelia was referring to.

"The keys are in the driver's side," James said, nudging me. "Please take it. It's at least faster than the bus. Plus, *no losers*," he whispered.

I giggled, even though Amelia's behavior was mortifying. "Thank you."

"You're welcome." He grinned, dimple peeking out. "And have fun at practice. I know how much you love running."

My foul look could rival one of Amelia's. I started to say something back, but the mailboat came into view, speeding toward the dock. A sick feeling settled in my stomach—I was leaving him for the day.

James sensed my discomfort immediately. "Hey." He

squeezed my hand—under my father's watchful eye, he didn't dare do much more. "Have fun, okay? Today's going to fly by. You'll do great."

"Thanks."

Becky snapped a few pictures of Amelia—and then, because my dad was there, of me. She even took one of me and James. Dad hugged me, then James briefly kissed my cheek.

I really didn't want to get on the boat, but I did it anyway. I swallowed hard as we waved goodbye. James smiled encouragingly, making my heart squeeze.

We sped off and the dock disappeared behind us, a tiny speck.

"Score," Amelia said as she settled in next to me. "I totally knew he'd give us the car!"

I frowned, first at her, then in general. The hours stretched out before me, every one of them without James. I didn't even enjoy the trip across Hart Sound, the sights and smell of which I normally loved. I was too busy pouting.

We reached the dock in Pine Harbor and scrambled out. The younger kids lined up, all cute with their haircuts and new backpacks, and waited for the bus. Amelia gloated as we followed two of the other high schoolers to the parking lot, quickly finding James's Yukon. She casually threw her stuff inside—but then looked around to see if anyone noticed whose car she was climbing into. I rolled my eyes but held my tongue. She was fourteen. There wasn't much use lecturing her, even though to be near her was to be annoyed.

My mood darkened further as I climbed into the driver's seat and searched for the keys. I hadn't let myself focus on it much, but I was dreading the first day of school. Who wanted to be the new girl?

I located the keys in the side compartment—they had a piece of paper wrapped around them with my name on it.

Dear Taylor,
I knew you'd read this before school because I knew Amelia would want to take the car. Premonition? Maybe. You know I'm good like that.
I hope you have a wonderful first day. I'm sorry that things have been so hectic since you've been home. But as much as I hate to let you go, I'm happy that you're starting senior year. Enjoy every second. You're smart, beautiful and talented, and I'm so proud to be your boyfriend. You're a gift to the whole world, Taylor—not to mention the best thing that's ever happened to me. So please, enjoy your day. For me, but more importantly, for you.
Love you, babe.

James

"What's that?" Amelia eyed the note with interest.

"Nothing." But that was a lie. I dreaded school, but at least I had James to come home to.

That was something. That was everything.

13

I'M NEW, TOO

MOUNT DESERT ISLAND HIGH was in Bar Harbor, about a ten-minute drive from the dock. I'd never driven the Yukon before, but for such a beast of a car, it handled easily. It was comfortable and quiet, gliding along the deserted roads in the early morning sunlight.

"So," I asked Amelia, "are you excited for any of your classes?"

"No." Her face was buried in her phone. "My mom's making me take all AP stuff. It's going to suck."

"At least you'll be able to get into a good college."

"Ugh," Amelia groaned. "I wish I could go *now*. You're so lucky you get out of here next year."

"Yeah." In fact, I had no idea what the next year would bring.

"Are you *going* to college?" Amelia looked at me as

though for the first time. She'd probably never wondered about my grades before—or if they'd let someone poor, with a dead junkie mother, into an institution of higher learning.

"I have the GPA for it. But I don't know." I sucked in a deep breath as we pulled into the MDI High. It was bigger than I expected, and so much nicer than my school back home. There was a football field surrounded by an enormous track and floodlights. The building itself was redbrick, with typical New England charm. There were solar panels across the roof, a modern touch. "This is nice. It's so pretty."

Amelia snorted. "Are you kidding? MDI's a cesspool. Look at the parking lot—it's all rusted trucks and old jeeps. Most of the kids here buy their clothes at Mitchy's."

Mitchy's was a discount store off-island. My half-sister needed to learn to read the room—my denim shorts were from Mitchy's. "That doesn't make it a cesspool."

I pulled into one of the open parking spots, careful not to get too close to the other cars, as Amelia smoothed her hair.

"Whatever." She shrugged. "But face it: in the winter, MDI is a frozen freaking tundra—it *sucks*. Nobody wants to live here. The summer residents leave because they can. The only people who stay are the ones who're stuck here."

"Dad and Becky seem to like it," I offered, not sure why I was bothering.

"Dad likes it because he's weird, Mom likes it because she hates change." Amelia unbuckled and rolled her eyes. "See you later."

"Yeah, see you." But she was already gone, adjusting her backpack and dangerously lowering her tank top.

I grabbed my own backpack and my sports bag, inwardly groaning. Talking to Amelia hadn't exactly set a great tone for the day. I took the note from James and shoved it inside my pocket. If nothing else, it would give me courage.

I navigated the busy lot, slipping between the cars that were dropping off students at the curb. A flashy black BMW sports car caught my eye. Sleek and expensive-looking, with dark-tinted windows, it stood out from the sea of pickup trucks and minivans. The driver slowed to let me pass, then sped around the parking lot.

My sense of dread intensified as I pushed through the doors. The hall was packed with students and rows of forest-green lockers. Everyone seemed to talk at once. Most of the kids I passed eyed me up and down; they recognized a new student when they saw one.

My cheeks heated and I ducked my head. I patted the

note in my pocket, reminding myself that I wasn't really alone. I didn't know where I was going, but I somehow found the office, two plain double doors near what appeared to be the nurse's station and an abandoned-looking water fountain.

A harried administrative assistant holding a stack of papers paused long enough to notice me. "Hey there." Her smile deepened. "Are you one of the new girls?"

I looked around, but there was no one else. "You know who I am?"

The woman laughed. "There's less than a hundred kids in the senior class. We've been expecting you. Which one are you—Taylor or Mali?"

"Taylor."

"Do you know where you're going?"

"Um." I felt my cheeks burning. "You sent me a class list and a map, but I'm still hopeless."

"Let me show you, honey."

Even though she was obviously swamped, the nice lady left her sheaf of papers behind and brought me to my first class, AP Statistics.

I felt eyes on me again as we headed down the crowded halls. The other students craned their necks to see the new girl following the nice office lady. The one upside was that a few of the other girls wore outfits similar to mine—jean shorts and hoodies. There was some comfort in that.

The woman brought me to my class and introduced me to my teacher, Ms. Greene. I made a beeline for the back of the room and didn't look at anyone as I chose my seat. My hands were a little shaky as I took out my pen and notebook, preparing to take notes.

Ms. Greene was taking attendance when the administrative assistant returned. Behind her was another student, a girl. She was curvy, with long, stick-straight ebony hair, pale skin and dark-framed glasses. She hung her head a bit, her shiny locks covering her face like a shield.

"Ms. Greene, here's your other student—Mali, from upstate New York."

Ms. Greene smiled at the girl. "Welcome to Statistics."

"Thanks," Mali mumbled. She picked her way to the back of the class to the only available seat—the one next to mine. By the time she sat down, her cheeks were pink.

"Hey," I said.

She peered at me, then quickly looked away. "Hey."

"Just give me a second, everyone—technical difficulties." Ms. Greene frowned and tapped into her laptop. I glanced at the girl next to me. She was beautiful, her pale skin contrasting with her glossy dark hair. Thick eyelashes framed her bright-blue eyes. She wore a plain white T-shirt, black leggings, and high-top sneakers. Her backpack was new, simple and gray. I recognized the intent behind the outfit: socially acceptable, while being simple enough to blend in.

Maybe she was as nervous as I was.

"I'm Taylor," I said. "I'm new, too."

"Hey. I'm Mali."

Ms. Greene began talking, and it forced us to turn our attention to the front of the room. I methodically took notes, but the period dragged on. Finally, the bell rang, and we gathered our books. I hadn't exactly enjoyed Statistics, but I was loath to go back out to the crowded hallway and try to find my next class.

"What do you have second period?" I asked Mali.

She scowled down at her schedule. "Um… Environmental Science. Except I have *no* idea where Room 32B is."

"Me either." I smiled at her, happy to at least have someone to talk to. "I'm in Room 32D—Human Biology. They must be the science labs. Want to try and find them together?"

"Yeah." She blew out a deep breath. "That'd be great."

We headed into the crowded hallway and I was

relieved to have her next to me. "So, you moved from New York?"

"Yeah, upstate." Her scowl deepened. "From one freezing hellhole to another. What about you?"

"Massachusetts."

"Are you a senior?" Mali asked me.

"Yep."

"Me, too." For the first time, the girl smiled at me.

"Hey, this looks like the right wing." I counted the room numbers, which finally led down to 32. "Have a good class."

"You too." She hesitated for a second, twisting her lips into a frown. "Um… Do you want to sit together at lunch?"

I exhaled deeply. "I thought you'd never ask."

"Okay," she said, sounding relieved. "See you later."

"Yeah, see you."

Mali and I had both packed our lunches.

"I didn't want to stand in line for food," I admitted. "I didn't know what it was going to be like, and I didn't want to have to ask."

"Me either." She unwrapped a delicious-looking salad with grilled chicken, corn and tomatoes. "This school's like the one I went to back home—it's *so* small. Everybody knows everybody."

"My school wasn't like this. It was big." I shrugged. "Maybe this won't be so bad."

Mali arched an eyebrow. "I'm pretty sure it will be. Being new sucks—especially senior year."

I unpacked my peanut-butter-and-jelly sandwich, which was sad compared to Mali's lunch. "Maybe it'll fly by." I said it just as much to cheer myself as Mali.

"I hope so." Her voice took on an icy edge. "I am *so* out of here once I graduate. We're on one of the islands —the house doesn't even have Wi-Fi. How am I supposed to do my homework?"

"Which island?" I asked. "Most of them have internet, at least."

"Not at my grandma's house." She frowned as she speared a tomato. "We're on Spruce. All our neighbors have satellite television and Wi-Fi, but not Grandma. She's too old-school. She wants nothing to do with it."

"We're practically neighbors—I'm on Dawnhaven." I had a sip of water. "I didn't see you on the mailboat this morning."

"My uncle brought me across. He booked the water taxi." She shrugged. "He had to go off-island early."

"So... You live with your grandma and your uncle?"

Mali snorted. "*And* my dad. *And* my aunts and uncles. *And* my little-brat cousins."

"Oh. Huh." Not wanting to pry, I waited to see if she'd elaborate.

"We just moved up here last week—I didn't want to come. We kept going back and forth about it. What about you?"

"I got here at the beginning of June."

"Yeah?" Mali's gaze flicked over me. "Do you like it?"

"I love it," I admitted, cheeks heating. All I could think of was James. "The summer was amazing."

"Huh. I probably should have come up then, before the weather turned. We haven't been here in the summer for a long time." She shook her head. "Anyway, my grandmother's getting old. She needs help with the house, so everybody is pitching in. She won't sell it, even though living on ten acres on a practically deserted island isn't exactly easy. So here I am."

"Maybe you'll like it." I smiled, trying to encourage her.

"Maybe. My mom *hates* it up here. She said she'd rather get a divorce than move—so that's what she's doing." She laughed, but it sounded hollow.

"Oh. Sorry. You couldn't stay with her in New York?"

Mali shook her head. "That wasn't an option."

"Sorry," I said again.

She groaned. "Not as sorry as I am."

The other students started gathering their things, so we did the same. "Are you taking the mailboat home after school?" Mali asked hopefully.

"Not till later. I have to stay after for cross-country." Dread filled me; I'd forgotten all about practice.

"Oh, good—I'm doing cross-country, too!" Mali smiled. "My dad says I need to get some exercise. He doesn't want me back on the island too soon. He said I don't need any more time to mope."

"That sounds like *my* dad." But of course, Big Kyle also wanted to keep me away from James.

"I'm glad we'll be on the team together, but..." Mali eyed me. "You've got long legs—I don't think I'll be able to keep up."

"Um, I'm the slowest runner on the planet. I'll be last at everything."

"Phew—I'll be right next to you. See you after school!" Mali seemed cheered as she headed to her class.

I, however, had mixed emotions as I wandered down the hall to Spanish. On the one hand, I was happy to have a friendly face on the cross-country team. On the other, Mali would see how very un-athletic I was. She was just another person to be embarrassed in front of...

I tried to quell the thoughts. Mali seemed nice. I

hadn't expected to make any new friends at MDI, but maybe I'd been wrong. In a similar fashion, maybe cross-country wouldn't be as bad as I was thinking... I vowed to at least give it a chance.

"OH MY GOD." I groaned and bent over. "This is so much worse than I thought."

"What are we training for, huh?" Mali panted beside me. "The freaking apocalypse?"

Coach Blaisdell—a very fit and cruelly perky forty-something year old—had made us run two miles. In a row. Then she'd lined the team up for sprints on the spare soccer field. She kept smiling, saying such stupid things as "good job."

"Why do we need to sprint?" I gasped.

Mali eyed Coach Blaisdell, who'd raised the whistle to her lips again. "Maybe so we can eventually run away from that crazy bitch?"

I didn't have time to agree with her. Coach blew the whistle, and we couldn't speak for the rest of practice.

I felt like I might throw up as Mali and I limped across the parking lot to the Yukon. I'd offered my friend a ride back to Pine Harbor, where we'd take the mailboat home together.

Amelia waited at the SUV, her perpetual scowl marring her pretty face. "What the hell happened to you?"

"Running. So much running." I opened the trunk and we threw our stuff inside.

"It *had* to be better than golf practice," Amelia complained. "It was me and two other freshmen who are complete dorks, three nerdy juniors, and one girl who's a senior and a *total* bitch."

She eyed Mali up and down. "Who're *you*?" she asked, rudely.

Mali raised her eyebrows. I had the sense that since Coach had kicked the shit out of us at practice, she didn't have much patience left. "I'm Mali. Taylor's giving me a ride to the mailboat. Who're *you*?"

"Amelia—Taylor's sister." Amelia's brow furrowed, as if it surprised her she'd admitted that out loud. "Where do you live?"

"Spruce," Mali said. She didn't elaborate. I had the sense she didn't care for Amelia's scowling scrutiny very much.

Amelia looked the unfamiliar girl up and down, taking her measure. Even sweaty and disheveled, Mali was very, very pretty. "I've never seen you before."

"I'm new—my dad and I just moved here." Mali navigated around Amelia and helped herself to the front seat. "Nice skort, by the way."

Even though the stitches in my side were killing me —and I still felt like I might puke—I smiled.

The first day had been rough, but it hadn't been *all* bad.

14

SOMETHING

Cowed by Mali's skort comment, Amelia made small-talk on the drive, perhaps in an attempt to win my new friend over. She asked her about where she'd moved from and what she thought of MDI High.

Mali answered her in clipped, one-word responses. For some reason, that made my half-sister even more chatty.

I parked the car in the Pine Harbor lot. We grabbed our things and headed directly down the steep ramp to the dock. The mailboat would be there soon. It hurt to walk down to the platform; my muscles were already sore and screaming.

I limped down, wincing, and then stopped: James waited at the entrance to the private section of the moor. He grinned, his dimple peeping out. "Hey Taylor."

Elated at the sight of him, I grinned back. "Hey."

He looked me up and down. "Are you...limping?"

"Yep. I can barely walk," I admitted as he grabbed my bags for me, throwing them over his big shoulder.

He leaned over to kiss me, but I frowned. "Don't get too close—I was sweating a *lot*."

"Doesn't bother me." His grin deepened as he bravely kissed my cheek. "You're such a jock. It's hot."

I laughed, then quickly stopped. It hurt. Everything hurt.

Mali and Amelia joined us on the dock. James turned his smile on them. "Hey Amelia. Hey..." His eyebrows quirked up.

"Mali." She sounded much more friendly than she'd been to Amelia. "I'm Taylor's friend."

He shot me a quick look, which I answered with an encouraging smile. James nodded at her politely. "It's nice to meet you, Mali. You need a ride across? I have my boat."

"Sure. Thanks." She smiled at James, but he'd already turned away.

A funny expression crossed his face. He looked... perplexed. But it only lasted for a moment, then he composed his features.

Amelia peered past him, down the dock. "You brought the Hinckley?"

James chuckled at her name-dropping. Hinckley was a famous brand of boats, well-known on MDI because of their beautiful craftsmanship, whopping price tag, and celebrity owners. Even Martha Stewart had a Hinckley. "Yup. Here, give me your bag, Amelia. You probably got a workout at golf."

She snorted. "Ugh, it sucked."

He smiled at her and cheerfully said, "Tell me how you really feel."

Amelia didn't miss a beat. "It *really* sucked."

We followed him down past several enormous luxury yachts and sailboats to the *Norumbega*. Its wooden hull gleamed in the late-afternoon sun.

Mali looked intrigued. "Interesting name—it's unusual, isn't it? Don't most boats have female names?"

"Some of them." James's sounded non-committal and vaguely unfriendly.

Mali didn't seem to notice. "But yours means something else—I've heard about Norumbega before. It was a mythical city, right? Weren't the European settlers looking for it or something?"

James shrugged. "Not sure."

Why was he lying to her?

Mali seemed unperturbed. "So... Are you from here originally? You must be, with a boat name like that."

"No." James didn't sound as though he cared to elaborate. He gave her a perfunctory smile and started the engine. "Where should I drop you?"

"On Spruce, please."

He concentrated on pulling out from the landing. "At the town dock?"

"Um, my grandmother's house is around the other side of the island. Would you mind taking me there?" Mali asked.

"No problem." But James's response was stiff.

Mali leaned closer to me. "I wouldn't ask, but we got our butts kicked at practice—I'm not sure if I can walk." She laughed, then winced. "Ow. Taylor, do your *ribs* hurt?"

"Yep." I shook my head. "I don't know why, except that everything hurts. So my ribs might as well join in."

We quieted down as the boat picked up speed across Hart Sound. I wondered why James had been so stand-offish, but it would have to wait. Amelia was texting and taking selfies, probably bragging about the Hinckley. I spied the Osprey standing aside its enormous nest and pointed it out to Mali.

"I know," she called over the roar of the engine. "It's really cool!"

The ride over to Spruce was quick. James slowed down as we approached the island. "Which part are you on?" he asked Mali. His tone, I noticed, was still unfriendly.

"The south side." She jutted her chin at me and lowered her voice. "I hope this is okay."

"It's fine," I assured her, even though I wasn't sure about that.

We were quiet as James circled the island, which was larger than Dawnhaven, and more populated. We saw enormous houses with private docks leading down to the water.

"It's right up here." Mali pointed further ahead. "With the blue awning."

The dock was large and weathered. The awning was sun-bleached and a little dilapidated—part of it was ripped, its shredded fabric flapping in the breeze.

James pulled alongside and began tying up, but Mali climbed out before he could finish. "Thanks for the ride. It was nice to meet you."

He nodded in response.

"Taylor, see you tomorrow." She flashed me a smile, but then winced as she started walking. "Everything hurts!" Her laughter echoed as she disappeared down a long, woodsy trail.

"Huh." Amelia scowled after her. "The houses on this side of the island are huge."

"It's her grandmother's, I guess." I shrugged. "Mali just moved up here."

"Really?" James asked.

I nodded. "Yeah, she said her grandmother can't take care of the property by herself anymore."

The muscle in James's jaw jumped. "I see."

See what? I wanted to ask, but I didn't think it wise to talk to him in front of Amelia. The boat picked up speed as we headed to Dawnhaven.

I wondered what was troubling him.

WE DOCKED AT THE BOATHOUSE, then James drove us home in his truck. I waited until Amelia was inside to ask, "What's wrong?"

"So… You made a new friend." His lips pressed together in a thin line. He was quiet for a moment. "Mali seems nice."

"Yeah, I think so." I tried to read his expression. "Do you not like her?"

"It's not that." He scowled out at Becky's pool. "There's just something about her. Something confusing."

"Her aura?" I couldn't imagine what else it could be.

"Yes." He shook his head. "But no."

"*James?* Can you please translate that for me?"

He frowned. "What's her last name?"

"I don't—I don't know."

His frown deepened. "Her aura was very *cheerful*."

"And that's a problem because—why is that a problem?"

"How did you meet her?" he asked instead of answering me.

"She's the other new girl. She was in my first class, so we talked a little. We ate lunch together."

"And she's also running cross-country?" He sounded suspicious.

"Just because she's new and she's running cross-country doesn't mean you need to sound like that."

"Like what?"

I shook my head. "Like you're planning on zapping her."

"Her aura reminded me of something." He looked perplexed again. "You need to be careful with her, Taylor."

"I think you're taking your protective instincts a little too far." I grabbed my things. I wasn't often annoyed with him, but he was being too suspicious. It reminded me of my dad.

Although Dad has some reasons to worry—I am *in love*

with an immortal who used to be a vampire. I shoved the thought aside. "I'll see you tonight?"

James nodded, but he still seemed lost in his thoughts. "I'll be here at the normal time." He absent-mindedly kissed me on the cheek.

I hopped out of the truck, then leaned back. "Wait—how's Eden?" This was the longest I'd been separated from my friend since James had turned her.

"She's hanging in there. She and Luke are probably tearing the house apart, though—I should get home before Patrick mutinies."

"Yeah, better safe than sorry. See you later?" He'd bothered me with what he'd said about Mali, but I still hated to be away from him so quickly.

"Yeah, see you." James nodded at me. "Oh, and Taylor?"

"Yeah?"

"I love you."

His steel-blue gaze burned, melting me, all my annoyance slipping away. "I love you, too."

I LIMPED up the stairs and into the shower, my muscles screaming in protest. I could barely lift my arms to wash my hair. *What the hell?* How did I hurt my arms *running*?

It didn't matter. Like Mali had said, even my ribs hurt. It didn't have to make sense to be true.

I blew my hair dry for the second time that day. *Note to self—start doing your hair at night.* I was so sweaty from practice, I'd had to wash it again. But if I did that twice a day every day, my hair would dry out and frizz into oblivion...

As I worked through my hair, my thoughts circled back to Mali, and to James. Why had he been so unfriendly to her? I didn't think he was being reasonable. I understood that he wanted to protect me, but not every person I met was a threat.

I headed downstairs and set the table for dinner. My dad was outside, grilling. Amelia was frowning over her homework in the living room. Becky was nowhere to be seen.

I ducked around the corner to the immaculate kitchen. Normally at this hour, my step-monster would be preparing a salad while sucking down a glass of white wine. But the room was empty.

I padded out to see Amelia. "I'm setting the table. Is your mom here?"

She scowled up at me. "No, she just texted me—she's staying off-island for a late barre class. She's taking Bud over after. She said to make sure we do our homework."

"Okay, thanks."

Big Kyle had grilled salmon, asparagus, and once again, fresh bread slathered in butter. He set out limes, lemons and mango salsa as toppings.

Without Becky around to shame her, Amelia ate three helpings of bread. "This is *so* good, Dad."

"Thanks honey—my little golfer needs her carbs." He smiled. "So. How was practice for my ace athletes?"

"It sucked." Amelia had her story, and she was sticking with it.

"My entire body hurts." I snagged another piece of bread. "My coach made us run two miles. *In a row.*"

Dad chuckled. "It's good for you. I'm proud of you both."

"Thanks, Dad." Amelia seemed in decent spirits, maybe because of the bread. "Did mom say what time she'd be home?"

"After she's done with hot yoga—whenever that is."

Amelia looked momentarily confused. "Oh, I thought she was going to barre."

Big Kyle shrugged. "Could be. I can't keep up with your mother and her trendy exercises."

"Why is she working out so late at night?" Amelia asked, her nose scrunching. "She's got all day."

"I don't know, honey." He smiled at his daughter, but I caught an undercurrent of something else—an edge. "Your mother's a mystery sometimes."

I wondered if my dad would ever realize how true that statement was.

I checked my phone after I finished the dishes. There was a text from Mali: *See you tomorrow! PS, I can't move. Even my texting thumb hurts lol.*

I laughed, then texted her back.

I hurt all over. I could barely dry my hair! See you tomorrow. Hope we don't die at practice. Then I sent her a smiley face, followed by a skull and crossbones.

I knew James thought I should be careful, and I would. But I was at least going to give my new friend a chance.

Where was the harm in that?

15

SURPRISE

RIGHT BEFORE MIDNIGHT, James appeared outside my room.

"Hurry babe, okay?" he whispered.

I sat up in bed quickly, then I moaned—sharp pain knifed through my muscles. The soreness had only increased as the hours passed. I limped to the window, then winced with each step down the ladder.

James kissed my head when I reached the bottom. "Poor thing. Here, let me carry you to the truck."

"I'm fine, really—"

"But we need to hurry." He lifted me up and moved swiftly across the silvery grass, lit by the moonlight.

"What's the rush?" I asked, my anxiety rising.

"It's nothing bad, I promise." James deposited me inside the cab, then hustled to the driver's side in a blur of speed. He drove faster than usual back to the Tower. Silence settled between us as we bumped over the dirt road, and I frowned out at the darkness, worrying.

But nothing seemed amiss as we passed the No Trespassing sign and pulled into the Tower's grounds. The moon hung in the sky, surrounded by thousands of stars. The ocean rocked gently in the distance. The Tower itself looked beautiful and impenetrable as always, its stone facade gleaming in the moonlight.

James took out his phone and checked the time — *11:59*, the illuminated numbers declared. "Ah. We just made it."

"Just made *what*?"

He grinned as the clock turned to midnight. "Happy birthday, Taylor."

"What? Oh...*ha*. I forgot!" With everything that had gone on, besides school starting, I had completely forgotten about my birthday.

"September first, the day the world became a better place. It's a big one, Taylor. Eighteen." He brushed the hair back from my face. "I can't believe it."

"So how much older than me are you *now*? I must be catching up," I joked. The thing was, I didn't know James's exact age—or his birthday. "When *is* your birthday? Is that the sort of thing vampires celebrate?"

"Sure we do. Mine's November 18th." He grinned. "I'm a Scorpio."

"Isn't that bad?" I asked.

"People love to hate on Scorpios—but it beats being a Virgo." He winked at me.

I couldn't argue about that—I knew nothing about my astrological sign. "You still didn't tell me how old you are."

"I think we're continuing to baby-step our way around that one." He nudged me playfully. "All right, c'mon. I've got a surprise for you."

We hopped out of the truck and James took several large steps out into the middle of the yard. "Stay there, okay?"

A familiar *caw* echoed down from the pines bordering the lawn. James laughed. "I guess Edgar also wants to wish you a happy birthday."

I couldn't see the crow in the darkness, but I felt his presence nearby. "Thanks, Edgar," I called. He cawed back, and I laughed too.

"Here we go—happy birthday, Taylor." Suddenly, James was outlined in a bluish-white light. *His* light. I sucked in a deep breath. I hadn't seen his power since the night of the gala.

He bowed his head and put his palms together. Light pulsated though him; he tossed a sphere of it into the sky. The blazing orb hung in the air for a moment, then changed shape. Suddenly, an enormous birthday cake hologram hovered over the yard, eighteen candles crackling with bluish-white light.

James moved his hands again, and the cake shifted, seeming to vaporize into a million tiny sparks. They spread out across the lawn, blanketing us from above, then fluttered to the ground, glittering fallen stars.

"James." My voice welled with emotion. "That was amazing."

"I've been working on it." He grinned, his face reflected in the fading embers. "I have something else for you, too."

He was suddenly right in front of me, holding my hand. That was one of James's other powers—the ability to run fast, even faster than other vampires.

I mean, *he* called it running. I was still convinced it was closer to teleporting.

James pressed a small velvet box into my hands, and my breath caught in my throat. "W-What's this?"

He didn't bother to glance above my head, but he still chuckled. My cheeks heated. He didn't have to read my aura to know what I'd been thinking.

"Not *that*. It's something else. Although you *are* eighteen now..." He laughed again. "I'm ready when you are."

I took a deep, shuddery breath. "Ha ha." But part of me hoped he wasn't kidding.

He pressed my fingers around the gift. "Here, open it."

James raised his hands so that they glowed with enough light so I could see.

"My own personal flashlight." I giggled. "I never expected you to be so *useful*."

"I know. In addition to my looks, it's a bit much," he joked. But he held still as I opened the box. I had the sense that he was holding his breath.

Nestled inside was a necklace. Attached to the slim golden chain was a pendant, engraved with a symbol—a segmented cross, outlined in what looked like tiny diamonds. The symbol matched the tattoo on James's bicep. It represented not only the cross, but a Native American image for balance.

"It's beautiful." I felt the pendant between my fingers. "But it's too much. Are those *diamonds*?"

He chuckled. "Maybe."

"I can't accept this, James." I could never reciprocate an expensive gift like this, not if I waited tables for a hundred years. "It's too generous."

"Taylor." He sighed. "I don't mean to make you uncomfortable, but you have to understand that the money is meaningless to me. As far as I'm concerned, I can't ever be generous *enough* with you. And it's not about the price tag of something—that's irrelevant."

He brushed the hair back from my face as he continued, "I want you to have this. You know this symbol is important to me—but I didn't realize how much it really meant until we were together."

James stepped closer, tentatively putting his palms against my hips. "You bring balance to my existence. Even through the hard parts, the challenges. I wouldn't want my world to ever go back to the way it was before, without you. The weeks we spent apart this summer taught me that. I *can't* ever go back to my life before you —it doesn't even exist for me anymore. I know what I want now, what I...need."

I leaned closer to him, the familiar heat rising between us.

"Do you want to wear it?" His voice was husky.

"Absolutely."

I lifted my hair and he clasped it around my neck. Though small, the pendant had a certain weight to it. It felt smooth pressed against the skin of my chest.

James put his fingers under my chin, raising it. "It's perfect. Not as perfect as you, of course."

I put my palm over the pendant protectively. "I love it. Thank you."

"It's my pleasure."

He leaned down to kiss me, and I responded hungrily. He sank his hands deep into my hair and I arched my back, anything to get close to him, my sore muscles be damned. James deepened the kiss, his tongue searching for mine. When they connected, I felt a powerful surge of electricity all the way down to my core. His eagerness was clear in his every touch. He pulled me closer and my body lit up with heat, fire for him. I wrapped my hands around his neck, wanting more—

"Sorry to interrupt your make-out session," Luke called gleefully from the deck, "but your presence is requested inside."

James cursed as we broke apart.

Luke's laughter rolled across the yard. "I *do* apologize, but there was baking involved. And balloons. Let's not let them deflate, shall we? Although I'm sure that's not the only thing deflating right now."

James cursed again as he gripped my hand and led me to the house. "Bye, Edgar," I called, trying to lighten the mood.

The big bird cawed back softly from the trees; I wondered if he was sleepy. The thought made me yawn —the long day was catching up to me.

But as soon as we entered the Tower, it was clear that I was alone in my fatigue. *"Surprise!"* Eden and Luke jumped out from the dining room. Tons of pink and red balloons crowded behind them.

"Happy birthday!" Eden bounded across the room, coming as close as she could before James frowned. "Yay, another year of Taylor!"

Luke came up beside her, waving fake pom-poms. "Give me a *T*! Give me an *A*! I could go on…"

"Ha ha, thanks guys. You got me balloons? That was so nice!"

"Yeah, and I baked you a cake. C'mon." Luke steered me by the elbow toward the dining room.

James hissed but I winked at him. "It's okay… It's my birthday. He *baked* for me. Come and have some cake."

Luke brought me to the head of the table and pulled out my chair. They'd filled the room with balloons and set the enormous table for four with linen napkins, the good silver, and china dessert plates. There was an open bottle of champagne chilling in an ornate gold bucket, and a plump-looking cake with white frosting atop a tall crystal stand.

"Patrick's sorry he had to miss this." Luke didn't sound upset about the absence of our friend at all. "That's the problem with being human—you can't keep up."

Luke winked at me as I yawned. "Present company excluded, of course."

"Ha. Sorry. Long day." I yawned again.

James stepped protectively toward me. "Taylor, you can go to bed—"

"Not so fast." Luke tsked. "I made this cake from *scratch*. The birthday girl needs a slice."

"I'd love some," I said, before James could get into another fight with his brother.

Luke cut the cake open, revealing a deep-red interior. He handed me a piece.

"Red velvet with cream-cheese frosting," Eden said. "Looks delicious, if you're into that sort of thing."

Luke beamed at her, then handed her a slice. "One for my red-headed friend."

Eden narrowed her eyes at her plate. "I don't think I can eat that, Luke. Sorry." She reached for the champagne instead.

"You should try it. I made it red just for you, Red." Luke smiled at her in encouragement. "That's the next thing you and I are going to work on—blending in with the humans. Eating food is a great way to do that. It gives you a reason to go out in public, too, a legit one."

Eden sniffed her frosting while I shoveled more cake into my mouth. "This is *incredible*."

Luke beamed while James scowled. "I made it just for you, Princess. Four-hundred years of baking experience can really help you perfect your technique."

I almost choked. "Four h-*hundred*?"

"Something like that." Luke glanced at a scowling James, then quickly back at me. "In other breaking news, James told me you made a new friend. Is she cute?"

I glanced at James. "Um…"

"What do you care if she's cute?" Eden narrowed her eyes at Luke, then turned to me. "Please don't tell me you've found a BFF replacement."

"Never," I assured her. "But I did meet someone today—her name's Mali—she's the other new girl at MDI. It was nice to not be the only new one, you know? There's safety in numbers. At least I had someone to sit with at lunch."

I turned my attention back to Luke. "Anyway, why do you ask?"

"James mentioned there was something a little… different…about her." He raised his eyebrows. "What do you think about that, Taylor?"

"I thought she was nice." I shook my head, confused.

"Can I meet her, too? I bet she smells good. Please don't leave me behind," Eden whined.

James sat forward with a start. "You know what…?"

Luke watched him with interest. "Go on."

"That was the other thing." James frowned out at the balloons, but he didn't appear to see them. "Mali didn't have a recognizable scent. I only registered that just now."

"You're losing your edge, bro." Luke drank some champagne.

James's frown deepened. "Her aura threw me off. And Taylor's scent overwhelmed me."

My cheeks heated. "I told you I was sweaty from practice."

"No, no—not like that." James squeezed my hand. "I meant your natural fragrance. It always overpowers me in the best way possible. And I don't pay much attention to other humans anymore, but I'm certainly aware of their scents. For instance, I could pick Amelia out blindfolded. But Mali didn't have one, at least not that I could sense… I didn't really notice it at the time, but I *should* have."

Luke and James looked at each other for a beat.

"Do you have her as a contact?" Luke asked me.

"Yeah, she texted me earlier."

James's frown deepened as I handed my phone over to Luke. "I didn't have a chance to mention it," I told him lightly. "And it's not like it's a big deal. It's a *text*."

Luke's eyes narrowed at my phone. "You spell it M-A-L-I, huh?"

When I nodded, Luke turned to James. "That's the ancestral spelling."

"What does that mean?" I asked.

Luke's eyes glittered. "It means I'd like to meet her. I hope Mali wants to make more new friends."

"Um." I looked back and forth between James and his brother. "Maybe?"

"What about me?" Eden pouted at Luke. "Did you forget *I'm* your friend?"

"Never. You know you're my girl." Luke waggled his eyebrows. "You've been so good, I was just going to ask James about that thing we discussed, remember?"

Eden's eyes glittered. "How could I forget?"

"What?" James frowned at his brother.

"I wanted to take Eden out into the woods tonight. The deer have been out there, I've heard them." Luke patted her hand. "She's been doing so good, I thought it might be time to take her out to hunt. Fully supervised, of course."

James started to argue, but Eden leaned forward. "*Please*, James. If you're with me, nothing bad will happen. I just want to see if I can do it—if I *can* hunt. And I want to drink from something alive, not a plastic bag..."

When I shuddered, she grimaced. "Sorry, Taylor."

"It's okay." Eden looked so hopeful I felt sorry for her. I nodded at James. "I'm going to bed, anyway. You and Luke will keep her safe. She's been trying so hard."

James grunted and sat back in his seat.

"Is that a yes?" Eden looked from Luke to James.

"It's a yes." James didn't look happy about it, but Eden hopped up and hugged him.

"Yay! A pulse, I'm finally going to drink from something with a pulse!" She shimmied her way out to the kitchen.

"Nice, bro." Luke clapped him on the shoulder. "I love it when you show a little mercy."

"Don't patronize me and don't let her out of your sight." James scowled at him. "I'm going to take Taylor to bed—then we'll go to the forest. And what do you think about going over to Spruce after? I want to check out Mali's family compound."

"YES! I'm all in on that. I do love a good field trip, especially in the middle of the night." Luke fist-pumped. "See you later, Taylor—happy birthday."

James got to his feet and held his hand out for me. "Time for bed, birthday girl."

"Woah, woah—wait a minute." My head was spinning. "I have questions, lots of them."

He led me up the back stairs. "Ask while we climb. It's late, babe."

"First of all, *why* are you going to Spruce?"

"I just want to look at where Mali lives, and whether I can pick up any scents over there." James said it matter-of-factly. "I'm double checking myself to see if I misunderstood what I experienced earlier."

"Isn't that dangerous, sneaking over to someone's yard in the middle of the night?" I asked.

He scoffed. "Who do you think's going to hurt me and Luke? We're immortal, remember? And I'm immortal-*undead*."

I gritted my teeth. "I think you're being a little too cocky."

"And *I* think it's adorable when you worry about me."

I really didn't want him to go. "Who will watch Eden? Aren't you worried about leaving her alone with me?"

James chuckled. "Nice try. She'll be full of deer blood, and I'll shackle her to her bed and lock her door before I leave. *And* I'll set the alarm, which has a motion detector. Patrick's still here. If she trips the sensor, he'll be up and on it. See? I thought of everything—you don't have to worry."

"I'm not worried about *me*." I scowled as we reached the bedroom and he turned down the covers. The sooner he got me to bed, the sooner he'd leave. "And I have more questions."

"You're running out of time."

"I'll be quick, then: What did Luke mean about Mali —about the spelling of her name? And did he say he's *four hundred* years old? How old does that make you, huh? And is Eden really going to be okay out in the woods?"

"I won't let anything bad happen to Eden, I promise." He tucked me in. "And as for the rest of it, why don't we worry about all that tomorrow? Like I said earlier—baby steps."

I frowned as he brushed the hair off my face.

"But I want to know *now*." I yawned.

"*Now* you sleep." He kissed my forehead, then each of my cheeks, and finally, my lips. "Happy birthday, my love. We'll get to all of this in good time."

I took his face between my hands. "Please be safe."

"Always." He kissed me again, gentle but firm. "Lights out. It's a school night."

"Ugh." I pulled the covers up to my chin.

I was worried about him and his night visit to Spruce. I also wanted to know everything, and I wanted to know it *now*, but my humanity—and cross-country practice—caught up with me. There was nothing I could do; my eyelids were heavy, so heavy.

"Love you," I mumbled as my eyes fluttered close. "Best birthday ever."

"I love you more."

His whisper was the last thing I heard before I fell into a deep, dreamless sleep.

16

OFF-ISLAND

I WOKE up to James gently shaking my shoulder. I squinted around, surprised to find myself in the cab of his truck. We were parked on the main road, just outside Becky's property.

"Huh?" I blinked, confused. The sky was still dark. "What are we doing down here?"

"It's almost morning—time for your dad to get up." James kissed the top of my head. "You were in a dead sleep, so I carried you out to the truck. Even the bumps didn't wake you, although as usual, your eyes were half open." He chuckled.

I suddenly sat up straight, remembering everything from the night before. "Wait—what happened on Spruce?"

"Nothing too interesting. Luke and I got out of there pretty quick." James drew me to him and kissed the top of my head, then my cheeks. He hugged me closer.

I nestled against his chest, protected and warm. I felt like I could fall back asleep in his embrace. "Ugh, I don't want to leave you again. And go to school. And *practice*," I groaned.

"You'll be fine." But James's expression tightened. "Promise me you'll be safe? I wish I didn't have to stay on the island to babysit. I'd come with you and hang out near MDI High all day, just to make sure you're okay."

"You don't have to do that." I kissed his cheek. "I'll be fine."

"Just promise me." He squeezed me close again.

I sighed in his embrace, warm and happy. "I promise."

James reluctantly released me. "I can hear your dad waking up. I better get you inside. Happy birthday, Taylor."

I brushed my lips against his cheek. "Thank you for the light show outside, and for my necklace." I clasped my hand around the pendant. "I'm never going to take it off."

"Good. I like the idea of something I gave you being with you when I'm not." He lifted my chin, his steel-blue eyes gazing into mine.

I stared back, momentarily dazzled. "Wait—how did Eden do last night?"

"She was fine. She enjoyed herself."

"That's good." I refused to think about the poor deer. "I guess I should go, huh?"

"I guess so." He kissed me briefly, too briefly. "Have a great day, Taylor. I love you."

"I love you, too."

I WENT through the motions of getting ready, my body achy and sore. I would never admit it to James, but leaving the house at night was going to be tough now that school had started. I was exhausted; the day stretched out endlessly before me.

Showered, dressed, hair brushed, I dragged myself down to the kitchen for breakfast. My dad was usually at work at that hour, but he greeted me with a big hug.

"Hey, there she is—the birthday girl! I got you a muffin to celebrate."

An enormous blueberry-corn muffin waited on the table. "Aw, thanks Dad." I made myself a coffee so I could wake up enough to act enthusiastic.

"Eighteen years young." Big Kyle shook his head. "I can't believe it."

Amelia shuffled into the kitchen, yawning. "Happy birthday, Taylor."

"Thanks." I didn't think she'd ever said that to me in my life. "When's *your* birthday, Amelia?"

"April 14th." She yawned again. "I can't wait till I'm sixteen, so dad here can buy me a Range Rover. Only two years to go."

"Ha ha *ha*," Dad said. "Don't hold your breath."

Amelia inhaled deeply and held it, her cheeks puffing out like a chipmunk's. I actually laughed. Who knew my half-sister could crack a joke?

My sense of humor subsided—and I became instantly awake and alert—as Becky entered the kitchen. She was dressed in her workout clothes as always, but she seemed off. Her movements were slower than usual, her eyes slightly puffy and bloodshot. I'd had enough experience with such things to recognize that she was hungover.

My dad visibly stiffened as she fumbled with the coffeemaker, but he didn't say a word.

"Hey Taylor." She forced a smile in my direction. "Happy birthday." Big Kyle must've coached her on that.

"Thanks Becky." I made a beeline for the table and my muffin, all the better to put some space between us.

The necessary formalities over, she nodded toward

her daughter. "Amelia, hurry up and eat. I'll take you girls down to the dock—I'm meeting Sylvie for a walk after."

"You're getting an awful lot of exercise lately," Big Kyle said. He watched her carefully.

She smiled at him, not missing a beat. "I'm committed to being my best self. You know that."

"Sure thing, Bec." Dad turned to me. "You ready to open your present, or do you want to wait for tonight?"

"Whatever you want." All *I* wanted was for the tightness around my dad's eyes to relax. "I'm ready when you are."

"I think you might want it for today." He grinned as he pulled a gift bag out from the pantry and handed it to me.

"Thanks, Dad." I spread out the tissue paper and laughed when I saw what was inside. "Is this, like, a cross-country survival kit?"

Big Kyle's grin deepened. "For my precious athlete."

"Ha, this is perfect." I placed an assembly of gifts on the table: colorful headbands to keep my hair out of my face, a brand-new water bottle, two pairs of running shorts, a cute T-shirt, super-padded running socks, and best of all, a heating pad. "Dad, this is awesome." I held up the pad. "This might be my favorite!"

I got up and hugged him.

"I have something for you, too." Becky disappeared into the study, then returned with an elegantly wrapped present. The large box was covered with heavy, gold-embossed white paper, tied with a pale-pink bow.

"Wow, thanks." My stepmother had never bought me a gift in my life, except for the cash she dutifully mailed me every Christmas. I unwrapped the present carefully, half-worried about what I might find. *A severed head?* I forced my thoughts to subside before I erupted into nervous, near-hysterical laughter.

There was a brand-new pair of running shoes inside, expensive ones, size seven. "T-Thank you."

"I noticed you were still wearing my old sneakers." She couldn't seem to muster any warmth into her voice, even in front of my dad. "So I figured you'd want something better for practice."

"I really appreciate it." I did, even if she was the devil. These shoes would be *way* more comfortable than her ill-fitting hand-me-downs that I hadn't thought to replace.

"All right girls, enough dilly dallying. Let's get a move on." Becky started making Amelia's lunch.

I scarfed down my muffin, then fled the kitchen to get my things together.

Both Dad and Becky walked us down to the dock

again. They didn't speak to each other, or to us. Amelia didn't seem to notice. She just complained about the morning fog, and how it was making her hair damp. We joined the other families on the town dock and waited for the mailboat. It was quiet and uneventful; the mist seemed to settle like a hush over everyone.

"Thanks again for my presents, Dad." I hugged him as the boat sped into view. "I love them."

"It's my pleasure, honey." He smiled at me, but he looked sad. "Happy birthday—have a good day at school."

If Amelia noticed anything off with Dad and Becky, she didn't mention it while we were on the mailboat. She scrolled her phone, only looking up once to ask, "Are we taking the Yukon today?"

"I have the keys."

"Good," she grunted. "We can blast the heat—maybe my hair will dry."

I rolled my eyes, deciding to ignore her for the rest of our commute.

SCHOOL CRAWLED BY. I resorted to caffeinated soda to make it through the day. The schedule was different, so I only saw Mali at lunch and at practice.

Coach Blaisdell had us run two miles, followed by sprints, push-ups, sit-ups, and some evil contrivance called "six-inches." I hovered my legs above the ground until my core was shaking so hard, I was certain I'd puke.

Mali and I couldn't even talk—we were too busy wheezing. She looked as sick as I felt by the time practice was over.

"Do you want a ride to Pine Harbor?" I asked, miserably.

"My dad's picking me up. We're supposed to go shopping, but…" She grimaced and wiped the sweaty hair off her face. "But I might just die instead."

"I hear you. I guess I'll see you tomorrow—if we both make it." I laughed, but it hurt, so I frowned.

Mali nodded. "Thank God tomorrow's Friday—we'll at least have two days off."

As if on cue, Coach Blaisdell called, "Don't forget to sign up for the group chat! I have some light training ideas for you over the weekend!"

"No way. 'Light training' my ass." Mali rolled her eyes.

I hitched my bag up on my shoulders, eager to get away from Coach and her group chat. "Let's get out of here before she makes us run more."

We limped up to the parking lot. Mali pointed to a

big pickup truck with New York plates. "That's my dad. See you."

"Yeah, see you." I watched as my friend hobbled away.

Amelia waited at the Yukon, scowling as usual. "Mali doesn't need a ride?"

"I guess not." I winced as I climbed into the driver's seat. I glimpsed myself in the rearview mirror—my face was a dark, beet red.

"What happened to you?" Amelia looked perfect, not a hair out of place, in yet another new golfing outfit.

"We ran. We ran a *lot*." I eased the car out of the parking space. It even hurt to drive.

"Hey listen," Amelia said, "can we stop really quick on the way home? I have to grab something."

I glanced at Amelia. She was using her "nice" voice, which immediately put me on alert. "Stop where?"

"My mom's apartment. She asked me to pick something up." Amelia tossed her ponytail. "It's close—right down the road."

She didn't wait for an answer. She punched the address into her maps app, streaming the directions over the Yukon's Bluetooth speaker.

I sighed as I drove into downtown Bar Harbor, a cute little city that was the tourist hub of Mount Desert Island. Main Street was largely deserted. The rustic, colorful buildings that housed the shops and restaurants were abandoned, hibernating until next summer came.

I followed the directions, taking a left onto a narrow residential road.

"That's it." Amelia pointed to a gray building. "Number Four. You can park in the back."

I pulled around the rear of the building. There were only two other cars in the lot, a dilapidated minivan and a dented Sentra. "Are you sure this is the right place?" I couldn't picture Becky parking her pristine Mercedes SUV anywhere near these cars.

"Yep. Wait right here—I'll be back." Amelia grabbed her backpack and leapt out before I could argue.

I waited for her, feeling confused. Why did my stepmother have an apartment? Why would she rent something in *this* working-class neighborhood, which was surely not her style?

Did my dad have *any* idea about this? I didn't want to be the one to tell him, but then again...

After a few minutes, Amelia threw the car door open and hopped inside. "All set." She shoved her backpack between her legs, and something clanged loudly within. "Shit!" She unzipped it and peered into the interior, making sure everything was intact.

"What's in there?" I asked.

"None of your business." She didn't look at me.

I turned the car off. "Amelia Hale, you tell me what's inside that bag or I am not leaving this parking lot."

"Fine." She opened the top and showed me: a gallon of vodka and two bottles of wine.

"Um, what the hell do you think you're doing?"

"Taking my mother's booze. Big freaking deal." She glared at me. "Let's go, we're going to miss the mailboat."

I pointed to her bag. "You are going to put that stuff back right now."

"Like hell I am." Amelia buckled her seatbelt.

"I am *not* helping you steal alcohol from your mother."

"Yes, you are." She lifted her chin defiantly. "Or I'm going to tell Dad that you've been sneaking out to James's house every night."

"How did you—oh, never mind." She was just nosy enough to have paid attention to what I'd been up to. I changed tactics. "What do you think your mother's going to say when she finds her stuff gone, huh?"

Amelia shrugged. "She won't even notice. She's stockpiling."

I sighed. "And what if she does?"

"If she *does* notice, then I'll remind her that dad doesn't know about her little fuck-pad. And then she'll shut the hell up."

I winced. "Amelia…"

Two hectic spots of color bloomed in her cheeks. "Can we just go now? Or do you need to lecture me more?"

"I'll lecture while I drive," I grumbled. There was no way I was letting her get away with this. "Don't you remember how sick you got the night of the gala? You puked *everywhere*. What're you doing drinking again? I thought you might've learned your lesson."

Amelia snorted. "I drank Peach Schnapps that night —and yeah, I won't make that mistake again. But some of the older kids are having a bonfire down on the beach Saturday, and I said I'd bring drinks. Now how about you worry about yourself?"

"How about *you*—" But I stopped short. A sleek-looking black BMW pulled into the lot. I couldn't see the driver behind the dark-tinted windows. The sedan paused in front of us, idling for a moment, then sped back toward the road.

"Do you know whose car that is?" I asked Amelia.

"No."

I frowned. "I think I saw it at school the other day…" I wasn't a big car person, but the BMW was immaculate and shiny, just luxurious enough to stand out and make an impression.

"So?" Amelia asked, rousing me from my reverie.

"Can we, like, get going? If we miss the boat, we're screwed."

"Fine. But I'm lecturing you the whole way," I said.

"Whatever. You do you." Amelia popped in her earbuds. "It's not like I care."

I cursed under my breath, but she didn't hear me.

17

A ROCK AND A HARD PLACE

THE REST of the day left me frustrated. The hours slipped by. I wanted to tell my father about Becky's apartment, and about the fact that Amelia was hiding vodka in her room. But Amelia and Becky were both home. Little necessities frittered away the time before bed—showering, homework, family dinner. I didn't have an opportunity to pull him aside.

The truth ate at me.

I slept at James's, but we didn't really talk. Cross-country had completely wiped me out. My limbs were heavy, and I could barely keep my eyes open as we bumped over the gravel road leading to the Tower. I must've nodded off, because I woke up as he tucked me into his gigantic bed.

"Stupid cross-country," I mumbled.

He chuckled as he kissed my forehead. "G'night, Taylor. Love you."

"Love you," I murmured, but I was already half-asleep.

I woke up the next morning in my own bed, wholly confused. Had he carried me up the ladder—or had he just *carried* me? I checked my phone.

You were in a dead sleep when I tried to wake you, so I brought you to your room, James wrote. *Have a great day. But maybe take it easy with the running? It's Friday, babe. Hopefully, we can spend some time together this weekend.* Winking emoji, red heart emoji.

My heart leapt. I'd made it to the weekend. Only one more day off the island, away from him. *Yes,* I texted back immediately, *I can't wait.*

I groaned as soon as my feet hit the floor, then cursed Coach Blaisdell. Everything hurt. I limped to my closet, pulled out my most comfortable leggings and sweatshirt, and took a hot shower. I groaned again, remembering the events from the day before: Becky's apartment, the booze stashed in Amelia's backpack, the secrets I was inadvertently keeping from my dad. Physical *and* mental pain...*yay.* Go, me.

Unfortunately, my dad had already left for the co-op

by the time I made it downstairs. My guilty conscience wouldn't be expunged before school.

Becky was the only one in the kitchen. She waited by the Keurig as her coffee poured out. "Good morning," she said, her voice icy.

"G-Good morning." I wished she'd get away from the coffeemaker; the only way to deal with her was fully caffeinated.

Becky finally moved to the side and I got out a coffee pod. I felt her eyes on me as I self-consciously used the Keurig. To stand in her kitchen, using her coffee and organic cream, was to feel every inch the interloper. I was the house guest who'd long overstayed her welcome, and we still had ten months till graduation.

Becky leaned against the marble countertop. She was, as always, dressed stylishly for her morning work-out, in a cropped sweatshirt and camouflage leggings, her hair up in a high ponytail.

She narrowed her eyes as I turned. "Is that a new necklace?"

"Yeah. James gave it to me for my birthday." I clutched it. To have Becky mention a necklace brought me back to the summer, when she'd accused me of stealing Amelia's aquamarine pendant.

"I take it those are real diamonds?" She attempted to sound friendly and failed.

"Y-Yeah. I guess so."

"So Taylor, I'm glad I caught you." All pretenses of nice evaporated from her voice. She gripped her mug rigidly, the veins in her hands standing out. "What were you girls doing in downtown Bar Harbor yesterday?"

I almost choked on my coffee. "I don't know…?"

Becky blinked at me. "What do you mean, you don't know?"

Amelia stumbled into the kitchen, and I sighed in relief. She looked pissed that she was forced to be awake. "Hey, Amelia. Your mom was just asking what we were doing in Bar Harbor yesterday."

"I was asking *you*, Taylor." Becky's voice was sharp.

Amelia shot me a death look. I knew what it meant—I'd better not rat her out.

"Um." I hesitated, not knowing what to do. "We got lost. I mean, *I* got lost. I needed to go downtown to pick up some poster board for a project I'm doing, but the art store was closed. So I just kind of drove around until I found my way back to the highway," I babbled.

Amelia rolled her eyes. Translation: *you suck at this.*

"Huh." Becky didn't sound remotely satisfied.

"Who told you we were there?" I asked, genuinely curious.

Becky narrowed her eyes at me. "A friend."

"Mom, do you think we can go shopping this weekend?" Amelia interrupted. "A girl at school had on a totally cute sweater—she said she got it at Aqua. Can you take me?"

"Sure thing, honey."

"Thanks, Mom. Can we go today?" Amelia whined. "It's starting to get chilly."

"Of course."

Amelia gave me a pointed look as she headed from the kitchen. "Taylor, go get dressed—we're going to be late!"

I was about to escape up to my room when Becky called me back. "Taylor—hold on a second, please."

I took a deep breath, then faced her. "Yes?"

My stepmother stepped closer. I had to physically restrain myself from backing away. Close enough for me to touch her—which I never would—the smattering of freckles across Becky's nose was visible, as was the bright-blue of her eyes, framed by her fake mink lash extensions. Even though I despised her, her beauty momentarily dazzled me.

"I don't know why you were where you were yesterday." She smiled at me, but it was pure poison. "But I'd like you to understand something. My business is *my* business, as is what's going on between me and your father."

"Okay." I licked my lips. "But... What are you

saying?" If she was giving me a directive, I needed it to be clear. I didn't want to run afoul of the stepmother from hell.

"I'm saying that you should mind *your* business." Her smile broadened, but then it became blurry.

Oh no. I rubbed my eyes, but it didn't help.

Becky was shaking—so fast, it looked like some terrible tremor. "U-U-U-Understand m-m-m-me?" The words came out in a stutter.

I jumped away from her and smashed into the door, rattling it on its hinges.

She suddenly stopped shaking, then blinked at me innocently. "Are we clear?" Her voice was normal.

"Yes." I backed up toward the staircase. "I have to go, okay?"

"Yep—you can't miss the mailboat." She took a sip of coffee as though she were an actual human, not a monster.

I was breathing hard when I made it to my room. I texted James immediately. *Becky was just shaking.*

My phone buzzed instantly. "Are you safe?" he asked.

"Y-Yeah. I think so. I'm going to catch the mailboat and get out of here."

"I'm coming down." He hung up before I could argue.

By the time I'd brushed my teeth and grabbed my backpack, James was at the front door.

"Hey, James. This is a surprise." Becky peered past him. "Where's your truck?"

James's gaze swept over her, searching for signs of trouble. "Patrick dropped me off—he went to see his mom."

"You boys are up early." She smiled brightly, no tremors in sight. "Good for you."

"Thanks." He grabbed my hand and pulled me outside, holding me close to him. "I'll walk the girls down to the dock today, Mrs. Hale. You have a good morning."

"Amelia will be right out. Take care." Becky was still smiling as she shut the door.

"Psycho bitch," I muttered under my breath.

"Now, now." James kept a fake smile on his face in case Becky still watched us. "Let's play nice until I can get you out of here."

"I thought it was over." To my surprise, my eyes filled with tears. "I thought she might not do it again, or that I imagined the whole thing."

"I *hoped* it wouldn't happen again. That maybe she'd adjusted…" James put his arm around me. "But it's okay —I've got you, Taylor. You're safe."

I clung to him, wishing I could believe what he said.

But how could I ever be safe while this strangeness gripped Becky? How could you be safe from something you couldn't understand, that seemed to have no rules?

Amelia came out, and James walked us down to the dock. Again, we had no privacy, no chance to talk about everything that had happened. I longed for the weekend to start, for time alone with him.

James sensed my mood. He kept me close as we waited for the mailboat and was dead serious as he kissed me goodbye.

He took my face between his hands. "I love you, Taylor. I'll keep an eye on things—I promise. I'll see you after school, okay?"

"O-Okay," I said, even though nothing was okay.

───

MALI and I had Statistics again that morning. After first period, we limped together to our science labs.

"I don't know if I can survive another practice," she whined.

"It's just one more before we get a break," I said, trying to sound upbeat. "We can do it."

She arched an eyebrow and I sighed. "Okay, it's going to totally suck. But then it'll be over, right?"

"Ugh, right. See you at lunch." Mali pushed her

glasses up on her nose and was gone.

I saved her a seat at lunch, but she was late getting there. "Sorry about that. We were doing an air-pollution lab, and I knocked over my team's Petri dish." Mali scowled. "I'm pretty sure the other kids hate me."

"Of course not. Everybody understands that sort of thing."

"Really? Because one girl gave me some major side-eye." Mali glumly opened up her lunch container. There was another colorful salad inside, with beets and tomatoes and yellow squash.

"That looks amazing," I said, trying to cheer her up. I attempted to enjoy my peanut-butter-and-jelly, which was lackluster by comparison.

"All these vegetables are from my grandma's garden." She shrugged. "I guess that's pretty cool."

"Yeah, it is." But I stiffened at the mention of her grandmother, remembering that James and Luke had stolen over to her property to spy on Mali and her family.

As if she could read my mind, Mali lowered her fork. "So…James seems nice."

"Oh, thanks."

She frowned. "He didn't seem to like me very much."

"Don't take it personally." I shook my head. "He's just kind of quiet until you get to know him."

"How long have you guys been together?"

"Since the beginning of the summer. I met him when I first got up here."

She nodded. "He lives on Dawnhaven, too?"

"Yeah."

She looked as though she wanted to ask more, but the bell rang. "Crap. I can't be late for Wellness. See you at practice, okay?"

"Okay." I couldn't shake the guilt that zipped through me. *See you at practice, and by the way, my undead boyfriend and his vampire brother are suspicious of you.*

For someone who didn't like to keep secrets, I sure had a few piling up.

IN WHAT MUST'VE BEEN an act of divine intervention, Coach Blaisdell dedicated that afternoon's practice to walking and stretching. Mali and I didn't even limp much as we headed to the parking lot afterwards.

Amelia waited by the Yukon. I unlocked the car and without saying a word, Amelia climbed into the SUV's backseat. Apparently, she'd ceded her co-pilot status to Mali. "Hey guys."

"Hey," we said in unison as we piled in.

"Thank God she didn't make us run," Mali said as she

collapsed against the cool leather seat. "I fell asleep at seven last night—I didn't think I was going to make it through more torture."

"I might actually stay awake enough to enjoy my weekend." My heart lifted at the thought. I couldn't *wait* to see James.

"What're you doing?" Mali asked.

"Nothing really. Just hanging out with James." I suddenly felt guilty; Mali probably didn't have any plans.

"There's a bonfire on Dawnhaven tomorrow night if you want to come," Amelia said. "It's going to start around eight."

Apparently, the more the pretty senior ignored her, the harder Amelia tried.

"Are you going, Taylor?" Mali asked.

"Maybe? I hadn't even thought about it yet." The last thing I wanted was to attend a bonfire where Amelia and her friends would be getting trashed. "Let's text tomorrow, okay?"

I drove to Pine Harbor quickly, eager to get back to the island. But my stomach lurched as I pulled into the parking lot—Becky stood there, waiting, her aviators perched atop of her head.

"Hey mom." Amelia hopped out of the Yukon. "What's up?"

"You wanted to go to Aqua, remember?" Becky smiled indulgently at her daughter. "I figured since you went to golf all week, you deserved a treat."

Becky nodded at me coolly. "Your dad's waiting down on the dock. He can bring you across. Take Amelia's backpack for her?"

"Sure."

Becky glanced at Mali, who was wincing as she slid down from the SUV. They both looked surprised when they made eye contact. "Hi," Mali said first. She sounded as if she recognized Becky.

"Hey." Becky gave her a fake-friendly smile, then quickly ushered Amelia toward Main Street. "See you girls later."

I wanted to ask Mali if she knew Becky, but my dad waved from down on the dock. He'd parked his little motorboat nearby.

His face split into a grin when he saw me. "Hey honey. I brought Becky across, and I thought I'd drive you home after such a long week."

"Do you mind giving my friend Mali a ride to Spruce?" I asked.

"Course not—it's on the way. Nice to meet you, Mali." Dad smiled at her. "Anywhere special I can drop you?"

"The town dock's fine. Thanks so much." Mali smiled back at him.

Big Kyle helped us with the bags, and we crowded onto the little boat. He drove slowly, carefully navigating over the wake in the harbor.

"Are you from up here, Mali?" Dad asked as we picked up speed across Hart Sound.

"My grandma is," she called. "My dad and I just moved back."

Big Kyle smiled and nodded. The wind, combined with the churning of the motor, made conversation nearly impossible. Once we got closer to Spruce, I asked my friend, "Are you sure you don't want us to bring you around to your house? It's no problem."

"Nah, I'm fine. I can actually walk today," she joked. "I'll text you tomorrow, okay? Maybe I'll see you at the bonfire."

"Yeah, sounds good."

Mali hopped out onto the dock. "Thanks again," she called to my dad. With another friendly smile, she climbed up the ramp and disappeared.

"She seems like a nice kid." Dad steered the boat back into the harbor, heading toward home. "Is she in your grade?"

"Yep. We have Stats together, and she's doing cross-country too."

"I'm glad you made a new friend." He smiled in approval.

I steeled myself as the boat picked up speed, the wind whipping my ponytail. Once we docked back on Dawnhaven, I was going to have a heart-to-heart with my dad. I didn't want to be the one to rat out Becky and her apartment, but I couldn't keep a secret like that from him.

No matter how bad Becky scared me. No matter what she might do.

We reached the dock quickly. Big Kyle tied up the boat and helped me off, then hoisted both my backpack and Amelia's over his big shoulders. We started walking up the ramp.

"We need to talk," he said. His tone was suddenly serious.

I blew out a deep breath. "Yeah, we do."

"Listen, Taylor. This isn't going to be easy. But I've thought about it a lot, and time's up." His expression darkened. "I can't take it anymore."

"Oh, Dad." I patted his arm, relieved that he at least had some idea what was going on. "I'm so sorry."

He looked anguished. "Not as sorry as I am. I can't keep a secret like this. It's killing me."

Secret? Confused, I hesitated a moment. "What… What do you mean?"

"We have to tell the Lamberts that Eden's home. I gave you the rest of the week, and I can't do it anymore. Every time I pass her mom down at the co-op, I feel sick." Dad shook his head. "I'm done lying. If you don't tell her the truth, I will."

"Oh." I wasn't prepared for this. "I'll talk to Eden, okay?"

"You need to do more than that. Jean doesn't look good—she's lost weight, she doesn't look like she's been sleeping. She's worried about her daughter. Little does she know she's right down the street." His eyes flashed. "I want you girls to go see her today. I mean it, Taylor."

I nodded, not sure if I could really agree to what he was asking. We walked up the hill towards the house. Our time together was running out; I tried to think of a way to talk to him about Becky.

"So." I gathered my courage. "I thought you might want to talk about something else."

He stared at me blankly. "What?"

"Um." I bit my lip. "Becky? I know you guys have been having some problems..."

He frowned. "Listen to me, you don't need to worry about that. Becky and I had a long talk today. We're dealing with our issues."

"Oh." I wondered how much she'd confessed. "Are you—are you sure?"

"Yeah. I appreciate the concern, but it's between her and me." He patted me on the shoulder. "You just take care of yourself, okay? And Eden. Take care of Eden."

"Sure, Dad." I hesitated. "But there's one more thing. Amelia thinks she's going to a party tomorrow night…"

"Honey, you need to stop worrying about everyone else." Big Kyle's frown deepened. "I know you had to take care of your mother, but things are different now. Let me be the parent. Let me take care of *you*."

"That's nice dad, really." I took a deep breath. He might not want to hear it, but I was still going to say it. "But I think Amelia's sort of out of control."

"Don't you worry about your sister—I'm watching her like a hawk. There's no way in hell she's going to pull something like she did this summer." Dad stopped walking and put his big hand on my shoulder. "Like I said, honey, I got this. Just worry about yourself. And *Eden*. Are we clear?"

"Yes." But somehow, his assurances didn't make me feel any better.

I texted James; he said he'd be down shortly to grab me. Dad went out to mow the lawn and I crept into Amelia's room. He said he'd watch her, but I intended to help a little by divesting her of the stolen booze.

I looked in her closet, under her bed, and in her drawers; the bottle of vodka and the wine were nowhere to be found. She'd hidden them well, the stealthy little shit.

I vowed to find them before the bonfire. Then Amelia could hate me even more.

NOT THE SAME

I CLIMBED into James's truck. The sky was already gray, the afternoon sliding inexorably toward evening.

I leaned back against the seat and sighed.

"That wasn't the welcome I was expecting." James chuckled. "What's the matter?"

I groaned. "My dad made me promise to bring Eden to see her mother *today*. Do you think she's ready for that?"

"No." James frowned. "But if I'm with her, I can make it work. We just can't stay for long."

"I don't know if Mrs. Lambert will like that." I shook my head. "She probably wants to talk to her daughter alone for five minutes."

"That's not going to happen," James said matter-of-factly. "It's not safe."

I blew out a deep breath, resigning myself. Facing Mrs. Lambert with Eden would make the whole thing real: the violence of what had happened to my friend, the finality of her transformation—the loss her parents didn't even know about. *Eden's a vampire.* Her human, mortal life had ended; there was no going back.

I'd known it for weeks, but this made it seem final. I shivered.

"It's better if we bring Eden to see her mother on our terms. If your dad tells Mrs. Lambert and she surprises us, that could end badly." James patted my hand. "It'll be all right."

"I hope so."

"It will be." He sounded sure of himself. "Eden's out on the deck. Let's grab her—we'll do it now. Get it over with."

I shook my head, not knowing what to say.

"How was the rest of your day?" James asked gently. "I was worried about you after what happened this morning."

"It was fine—I was happy to be away from Becky. I still feel kind of weird around Mali, though. She wanted to hang out this weekend, but I didn't know what to say. 'Sorry, but James thinks you have a suspicious aura so we can't be friends.' It's not exactly a conversation we can have."

He shrugged a big shoulder. "Hang out with her if you want to."

I looked at him, surprised.

"It's fine—as long as I'm there to protect you."

I groaned.

"Speaking of protecting you, I watched Becky for a while today. She seemed like she'd calmed down—no more shaking."

"That's because I wasn't around." I blew out a deep breath. "I'm the one that makes her upset."

"No, it's not you. I'm pretty sure it's me." His frown deepened. "Or us."

My stomach sank. The last thing I wanted was for James to get agitated again about us being together, thinking it was somehow bad. "What was she up to?" I asked, eager to keep the conversation flowing away from dangerous territory.

"She went for a walk with Sylvie after you left for school," James said.

"Yeah, she does that every day. They get dressed up for each other in their fancy workout clothes and then stalk around the island."

James eased onto the Tower's long drive, and the rose bushes scratched the sides of the truck. "I overheard part of their conversation."

"Yeah?" I perked up. "You overheard, as in, you were spying on them?"

"Yup."

"Nice." That cheered me.

He smirked a little. "I hid in the woods when they came down toward the beach. I wanted to see how she was after her episode this morning."

"And?"

"She was better." The smirk disappeared. James looked slightly uncomfortable. "She was talking about your dad."

"What did she say?"

"She told Sylvie they had a date this weekend, and they were going to…" His brow furrowed. "She made it sound as though they were going to be, err, intimate. So that your dad would stop thinking something was going on."

I opened my mouth and then closed it. *Ew.*

James coughed. "Sylvie had some colorful suggestions for her, which I'm attempting very hard to forget. But my takeaway was that your dad's suspicious, and Becky's trying to take his mind off it."

"So she's definitely having an affair," I said.

"It sounds like it." James nodded, looking miserable. "I'm sorry, Taylor."

"I already knew. I saw her with that guy at the gala."

Still, I felt a little nauseous. "Amelia made me stop by Becky's apartment yesterday off-island. That's why Becky was upset this morning—someone told her we were there."

"What?" James clutched the wheel. "Why didn't you tell me?"

"Because I was asleep, remember? And then Amelia was with us before school… It wasn't the sort of thing I thought I could text you." I sighed.

James nodded. "Just explain what happened, okay?"

"Amelia asked me to take her there after practice. It's in downtown Bar Harbor. She went in and took some vodka and wine for the bonfire tomorrow night. I tried to talk to my dad about it, but he cut me off."

"Does he know about the apartment?"

I shook my head. "He told me to mind my own business. He said that they're working on their issues."

"But Becky knew you were there and confronted you? How did she find out?" James parked in front of the Tower.

"Someone must've seen us—there was a fancy car that pulled into the lot while we were there, that could have been who told her." I shook my head. "She told me to butt out, that what was between her and my dad was private. That's when she started shaking. But it stopped pretty quick."

The muscle in James's jaw popped. "I'm so sorry that you were afraid again."

I looked him in the eye. "It's not your fault, so don't apologize."

Music wafted down from the deck, and I took a deep breath. "We should tell Eden and get this over with."

He nodded.

I glanced at him once more. "Do you really think this is going to be okay—bringing her down there? What will happen?"

"It won't be the same." He squeezed my hand. "It can't ever be the same."

"But it's something, right?"

His only answer was to keep me close as we headed for the deck.

WE PARKED at the Lambert's house, but Eden wouldn't get out of the truck. "What if I don't *want* to see her, huh?"

James sat behind the wheel, and I was in the passenger seat, Eden between us. We looked past her to each other.

"Your dad's off-island, so it's just your mom," I said. "It'll be a quick visit, I promise."

"We'll be with you the whole time." James sounded encouraging.

"I don't see why we have to do this today." Eden scowled.

I hesitated. "My dad said if we didn't bring you down here, he was going to tell her you're at the Tower. We don't want her coming down there and surprising us, right? This is safer."

Eden narrowed her eyes at me. "Why the heck did you tell your dad, anyway?"

"I suck at lying," I said lamely.

"Well, you better get good at it real fast, because we're about to see my mom and she can't know I'm a vampire." Eden's nostrils flared as she glanced at her family home. "I don't want to do this."

"You'll be fine—I promise," James assured her.

"What if I decide she smells good, huh? What if I want to eat my own mother?" Eden looked as though she might cry.

"You won't. And if you start feeling out of control, we'll get you out of here." James opened his door. "You can do this, Eden. Five minutes—that's all I'm asking."

"Five minutes, five minutes." She took the rearview mirror and inspected herself. "Ugh, I don't look the same. I don't even remember exactly how I looked before, but I know it wasn't *this* good."

Eden wasn't wrong about that. She'd always been pretty, but now her looks stunned. Her creamy complexion was clear, sparking. Her eyes were different, a steel-bluish gray, similar to James's. Her eyelashes were thick and luxurious, and her hair was more lustrous, a deeper shade of scarlet.

"You still look like you." I nodded. "Your mother will be happy to see you no matter what."

"She wouldn't be happy if she knew the truth." Eden shakily followed me out of the truck. In an attempt to look more like her old self, she wore sneakers, running shorts and a faded Portside T-shirt. "I-I don't know what to say to her."

I took her hand. "Just say hi and let her see you're all right. That's all she wants, I bet."

Mrs. Lambert opened the door before we reached it. She stood, staring, pale and worn beneath her flannel shirt. "Eden?"

"Hey, Mom." Eden took a tentative step forward.

They looked at each other for a beat.

James went and stood on Eden's left side; I went and took the right.

Mrs. Lambert ran out from the house to her daughter. She touched her cheek, her hair, her forehead, as if she were worried Eden wasn't real. "Are you all right?" she whispered hoarsely.

"I'm good, Mom." Eden smiled, her teeth a flash of blinding white.

"Thank God." Mrs. Lambert wrapped her in an embrace and Eden stood frozen beneath her, holding her breath.

When she released her, Mrs. Lambert looked her daughter up and down again. She narrowed her eyes. "Something's different."

"No, there's not." Eden shook her head, curls flying. "I'm just rested—my friends have been taking good care of me."

"Okay." Mrs. Lambert inhaled deeply, as if she were trying to gather her courage. "Why don't you come on in? I made crab cakes. Tell me what's been going on. I've missed you so much."

"Um." Eden's gaze flicked nervously to James, then back to her mother again. "I'm not sure that's a good idea."

Mrs. Lambert didn't tear her gaze away from her daughter when she said, "Taylor, you're welcome to come inside, too."

"Actually Mom, you know what? We can't stay." Eden shook her head. "I just wanted to say hi."

"Why won't you come in?" Mrs. Lambert's face flushed.

"I have to…" Eden quickly glanced at James again.

"We're having dinner."

Mrs. Lambert's complexion became fiery beneath her own red hair. She turned to James, her jaw set. "I would like some time alone with my daughter."

"I understand," James said calmly, "but I don't think she's ready."

"Last I knew, my daughter was an adult—capable of making her own decisions." Mrs. Lambert pointed at James. "You get back in that truck and get out of here. *Now.*"

James raised his hands, as if in surrender, and took a step back. "I'm not trying to insert myself into your family business—I'm just doing what your daughter asked."

"He didn't do anything, Mom." Eden shook her head again. "He helped me when I needed help, is all. James isn't the enemy."

"Then who *is?*" Mrs. Lambert's eyes filled with tears. "Why won't you come in the house, huh?"

"I don't—I'm not ready," Eden said quickly.

"What's wrong with you?" Mrs. Lambert asked. She took a step closer and Eden backed away.

"N-Nothing." Eden's pretty face twisted into a scowl. "I'm good, like I said. I just needed a break after what happened."

"Why do you keep looking at *him?*" Mrs. Lambert

motioned at James. "Why don't I feel like you're speaking for yourself, huh?"

"I am, Mom." Eden sounded miserable. "You know, maybe this wasn't a good idea. We'd better go."

"Please don't—not yet." Mrs. Lambert's tears spilled over, her face red and crumpling.

"I'm sorry. I'm sorry, Mom. I'll come back soon. I'm fine, okay?" Eden hurried back into the truck.

"Well *I'm* not fine!" Mrs. Lambert sounded anguished.

James stepped forward. "Mrs. Lambert, I'm so sorry—"

"Oh no, you don't. I trusted you," she said, voice shaking. "When everyone else was saying that this whole thing was suspicious, that you'd been doing funny things down at that house all summer, I defended you. I told them it wasn't a cult—that you kids were just different, maybe trying to enjoy a simpler life. But that's a *lie*. You've done something to my little girl, my baby. I want you to stay away from her!" Her voice rose into a shriek. "I want my daughter *back*, dammit!"

"James," Eden called from the truck, "*please!* Get me out of here."

I nodded at him as he followed her. "Take her home. I'll stay here—I'll walk down."

"Eden!" Mrs. Lambert started toward the truck, but

James was already inside. He threw it in reverse and barreled out of the driveway.

"No." Mrs. Lambert fiercely clenched her hands into fists as they drove away, dirt kicking up from the tires. *"No."*

"Mrs. Lambert… Hey." I moved closer, patting her arm. "It's okay. She's okay."

Mrs. Lambert straightened herself and wiped her face. Then she looked me in the eye. "No, she's not, Taylor. She's not the same and you know it."

"You're right." I nodded. "She's not the same."

"Why is she acting like that toward James, huh? Like he's in charge of her." Her voice shook.

"It's not like that." I licked my lips. "They got close after what happened. I think she looks up to him. Mrs. Lambert—I understand why you don't trust him, given the situation. I'm sure it seems strange. But I swear to you, James is a good guy. He's been a good friend to Eden. He wants what's best for her, too."

"It's not the same thing as family." She raised her chin. "Someday when you have a child, you'll understand. I *know* my daughter. I *know* something's wrong. I don't want some stranger thinking he understands what's best for her."

Jean Lambert turned, staring down the road where Eden had disappeared. "Do you think… If I tried… If I sent her father down there to bring her back, what would happen?"

I swallowed hard. "I think it would be a mistake."

"Do you think…" She kept staring down the road. "Would something *bad* happen?"

"M-Maybe." I wanted, more than anything, to just tell her the truth. But that would only make things more dangerous for everyone. "I think you should let Eden come to you—and she *will*. I know she will."

Mrs. Lambert didn't look at me when she asked, "How long before you'll bring her to see me again?"

"Soon." I hoped I had the authority to promise her. "I'll bring her back soon, Mrs. Lambert."

19

AGREEMENTS

I COULDN'T HELP but think of my own mother as I trudged down the long gravel driveway to the Tower. She, like Mrs. Lambert, would have been crushed if I'd stayed away from her. And if I'd kept a secret from her—even though she kept many of her own—it would have broken her heart.

My own heart was heavy as I reached the grounds. Eden, Patrick, and James were out on the deck. Eden clutched a bottle of red wine; it looked like she'd already finished half of it. There were several empty blood bags discarded on the ground near her lounger.

Patrick quickly picked them up as I joined them. "Hey, Taylor," he said.

"Hey." I glanced from Eden to James. He stared out at

the water; she chugged from her wine bottle. "You guys okay?"

James sat a little away from everyone else, an island unto himself. "I'm good," he said. But his expression was distant and dark.

"And *I'm* ready to party." Eden slammed the bottle down, empty. "I'm psyched it's the weekend—not that vampires really have weekends. Or do we?"

James didn't appear to hear the question. He didn't turn around.

"You need to take is easy." Patrick eyed Eden's empty bottle. "You can make a bad day worse, you know what I mean?"

"I'm chasing my blues away." Eden arched her eyebrows. "It's not every day a vampire's faced with her old human past. And her hysterical mother. How was she after we left, Taylor?"

"You know." I shrugged. "Okay."

"Yeah, right." Eden grabbed another blood bag from the nearby cooler.

"You're going to make yourself sick," Patrick warned.

"We'll see about that." Eden smiled. "Luke said he'd take me back to the woods tonight to cheer me up—I'm going to *gorge* myself on deer! I'm binging all weekend. That's my reward for dealing with messy leftover human crap."

She flicked the plastic cap off of the blood bag. It sailed across the deck as though it were a champagne cork. "*Yeehaw!* Cheers."

Patrick sank down onto a lounger and frowned at her. "You shouldn't be going back into the woods tonight. You need to calm down."

"C'mon Patrick." Eden straightened herself, curls bouncing. "Why do you have to be such a buzzkill all the time, huh?"

"I'm not." Patrick's jaw tensed.

"Compared to Luke, you're practically a nun. A grumpy one." Eden stuck her tongue out at him playfully, but his scowl only deepened.

"Luke's an ass," Patrick grumbled. "He shouldn't be plying you with booze and making questionable choices on your behalf."

Luke threw the door to the deck open and ambled out from the house, a fresh bottle of wine in his hand. "What questionable choices am I making now?" He glanced between Patrick and Eden.

"Nothing." Eden smiled at him, eyes sparkling more brightly.

"You shouldn't bring her into the woods tonight." Patrick looked as though he'd like to wrench the wine from Luke and whack him over the head with it. "She saw her *mother* today. That kind of shock's hard on a newborn."

"Um, you don't need to tutor *me* on being a vampire. Because unlike you, I *am* one." Luke's lips curved up into a smile. "But thanks for the help, half-breed."

Patrick rose, hands clenched into fists.

"Really?" Luke smirked. "You're going to *fight* me?"

James turned around. "Cut the shit, Luke." He glared at his brother. "We don't talk like that in my house, not *ever*. Are we clear?"

"I didn't mean it in a bad way." Luke sounded innocent.

"There's a good way to mean 'half-breed?'" Patrick asked.

Luke scowled at Patrick. "I was only joking. I didn't intend to insult your ancestry. Sometimes my mouth gets me in trouble."

"Sometimes?" James deadpanned.

"Apology not accepted—if you even apologized." Patrick sank back down in his seat. "By the way, you're an asshole."

"True, true." Luke grinned, seemingly unfazed. He held out the wine toward Eden. "You ready for more, girl?"

"Absofreakinglutely." Eden beamed at him. "And you *are* going to take me to the woods tonight, right?"

"Whatever my number one baby vampire wants, she gets." He winked at her while Patrick fumed in the background.

James stood up. "I'm going to make dinner." He headed into the house without another word.

"What's his problem?" Luke asked.

I shrugged. "I think he's upset about Eden's mother."

"Ah." Luke smirked. "Daddy issues."

When I looked confused, Luke explained, "I mean with Eden. He's her vampire daddy."

"Oh. Huh."

"He's probably beating himself up over Eden's mom." Luke rolled his eyes. "He loves a good wallow."

"I should go check on him." I headed inside, wanting to make sure James was okay.

He was in the kitchen, staring out the windows above the sink. "Are you all right?"

He didn't look at me. "No."

"Do you want to talk about it?"

"Not really." His shoulders sagged. "Want to help me make dinner?"

"Sure," I said, relieved that we had a normal activity to occupy us.

We didn't talk as he assembled the ingredients on the counter—fresh-ground salt and pepper, heavy cream, a bundle of fresh chives, a box of wide-noodle pasta labeled *tagliatelle*, and two sticks of organic butter.

"I'm making pasta. Is that okay?"

"You know it's my favorite," I said.

"I wanted to do at least one thing right today." He set to work without another word, putting water in the stockpot, chopping the chives.

I didn't help so much as stand there, watching him.

"Taylor?" He asked, after a few minutes of silence.

"Yes?"

He looked over at me, his eyes hollow. "I don't ever want your father to go through what Eden's mom is feeling right now."

He'd caught me off-guard. "O-Okay."

He squared his shoulders, then nodded. "Okay."

———

BY THE TIME we'd finished dinner and cleaned up, it was late. Patrick had gone to bed, citing a headache. I couldn't blame him. Eden and Luke were still out on the deck, cranking the music and laughing. I hadn't meant to count, but I'd collected their empty wine bottles—all thirteen of them. They showed no signs of slowing down.

"Are you really going to take them out to hunt?" I

asked James. "Aren't they trashed? And do you *ever* run out of wine?"

"We have a massive wine cellar here. Even at this rate, it'll last another decade." The corners of his mouth turned down. "And to answer your other question, vampires can't get drunk. Alcohol just makes them wilder."

He sighed. "I'll go with them to the woods—it's better to let Eden blow off some steam after today."

"Um, I was wondering…" I twisted my fingers together. "D'you think I could come with you?"

"Come with us into the woods?"

I nodded.

"So that Eden can hunt in front of you?" James looked at me as though I had three heads. *"No way."*

"I don't have to get up early tomorrow," I reminded him. "And it's not like Eden's going to hunt *me* when you and Luke are right there. She's hunting deer."

"Why would you want to see that?" James shook his head, confused.

"I don't want to go to bed by myself again."

James scowled. "That's hardly a good reason to go out into the dark and watch vampires attack the woodland creatures."

I'd had time to put my thoughts together during our

quiet dinner. "I just… I just want to see what Eden can do. It's all so—*removed*, you know?"

"Taylor—"

"Please listen to me," I said quickly. "I know what you are, and I know all about your family and Eden, but the only time I've ever seen anything supernatural happen was when you zapped Drunk Guy, and that night at the well. Oh—and when you showed me your fangs."

"So?"

"*So*—if I'm a part of your world, I guess I want to be more comfortable there. With all of it."

"You don't need to see that part of my existence." He frowned.

"I belong with you, James. And Eden's my best friend. I feel like you're shutting me out when you leave me behind. I know I've had things to deal with this week —school and practice—so I had to sleep. But living like this makes it seem like we're separated in two different worlds. And we're not."

He shook his head. "I need you to be safe. Do you understand that?"

"Of course. But hear me out? Just because I'm human doesn't make me weak. And you might feel like you need to protect me from a bunch of things, but you *don't* need to protect me from the people I love. I've *chosen* to have you in my life. So don't leave me behind, okay? It's

Friday night. I just want to hang out with my boyfriend and my friends."

He opened his mouth, then closed it.

"Well?"

"I want to be with you too, Taylor. I want that more than anything." James took my hands, tugging me closer. "And I don't think you're weak—far from it. You're one of the strongest people I know."

"So that's a yes?" I grinned up at him.

"Like I can say no to you." He nuzzled my neck, giving me chills. "*But* I have conditions."

"I'm listening." Even though all I was really doing was feeling butterflies as he wrapped his big arms more tightly around me.

"Two things," James said. "Number one—I know you're tough, but we're talking gentle herbivores versus bloodsucking vampires. If you get upset or sick over Bambi, I told you so."

"What's number two?" I asked.

"If there's any trouble out in the woods, we're gone. No questions asked."

"Fine. No questions asked." I tossed my hair over my shoulder, clearing a straightforward path for him to kiss my neck.

He obliged, planting tiny kisses up to my jawline. I moaned.

"We could always stay in, instead…" he murmured, his breath cool against my skin.

My body said *yes!* But I knew better. He was disarming me with his proximity, all the better to leave me behind. He'd never let Eden and Luke go outside by themselves.

"Mmm, hold that thought." I kissed his cheek, which had a bit of stubble. "I know you don't want Eden going out to hunt without you."

"Fine." James kissed my temple, then released me. "Then let's go. But just remember, I told you so. Don't come crying to me when Bambi gets a boo-boo."

20

FRIDAY NIGHT LIGHTS

I GRINNED—I didn't want to see a deer get hurt, but I was positively giddy at not being left alone in James's enormous bed again. We grabbed jackets and zipped them up before heading outside. Even though it was early September, the nights on the island were already getting much colder.

Luke and Eden sat on the railing overlooking the waves. Neither the chill in the air nor the whipping wind seemed to bother them. The music was still blasting, but it was being swept out to sea by the heavy breeze. The sky was full dark, the waxing moon visible behind quickly moving wispy clouds. The stars winked intermittently overhead.

"You two ready?" James asked them.

Eden jumped up and clapped her hands together. "Is it time?"

"It's time for you guys to turn the music down and stop acting like this is a frat house," James said.

Eden turned the speaker off. Luke drained his current bottle of wine and set it down. He eyed me with interest. "Is Princess here joining in?"

"Don't call her that, and yes, she's coming with us." James gave him a warning look. "I expect you to help keep her safe."

"There isn't exactly anything dangerous in the woods. Just the deer and maybe a skunk or two." Luke held out his arm for Eden. "Let's try to make the best of it, shall we?"

He led us down the steps to the yard. The grass blew in the breeze; the dark fir trees swayed, outlined against the night sky. Luke started across the grounds toward the forest, but James called, "Not that way. Go down the drive a bit—there's a field down to the right."

I clutched James's hand, grateful to take a different route. If we'd entered the woods at the edge of the yard, we would've been too close to the abandoned well. I never wanted to go back there, to the place where Becky had sent Eden and Brian to meet the end of their human existence...

"Hey." James held me close. "You don't have to be

afraid out here anymore. The well's been sealed. Not only that, but it's over. I'm here to protect you. I won't let anything happen to you. Not ever."

"I know." I moved closer, so I was pressed against his big body. "I still don't want to go back there."

"Fair enough." He wrapped his arms around me protectively, making me feel safe and loved.

We started down the gravel driveway, and something rustled in the firs above us. A caw issued down from the boughs. "Hi Edgar," James called up into the darkness. "Come with us—we're going into the forest."

The only answer was the beating of the crow's wings as he followed us down the drive.

A few minutes later, James veered off to the right, picking up a path through the woods. "This is it. You ready, Eden?"

She skipped along beside us, clearly excited. "I can't wait. Hunting is *such* a rush."

"You're a natural," Luke said. "I love to watch how you move."

"Aw, Luke." Eden's smile widened in pleasure. "Thank you."

We quieted as we went deeper into the forest. My eyes adjusted to the darkness, but I still had to lean on James to navigate over the twisty roots that knotted the path. Luke and Eden had no such concerns—they darted in between the trees, seeming to chase each other, occasionally laughing.

Soon enough, we reached a small clearing. The grass was silvery white in the moonlight. It was quiet, hushed; the only noise was the pines and firs swaying in the breeze, and the ocean crashing against the shore in the distance.

I took both of James's hands in mine and smiled. I was just happy to be near him. "Thanks for letting me come with you," I whispered.

He loomed over me, the moonlight reflecting off his pale skin. "Thanks for being my girlfriend. And making my life complete."

I decided I didn't care that Luke was probably laughing at us—I threw my arms around James's neck. "I love you. Happy Friday."

"Happy Friday to you, babe." He brushed the hair back from my forehead. "And I love you more." James kissed me deeply, and electricity shot through me.

But then something rustled from the trees behind us. He whirled to face it, crouching protectively in front of me.

"Easy, little brother," Luke teased, his voice a whisper. "You know how the deer love to sneak up and attack."

"Shh." Eden backed up into the shadows, watching the tree line eagerly. "You'll scare them away."

No one moved or said a word as a lone doe emerged from the trees and wandered into the clearing. She sniffed the air gingerly, as if determining whether or not it was safe to graze. After a minute, she bent down and nibbled on the blades of grass. Soon three other deer crept out of the dark to join her.

For a moment I forgot what we were doing in the woods. I watched them, enthralled. The deer flicked their tails as they stepped around the opening, searching for food. They grazed quietly, occasionally lifting their heads and pricking their ears, checking for signs of danger.

But they were no match for Eden. She crouched down low, her fingers resting on the ground, as if she were about to start an Olympic sprint race. Her total stillness was unnerving.

Eden stared at the deer, waiting. When Luke nodded, she sprung out into the glade.

She hissed as she sailed into the air, landing directly in front of the closest doe. It startled, raising back on its hind legs. Eden wrapped her arms around it and wrestled it to the ground. She raised her face up toward the sky, fangs flashing in the moonlight.

The other deer scattered, leaping to the safety of the trees.

Eden sank her fangs deep into the deer's throat. It thrashed beneath her, then shuddered. I had to look away. I turned so I couldn't see anything else.

But something stared at me from deep in the dark forest.

Something had been watching us.

A set of huge, wide-spaced, bright amber eyes gazed out from the darkness of the trees. They were surrounded by what looked like a mountain of fur.

I stared at the creature dumbly, not comprehending. What had Luke said? There were deer in the forest, and skunks, and... *Mountain lions?* Was that what I was looking at?

"J-James." But my voice was a weak croak, not audible above the thrashing of the dying deer behind me.

The beast in the woods took a step closer, parting the surrounding brush. It growled lowly. There was the faint outline of cropped ears, and of a long, protruding snout. *Oh, my God.*

Edgar must've sensed something—he began squawking loudly from his perch.

"Taylor?" James whirled around while I desperately reached for him. "What's wrong?"

"I-It. There." I couldn't get the words out. I clutched his shirt with one hand and pointed at the forest with the other.

The creature in the woods turned and ran. It crashed through the underbrush.

James pushed me behind him, further into the safety of the clearing. "What was it?"

"I don't know."

James didn't hesitate; he hurtled into the trees. "Luke, over here!"

Whatever the animal was, it ran fast—James took off after it.

"Luke!" James bellowed again. "Follow me!" His bluish-white light illuminated the woods as he chased the beast. For one split second, I glimpsed what it was: a wolf.

A giant, monster wolf.

"I'm coming!" Luke yelled. He flew past me into the forest, running so fast it was impossible to see him.

James's light disappeared deeper into the trees.

"Taylor." Eden was suddenly next to me. There was blood smeared across her cheek, her eyes were blazing, and her hair was wild. "What happened?"

"I don't know." I instinctively stepped away from her.

"They're *gone*?" She peered into the forest. "Luke and James?"

Why does she sound...pleasantly surprised?

"They're chasing something—a wolf." I licked my lips. "Maybe you should go and help."

She looked at me funny. "I will, but... You're afraid, huh? Your heart is pounding. Are you afraid of the wolf, or"—she edged closer—"something else?"

"I'm fine." But my heart skittered in my chest. I didn't care for the way her blazing gaze raked over me, making me feel exposed. The blood on her cheek, still fresh, glistened in the moonlight.

Eden closed her eyes and inhaled deeply. "Your heart is so *loud.* How am I supposed to think about anything else, huh? It's like it's pounding inside my freaking *head.* And your blood—I can hear it rushing through your veins."

"Eden, stop." I stepped back. "Snap out of it. You don't want to hurt me."

"Of course not." But she leaned closer.

Her bright gaze was on me. I stood, transfixed. I couldn't help but stare into those eyes. What did some predators do—hypnotize their prey? I felt very much as though I was under Eden's spell; it was impossible to turn away. Like in a nightmare, my limbs were heavy.

"Stop," I whispered again. I wanted to back further from her, but my feet were rooted to the spot.

"You could be my first," she said, her voice seductive.

"I'm still hungry, and you smell *so* much better than the deer."

"Eden, *no*." The words came out strangled, like a moan.

Her eyes blazed brighter as she moved closer. "I won't hurt you—I promise. But I need to have a taste. Just *one* taste!"

Panicked, I tried to clear my head. If I ran, would that make it worse? Would her natural hunting instincts completely take over?

"Taylor, listen to me." Her voice was sweet but firm. "I know you didn't want to kill me, but this is all your fault. I'm a vampire because of you. Becky wanted to throw *you* down that well. I gave my life for you. You owe me."

"I… You…" Her glowing eyes, so blue—or were they gray?—hypnotized me. "I know… I'm so, so sorry…"

"That's right," she whispered. "I understand why. I can make the guilt go away. Come to me—that way it's your choice. No one can say it's my fault. You don't want to get me in any more trouble, do you?"

"N-no," I stammered.

"You want to help me, don't you?"

"Of course." In that moment, I wanted it more than anything.

Eden reached for me, pale fingers extended in the

moonlight. "That's it, come here. Just a little taste, remember? I won't hurt you. No one ever has to know."

I closed the gap between us, but something shrieked down from the trees. Black wings flashed in the darkness.

Eden screamed in surprise and pain.

"Get *off* me!" Eden beat at Edgar as he dive-bombed her hair and pecked her face. She swatted at him, but the crow eluded her. He rose into the sky, then quickly dove back down to attack.

"Eden!" A burst of bluish-white light erupted from the forest. "Eden—get away from her!"

She ducked, cradling her arms over her head. "I'm the one being attack—"

But James didn't wait for her to say more. A powerful surge of light shot from his hands. Eden collapsed onto the ground.

James rushed to my side, gathering me in his arms. He lifted me up and ran from the forest.

"James! We need to see if she's okay—"

"No." He didn't say another word as we whipped through the trees, moving so fast it felt like we were flying.

Before I knew what had happened, we reached the Tower. He dropped me on the deck. "Go to your room and lock the door."

"James—"

"Now!" he snarled. He disappeared back into the darkness.

I did as I was told. I ran to his room and locked the door behind me, more miserable than I'd ever been in my existence.

21

CONSEQUENCES

I WAITED for as long as I could for him to return, but I eventually fell into a restless sleep. I tossed and turned. Images of giant wolves, Eden's blazing eyes, and a desolate-looking James haunted my dreams.

When I awoke, the sun was peering over the horizon.

Oh crap. I'd never texted my dad. I reached for my phone, finding ten different messages from him. They started out conversational and went significantly downhill from there.

The last one read: *You're grounded. Come home as soon as you get this.*

My heart sank further as I noticed the bed beside me hadn't been slept in. There was no sign of James.

I crept downstairs, worried about what I might find. The kitchen was empty, as was the living room. I peered out the window. Patrick, Luke, Eden and James were down on the beach. My spirit lifted—even though Eden had tried to drink from me last night, it relieved me to see her in one piece.

I wrapped my jacket around me and headed outside.

No one looked in my direction as I approached. They appeared to be deep in conversation, listening to James. His back was to me, his shoulders hunched. He gesticulated again and again with his hands. I didn't have to look at his expression to know that he was extremely pissed. As in livid.

"Hey Taylor." Luke was the first one to greet me. His smile was tight.

"Hey."

Eden's gaze skittered over to me, then quickly away again.

I joined their circle, taking the spot next to James. There were traces of dark circles underneath his eyes. His lips were pale.

"Hey." I squeezed his arm, but he was cold and stiff beneath my fingers.

"I need to get you home." His voice was hoarse, as if he'd been up all night shouting.

"Wait—I didn't mean to interrupt you guys. What's going on? Did you see the wolf again?"

He frowned. "Let's go."

I looked to Patrick, but he just shook his head. "I'll stop by your house later," he said.

"You don't have to—I'll be here."

"No, you won't be." James steered me by the shoulder toward the truck.

"W-Why not?"

"Didn't you check your phone?" His tone was curt. "You're grounded. Your dad was texting us both all night."

"He'll understand. I fell asleep."

"I don't think he's going to let you off that easy." James didn't look sorry about it.

I frowned at him. "Well, I'm eighteen years old. There's not a lot he can do."

He said nothing. He climbed inside the driver's side and slammed the door.

"Hey." I didn't get in. "Aren't you going to tell me what happened?"

He refused to look at me.

"Is Eden okay? And what about Edgar?"

"They're fine." He nodded toward the passenger seat. "Get in the truck, Taylor."

"Not unless you promise to tell me what happened last night—and also, stop acting like this."

James raised his eyebrows ever so slightly. "Like what? An asshole?"

"Well…yeah."

He finally looked me full in the face. "Why would I stop acting like that, huh? That's exactly what I am. Only an asshole would put his girlfriend in danger *again*. Only an asshole would almost get her killed *again*."

"I'm fine. Nothing happened—"

"The only reason you're alive is because Edgar protected you when I didn't." The muscle in his jaw jumped. "Now get in the truck. Your dad's worried about you, and he's pissed at me. He should be."

"James." I sighed as I climbed in. "You got back to me in time."

"Barely." He choked the word out.

"Eden wouldn't have hurt me," I lied. "She was just excited because of the deer."

"Please don't say stupid things like that," James said flatly. "She was going to drain you dry, and we all know it—including Eden. She confessed everything to me as soon as she came to."

"It's not her fault." I shrugged. "She's a newbie. I smell good."

"You're making it sound as though she was about to cheat on her diet, not *mangle you out in the woods and leave you for dead*. It's a little different from sneaking carbs."

He started the truck, but I put my hand over the gearshift. "Can we please wait—just a minute?"

He blew out a deep breath. "What do you want, Taylor?"

"I want to know what that thing was last night. It looked like a giant wolf."

He said nothing.

"Is that what it was?"

"Not exactly." He moved my hand away and shifted into drive.

I waited while we bumped over the gravel. When James didn't elaborate, I said, "You're not doing me any favors by keeping the truth from me. It's probably more dangerous if you don't tell me what's out there."

"Fine." He shook his head. "It wasn't *just* a giant wolf —it was a giant werewolf."

I gaped at him. "What happened to it? Did you...*catch* it?"

"No." His lips set in a grim, pale line. "It got away. It made it to the beach, and Luke thinks it took to the water."

"Huh. Woah."

James's scowl deepened. "And I don't think knowing that's any real benefit to you."

I watched his profile. "I need to know the truth."

"You really don't. What you need to do is stay out of

the woods, and probably away from me." He stared straight ahead as he drove faster than he should down the sleepy street to Becky's house. It was Saturday morning and the road was empty, silent. This late in the season, most of the fishermen took the day off.

"I don't agree with you." My voice shook a little. "Like I said last night, I'm part of your world. If there are supernatural things other than vampires, I should know about them."

James pulled up in front of the house before I was ready. He pursed his lips. "Now it's my turn to disagree."

"With which part?"

His blue-gray gaze focused on me. "With all of it. You don't need to be exposed to werewolves, just like you don't need to be exposed to other creatures who'd be more than happy to hurt you. Like your best friend, who I turned into a vampire not so may weeks ago, who almost killed you last night."

"It's not Eden's fault, just like it's not yours."

"Whose fault is it, then?" James looked incredulous. "Yours?"

"Can you tell me more about werewolves?" I asked, instead of answering his stupid question.

"They're dangerous—*extremely* dangerous. They're natural enemies of our kind."

"Why is that?" I asked.

"Vampires don't like to be second in the super-natural world—they like to rule. So we've always fought them. We almost made them extinct a while back."

I tried to wrap my brain around what he was saying. "Are they…endangered?"

"The one from last night is—I'm going to kill it as soon as I find it."

"James." I reached for him, but he pulled away. "You don't mean that."

He shook his head. "Don't worry about it. Just go inside, Taylor. Your father's waiting for you—I can sense him."

He was trying to get rid of me. That was obvious.

"Are you… Are you *mad* at me?"

His jaw set in a grim line. "No. I'm mad at myself."

Panic rose, gripping my chest.

"Well, I don't think it's safe for you to leave me alone with Becky all day." My voice wobbled. "Let's not forget who *my* natural enemy is."

I didn't want him to drop me at the house. Not because of Becky, but because of the way he was acting: I was afraid he wouldn't come back.

"I'll watch from the woods, or I'll have Luke do it," James said indifferently. "I won't let anything happen to you—at least, this time."

"Can you please stop?" I put my hand on his thigh. "*Please.* I can't handle it when you act like this."

"Like what?" The question was bitter, distant.

"Like you don't love me anymore." My cheeks heated. I suddenly felt sick to my stomach.

"Oh, I *love* you," he said immediately. "I just don't think that's what's best for you."

"James Champlain, don't you ever say that again." I hopped out of the truck, fuming. "You don't know what you do to me when you talk like that!"

I knew my dad was inside, and that it was too early in the morning for such a scene, but I couldn't help it. I kept yelling. "Last night was bad enough without you threatening to break up with me!" I slammed the door.

"I'm not threatening to—"

"What's going on out here?" My dad came out onto the front steps. "Taylor?"

"Sorry, Dad. I was just coming in." I ran up the stairs past him.

"My apologies, Mr. Hale," James said. "It won't happen again."

My dad looked perplexed as he followed me inside. "What did he mean—which thing won't happen again? That he won't bring you home twelve hours late, or that you won't scream at each other in my driveway at the crack of dawn?"

My heart twisted as the truck's tires crunched over the gravel. James was leaving. "He meant he won't ever bring me home late again, because he's breaking up with me."

"Hmm. You know, my mother used to have a saying: if it seems too good to be true, it probably is." Dad scrubbed a hand over his face. "You want some coffee?"

"Sure." I sank down onto the couch, relieved that it was the weekend, too early for either Becky or Amelia to be up. "Sorry about the noise."

Big Kyle grumbled something, but I couldn't make him out. He came back with two large mugs of coffee and handed me one.

"I don't appreciate the fact that you never texted me last night. Not to mention that you didn't come home." He had a sip from his mug and frowned. "I almost went down to the Tower and dragged you back. That could've been embarrassing for all of us."

"I was asleep, Dad. It wasn't anything more than that." I raised my right hand. "I swear to you: there was no drinking, and there was no sex. I fell asleep alone and I woke up that way. I'm sorry I forgot to text you."

Big Kyle coughed.

"Sorry to be blunt, but I don't want you to have the wrong idea. It was inadvertent—I wasn't trying to be sneaky." I suddenly perked up. "Cross-country's been making me exhausted. Do you think maybe I could quit?"

"No, but nice try." Dad rolled his eyes. "So what're you two fighting about?"

"Nothing." I had a gulp of coffee. I wanted to be alert enough to fume all day, to go back over the crazy details from last night, and to prepare an argument to rebuff James's position from that morning. "I think he's breaking up with me."

My dad raised his eyebrows. "I doubt it. Kid stayed up here on the island, even though everybody else's left and there's nothing to do. Seems to me he's a little…"

"A little what?"

"Obsessed." Dad frowned. "He's awful serious about you, Taylor."

"Maybe not anymore," I mumbled.

"Would that really be the worst thing?" His voice brightened.

I scowled at him. "Yes."

"Fine." Big Kyle sighed. "Back to last night—I know you're eighteen, and you can do what you want. I also know you care about him. But you're my daughter. I'd appreciate it if you didn't spend the night over there, and if you're going to be staying out late, please send a text."

I waited for more of a punishment. "I thought I was grounded."

"You are." He smiled at me. "You get to babysit your sister tonight while Becky and I go off-island to dinner."

"Dad, c'mon—does a fourteen-year-old really need a babysitter?"

Dad raised his eyebrows. "This is your sister we're talking about."

I groaned. "She wants to go to a bonfire."

"So take her to the bonfire and keep an eye on her. It'll just be some local kids, they do it all the time. I'll talk to her today. She's got to understand that her partying days are over. If she can't act responsibly, it's going to be no more bonfires, no more phone, no more *anything*. Both of you have to be home by ten tonight, no exceptions, and on best behavior. Are we clear?"

"Y-Yes." I hesitated. Should I tell him about the vodka, or deal with it myself?

"There's one other thing I need to speak with you about." Big Kyle leaned forward. He looked tired, and I felt bad for making him lose sleep. "I heard you and James took Eden over to see her mother. I appreciate that."

"Did you talk to Mrs. Lambert?"

He nodded. "She was upset, but I think she was

relieved, too. She said Eden wasn't her normal self, but that she was happy to have her back on the island."

"That's good."

"You know what's bothering me, though?" My dad shook his head. "I don't understand. Why's she still *hiding* down at the Tower, huh? I've known Eden forever. That's not like her—she's always had a good head on her shoulders. Always been real friendly, close to her family."

I licked my lips. "Like I told you, she needs some time. Her boyfriend *died*, Dad. It was terrible."

"I know—but something doesn't seem right. I can't put my finger on it." My father watched me closely. "Is there anything else you want to tell me, honey?"

There's a list, Dad. A long list.

"No."

"Okay, if you say so." He scratched his head. "But you know you can come to me with anything, right?"

"Of course I do," I lied.

22

BALANCING ACT

I DECIDED to spend the day in my room, pouting while clutching the necklace James gave me.

I'm sorry about last night, I texted to Eden.

You are literally out of your mind—you know that, right? She wrote back.

I called her. She picked up immediately; I could hear waves crashing in the background. "Are you okay?" I asked.

Eden snorted. "Shouldn't I be asking you that?"

"Maybe—I'm definitely not okay." I rolled over on my bed, tracing a pattern on the comforter. "I think James wants to break up with me."

"Is that why he's down at your house, moping out in the woods?"

I sat up straight. "He is?"

"Oh, please." She sounded annoyed. "It's not like he's ever going to let you out of his sight again. I screwed up big time, Taylor."

"It wasn't your fault. They had to run after that thing." I sighed. "They didn't mean to leave us alone."

"I know, but—*woah*. That was a close call. I was in, like, some blood frenzy because of hunting the deer. I'm so glad that stupid crow attacked me, because otherwise you'd be dead. We'd *both* be dead."

I took a deep breath. "It wasn't exactly the sort of thing you can plan for."

"And now we're in even more trouble," Eden said.

"What do you mean?"

"You saw it for yourself—the wolf. The *were*wolf. James thinks it was spying on us." Eden lowered her voice. "Luke wants to go out tonight and hunt for it."

"Does James know that?"

She sighed. "I don't know. James won't speak to me. He told me last night that if I ever go near you again, he's going to stake me himself."

I shivered. "He didn't mean it—he was just upset."

"Oh no, he absolutely meant it. Luke said he'd whisk me away from here as soon as he gets freed by his dad, but who knows how long that'll take…"

"Can I ask you something?" I hadn't broached this subject with her. "Are you… Are you into him?"

The sound of the waves became louder; she must be walking down the beach. "It's kind of hard not to be. Luke's hot, and he's the only one who treats me like I'm normal. Even though I'm not."

"You *are* normal, Eden. You're just different from how you were before." I hesitated. "What about Patrick? I thought you liked him."

"I *did*. I *do*. And I certainly appreciate everything he's done for me, but he acts like I'm a toddler." She snorted. "It's hard for me to be into that. I want an equal. I want someone who wants to let me explore myself. Not someone who's going to put me in time out for misbehaving, you know?"

"I get it, I guess." Poor Patrick. "But about Luke… Just be careful."

"Ha! Says the human who's in love with a vampire— or whatever James is—and almost got drained by her best friend last night. You're something, you know that?"

"Yeah, I do."

"So what're you up to for the rest of the day?" Eden asked. "I'm on probation. The only thing I get to hunt for is sea glass."

"I have to babysit Amelia tonight." I groaned. "She wants to go to some stupid bonfire and get trashed with her friends."

"Good luck with that. Which beach are they having the bonfire at?" Eden sounded a little too interested.

"For your own good, I'm not going to tell you. Try to behave today, okay?"

"You bet. And Taylor? I'm really sorry."

"I know."

Once we hung up, I headed to the top of the stairs, listening for signs of life below. The house was blessedly quiet. Eager to see James, I quickly sneaked downstairs and outside. The yard was empty. My dad must've gone down to the co-op. I had no idea where Becky and Amelia were, maybe off-island.

I scanned the woods. James was in there, somewhere. Most likely he didn't want to talk to me. I walked around the house, scanning the trees, hoping to catch a glimpse.

I texted him. *Are you out here?*

Becky's about to pull into the driveway, he texted back immediately. *You should go inside.*

Instead, I ran for the forest as tires crunched on the gravel. I needed to talk to James face to face. I searched beneath the canopy of dark fir branches, but he was nowhere in sight.

The car doors slammed. "Just bring the bags inside," Becky instructed. "I'll be right in—I have a quick call to make."

I slipped behind a large tree trunk as she walked around back, cellphone pressed to her ear. She wore brand-new sneakers, leggings, and a cropped, hooded sweatshirt. I'd never met somebody who spent so much money on workout clothes. She stalked across the grass, ponytail swishing, probably trying to get in more steps as she exercised her jaw muscles.

"Hey, it's me," she said. "Listen, I don't appreciate what you did back there."

She was quiet for a minute, listening. "I understand, but *you* need to understand that was my daughter. You can't be coming up to me and saying things in front of her."

Becky stopped walking. She scowled as she listened.

"I know you're not thrilled about it, but what am I going to do? He wants a date night. He's still my husband."

She went quiet again. She didn't look happy.

"I don't remember ever promising you that," she said, after a minute. "I need to figure it out for myself. I'll talk to you later, okay?"

She hung up the phone. For a moment, she stared out at the forest, frowning. Then she stalked back around front.

A sudden gust of wind blew by me—and then James

was standing right next to me, the muscle in his jaw taut. "That wasn't good."

"Who was she talking to?" I asked.

He shook his head. "A man. He sounded angry. I couldn't catch all of it, but he said he didn't want her with your dad tonight."

"Great." I groaned. "That's just perfect."

James watched me carefully. "You shouldn't be out here. It's dangerous in the woods, and it's dangerous to be around Becky when she's mad."

"I wanted to see you."

He frowned. "You don't always want what's best for you, do you?"

"Are we really doing this again?"

He kicked at the orange pine needles that littered the forest floor. "You could've died last night."

"That's not true. Edgar protected me, and so did you. And now we know better—I can't be left alone with Eden when she's in hunting mode."

"You can't be left alone with Eden *ever*." James looked as though he wanted to smash something.

"Fine." I shrugged. I was more than willing to concede his point—I just wanted him to stop looking so miserable.

"But that's the least of our worries." His expression

darkened further. "I talked to my father about the were-wolf. He's concerned—*very* concerned."

"What did he say?"

"He thinks its appearance is further…evidence. Of what I was worried about earlier this summer." He raised his gaze to meet mine. "About you and me, and what we're doing to the balance."

I groaned. "Here we go."

"Taylor—think about it."

James had a theory about "the balance," which was his term for the equilibrium between good and evil, dark and light. He also had a pact regarding it—with Patrick, Dylan and Josie. They'd sworn to work together to protect the balance.

James was worried he'd inexorably shifted things by falling in love with me, a mortal. He feared there were larger implications to our relationship—consequences.

I remembered exactly what he'd said when he'd explained the concept to me. *"When things are in balance, things stay in place, or stay moving like they always have. When there's an unbalanced force—like maybe you and me—there's acceleration. Things happen. Things change. And because of that, there might be pushback. There might be a scramble from some other force to restore order, to restore balance."*

"So you think—or your dad thinks—that the werewolf is some opposing force?" I still hadn't wrapped my brain around exactly what that meant.

"It definitely is." James nodded. "My father said he'd never caught sight of one up here. We haven't had reports of werewolf activity in this area for a hundred years. This absolutely has something to do with the fact that I'm here, that I've found you."

"We could leave," I said quickly. "I'm eighteen now. I don't have to finish school the traditional way, I could get my GED or go remote—"

"Taylor." James winced. "It doesn't matter where we are. If it's not here, it'll be at the next place we live. The supernatural order's not exactly the sort of thing you can outrun."

"Yeah, but… Maybe we just have to wait for things to calm down." I reached for his hand. "Maybe it's just going to take some time for the balance to adjust to the changes, or whatever."

"It's not *whatever*, and that's hardly our only problem." He squeezed my hand and released it, leaving me cold. "Being with me isn't safe for you. I have Luke to handle now, and Eden. And we both know how well that's going."

I took a deep breath. "We knew it wouldn't be easy. It comes with the territory. We just have to be more careful."

"What if I can't keep you protected, huh? Not only do we have Becky to deal with, there's a werewolf—and where there's one, there's always more. And in my own house, I have my criminal brother and a starving, out-of-control newborn." He shook his head. "There's no place in my life that's safe for you."

"That's not true. You're my guardian angel, remember?"

He smiled, but it didn't reach his eyes. "You've heard of Lucifer, right? Not all angels are created equal."

"Stop being ridiculous." I reached for him again, and this time, he didn't pull away. I stepped closer, pressing my face against his massive chest. "We'll find a way through this together. That's the only solution."

He finally wrapped his arms around me. "What if it's not?"

"It's the only one I can live with." I sighed, happy in his embrace. He could try to push me away, but I would always find my way back. "I don't care about the trouble —all I want is you."

"That's part of the problem." He kissed the top of my head. "You have to care, and so do I."

I raised my gaze to his. "I'd rather face a werewolf and a frenzied newborn vampire than walk away from you. Any day of the week, I'd make that choice."

"That's because you're human. Your thinking is

clouded by the wrong things." He kissed me suddenly and sank his hands into my hair.

His kiss was full of need. He clung to me.

My entire body lit up for him. Our tongues connected and I moved closer, desperate to touch as much of him as I could. I wanted to moan, and I also wanted to cry, but I wanted *him* more. He couldn't talk about leaving me. He couldn't think staying away was best for us.

We broke apart, breathing hard. I stared up at him, drinking in every line of his face. "I love you."

"I love you, too. But we can't decide about your future based on this." He motioned between us.

"*This* isn't some hormonal mistake." I took a step back from him. "You said you loved me. Do you?"

His shoulders sagged. "Of course I do."

"Then start acting like it."

"Taylor." He looked as though he might cry. "I am."

I didn't ask what he meant as he pulled me to him and cradled me against his chest one more time.

23

PARTY HARDY

I GOT a text from Mali a little while later.

Are you going to the bonfire tonight?

It seemed like a hundred years ago that we'd talked about it. I'd almost forgotten all about my pretty friend and her questionable aura.

Yes, I texted back. *I have to watch Amelia. Can you get a ride over?*

She responded that a boy from Spruce was planning to come to the party. He'd offered to bring her on his boat.

Great! See you later, I texted. One more thing for James to be pissed at me about.

We had resolved nothing out in the woods. He'd kissed me some more, but just when things were getting interesting, James made me go inside. He didn't want Becky looking for me, he'd said.

I felt more than a little cheated, but I'd done what he asked. I was back in dangerous territory, and I knew it.

James probably wouldn't come out to the bonfire tonight. He said he'd be nearby, watching. What he meant was that he'd be stalking me and preparing to fight anyone who came too close. But so long as he was near, and not breaking up with me, I wasn't complaining.

Big Kyle and Becky were dressed up for dinner at Bebe's, a stylish tapas restaurant located off-island. Becky had paired a pale-pink cashmere sweater that probably cost as much as a kitchen appliance with her favorite white jeans. She'd blown out her hair. She looked very pretty—the kind of pretty you'd want to be close enough to stare at—Exhibit "A" that looks could be deceiving.

"Have fun tonight, you guys." I smiled at them tightly.

"We will." My dad grinned. He looked handsome, and as if he were trying a little too hard, in his carefully ironed button-down shirt. "By the way, I talked to your sister. She knows she has to be on her best behavior." Dad gave me the thumbs-up.

Really? Did she tell you where she hid the booze?

"Of course she will be." Becky scowled at my father. "You don't need to single her out. Taylor here was the one who just stayed out all night."

Love you too, Bec. I kept my smile intact. "We'll be fine. See you."

I didn't want to be alone with Amelia, but I still breathed a sigh of relief when they left.

"Is the coast clear?" Amelia hustled into the kitchen, assembling various snacks and drinks on the counter. I was relieved that she was packing chips, soda and juice, not vodka and wine.

But her outfit was another story. Her tank top was open on the sides, the red lace of her bra peeking through. A solid inch of butt-cheek protruded from beneath her tiny denim shorts. I wasn't one to clothes shame, but she was fourteen years old and that was her *ass*. I took a deep breath. "We need to talk."

"No, we don't." She didn't look at me as she pulled out a soft cooler and started packing it. "Dad said we have to be home by ten. We can do that. And you don't have to come with me, you know. I don't need a babysitter."

"I think I'm actually more of a parole officer." I smiled at her. "Won't you be cold in that? It's going down to forty tonight."

"Why don't you let me be me? You wear your"—she

looked me up and down, scowling at my leggings and oversized sweatshirt—"*stuff*, and I'll wear mine. I'll bring a jacket. Jeez."

"Where's the vodka?" I asked.

"I don't have it anymore," she snapped. "Freaking relax, okay?"

I was anything but relaxed as we reached the small secluded beach where the bonfire already roared. Smoke rose into the air, and a Bluetooth speaker pumped out a popular country song about drowning your sorrow in whiskey. There were about ten kids on the sand, all younger than me, all with big plastic cups in their hands.

"Amelia." I stopped before we trudged across the beach to join them. "You can't drink tonight. You promised dad, and I guaranteed I'd watch out for you."

"You're like an eighty-year-old in a teenager's body." Amelia snorted and kept walking. *"Chill."*

I whipped out my phone and texted James. *Are you out there? Because someone's going to get hurt.*

He texted back immediately. *What's wrong?*

Amelia's being a pain. I might need backup.

Those kids look like preschoolers. He sent an emoji of a pacifier. *I'm staying in the woods, at least for now. Have fun.*

I grumbled and took off after Amelia, who was making a beeline for the bonfire.

"Did you bring my stuff, Keith?" She narrowed her eyes at a skinny kid wearing a fleece.

"Course I did." Keith smiled at her shyly. He had a smattering of adolescent acne across his chin and a hopeful look on his face. He pulled out two bottles from a shopping bag, and I cursed.

"Perfect." She swiped the bottle of vodka and sashayed away, leaving poor Keith to stare after her butt cheeks.

"Amelia." I kept my voice low so the others wouldn't hear me. "No freaking way."

"What?" Her tone was innocent as she poured vodka into a plastic cup and then dumped in lemon-lime soda. Its fizz sloshed over the top.

I reached for the cup. "You give that to me right now—"

She tipped it back and chugged the entire thing.

"You little *shit*."

She finished, grinned at me, then hiccuped. "Keep your panties on, Taylor. It's a party, sheesh."

A boat pulled up to the nearby dock and everyone cheered and waved.

"Glad you made it, Bodie!" the tallest, handsomest boy at the party called. He wore a braided belt and a smug expression—I took an instant disliking to him.

He elbowed the kid next to him. "Who's the hot girl he brought?"

"That's Mali—she's a senior. She's my sister's friend." Amelia puffed her chest out proudly. The handsome boy didn't look at her, and after a second, she frowned. "D'you want a drink, Chris?"

"Yeah, sure." He held out his cup but didn't look in Amelia's direction. Instead, he ogled Mali. She looked stunning even though she was dressed casually, in jeans and a plaid shirt, her hair in a braid. "I intend to yank that braid by the end of the night," Chris bragged to his friend.

"Not if I yank it first," his friend said.

"Those glasses are *hot*, right?" Chris chugged some of his drink. "She's got that good-girl thing going on."

I groaned. At this rate, *I* was going to start drinking.

"Taylor, hey!" Mali jogged up the beach and hugged me. "I'm so glad you're here." She glanced at the other kids. "Do you know any of these people? They look a little young..."

"No." I scowled. "Except for Amelia, who stole booze from her mother and is intent on getting lit. And I'm supposed to be keeping her in line."

"Oh, boy." Mali linked her arm through mine. "How can I help?"

"Maybe we could dump her vodka in the ocean?" I wrinkled my nose. "Or would that kill the fish?"

Mali frowned as we watched Amelia tote the bottle of booze around, offering shots to the others. "Looks like we're going to have to pry it away from her."

I cracked my knuckles. "Good. I hope she puts up a fight."

"Now, now, ladies." A tall, handsome, sinewy figure suddenly appeared next to us. Luke wore a tight-fitting T-shirt that prominently displayed his broad chest, an unzipped sweatshirt with a shearling hood, and artfully ripped jeans. He waggled his eyebrows. "Let me handle this."

Luke sauntered down the beach toward Amelia.

Mali fanned herself. "Who the heck is that?"

"It's James's brother. Luke." I watched him, confused. Had James sanctioned this?

My phone buzzed. *Sending him in as backup. I have a theory.*

Is it safe? I texted back. This was my first experience seeing Luke out in civilization.

James texted back a shrugging emoji.

"Where *is* James?" Mali asked, looking around.

"Um, he might show up later. Parties aren't really his thing."

She nodded, then we both watched Luke in action.

Half of the people at the bonfire were girls, and all of them stopped to stare as he strutted across the sand toward Amelia. He grinned, obviously enjoying the attention.

"Hey there, beautiful." He gave Amelia an overpowering smile. "How about some vodka for little old me?"

"Uh, sure." She gaped up at him, dazzled. "Who *are* you?"

"Aw, you don't know?" He fluttered his thick eyelashes. "We're practically family. I'm Luke Champlain, James's brother. And you must be Amelia, Taylor's gorgeous younger sister."

Amelia blushed scarlet. Luke looked at least twenty-five, he was as handsome as a rock star, and his outfit was all luxury brands and must've cost three thousand dollars—something Amelia would be acutely impressed by. She glanced around. Everyone was watching them.

"Of course, Luke." She tried to sound casual and failed. "No problem." She reached for a fresh cup, but Luke intercepted her hand. "That won't be necessary. I need a lot more than just that."

He gently took the bottle from her and helped himself to a swig. "Ah. That's better. So, do you come here often?"

Amelia seemed dumbstruck. Mali giggled next to me. "He's a piece of work, huh?"

"You have no idea." We watched as he chatted Amelia up, a veteran lion tamer and a brand-new kitten.

"So." I tried to relax a little. "How has your weekend been so far?"

"Boring." Mali shrugged. "I iced my calves last night. That was about it for excitement."

"Did someone say excitement?" Luke suddenly joined us again. He took another swig of vodka. "I love excitement."

Mali seemed as stunned by his presence as Amelia had. "Hi." She stuck out her hand. "I'm Mali—Taylor's friend."

Luke's smile widened. "Nice to finally meet you, Mali with an 'i.' Taylor's told me all about you."

"Oh. That's nice. I mean, I hope it was." Mali laughed.

"It was all good." Luke held out the bottle to her. "Care to share? The alcohol kills all the germs—it's safe."

She shrugged. "Sure. Why not?"

From the other side of the bonfire, Amelia scowled while Mali had a sip of vodka.

"I'll be right back," I said. I leaned closer to Luke. "Please behave."

"Like I have a choice." He grimaced. "My jailor's in the woods."

"Huh?" Mali looked at him funny.

"Nothing," Luke said smoothly. "Has anyone ever told you that you have beautiful eyes?"

I shook my head as I made my way over to Amelia. Luke was ridiculous. "Hey."

Amelia didn't look up as she dug through another cooler. "Why didn't you tell me James had a super-hot brother?"

I sighed. "He's a little old for you." She didn't know the half of it.

"Like I care." She found a beer and pulled it out. "Do you think you can get my vodka back for me?"

"No—and give me that." I wrestled the beer out of her hand. "If I catch you drinking anything else tonight, I'm dragging you home and telling dad everything."

"I'll tell Dad about *you* sneaking out every night of the week. And I'll tell my mom you've been bullying me. Give me that!" She tried to yank the beer back.

I threw it in the ocean. I felt bad about littering but thrilled at how pissed Amelia looked. "No more drinking. You're probably buzzed from the vodka anyway—enjoy it while it lasts."

She glared at me, and I glared back.

"Listen—if you're good for the rest of the night, I'll have James take us out on the Hinckley. In broad daylight, so everyone can see you. And I'll make him bring Luke. *And* insist he pose with you for selfies."

She looked slightly mollified. "Deal."

Amelia raised her nose into the air and went one way; I went the other. Luke still chatted Mali up. I thought briefly of Eden, who was probably locked in her bedroom at the Tower with a pint of blood and a bottle of wine. She wouldn't care for the way Luke was looking at the dark-haired beauty, as if she were definitely the most appetizing thing on the menu.

"So tell me more about your family," Luke said. "Taylor mentioned you moved up here recently. Your grandmother has a property over on Spruce?"

"Yeah, that's why we came back." Mali nodded. "She has a lot of land and animals, and she couldn't keep it all up anymore. So we *all* moved back—me, my dad, my uncles, my aunts and my cousins. The property's been in our family for generations."

"Sorry, what's your family's last name?" Luke asked. "I don't think I caught it."

"Pierce," Mali said.

24

JEALOUS

WE STAYED at the bonfire until curfew. To her credit, Amelia didn't touch another drop of alcohol. She must've really wanted those selfies on the Hinckley.

I felt like a third wheel next to Mali and Luke. They sat beside each other for hours, laughing and chatting. Luke drained the entire bottle of vodka. Luckily, Mali seemed just buzzed enough that she didn't notice he wasn't even slurring his words.

Mali and her ride left at the same time Amelia and I had to head home. Some of the kids put the bonfire out, its embers smoldering in the darkness as the revelers abandoned the beach.

Luke disappeared without saying goodbye. He'd probably gone to join James in the woods.

It was dark, but it was a short walk to Becky's house.

I knew James was watching us, so I wasn't afraid. At least, not much.

Now that the party was over, Amelia wore her fleece and rubbed her arms, as though she were chilled. "That kid Hayden's an asshole," she confided.

"How come?"

She whipped her head at me. "Didn't you see what he did? He puked in Brynn's tote. Then he laughed about it."

"Ew."

I stopped short when we got to the house. The lights were on upstairs, and music wafted from the windows. "Are Dad and Becky back already?"

"Looks like it." She went quiet for a second and listened to the song that was playing. "Gross, they're listening to old-people sexy-time music."

We looked at each other.

"You don't think they're…" I refused to say it.

Amelia glanced up at their bedroom window and clutched her stomach. "Now *I* might puke."

"At least my bedroom's on the other side of the house." I couldn't help it; I giggled. "Have fun in *your* wing!"

She groaned as she went inside, but I stayed out for a second. I wanted to see James. That he'd been nearby all night but had stayed away from the party made me ache.

The last time I'd seen him, we'd been making out in the woods…

Hey, I texted, *can you kiss me goodnight?*

Three dots appeared on my screen, the universal sign for a forthcoming reply. I waited. But then I heard rustling coming from the backyard. I headed around the corner, eager to reunite with James.

But I stopped dead in my tracks.

James wasn't the one waiting for me in the moonlight.

It was a giant wolf—a giant *were*wolf.

The same enormous amber eyes I'd seen last night burned through the darkness. The creature stared. I took a stagger-step—I thought the wolf's gaze was trained on *me*—but I slowly realized it was focused on the house. It gazed, fixated, at the light coming from the bedroom window.

I ducked behind the propane tanks and prayed it didn't see me.

Heart thudding, I peered out. The wolf hadn't budged. It was larger than I'd expected—as big as an SUV. Its fur was inky black, shiny in the moonlight. Still staring at the up at the house, it laid its pointy ears back and whined.

My phone vibrated and lit up with a text from James. *Don't move.*

The wolf whimpered again, and I looked up—it trained its amber eyes in my direction, probably alerted by my glowing cell phone.

I froze.

Something streaked past the beast, a blur of movement, ruffling its fur. It sniffed the air. Then it tensed, big muscles coiling.

At the same time, a figure silently landed beside me in the darkness. "Don't move." Luke clamped his hand over my mouth. "We're going to lure it out of here."

"Where's James?" I tried to ask, but his hand muffled my words.

The wolf looked in our direction again, and Luke tightened his grip. *Crap.*

Thin tendrils of silvery-blue light slid across the yard. The bright, smoke-like wisps curled around the wolf's feet. It distracted the beast. It nipped at the smoky brightness, making it disappear into little puffs. The light seemed to play with the wolf—circling him, then retreating a bit. The beast kept nipping at it and trying to flatten it with its paws.

The bright tendrils slowly, tantalizingly, withdrew into the woods. Seemingly transfixed, the wolf followed them.

"Go inside. *Now.*" Luke released me. "And if anybody's awake, make up a good goddamned excuse for the noise out here. Your family can't find out about this, Taylor. It would be a death sentence for them." He silently darted away in the same direction as the giant wolf.

I wanted, more than anything, to follow them. What if something happened to James? What if he got hurt?

A blaze of blue and white light illuminated the forest, then faded away. I couldn't see anything—not the beast, not James, not Luke. I cursed. If I went out there, James would never forgive me.

Cursing again, I fled for the safety of the house.

I WAITED for hours by my bedroom window, which faced the woods.

I saw two more flashes of light, but nothing else. James didn't return my texts or calls. After a while, I stopped bothering. But I never stopped pacing. Surely, he'd come for me.

Wouldn't he?

He would, *if* he was okay...

I texted both Eden and Patrick. Patrick must've been asleep, but Eden reported that neither Luke nor James had returned home. She was locked in her room, but still. They'd have checked on her if they'd reached the Tower.

My heart thudded as I paced, clutching my necklace. He had to be safe. He *had* to be.

Around three a.m. my phone buzzed from my nightstand. I lunged for it.

You should be asleep, Taylor.

My eyes pricked with tears. *How can I sleep when I'm worried you're dead?!*

He replied with a vampire emoji, followed by an angel. *That's kind of a moot point.*

Not funny. I sighed. *Please tell me you're here.*

The three dots graced the screen, swimming in front of me. *Coming up.*

A moment later, his handsome profile appeared outside my window. "Hey."

Tears pricked my eyes again. "H-Hey."

"Do you want to sleep over?" he asked. "Even though it'll only be for a few hours?"

"Of course I do." I grabbed my sweatshirt, slid the screen over, and eagerly climbed out. I was exhausted, but there was relief underlying my relief. Not only was James alive and in one piece, but: he'd come back for me.

"You haven't slept at all, huh?" He helped me from the ladder and gently took my hand.

"I didn't know if you were okay," I whispered. We headed to his truck. "Why haven't you called me?"

"My cell was out of range."

We ran to the truck. The sound of the engine turning over cut through the night's silence, and I prayed that neither my dad nor any nearby werewolves heard it.

"Why?" I asked. "Where were you?"

"In the ocean."

I blinked at him. His hair was, in fact, still a little damp. "You need to explain that. And you need to explain the—you know."

He glanced at me. "I don't have to read your aura to tell that you're beyond exhausted. We should wait until tomorrow, huh?"

"James Champlain, you will explain as long as this truck is in motion. And then you will *keep* explaining for as long as I am walking across your big-ass yard into your house. Okay?"

"Fine." He sighed. "You saw what I did with the wolf —I lured it into the woods. As soon as it figured out that it was a vampire playing tricks on it, it took off. Luke and I chased it for hours. The thing about shifters is, they're beholden to their animal instincts. So the beast couldn't help itself—it wanted to play with my light. Just like a dog will chase a reflection and try to snap at it.

You can amuse them with such things until they tire out."

I frowned. "So werewolves are easy to trick?"

"Not exactly—like I said, the wolf figured out pretty quick that I was toying with it." James slowed the truck as we bounced over the gravel. "The flip side of their intense animal instincts is that they excel at certain things: tracking, concealment, instinctively knowing the best places to hide. They're natural predators. One advantage vampires have over shifters is that our scent is not detectable to them—which is extremely helpful."

"So that's good." I nodded. "Right?"

He shrugged. "It would be, but I realized something tonight. *I couldn't smell the shifter.* Neither could Luke. That's how it was down at your house without me knowing about it."

"Huh."

He gave me a long look. "Does that ring a bell for you?"

I wrinkled my nose. "Why would it?"

"Because of your new friend. Mali."

I almost fell over. "You think *Mali's* the werewolf?"

"No, because she was at the party with you. But this could involve her. I didn't detect an odor from her, remember?"

"Yeah, I guess." When he'd met Mali, he'd mentioned

something about that to Luke: *Mali didn't have a recognizable scent.*

"Tonight I put the pieces together. I need to talk to my father about it as soon as possible—this is a big deal." His brow burrowed. "There's been stories circulating recently about their kind. I've met plenty of shifters, but their fragrance has been clear to me, distinct. But rumor has it they're evolving. Because they almost reached extinction, they've had to adapt to survive. Historically, their scent was always a powerful means for vampires to identify them."

"So you think they can hide the way they *smell*?" I found that baffling.

He nodded. "This is the first time I've experienced it, but yes. It's actually not too surprising. Shifters are masters of deception. In their human form, they're the best of all our kinds at blending in."

My brain, already tired, felt as though it were being scrambled. "I want to know more about them." I yawned.

"But you should get to bed."

"You have to at least tell me what else went on tonight," I complained. "You chased the wolf and it hid. What happened after that?"

"It eventually went to the beach. We stayed behind and watched, keeping some space between us. It took off into the water, just like the other night. We followed it, but we kept our distance. I wanted to attack but Luke felt it might be smart to trace it to its den."

I raised my eyebrows. "Maybe he's not as out of control as you thought."

"Maybe you don't know him as well as I do. He's playing the long game." He frowned. "He's not just itching for a fight. He's itching for a *war*."

"Oh." There went that theory.

"We swam after it. It's harder to track in the water, but then again, it's also harder to *be* tracked. We kept a safe distance. The wolf came ashore on Spruce." James glanced at me. "He disappeared into the woods right near Mali's grandmother's property."

I didn't know what to say. I understood that he believed there was a connection between Mali and the wolf, but I wasn't prepared to go there. I couldn't picture my pretty friend as anyone or anything other than herself—an ordinary high-school girl. "But when you went over there the other night, everything looked normal," I reminded him.

"True. But that's a secondary concern for me." James shook his head. "The fact that the wolf was outside of *your* house… That's what's going to break me."

"What do you think it was doing there?" I asked.

"When I found it, it was sitting there in the yard. I felt like it was watching the house."

"It must've been looking for you. I just don't know why…"

"I don't think that's it. I was easy enough to find down at the bonfire." I frowned. "The wolf was looking upstairs. I felt like it was watching my dad's bedroom."

"That doesn't make any sense." James's brow furrowed as he pulled into the lot and parked the truck. "But it's not something we have to figure out tonight. You need to sleep. C'mon."

As we headed into the house, he wrapped his arms around me. I was grateful for his warmth, to be pressed against him. Voices floated out from the dining room and James tensed. "Wait here."

I didn't—I followed him as he glowered at Luke and Eden. They sat at the table, sharing a bottle of wine.

The muscle in James's jaw jumped. "I told you she's not allowed out of her room when Taylor's here."

Eden stood up. "I'm sorry—I'll go back upstairs."

"You don't have to." Luke frowned at his brother. "I'm watching her. Take Taylor to bed."

James scratched his neck, looking annoyed. "I don't remember agreeing to take orders from you."

Luke groaned. "I'm not giving you an order—I'm giving you an out. You're both exhausted. I can watch

Eden. I *swear* we won't leave this room. All I want is to hang out with her, catch her up on our wolf situation, and drink a shit-ton of wine. Scout's honor." He raised his hand.

Eden still wouldn't glance at James. Or me. She frowned down at the table, awaiting her sentence.

I put my hand on James's arm. "Please?"

He blew out a deep breath. "Luke, I swear to God, if you let her out of your sight—"

"I won't. I promise."

"And *I* promise to behave," Eden added, her voice small.

James didn't look at her, only Luke. "Fine." But his big shoulders were still tense as he led me up the staircase.

"Hey, it'll be okay. And you maybe need to give Eden a break," I said.

"I'm going to need some time before I can do that."

"How much? A day or two? Or are we talking eternity?"

"Ha ha." But he didn't answer.

I drew back the covers and was thrilled when he climbed in. It had been a long time—much too long—since he'd come to bed with me.

He sighed and pulled me against him. He played with my hair, gently curling the locks around his fingers.

I clung to him. I felt the familiar heat kick up between us, and I traced a pattern over his broad, muscular chest.

He turned and looked at me, his eyes gray and intense. He had a certain set to his jaw that I recognized: he was upset. Worried. Brooding.

"D'you think you could stop frowning long enough to kiss me?" But I didn't wait for an answer. I placed my lips to his and gently kissed *him*.

He surprised me by responding immediately, almost fiercely. He rolled over and crushed his lips against mine. Heat coursed through me as our tongues connected. He kissed me again. And again.

I moaned and moved closer. I deepened the kiss, and I had the sensation that I was drowning in James, in the best way possible. I would never come up for air again if I had a choice: it was heaven.

He pulled away for one moment and cradled my face in his hands. "I love you, Taylor." He kissed me repeatedly, hot and intense, his tongue searching my mouth.

I rolled on top of him, feeling his strong, rock-hard body beneath mine. I luxuriated in the sensation; he wanted me as much as I wanted him.

"Hey." He drew back, breathing heavy. "Don't you have to work today?"

"What? *No.*" I almost cried.

I'd forgotten I'd told Jenny I'd start waiting tables Sunday mornings at the Portside. My shift started at seven a.m. I glanced at the clock on the nightstand: it was four o'clock in the morning.

"You need to go to sleep. *Now.*" He gently rolled me off of him. With a chaste kiss on my cheek, James scooted to the far side of the bed.

He closed his eyes, but a small smile played on his lips. "Love you, Taylor."

"You're seriously pretending to go to sleep?" I grumbled.

"Shh," he teased, "I need my beauty rest."

"As if," I mumbled, eyelids heavy. Being human was *so* annoying.

Mere mortal that I was, I immediately fell asleep.

AT YOUR SERVICE

I'D NEVER BEEN HUNGOVER. But the next morning, as I assembled plates of eggs Benedict and roast-beef hash for my customers, I felt as though I might have some idea what it felt like. I was shaky. And nauseous. And I had a headache. Less than three hours sleep could do that you, I supposed.

I plastered a smile onto my face and did not look at my tray as I headed out to serve my tables. Dawnhaven was a ghost town this time of year, but the Portside still managed to be packed. Locals from all the neighboring islands had driven their boats over for Sunday brunch. Even the bar was full. There was a wait list for seating. Parties waited outside on the dock, skipping rocks and poking around for sea glass until Jenny called their names.

Thank goodness I wasn't a new waitress anymore. I hustled through the morning, filling maple syrup dispensers, restocking jams and jellies, and refilling coffee for all I was worth. I missed Eden terribly; the other two servers were older men, both retired teachers, who appeared to be best friends. They barely spoke to me. I also missed Elias. The kitchen was quiet, the cooks grumbling and sweating behind the lines, but no one joked around. It was good that I was slammed with customers. Otherwise, I might've felt a little sad.

I consumed enough coffee to stay alert. I stayed on top of my tables, delivering everyone's meals on time, keeping coffee cups full and waters replenished. People tipped me generously, and I remembered why waitressing wasn't *that* bad.

Jenny sat a party of two in my section, and I hustled over to bring them waters. To my surprise, it was Mali and a handsome, older man—Bryant Pierce, Becky's "friend." The one I busted her with at the gala.

Mali said her last name was Pierce. I never put it together... I almost dropped the drinks. "Oh. Hey."

"Hi Taylor." Mali grinned at me. "I didn't know you worked here."

"Y-Yeah. I waitressed this summer, and now I'm just working Sundays." I smiled at them stupidly, then remembered to take out my pen. "Would you guys like some coffee?"

"Sure." Mali smiled brightly.

Bryant Pierce cleared his throat. "I'd love some. And I'm Bryant, by the way. My niece seems to have forgotten her manners."

His niece. Better than his daughter. "I—hi." I smiled again. "I'm Taylor Hale."

"Nice to see you, Taylor." Bryant Pierce was well-dressed, fit, and extremely handsome. He had thick, black hair that curled above his prominent forehead. His skin was smooth and evenly tanned, and he had light-brown eyes and a large, patrician nose. A tuft of dark chest hair protruded from the lavender polo that strained against his powerful chest. I didn't look at it; it seemed impolite.

He smiled back at me without warmth.

"I'll just go grab that coffee." I almost tripped over myself to get away from them.

I tried to process this recent information while I poured cream into a little aluminum creamer. Bryant was Mali's *uncle*? My mind was reeling.

I came around the corner and stopped dead. My dad, Becky, and Amelia were being seated in my section, a few tables removed from Mali and Bryant. I wanted to hide in the kitchen, or maybe jump in the ocean and swim away. Instead, I placed coffee cups before Mali and Bryant, shakily took their order, then went to bring my family waters.

I didn't miss that Bryant Pierce was gazing at the back of Becky's blond head. Didn't he see how big my dad was? Bryant was a large man, but he was no match for my meat-locker of a father—not that I thought Becky was worth fighting over.

"Hey Dad." I smiled at him, ignoring Becky and Amelia. "Do you want some coffee?"

"*I* do." Apparently, Amelia would not be ignored.

"Since when did you start drinking coffee, young lady?" Dad asked her.

She tossed her hair over her shoulder. "I'm in high school now." For good measure, she tossed her hair again.

"What about you, Becky?" I was too exhausted to hide the edge in my voice. "What do you want?"

"Coffee, please. Can you make sure it's the organic brew? I don't like the regular."

Of course she didn't. "Sure thing."

Her skin, I begrudgingly noticed, looked great. I suddenly remembered the old-people sexy-time music they were playing last night. What was it I'd heard…that sex was good for your complexion?

Ew ew ew. My brain was too tired to keep out the

rampant thoughts. I glanced from Becky to my dad—he looked great, too. Healthy, glowing. *Gross.* I glanced over at Bryant Pierce, who was scowling at us. All these adults needed to stop having sex. Or feelings. Or whatever.

I went to get Becky's stupid organic coffee, vowing to mix it with the cheap stuff.

Mali kept smiling in my direction throughout her breakfast, but I was too busy to talk. Bryant Pierce was still staring daggers into the back of Becky's head. I monitored the situation: she hadn't turned around once. She seemed completely focused on my father and Amelia. I didn't catch all of what they were saying, but it seemed to be something about checking out the foliage the following weekend.

I delivered my family's breakfast. My father had Eggs Benedict, hash browns and, inexplicably, a side of baked beans; Amelia had a spinach-and-mushroom omelet—no toast, because her mother wouldn't allow it—and Becky had fruit salad sprinkled with flax seeds.

They settled in and started talking again, and I wondered if I was imagining the whole thing. But a glance at Mali's table indicated otherwise: Bryant Pierce had barely touched his food. He was still scowling in Becky's direction.

Two of my tables finished and left. I was busy

bussing the dishes when I heard someone say, "There she is—my favorite waitress."

James grinned at me from the hostess stand.

He wore a tight-fitting gray T-shirt and dark jeans, oh my. Luke ambled in behind him, wearing a white button-down shirt and black ripped jeans. James looked like he was fresh from a modeling job, and Luke appeared as though he'd just stepped off-stage from his concert.

I wasn't the only one staring at them. Curious looks came from the bar, and the other tables. Amelia and Becky openly gaped. I glanced quickly at Bryant Pierce; a grimace had replaced the scowl as he sized up the two handsome young men. Maybe he was worried they were more competition for Becky's attention.

Jenny winked at them and led them to my section. "I have the perfect table for you." Even though she was gay, she seemed to ogle them both.

"Thanks, Jenny." I almost whacked her with the menus.

"Just a sec—I need to say hi to my people." Luke went to my family's table and offered my father his hand. "You must be Taylor's father. I'm Luke Champlain, James's older brother. It's a pleasure to meet you, sir."

Big Kyle looked surprised, but he smiled at Luke. "I didn't know James had a brother."

"He likes to keep me a secret because I'm better looking than him—he can't handle the competition." Luke winked at my dad and patted him on the arm. "I'm sure you know what a pain he is."

Big Kyle's face brightened. "I sure do."

Luke turned his megawatt smile on my stepmother. "And you must be Becky. Just as lovely as I've heard."

Becky grinned widely. "James has been holding out on us."

"You don't know the half of it, Mrs. Hale." He shifted his attention to Amelia. "There she is—Taylor's beautiful little sister. Nice to see you."

"Hi." Amelia blushed scarlet.

"What a gorgeous family you have, Mr. Hale." Luke sounded impressed. "It's so nice to meet you all, I've heard such great things from James and Taylor."

"Would you boys like to join us?" Big Kyle asked.

"No, we couldn't impose. But some other time—I'd love to get to know you all better." With a friendly wave, Luke ambled down the aisle to Mali and Bryant's table.

"Oh boy," I said, under my breath. "Here we go."

"Who is that with Mali?" James asked.

"Tell you later."

James tensed as he watched his brother. Bryant Pierce's scowl etched deeper into his handsome face as

Luke reached them. "Hi Mali—I don't want to interrupt, I just wanted to say hello."

"Good morning." Her smile was friendly, and her eyes sparkled as she looked up at him. "I definitely recommend that French toast—the powdered sugar makes it sweet, but the boysenberries give it an edge."

"I love a good edge." The smile slid from Luke's face as he faced her companion. "I'm Luke Champlain, Mali's new friend."

"I'm her uncle—Bryant Pierce."

"Nice to meet you." Neither man offered to shake hands. "Well Mali, see you around." With a final waggle of his eyebrows, Luke ambled back to us.

Luke snatched a menu from me and sat down. "I hear the French toast's to die for."

"Sounds perfect for you." James frowned at his brother. "Eat up."

Luke smiled calmly back at him. "You don't want me dead—not just yet. You're the one that thinks everything happens for a reason, right? Maybe there's one I came up here."

"Other than being grounded by Mom and Dad?" James asked. "I'm all ears."

Luke winked at him. "I think things are more interesting on the island than I expected."

James grimaced. "It's getting more fascinating all the time."

I wanted to hear more, but one of my customers beckoned to me. "I'll be back to take your order, okay?"

James's expression softened. "Of course, babe."

I heard Luke teasing him as I turned on my heel, but it didn't bother me. I almost bumped into Mali. "You guys leaving?" I asked.

"Yeah, see you tomorrow." She grinned. "I can't wait for another week of cross-country, *yay!*"

"Ha. See you in class."

"Hey Amelia," Mali called. "Enjoy your day."

Amelia flushed, probably pleased that the pretty senior had said hi. "Yeah, you too." She briefly glanced at Bryant Pierce, frowning.

But he didn't seem to notice. His gaze slithered over to Becky again.

Becky didn't look at him. She stared at my father instead, smiling.

I hadn't seen her smile at him like that in forever. Not for the first time, and unfortunately probably not for the last, I wondered what the hell my step-monster was up to.

BUZZKILL

THAT NIGHT AT DINNER, Dad and Becky announced we were taking a "family day" the next weekend. Dad was picking out trails for us to hike in the park so we could enjoy the early fall foliage.

Both Amelia and I groaned. Where was the down-time? More importantly, where was the *James* time? I gave my dad side-eye as he passed the roast chicken. He seemed all too pleased with himself for keeping me busy.

"James's brother seems nice," Becky said nonchalantly.

"Who cares about nice? He's *hot*." Amelia's eyes got glassy. "Did you see him in those jeans?"

"He's *way* too old for you." Becky pursed her lips. "You can look, but don't touch."

"Don't even look," my father growled.

"Where does he live, Taylor?" Becky asked.

"Um, with James's parents, I think? In Oregon. But I guess he travels quite a bit." I had no idea where Luke had been before coming to the island—except in trouble.

"How's Eden doing?" Becky asked. "Your dad said she finally went down to see Jean, but that she's staying at the Tower. That's sort of strange, isn't it?"

I coughed. To hear Becky talk about Eden so casually rattled my nerves. "It's just more comfortable for her, I think. The Tower's pretty private, it's not like her parent's house where people are stopping by all the time. And she's doing better—t-thanks." To thank her for checking on Eden was to feel as though I'd gone completely, utterly insane.

I didn't miss that my dad and Becky seemed awfully chummy during dinner. She even had her hand on his thigh at one point.

"May I be excused?" I asked. I needed to leave the table before I puked.

In another annoying development, I fell asleep while reading my American Lit assignment. I woke up at midnight. My lights were out, and I was neatly tucked into my bed, my book on my nightstand. There was a note on my pillow.

Hey babe.

You were asleep when I got here. I tucked you in and kissed you goodnight.

I'll miss you so much tonight, but you need your rest.

Luke and I are taking turns keeping watch over your yard.

Edgar's out there, too. It's quiet—no signs of trouble. So sleep tight.

Love you,

James

PS - I closed your eyes for you. :)

I wanted to call him, but I rolled over and immediately fell back asleep. When I woke up in bed the next morning, I cursed: every night without him was a wasted one.

Amelia and I were almost late for the mailboat. We both staggered down the ramp in the early mist. The weekend hadn't been nearly long enough, and now the hours stretched out in front of me. I wouldn't see James, and I couldn't find out anything else about the werewolf. The whole school thing was seriously cramping my style.

We were mostly silent as I drove the Yukon over the winding road that led to MDI High. I parked the SUV and glanced at Amelia, who was staring at her phone. "I'll meet you here after practice, okay?"

"Yeah." But she seemed distracted. I wondered if she'd even heard me as she got out and slammed the car door.

It wasn't as misty in Bar Harbor, but gray clouds hung over the sky. The trees were changing color, their deep green edges tinged with red and orange. It was beautiful, but for some reason, it made me sad.

I hustled to the school's entrance but stopped short when I saw Mali getting dropped off. She was climbing out of a sleek-looking black BMW, the same car I'd seen at Becky's apartment.

I took a stagger step, missing the curb and twisting my ankle. "Ow!"

"Are you okay?" Mali came toward me quickly.

"Yeah, I just missed a step." I rubbed my ankle and adjusted the cuff of my jeans. "I don't think I hurt myself bad enough to skip cross-country, unfortunately."

"Want me to trip you?" she joked.

"Ha ha. No, I'm clumsy enough all by myself." My leg throbbed a little as we headed inside. "Who drove you today?" I asked.

"My uncle—the one you met yesterday. He works in town, so he dropped me off." She shrugged.

So Bryant Pierce drove the fancy car I'd seen pull into Becky's. If I'd needed any more evidence, confirmation of my suspicions had been deposited squarely in my lap. *Yay.*

"How was the rest of your Sunday?" Mali asked. "The restaurant was packed, huh?"

"Yeah, it was." Despite everything, our conversation managed to be normal. We chatted the entire way to class, and I found myself pleasantly distracted. Distracted from the werewolf in my yard the other night. Distracted from the fact that Mali's uncle was likely having an affair with Becky—and that my father's world could easily be shattered.

From that perspective, school didn't seem too bad.

That afternoon, my teacher sent me down to the media room to pick up a projector for class. I spotted Amelia in the hall. Her back was to me. She was deep in whispered conversation with one of the boys from the bonfire—Chris, the handsome one who'd been eyeing Mali.

He had paid no attention to Amelia the other night, but he sure looked interested at that moment. He leaned against his locker and grinned down at her, then said something that made her giggle.

I vowed to ask her about it later, after practice, and went on with my day. But as I limped to the parking lot after cross-country, Amelia wasn't waiting by the Yukon like usual. I checked my phone—she'd texted an hour before. *In town,* she wrote, *can you pick me up when u r done?*

I gaped at my screen. In town, *what the what*? She was supposed to be at practice! My stomach sank. Amelia was always up to something, even on a Monday.

Luckily, Mali had gone home with her dad—I could yell in private. I slammed the car door and put my sister on speakerphone. "Where the hell are you? You're supposed to be at golf!"

There was music in the background, and voices. "I'm at mom's apartment. Can you come grab me? I don't want to miss the mailboat."

"Who are you with?" But she'd hung up before I even got the question out.

I drove quickly, gripping the steering wheel so hard my knuckles were white. What the *hell* was she doing, skipping practice and going over to Becky's apartment? I had a pit in my stomach as I pulled into downtown and navigated over to the building. I parked in the back, next to the dilapidated minivan. There was a shiny Volvo SUV in the lot—whoever Amelia was with, they were definitely a rich kid.

I texted her. *I'm here. Come out now or I'm coming in.* I hoped she obeyed. The idea of going into Becky's apartment made me feel sick.

"There you are!" Amelia's voice was too bubbly as

she hopped inside the car, stuffing her backpack between her legs. "We gotta go!"

I sniffed the air—she smelled like weed. Just slightly, but still. "Amelia, look at me."

She was, of course, staring at her phone. "Why? I'm busy. Gotta text my peeps."

"Look at me right now, or you're walking." I waited as she reluctantly turned my way. Her pupils were huge, and there was a stupid expression on her face, like she might start laughing hysterically at any second. "You're high."

"No, I'm not."

"Don't be an idiot. Your pupils are as big as saucers. Even *Dad* would know you were high."

She frowned. "Don't tell him, okay?"

"Amelia." I turned the car off.

"We're going to miss the mailboat." A note of panic crept into her voice.

"Are there still people in Becky's apartment?"

She shrugged. "Maybe."

"That's really freaking stupid. Go in there and tell them to get out."

"I told them they could stay." She looked miserable.

"You don't want me going in there—or Becky. What if she just shows up, huh?"

"What's she going to say? She can't tell me I'm bad

when she's even worse. But *whatever*." She huffed and slammed the car door behind her.

Amelia marched back to the apartment, looking a little unsteady on her feet. It took a few minutes, but then she returned with two boys I recognized from the party: Chris, the handsome one, and Kevin, the one who'd stashed her booze.

Amelia headed for me, while the boys went directly to Chris's SUV. "Hey!" I jumped out of the Yukon. "No way. You two can ride with us."

Chris snorted. "We're fine—"

"Get in my car, dammit, or I'm calling your parents."

"Taylor." Amelia's face heated. *"Chill."*

"What do you want to do, huh?" I faced Chris, whose expression had turned from dismissive to deeply annoyed. "Your choice—I give you a ride, or I call your mom."

I hopped back into the driver's seat and waited. It didn't take long for them to join me. No one looked happy. "I'm actually okay to drive," Chris said, sounding superior and pissed. "So this is unnecessary. I don't exactly want to leave my car here."

His new Volvo SUV was certainly out of place next to the minivan. I hoped someone keyed it, at the very least. "It'll be fine."

"We weren't doing anything," Keith said. "We were just hanging out."

"Yeah? Look at me." I swiveled around in my seat. Keith's pupils were dilated, and Chris pretended to be studying something out the window. "You've been smoking pot. Probably vaping it, cause the smell isn't that bad. But I can still tell—your pupils are huge."

"What're you—a hall monitor?" Chris laughed at his own joke and then stopped when he found me glaring.

"No, but I'm someone who's had a lot of experience being around drugs," I said matter-of-factly. "Did you know vaping can fry your lungs? Did you *also* know that the THC levels are, like, ninety percent higher when you vape?"

"Isn't that the point?" Chris smirked.

I shook my head, then started the Yukon. I'd dealt with enough drugged-out idiots to know when someone was a lost cause—not to mention a bad influence.

We sat in strained silence on the ride to Pine Harbor. When the mailboat came, the boys moved as far away from us as possible. Fine by me. "That kid Chris is bad news," I told Amelia.

Her high seemed to have faded a bit. She looked kind of crappy, pale. "He's nice."

"He's an asshole," I said.

"He's not the only one," she muttered under her breath.

I crossed my arms against my chest and glared at her the rest of the ride home. It was two steps forward, twenty steps back for me and Amelia. When we got to the dock, Chris climbed out without saying goodbye. Keith gave her a tentative wave, which she ignored.

I hoisted my bag over my shoulder. "I told you he was an asshole."

She whipped her head at me. "He's pissed, and he should be. You had no right to do that. He shouldn't have left his car there—it's brand new."

"I couldn't exactly let him drive to Pine Harbor when he's high as a kite. What if he got into an accident? What if he killed someone? Is that better than leaving his precious Volvo there?"

"They were going to wait for a while." Amelia scowled. "Plus, driving while you're stoned isn't the same thing as driving drunk."

"Oh, really? You're so experienced at fourteen, I guess. You just know everything." I held onto my back-pack straps, so I didn't reach out and smack her.

We reached the end of the ramp and crested the parking lot. She stopped walking. "Are you going to tell dad?"

"Of course I am." I shook my head. "It's *Monday,*

Amelia. If you're skipping practice to go smoke with preppy losers on a Monday, you're in pretty bad shape. You need help."

"No, I don't." Amelia's expression turned pleading. "Chris found out about the apartment, and he wanted to check it out. That's all. He wanted to smoke, so I said okay. It's not like I went over there to get high, I just wanted…"

I knew what she wanted. Chris was an upperclassman, handsome and popular. "You can't get sucked into something like that. He'll tell everybody. Next thing you know, he's going to be asking to have a party over there."

Amelia bit her lip.

I sighed. "Listen, I know the type. You just have to be firm with him. Tell him your parents found out you guys were over there, and you can't go back. Tell him they said they'd call the police. That way it's not your fault—he can't be mad at you."

"Are you going to tell dad?" She twisted her hands together. "I swear to God I won't go back over there. Not *ever*. I won't smoke weed or drink anymore. Just don't tell him."

We faced each other. Amelia had a pleading expression on her face, and I still had that pit in my stomach.

"*Please*, Taylor. I just wanted to hang out with Chris. He's a junior, and he's captain of the lacrosse team. You understand, don't you?" She wrung her hands some more. "I *swear* I won't do it again—I didn't even like smoking. It tasted like crap."

I took a deep breath. "*I* swear to God, one more strike and you're out. If I catch you doing *anything*—and I mean it—I'll tell Dad and Becky. This is the last chance you don't deserve."

"Thank you!"

She was relieved, buoyant, as we walked home. But the pit in my stomach weighed heavily. Was I helping her, or hurting her? Having dealt with my mother for so long, I knew the answer. I was repeating a pattern. I was protecting Amelia, but that wasn't the same thing as helping her.

The clouds stretched out above me, dark and foreboding.

If I knew better, why wasn't I doing better?

I took a deep breath, vowing to tell my father the truth. I just needed more time. Once I told him about Becky's apartment, everything was going to erupt. I stared back up at the sky: the clouds looked as though they might burst.

I felt the same way.

SHIFTY

IT WAS VERY difficult to sit through dinner that night.

Becky and my dad still seemed to be getting along. She complimented the way he'd prepared the grilled corn. "What did you use?" she asked. "It's so delicious."

"Um, a little lime juice, sriracha, fresh cilantro. I'm glad you like it." Dad had a sip of water and grinned at her. She grinned back.

I almost threw up in my mouth.

Amelia barely said a word. She ate only protein and vegetables, possibly in an attempt to fly below her mother's radar. She looked better, less pale, and her eyes were back to normal. She was probably counting her blessings while I was busy counting my secrets.

"May I be excused?" I rose from the table. "I was

going to bring my homework down to James's, if that's all right."

"Just be home by nine," my dad said.

That didn't give me much time, so I raced upstairs. The truth is, I'd already finished my assignments. I was desperate to see James, to hear more about the wolves, and to tell him what I suspected about Bryant Pierce.

James was in the living room, talking to Becky, when I made it back downstairs.

"Your brother seems nice," Becky said. "Is he older than you, or younger?"

"Older. But he's much more immature." James smiled when he saw me. "Ah, there she is. Good to see you, Mrs. Hale. I'll have Taylor home by curfew."

I breathed a sigh of relief once we were outside, in the cool September evening. The clouds had blown out and the air was fresh, free of humidity. James glanced above my head. "You've had a day, huh?"

"You don't know the half of it—even my aura can't explain it all."

He laughed. "I'm all ears. Tell me what's going on."

I sighed as I climbed into the truck. "First of all, Amelia is a royal pain in my ass. She skipped golf today. She went to Becky's apartment with some losers and got high. I had to drag them out of there."

He whistled. "What did your dad say?"

"Nothing. I didn't mention it to him."

James frowned. "Why not?"

"Because," I groaned. "Amelia begged me not to. She asked for one more chance."

"So?"

"*So* I figure I'll give her one. She's got two strikes already—drinking at the bonfire and now smoking weed."

"It's three if you count the fact that she stole the booze in the first place," James reminded me. "Not to mention getting trashed at the gala. That's actually four."

"Ugh, I know. I'm going to tell him—it just needs to be the right time."

He glanced at me. "What's going on here? Are you softening up on Amelia?"

"No. She's a brat."

"True, but she's still your sister."

I grimaced. "Don't remind me."

"What else?" James asked, as we turned down the drive for the Tower. The rose bushes screeched against the truck.

"I saw Mali getting dropped off at school today. Her Uncle Bryant drove her. He was driving the same BMW I saw last week, the one that was at Becky's apartment. Which seems to confirm...you know."

"Ah. Sorry about that." James maneuvered the truck into its space.

"Not as sorry as I am."

"I saw the way he was looking at her yesterday at the restaurant," James said. "Her aura was reacting to it, even if she wasn't."

"What was it like—her aura?"

He frowned. "Red. Pulsing."

"What does that mean?"

"Nothing good for your dad." He scowled in distaste. "She likes the attention. And I think she's powerfully attracted to him. The fact that she shouldn't be only heightens the feeling."

My heart sank. "I should tell my dad about the apartment."

"You should probably tell him about Amelia, first."

I groaned. Then I distracted myself by looking at the moon. It hung bright in the dark sky, the stars holding court all around it.

"Can we change the subject?" I begged. "How is Eden doing?"

His expression darkened, and he shrugged.

"Is something wrong—or are you just still upset?"

His gaze flicked to me. "I am still upset because something *is* wrong. She tried to kill you."

"It was more in word than in deed."

He laughed without humor. "Really? You're still trying to protect her?"

I faced him. "And you're still trying to punish her?"

He straightened his shoulders. "I'm going to need a little more time. Almost losing you isn't exactly something I'm going to forgive easily—and that applies to both Eden *and* me. I'm more pissed at myself than I'll ever be at her."

"James... Let's not do this." I shook my head. The more he blamed himself, the more guilt I felt. It was a never-ending cycle, push-pull of negative emotion. "It's over now, so we should move on. Okay?"

"Fine." He took my hand in his. "C'mon."

Once he checked on Eden, Patrick and Luke, we sat out on the deck. As the air chilled over the past few nights, the mosquitos had begun to disperse. It was lovely to sit outside with the waves crashing against the rocks, the spectacular view of the stars stretching above us.

Our almost-fight in the truck seemed far away, almost forgotten. James dropped onto a lounger and pulled me to him, positioning me between his legs, wrapping his arms around me from behind. He hugged my back against his chest. It was heaven.

He moved my hair over to one shoulder and kissed the side of my neck. "Are you warm enough?"

"Yes." I leaned against him, and he pressed his cheek against mine. "I'm perfect."

"Yeah, you are." He grazed his lips across my jawline, right underneath my ear.

"Did you talk to your father?" I asked.

"I spoke to him for a couple of hours today." He sighed, the peaceful mood between us evaporating. "He said he might have to come up here again. He's very concerned about the wolves."

"Did you tell him about the smell thing?"

"I did." James pressed his forehead against my shoulder. "He said that we need to be prepared."

"For what?"

"An ambush. An attack. Something."

I craned my neck to look back at him. "Are we prepared?"

"*We* are not going to worry about that." He kissed the tip of my nose. "*I* am taking care of it."

"James." I sat forward, breaking our embrace. "I don't think I need to remind you that there is no 'I' in 'we.'"

He said nothing for a moment. Then, "I can't put you in harm's way again, Taylor. After everything that's happened… Don't ask me to do that."

"You sound like a broken record."

He stiffened. "You and the werewolves have got nothing to do with each other."

"Except that one was sitting outside of *my* house the other night."

He scrubbed a hand across his face. "I have a feeling that has way more to do with me than with you."

I sighed. "I don't want to fight with you."

"Then don't."

He reached for me and I settled back against his chest, but it didn't feel the same. We were at an impasse: I wanted to be involved with everything, and he wanted to shield me from all of it.

"Do you understand that I could never live with myself if something hurt you?" he whispered against my hair. "Don't you know how much I love you?"

I melted against him. "Of course I do—it's how much I love *you*. I would do anything for you."

"Then stay safe and don't put yourself in harm's way. Okay?"

I kissed his cheek. "Okay." It seemed a reasonable enough promise to make.

"I love you." He nuzzled my neck, then craned his face around so he could press his full lips against mine.

I turned, clinging to him, and lost myself in his embrace.

Kissing was so much better than arguing. Our tongues connected, and I ran my hands down his strong back, forgetting all about the possibility of a werewolf ambush, at least for the moment.

LATER THAT NIGHT, James snuck me out of my house. He'd made me promise, though: I had to sleep.

Back in his bed, I did. "I promise," I said, luxuriating against his broad chest. Patrick and Luke were taking turns watching Eden. James had said he needed to go relieve them soon, so I intended to enjoy every second I had with him.

"Promises, promises." He kissed me slowly, almost lazily, until I was panting for more.

He pulled away before I was ready. "You *have* to sleep."

"I will, I will. Just don't go yet." I nestled against him, unable to stifle a yawn. "Will you tell me more about the werewolves? Pretend it's a bedtime story."

He chuckled. "Okay, but only for a minute, and only because I can't say no to you."

I pressed my face against his chest, utterly content.

"Once upon a time, there were creatures called werewolves. But that's a bit of a misnomer." He kissed my cheek and continued, "They aren't just wolves. We correctly call them *shifters* because they're a multifaceted group. Some shifters can only turn into wolves. But there are other kinds—they can turn into other animals, and some of them can even change their *human* appearance."

"Woah. I just...*woah*. That's pretty cool." But my brain was too tired to tackle it.

"They *are* fascinating, if you can get past the part where they want to destroy all vampire kind."

"But why do they want to do that? Isn't there some sort of paranormal, I don't know...alliance or something?"

"You would think so," James said. "But after we hunted them almost to extinction, maybe not so much."

I shook my head. "Why did the vampires do that?"

"Why does anyone do anything bad, huh?" He ran my hair through his fingertips. "I guess it was because they were afraid of losing something. The vampires who came to MDI so many years ago were used to ruling the supernatural world. When they learned that the were-wolves were the predominant leaders here, they hunted them down. They didn't want to share this rich, new land."

"I guess they weren't so different from the human explorers," I said.

He kissed the top of my head. "Guess not."

I could feel sleep on the edge of my consciousness,

creeping closer. I didn't want to drift away from James. I struggled to stay awake. "We can do better than that."

"We *have* to do better than that."

"Then don't fight them," I mumbled.

"I don't want to, but…" James held me as my eyes fluttered close against my will. He gently kissed my cheek. Sleep tugged at me, pulling me into its inevitable embrace.

"*But* I'll protect you no matter what," he whispered.

Those were the last words I heard before I drifted off.

28

NC-17

THE NEXT FEW days passed in a blur of school, cross-country practice, complaining about cross-country practice, and falling into an exhausted sleep in James's arms. There were no werewolf sightings. James still wouldn't look at Eden. I checked Amelia's pupils every chance I got, but she appeared to be clean.

I still had said nothing to my father.

I watched Becky—for signs of having an affair, for signs of unnatural shaking. She gave me nothing. All she did was play nice with my dad, argue with Amelia over homework, and go to barre class. I couldn't tell if her relatively normal behavior was because she was hiding something, or because she had nothing to hide. Except what she'd done to Eden and Brian, of course.

But the further we got away from that night at the

abandoned well, and the longer she went without shaking, the more insane I felt.

Finally, Friday arrived. I was eager to get out of practice and get to the mailboat—the sooner we were home, the sooner I was back in James's arms. Mali's dad was picking her up again. We said a hasty goodbye before I hustled to the parking lot. Amelia waited by the Yukon, bouncing her knee, a hopeful expression on her face.

"Can we stop on the way to the mailboat—super quick?" She used her nice voice again, which immediately had me on guard.

"Why?" I sighed. "I really want to get going."

"I know, me too," she said immediately. "But we *have* to go by the apartment."

That stopped me dead in my tracks. "I'm sorry?"

Her shoulders slumped. "C'mon Taylor, *please*. Chris thinks he left something there—I have to go get it. If my mom finds it, I'm dead."

"What is it?" I asked, even though I had a pretty good idea.

Amelia shook her head. "His pen and some of his cartridges, I dunno. Maybe some other stuff."

We hopped into the car and pulled out of the parking lot. "Like what other stuff?"

"I don't know, but I know that Mom can't find it. I told him he could keep his things there for a few days—I guess his parents keep going through his room. But he was supposed to deal with it today, and now he has to meet his mom." She blew out a shaky breath. "If *my* mom finds that crap, she will literally kill me."

That was true. "Did he leave it there the other day?" From what I understood, people couldn't easily tolerate being separated from their vapes for that long.

"Not exactly. Don't be mad, okay?" She started cracking her knuckles. "I gave him the key. He's been going over there on his breaks from school, I guess. He said he's been really stressed because of his parents, so it's been helping a lot."

"So he's been using Becky's apartment, probably every day, to get high," I said. "And now he can't grab his stuff because he's in trouble. Does that sum it up?"

Amelia looked miserable. "Pretty much."

I almost didn't take the turn for downtown. "He *should* get caught, Amelia. He's messed up."

"I know, but this isn't just about him—it's about *me*, because I'm the one who'd be busted. And I didn't do anything wrong!" she wailed.

"That's not true. You're letting Chris use you. You're bartering with something that isn't even yours—your mom's secret apartment. She's going to lose her shit if she finds out."

"Don't make me anymore stressed! I know it was

stupid, okay? He just asked me, and I didn't know how to say no!"

"Just say it, dumbass." I cursed some more under my breath as we cruised through downtown to the apartment building. There were no cars in the lot besides our old friends, the dilapidated minivan and banged-up Sentra.

I parked, and Amelia hopped out. "I'll be quick."

I fumed as she hustled inside, fumbling with her key. Not only had I protected her—twice—she'd lied to me again. Not telling me what Chris had put her up to counted as a lie. That was it. I would tell my dad the entire story as soon as we got home. I just wasn't sure how I would explain about the apartment…

A minute passed, and then another. I drummed my fingers against the steering wheel. *What's taking so long?* I checked the time on my phone: if she didn't come out quickly, we were going to miss the mailboat.

Another minute passed. I sighed, then got out of the Yukon.

I hesitated, not wanting to go into Becky's apartment. I knew once I crossed the threshold, once it became real to me, I would have to tell my father the truth. I didn't want to be the one to bring that sort of pain to him—he'd been through enough. But Becky was bad, I reminded myself, and not just because she was renting a secret apartment in order to rendezvous with her lover. She was bad because she was…*bad*.

The door was unlocked. I went into the entry, which opened on a hallway. All the lights in the apartment were off. There was thin, stained beige carpet on the floor. The walls were whitewashed, bare. Having lived in several crappy rentals in my life, I recognized the atmosphere as cheap, the finishes bare-boned.

I couldn't imagine Becky spending time in a place like this.

There was a room down the hall to the right. I headed that way. "Amelia?" But I didn't hear anything. Except…

A few more steps in, I heard a low moaning. I froze. The moans were rhythmic, mesmerizing. "Amelia?" I whispered. "Are you okay?"

No answer. I took a deep breath and rushed around the corner. To my left was a small kitchen, open to what must be the living room. A brand-new couch sat along the wall to my right.

Amelia stood in the middle of the room, clutching a bag to her chest. Her face was pale, so pale.

"What's—"

But she swatted me, hard, then put a finger to her lips.

The moaning started up again. It was definitely a

woman's voice. It was coming from a room on the opposite side of the living room, its door half-closed.

Another sound joined it. An intense, guttural groan —a man's. I reached for Amelia's hand. She did *not* want to be here, not any more than I did.

She swatted me off again. *Listen*, she mouthed.

The moaning intensified. And then—something snarled. It growled, then snapped its teeth. It sounded like an animal.

The woman's moans came faster, reaching higher, a new pitch. She cried out. I'd thought the noise was coming from pleasure, but was it pain?

There was more snarling from within the room, a growl that seemed rabid, out of control. The woman screamed.

What the fuck? Amelia mouthed. Her face was alabaster. I worried she'd pass out.

I shoved her behind me. I needed to get her out of here, but I'd never forgive myself if someone was being hurt. I crept closer to the door—it was open just enough that I could peer inside.

But what I saw made me wish I didn't have eyes: I would never be able to unsee it.

Becky was on the bed. Bryant Pierce was on top of her. They were both naked, his hairy chest visible in the dim light. But he wasn't...normal. His eyes were glowing—a bright, familiar amber. He growled as he thrust into her, teeth gnashing together. Becky cried out again.

And then she started shaking.

They were so lost in each other that they didn't notice me. Becky shook beneath him, wildly, even as she dug her nails into his back to pull him closer. He snarled again, and then fiercely roared as he buried himself in her, his amber eyes blazing.

I backed away, grabbed Amelia by the arm, and ran.

Her chest was heaving by the time we reached the Yukon. She was visibly trembling, her complexion snow-white. I shoved her into the car and buckled her in.

"What the… What were they… Why were his eyes…" She blinked at me. "Did you see his eyes? And why was mom *shaking* like that?"

"Um." I threw the car in drive and peeled out of the parking lot. I had no idea what to do, what to tell her. What I'd just seen was so wrong, I needed a new word for wrong.

We drove past a grocery store, and I saw Becky's Mercedes SUV parked there. A block later, I spotted Bryant Pierce's BMW in a drugstore lot. They'd been very careful to cover their tracks.

Amelia didn't say anything else. I glanced at her—her

eyes were glazed, her mouth hanging open. I worried she might be in shock.

"Are you okay?"

"I don't…I don't understand what I just saw. And I don't think it's just because I'm a virgin."

"Yeah. I…" I literally had no words. She still clutched Chris's bag. "What're we going to do with that?" I asked, in order to distract her.

She just shook her head.

"I'm going to see if James can pick us up, okay? That way we don't have to take the mailboat." I dictated a text over Bluetooth and nodded when he responded. "He's going to leave now, okay? He'll meet us at the dock. Everything's going to be okay."

Amelia stared straight ahead. She didn't look convinced. I gripped the steering wheel and drove well above the speed limit.

I knew I couldn't put enough distance between us and Becky, but that wasn't going to stop me from trying.

29

CLOSE WATCH

JAMES MET us in Pine Harbor. His smile quickly turned to a frown as he took in Amelia's rattled appearance. She was pale, mascara streaked beneath her eyes. Her arms were locked around Chris's stupid bag. She had it pressed to her chest in a vice-grip.

"You guys okay?" He gently helped her on board the Hinckley. She went and sat down on one of the couches, not answering.

"What happened?" he whispered.

"B-Becky. It was bad." I glanced at Amelia, who was staring listlessly out at the water. "I think she might be in shock. Can you bring us to the Tower? I don't want to run into my dad. He shouldn't see her like this."

"Sure." He navigated out of the harbor and made good time across Hart Sound. I barely noticed all my favorite landmarks; all I could picture was Becky with Bryant Pierce.

James glanced above my head a couple of times. He looked worried.

I went and sat with Amelia. Neither one of us said anything as the wind whipped our hair. She'd wiped her eyes. The mascara traces were gone. She put Chris's stash inside her backpack, zipping it up neatly.

Amelia didn't appear surprised when we circled Dawnhaven and pulled up to the Tower's dock. She helped with the bumpers and then climbed out of the boat. We headed up to the deck and she shuffled beside us, saying nothing.

I nodded toward her. "I'm going to call Dad real quick, okay?"

She shrugged.

I told him we'd stopped at the Tower to hang out but would be home soon. "That was nice of you to include your sister," he said.

"Sure thing, Dad." I sighed when I hung up. What was I supposed to tell him about that afternoon?

Luke ambled out onto the deck and joined us. "Hey guys."

"Where's Eden?" James immediately asked, his voice tense. He was probably worried about Amelia, another human to tempt her.

"It's fine—she's in her room." Luke rolled his eyes and turned his attention to Amelia. "What's the matter, girly? Did you have a rough day at school?"

She glanced at him, then looked away. She promptly burst into tears.

"Oh, boy." Luke made a hasty exit. "I'm just going to…" He didn't bother finishing the sentence as he disappeared back into the house.

I went and sat by her. "Hey. It's okay." I nodded at James. "Give us a minute?"

"Of course." He followed Luke inside.

I drew Amelia in for an awkward hug, patting her hair. "I know that was a terrible thing to see. I'm sorry that you had to deal with that."

She pulled away and wiped her eyes. "My mother is a *whore*."

"Okay. Well…" I cleared my throat. "We all do things that we regret. She's making a bad choice."

"A bad choice is wearing denim on denim—not having sex with a guy who snarls like an animal and who's eyes glow." Amelia wrinkled her nose. "He was, like, a *demon*. A sex-animal demon."

"Yeah, about that…" I took a deep breath. "Maybe we didn't see what we thought we saw. Maybe they were just being really freaky, or something."

Amelia shook her head. "What do you mean?"

"Well, you know." I shrugged, even though *I* didn't know what I was talking about. "Maybe they're just into some weird stuff. Like making strange noises. And wearing crazy contact lenses. Maybe it's, like, role-playing."

Amelia eyed me up and down. "Role-playing *what*?"

"Sex-animal demons?" I asked hopefully.

She looked at me as though *I* might be a sex-animal demon. "I just wish I could forget it. I'll never be able to look at Mom again—and *Dad*, oh my god, what're we going to do?"

"I don't know. But I don't think we should say anything to him. Not yet."

Her eyes almost bugged out in her head. "So what—we're gonna go home and pretend nothing happened? That's *insane*, Taylor!"

"Yeah, you're probably right." I had no idea how to handle this. Amelia had a point—we shouldn't keep this from our father—but there were other, possibly more insidious, factors at play. "I'm going to grab a glass of water, okay? You want something?"

She blew out a ragged breath. "Water would be great."

I hustled inside. James and Luke were standing in the living room—they'd obviously been watching us. "Can you help me?" I asked James.

"Of course. Anything."

"Good." I inhaled deeply. "Amelia needs to be... zapped. Like, right now."

Luke smiled eagerly. "You mean—with the white knight's light?"

"Yeah, that's exactly what I mean."

"Awesome," Luke said. "He never lets me see it."

James gaped at me.

"I need you to erase her memory from today. Can you do that? She saw something she shouldn't have—something dangerous." Luke and James waited, and I sighed. "We walked in on Becky having sex with Bryant Pierce."

Both of their jaws dropped.

"By the way, I'm pretty sure I know who the were-wolf is," I continued. "And Becky was shaking while they were doing it—like, *shaking* shaking."

I stalked back outside to my sister. She was a pain in the ass, but she was *my* pain in the ass. I had to protect her.

Amelia looked confused. "Where's the water?"

"I didn't get any. I got James instead. Listen Amelia, I asked him to help you. Do you trust me?"

She arched her eyebrows. "Not especially."

I couldn't help it; I laughed. "Can you try to start?"

Her shoulders sagged. "It's not that I don't trust you

to do the right thing—you're a total goody-two shoes. But what are you talking about?"

"Something that will make you feel better."

She looked wary. "I thought you didn't like drugs."

"It isn't drugs." James joined us outside and I motioned to him. "James is going to help you. He'll make you forget all about this afternoon."

Amelia scrunched her nose. "I won't remember what happened?"

"No." I shook my head. "It's to protect you, Amelia. I promise you that I am going to take care of this. You don't have to be afraid, and you don't have to worry about telling Dad. I'll handle it. Okay?"

She nodded, almost imperceptibly.

"You won't remember this, so I'll just say it now: you're welcome."

Amelia raised her eyebrows. "Thank you?"

James went closer and smiled at her kindly. "This won't hurt at all," he promised. "Just don't make any sudden movements."

Amelia held perfectly still, a puzzled expression on her face.

I watched as James worked his magic. But in the back of my mind, I wondered what in the hell I was going to do next.

WE KEPT a close watch over Amelia.

After James used his light on her, she'd seemed dazed for a few minutes. But then she returned to her normal, scowling, pubescent self.

She didn't appear to remember a thing about her mother and Bryant.

We ran a test: Luke came out to the deck, smiling and chatting. Amelia's scowl disappeared. She stuck her chest out, and when he asked about her day, she said it was "boring." Boring was good. Boring was *great*. She seemed normal, and as though she had no memory of going to the apartment that afternoon. I just hoped that seeing Becky wouldn't produce some kind of flashback.

James didn't know what would happen. He'd never used his power that discretely before. "It's actually pretty handy," he said. "I used a very light touch, and I could control it. I'm impressed by the results."

I wasn't certain what to make of that, but I didn't have time to ponder. There were too many other things to worry about.

James drove us home. "Wait—can you go the long way?" I asked.

"Sure." He went straight instead of turning right.

The "long way" was simply a diversion down another

road, past several of the island's more upscale homes. I knew Chris lived on that street. That was the thing about the island—everybody knew everything, including where everyone else lived.

"Wait, can you stop there?" I pointed to Chris's house.

James pulled over and I took Amelia's backpack. She watched me blankly, as though she had no idea what I was up to. "Why're we stopping at Chris Fitzpatrick's house?"

"No reason," I lied. I hustled to the front door. I took Chris's stash out, unzipping it and leaving it open on the top step. I grabbed a sticky note and a pen from Amelia's backpack. *Chris, just returning your stuff. You're welcome!* I scribbled a smiley face, then stuck it on top of his vape supplies.

It only made me feel mildly better. Still, it was something.

Amelia was texting the rest of the ride home. I glanced at her cell, to make sure it wasn't a warning to Chris. Instead, it was just a note to Brynn about an upcoming French quiz—and how much of a douche their teacher was. We pulled up to the house, and Amelia hopped out of the truck. "Thanks, James." She seemed oblivious and completely, utterly back to normal.

"I need to talk to you, but you can't leave her alone." James nodded toward Amelia, who was scowling at her phone as usual. "Keep an eye on her. If she says anything about what happened, or seems to remember, let me know right away."

The last thing I wanted was to be separated from him again. "Do you want to come in?"

James sighed. "I do, but I have to get back. This changes things... Luke and I need to make a plan. Am I correct in assuming that you think the werewolf is Bryant Pierce?"

I couldn't say it out loud—not yet—so I nodded.

I wanted to talk about it more, to piece it all together, but Amelia headed for the door. "I'll talk to you later—love you. And thank you." I kissed him briefly and then hustled after her.

The house was quiet—my dad must've been at the co-op, and Becky... I shuddered. I didn't want to think about that.

"I'm going to take a shower and put my sweats on." Amelia yawned. "I'm *so* glad it's Friday—school sucks!"

"Yeah, it does." I watched as she padded upstairs, still on her phone, seemingly without a care in the world.

I showered too, hoping I could somehow scrub the grossness of the day away. I washed my hair and blew it dry, then changed into my coziest clothes. But even my favorite sweatshirt couldn't comfort me. I felt chilled inside, inconsolable, deeply disturbed by what I'd witnessed.

Becky, shaking uncontrollably and moaning. Bryant Pierce on top of her, snarling, his eyes glowing a fierce amber.

Big Kyle got home first. He hummed as he headed for the kitchen, where he ate chips and salsa, chased by several cookies. He looked sheepish when I came in. "Don't tell Becky. She's making low-carb pizza tonight, and I just had to eat something real before she gets back."

"I won't say a word, Dad." I was getting good at it.

I wanted to explain what had happened, but I couldn't. Not yet. I needed to keep him safe, and the best way to do that was to keep him as far away from the supernatural truth as possible.

I grabbed a couple of cookies. "How do you make low-carb pizza?"

He shuddered. "You don't want to know."

Becky came home a little while later, laden with grocery bags. She wore zebra-striped athletic tights and a furry black sweatshirt. Had I been in the mood to crack jokes, I would've asked if she was connecting with her inner animal.

But it wasn't funny, and I knew it.

She acted as though nothing was wrong, kissing my dad hello, complaining about someone who worked at Main Street Market, pouring herself a glass of white wine. I hoped she'd at least taken a shower.

I headed to the living room, staying close to the kitchen so I could eavesdrop. But they only discussed the weather, and whether it was going to be good enough for our family hike in the park. They concluded it was going to be fine. I groaned inwardly. I couldn't *wait* to spend all day with Becky, *yay*.

Dinner that evening was indeed low-carb pizza. The trick was that Becky made the crust from cauliflower, which tasted like cauliflower mixed with cardboard.

"Thanks, Becky. This is good," I lied. I couldn't look at her without imagining her writhing naked beneath Bryant Pierce. *Ew ew ew.* The cauliflower crust was almost as gross.

"You're welcome." She smiled, and I noticed her complexion was stunningly perfect. She was glowing again. Quadruple *ew*.

The positive news was that Amelia seemed completely oblivious. She had truly forgotten what she'd seen that afternoon. She complained about the cauliflower crust. She complained about golf. She complained about hiking. I'd never been so happy to see her act like her normal, bitchy self.

I pretended to enjoy my pizza, sighing inwardly. There was no chance of going back to the Tower that night. If Amelia remembered what happened, if Becky started to shake, or God forbid, if Bryant Pierce showed up at our door in human or wolf form—I couldn't leave my family alone. Too much could happen. So after dinner, I found myself stuck in the living room with them. Dad, Becky, Amelia and I watched some show on Netflix about a music festival gone wrong.

James texted me several times, but he didn't tell me much. He'd updated his father with the recent information, and they were working on a plan. His vagueness alarmed me. He was keeping me in the dark. I didn't know if it was because he was protecting me, or if he was shielding me from the danger he planned to put himself in. I hated being left out, but I hated worrying about him more.

There would be no sneaking down to the Tower after hours. James informed me that Eden would be locked in her room, with Patrick and the alarm system on duty. Luke and James would come down to Becky's house. They'd set up watch around the perimeter, taking turns on guard.

They were watching for the wolf.

It wasn't exactly the Friday night I'd hoped for. I went to bed early, and in a sour mood.

"Don't forget we've got chores tomorrow," my dad reminded me. "We have to winterize the pool."

"Okay, Dad." I didn't have the heart to complain to him.

James texted me before I fell asleep. *We are out here. It's quiet.*

Thank you, I texted back.

Love you.

I love you, too. It wasn't the same as falling asleep in his arms. But knowing he was outside, protecting my family, made me love him that much more.

In spite of everything, sleep came easily. I had cross-country to thank for that. But my dreams were dark and scary, haunted with images of glowing eyes, and filled with the sound of Becky's low moaning. There was no escape, no relief.

Still, morning came far too quickly. My stomach was heavy with dread. I had to face another day, and I had no idea what would happen next.

SHUDDER

"PUT YOUR SWEATSHIRT ON, PUMPKIN." Dad winked at me over his steaming mug of coffee. "It's chilly out there."

I grabbed my heavy *Portside* hoodie and pulled it over my head. "Is this going to take long?" I asked. I'd never winterized a pool before. I had no idea what it entailed.

"Well, there's a couple of steps." Dad seemed to be mentally checking off a list as he continued. "We have to balance the levels, clean the pool, let some water out, add some different chemicals... And then we have to deal with the cover. So we're looking at two, three hours."

Ugh. "Can I go down to James's after?"

"Sure, but I don't want you staying out too late. We're hiking tomorrow, remember?"

"Yep." I groaned inwardly. Jenny hadn't put me on

the schedule for that weekend, so I was unfortunately free for our family hike in Acadia. All day with Becky the next day, *yay*.

I watched my dad carefully as we worked. Amelia was sleeping in, and Becky had gone for a power walk with Sylvie. Big Kyle seemed cheerful as he checked the chemical levels of the water, explaining the balance of compounds to me. Private pools were outside of my realm of experience. The chemical names and proper balances meant little to me. Still, I listened. I liked spending time with him.

"Did anyone actually swim in the pool this summer?" I asked as we cleaned out one of the filters. The only one I'd seen jump in was Drunk Guy, aka Adam—the first person I ever saw shake, the first person to attack me— but he hadn't exactly been an authorized guest.

"I don't think so." Kyle frowned as he pulled wet leaves from the filter. "But Becky thought it was a necessity—she says all luxury homes should have a pool."

"Oh." Again, outside my experience.

"Everything all right with you? You seem a little quiet." His gaze swept over me briefly.

It was seriously annoying how observant he was of my moods, and how clueless he was about his own relationship. "I'm good, Dad. Everything's fine. What about you?"

"You know what?" He grinned at me. "I'm feeling pretty optimistic these days. You and Amelia seem like you're getting along, which I love. And Bec's doing—I think she's doing okay. Maybe the therapy's helping. Or could be all the exercise."

"Y-Yeah." I felt deflated. How could I tell him the truth? I didn't even know where to start. *A secret apartment, an affair...a werewolf.* It wasn't exactly a simple conversation.

"Ah shoot. We need a special wrench for this. There's one down at the co-op. Be right back." Dad chuckled. "Don't have too much fun without me."

"Ha. I'll try not to."

As soon as he disappeared around the corner, Amelia stormed outside. She wore flannel pajama bottoms and a severely pissed look on her face. "Taylor! What did you do? Chris just texted me—he said he's in a crap-ton of trouble because someone left his vape stuff on his front step. His mom found it."

"Huh." I pretended to study the chemical levels in a beaker. "What would I know about that?"

She put her hands on her hips. "You were the one who found us, and you *yelled* at him."

"So?" I kept my eyes on the beaker.

"*So* you have to explain to him I had nothing to do

with it. He's grounded for a month, and he thinks it's all our fault."

"If he asks, tell him I have no idea. Tell him he should keep better track of his things." I glanced back at her. "Oh, and tell him I think he's a douche, okay? Because I think he's a douche."

Amelia groaned, but then a funny look crossed her face. "You know what's weird? I feel like I'm forgetting something. Like, I can't remember some of the stuff he was talking about."

"I told you not to vape. That crap will fry your brain! The number one side-effect of THC is short-term memory loss." I watched her, hopeful she would leave it at that.

She scratched her head. "But it's *weird*. He said I told him I'd go to the apartment and grab it for him yesterday, but I don't remember ever saying that."

"I'm telling you—your brain's fried."

When she still looked confused, I asked, "What about your texts? Did he text you something about it?" My heart sank. If he had, she might recall what James had made sure she forgot. It would be better to deal with it as soon as possible.

"Nah, we only talk on Snap Chat." She shrugged. "Everything self-deletes. That's sort of the whole point."

"Well, I don't know what Chris's problem is," I said. "I just know it's not *my* problem. Or yours."

"Whatever." Amelia appeared over it. "He's cute, but you're right—he *is* kind of a douche. He totally asked me to have a party over there. When I said no, he started ignoring my texts. I don't need that in my life."

"You're right—you don't." Maybe she was coming around. "You want to help out with the pool? We're almost done."

"Nah, I'm going to watch makeup tutorials on YouTube. But you have fun with that." She snorted.

I sighed. Then again, maybe she wasn't.

I waited, amusing myself by reading the ingredients list on the balancing chemicals. But unfortunately, the next person who came up the driveway wasn't my dad. It was Becky.

Her lips were pursed as she power-walked toward me, ponytail swishing, cheeks ruddy from her walk with Sylvie. She frowned as she got closer. "What're you doing, Taylor?"

"Waiting for Dad. He went down to the co-op to get a wrench."

She motioned to all the chemicals and the pool supplies. "I *mean*, what're you doing with all this stuff?"

She sounded so accusatory, I took a step back.

"N-Nothing." I licked my lips. "I wasn't touching

anything. I was just following Dad's directions." She made me feel like a naughty four-year-old who'd been caught playing with something off-limits.

"Make sure you wait until he gets home. That pool cost me over a hundred thousand dollars," she snapped.

"Too bad you never even swim in it." The words tumbled out, a bit rudely, before I could stop myself.

Her eyes widened in shock. "Don't you take that tone with me!"

My half-sister got away with murder, but I wasn't allowed one minor, knee-jerk retort. "Sorry. I've just been thinking it's a shame we're draining the pool—no one ever used it." Even as the words left my mouth, I knew she'd find fault with them.

Becky's nostrils flared. "I don't need you judging me or how my family chooses to live in *our* house."

I coughed. Then, because I could not stop myself, I said, "If I was judging you, it wouldn't be for that."

"Oh, that's just perfect." Becky drew herself up to her full height. "It's every time your father isn't around. That's when you show your true colors."

"Becky, I—"

"Don't you dare try to defend yourself! We both know the truth." A tremor, almost imperceptible, made her shiver. "You think you're better than us. You're on your high horse, a martyr, thinking you know better—but you know *shit*."

"I know some things. Things I wish I didn't." My voice, like her face, trembled a bit.

"*Pfft.* I'm not afraid of you. Who do you think you are, huh? You're running around with James like you think his family could somehow rub off on you. Well, *guess what?*" She shivered again, this time more violently. Her entire body trembled. "H-h-he d-d-doesn't belong to you. He doesn't make you safe. You're nothing without him, nothing."

She took a step closer, shaking so fast her face became a blur.

"Get away from me!" I ran to the other side of the pool.

Becky chased after me, her body convulsing.

My mind raced. Could I throw her in the pool? Would that even do anything? What would happen if I touched her?

She got closer. "The only r-r-r-reason you're s-s-still h-h-here is because I'm l-l-looking out for M-M-M-Melia. I-I-I'm c-c-coming out on t-t-t-top—"

"Mom?" Amelia slammed the front door and ran down the steps. "What's the matter?"

The moment she heard her daughter's voice, the

shaking stopped. It was immediate and complete—like some sort of switch had been flipped.

I'd never been so happy to see Amelia in my life.

"Oh! Nothing, honey." Becky's ponytail flicked as she whipped her head at her daughter, a big smile on her face. "I was just talking to Taylor about closing up the pool."

Amelia looked from her Becky to me. I made certain my expression was neutral.

Amelia peered at her mother. "You looked funny. Are you sure you're all right?"

"Yes, I'm fine." Becky sounded so normal, I almost smacked her. She went and put her arm around her daughter. "Let's go make smoothies, okay? And then maybe we can go shopping."

Amelia glanced over her shoulder at me as Becky led her toward the front steps. I smiled as though everything was just fine. All I wanted was to be away from Becky.

I texted James as soon as they went inside. *Where are you?*

At the house. Something came up. Are you okay?

Becky just went off, I typed quickly. *But she's fine now.*

My phone rang. "I don't want to talk about it, all right?" I felt drained, close to tears. I was sick of my stupid step-monster, her infidelity, her shaking, but most of all, the way she treated me like trash. "I'm fine—I just wanted you to know."

James exhaled deeply. "I'll come down and pick you up right now."

"Let me finish up with my dad, okay? I'll text you after."

James was quiet for a second. "I'm sorry, Taylor."

"It's not your fault."

I hung up quickly, before he could say it was.

31

RED CARPET

ALTHOUGH I WAS WORRIED about leaving Amelia alone with her mother, she looked okay when they came back outside a few minutes later and took the truck. They were going off-island to shop. Becky barely glanced in my direction.

They both seemed fine. Normal, even.

I, however, was *so* not fine. What did Becky mean, the only reason I was still here was because of Amelia? What else had she said... *"I-I-I'm c-c-coming out on t-t-t-top—"*

What the heck?

My dad came back, clueless as ever. I wanted to explain everything to him. He needed to get the hell away from Becky. But how could I say that? How could I tell him the truth? Knowing about the wolves, not to mention the vampires, would put him at terrible risk.

Becky had never gone after my father. She'd never had one of her "episodes" when either he or Amelia were near. When either of them had come close, she'd ceased shaking immediately, before they could notice anything. I had to trust that they were both relatively safe around her—that her episodes were reserved for me, her terrified target audience of one.

We finished with the pool cover, and Dad went back down to the co-op to return the wrench. James picked me up as soon as I texted. It was a relief to see his handsome face, to climb into the safety of his truck.

"Hey." He kissed my cheek, lips lingering for a moment. "Are you really okay?"

"Yeah. I mean, *no*. But yeah."

He raised his eyebrows as we drove.

"She didn't do anything, except shake and say nasty things."

"What provoked it?" James asked.

I shook my head. "She saw me with their pool chemicals. She wanted to make sure I wasn't messing up her precious salt-water that she never swims in."

He put his hand over mine. "What else?" His voice was gentle, not pushing me.

I sighed, then told him what she'd said about Amelia and coming out on top.

James's brow furrowed. "I don't like that."

I groaned. "I don't either. But I don't know what it means."

"Me either." He said nothing else for the rest of the ride; he seemed lost in his thoughts.

When we parked, he said, "I have a surprise for you."

"You do?" My heart rate kicked up. I wished that he'd surprise me with the promise of an afternoon alone, without trouble or interruption.

He chuckled. "I don't have to read your aura to know what you're thinking—and I wish that we could spend some time alone, too. But unfortunately, that's not it."

I studied his high cheekbones, drinking him in. How was it possible to miss someone so much, when you lived right down the road from them?

"So what's the surprise?" I finally asked.

"You'll like it, trust me."

James held my hand as we walked across the lawn. It was a gorgeous afternoon. The morning cloud cover had blown out, revealing the sun high in the sky. Edgar cawed from the trees and I waved in his general direction. I should bring him something shiny, a reward for saving me from Eden the other night.

I smiled, and my heart lifted. Being close to James was my favorite place in the entire world.

We reached the deck and a familiar voice called, "Finally, Taylor! I drag myself all the way up here to see you, and you're winterizing a pool."

Josie waved to me from the far end of the deck. I hadn't seen my friend in weeks, not since I'd fled the island with Eden. She looked stunning as always, with her short dreadlocks and glowing, flawless dark skin. The diamond stud in her nose winked in the sunlight.

"Josie!" I ran and hugged her. "I didn't know you were coming."

"I didn't know either. But since you fools are messing around with werewolves, I didn't have much choice, did I?"

"Where's Dylan?" I asked. Dylan was Josie's girlfriend. They lived together in Brooklyn.

She shook her head. "She has an exam; she couldn't miss it."

Luke ambled out onto the deck, and a deep scowl replaced Josie's smile. "Speaking of fools. Here's the original one, himself."

"Aw c'mon Josie, you know you missed me. At least a little." Luke winked at her. "It's been too long. Although you're even more dazzling than the last time we met."

She shook her head. "You haven't changed."

"But you have." Luke's grin widened. "Unless you were always that hot."

"Oh, I was." She arched an eyebrow. "But *you* haven't changed a bit: pretty on the outside, rotten to the core."

He put a hand over his heart. "*Ouch.* You wound me. And I don't even think that's true anymore—about my rotten core—right, James?" With a pleading expression, he turned to his brother. "You think I'm better, right?"

James crossed his arms against his chest, his mouth set in a grim line.

Luke swung his megawatt smile back on Josie. "Don't fall for his act—we're getting along great. I'm his second, his go-to. He even lets me babysit Taylor every once in a while."

"Ha—things must be bad, then," Josie said. "James?"

"Yeah, it's bad. I'm glad you came back."

"Me too. I mean, mostly." She eyed Luke with disdain again, then turned toward the water. "Maine's so much better than the city. I don't know how I'm going to make it through another year there."

"Then come home for good—we need all the help we can get." James sighed and sank down into a lounger. "There's a lot to catch you up on. I wanted to wait until Taylor was here. We'll give you the abbreviated version…"

He told her about meeting Mali, and how the werewolf

tracked us to the woods when Eden was hunting. He told her about the enormous wolf sitting outside of Becky's house, and how it swam to Spruce to escape them. He told her about Bryant Pierce—the fact that I'd seen him with Becky at the gala, and subsequently, on the *Breathless*—and that Becky had been keeping a secret rental off-island.

I jumped in and completed the story, including the scene at the apartment the day before. Josie's jaw dropped as I listed every sordid detail. Then I told her about that morning out at the pool. I shook my head once I finished. "It's been...hectic."

"It's been crazy, that's what it's been." Josie scrubbed a hand over her face. "Not to get too much in your family's business, Taylor—but Becky is into this guy, right?"

I shrugged. "It seems like it. But then again, she and my dad had 'date night' the other night... But she was with Bryant after that. So I have no idea."

"You said she was shaking when she was with him?" Josie watched me carefully. "Was it like...before?"

I nodded. "She was moving so fast her face was blurry. It was the same thing at our pool this morning." Thinking about it still made me feel sick.

"We're going to figure this out. It'll be okay." Josie's voice was gentle. "I'm wondering, though, what sort of control this wolf is exercising over Becky. It's no joke when a human has sex with a supernatural. It's power-ful, addictive."

Luke winked at her. "Is that your way of saying you miss me?"

"Ugh, shut *up*." Josie looked disgusted. "It's my way of saying that Becky is probably in over her head. Not that I'm trying to make excuses for her. Becky's not exactly my favorite."

I wanted to ask what she meant, but Patrick burst out of the house. "James. I've got news—*bad* news."

James jumped to his feet. "What?"

"Your mother just called the landline. She's coming to the island. She'll be here in a few minutes."

"What?"

Eden came out behind Patrick, peering out at the water. "She said she was arriving by boat this time. D'you guys see anything?"

Everyone watched the horizon. Finally, Luke pointed west. "There. That's got to be her—that enormous yacht."

James scowled as it drew near. "Not exactly understated."

Luke shrugged. "This *is* mom we're talking about."

Once it got closer, I saw what they meant. It was a large white yacht. It stopped outside the channel, near

Moss Head. A smaller boat, a tender, lowered into the water and sped toward us.

"What does your mother want, James?" Josie sounded grim. "She's not exactly one to just drop by and visit."

"I don't know." James frowned, then glanced at Patrick. "Did she say anything specific? I talked to Dad earlier, he mentioned nothing about this."

"I'm sure he didn't want to give you too much of a heads up," Luke said. "You know how it is. When mom gets something into her head, there's no stopping her. He probably didn't want you to put up a fight about it."

James's scowl deepened. "This can't be good." He glanced at Eden. "I see you're out of your room. Stay away from Taylor—if you get too close, you're getting locked up again."

Eden meekly nodded. She made sure to stay on the opposite side, close to Luke.

We all walked around the Tower to greet Marietta. What I really wanted to do was run in the opposite direction. Running sucked, but it was *so* much better than facing James's terrifying mother again.

My heart sank as the tender approached the dock. Marietta Champlain was just as lovely and intimidating as I remembered. Her long auburn locks blew back from her face. Enormous round sunglasses were perched atop her nose, and her crimson lips curved into a pout. She wore a deep-emerald silk jumpsuit, and multiple, thick gold necklaces.

The vampire captain helped her off the boat. Her spike-heeled boots purposefully clicked down the dock as she approached, chest thrust out and bouncing, hips swaying. She was mesmerizing.

The harried-looking captain followed her, carrying a large sack that was…moving.

"Your mother is a crazy bitch, but *damn*, she always looks good. It's like she's hypnotizing me with those hips." Josie shook her head as if to clear it. "Um—is it too late for me to hide?"

"Why would you want to hide? I just want to stare—I want to be just like her when I grow up." Eyes wide, Eden drank in the sight of the stylish, gorgeous vampire stalking toward us. "Can vampires get breast implants?"

Luke chuckled. "My mother has great style, but she's not exactly someone you can emulate. She's very…"

"Scary?" I asked.

"Unique," Luke offered. "She's one of a kind."

"Thank God for that." James was still scowling when Marietta reached us. "Hello, Mother."

"James." She air-kissed him on both cheeks, then motioned for Luke to come closer. "There's my baby. How are you holding up?"

Luke grinned. "Fine, Mom."

She pulled her sunglasses down and inspected Eden, Josie, Patrick and me. "Even with all the riff-raff?"

Despite her insult, I couldn't help but stare at her stunning aqua eyes.

"Aw c'mon, Mom," Luke said easily. "You know you shouldn't say stuff like that out loud."

"Fine, fine." She looked past her son to Patrick. "Patrick Cavill, I have a bone to pick with you."

He nervously scratched at his neck. "Yes, ma'am?"

"Where has your mother been, young man? Why isn't she here? Nelson said she's been practically useless."

Patrick visibly stiffened. "She's got her own stuff going on, Mrs. Champlain."

Marietta rolled her eyes. "I've told my husband for years that she's a weak ally."

"*Mother.* Patrick's been an excellent friend to me," James said. "Mrs. Cavill has helped a lot this summer, with advice about Eden. She has a very strong maternal instinct. Not your area of expertise, of course."

Marietta shrugged. Behind her, the captain wrestled with the sack. Something yipped from inside of it.

"What's in there?" James asked.

"Oh." His mother waved her hand dismissively. "I brought ammunition for us to use—it's symbolic."

James pointed at the bag. "It's *alive.*"

"It's not an *it*, it's a *they*." She snapped her fingers and the guard placed the sack on the lawn. He loosened the top so we could peer inside. Four small, gray-and-black pups peered back out at us, their ice-blue eyes shining and curious. One of them whined.

"Puppies?" Luke's brow furrowed. "I don't get it, Mother."

"Oh, honey—it's a good thing you're so handsome, otherwise, I would worry about you." She nodded and the guard took out one pup. "They're *wolves*. Baby wolves."

"Why did you bring wolf pups up here?" James gave his mother a strange look.

"Because I'm going to *drown* them, darling, and then toss them onto the werewolves' front lawn. *Symbolism*, get it?" She tossed her hair over her shoulder and headed for the house.

James stood rooted to the spot. "Why are you here, Mom?"

"Because I hate werewolves. You know that." She didn't look back. "And I intend to help you kill them all —with some *flair*."

The captain picked up the sack and followed Marietta. Luke, Josie, Eden, and Patrick trailed after them.

But I stayed in the yard, gaping.

James gripped my hand. "You need to go home, Taylor."

"What? N-No." I pulled away. "I need to know what she's planning—it involves me."

"You're wrong." The muscle in his jaw was taut. I knew how much Marietta pushed him—he appeared about to go over the edge. "It has nothing to do with you, that's the whole point."

"It does, though. Becky, Bryant…" I faced him. "I'm in this, James. Whether you like it or not."

Before he could try to stop me, I followed his very scary mother to the Tower.

32

DANGER ZONE

MARIETTA FROWNED as we crowded into the living room. "Boys. Don't we need some privacy to discuss logistics?"

She looked from Patrick to Josie. "This isn't a conversation about the balance, or whatever it is you think you're defending. This is about protecting *vampires*, and making sure that the dogs know who their master is."

"Guys, give us a minute?" James asked. Patrick and Josie headed out to the deck. They both looked relieved to get away from Marietta.

"What about me?" Eden asked.

"You're one of us," Luke said.

"I heard you almost attacked Taylor the other night," Marietta said. Her eyes sparkled. "You're more than welcome to stay."

Eden beamed at them, then eagerly took a seat on the couch, far from me and James.

I leaned close to him and whispered, "What about *me*?"

"You're directly implicated in this," Marietta said coldly. "You stay."

James didn't look at me, but he gripped my hand.

The captain set the sack down, and Marietta nodded at him. "Let them out—let them stretch their legs while they can."

He opened it and the puppies spilled out, nipping and yipping at each other, tumbling all over the carpet. They took off across the kitchen, giving chase, and careened out of sight.

James watched them, then turned to Marietta. "You can't drown them. That's... It's wrong, Mother."

She arched an eyebrow. "Since when have I shared your weighty moral compass? You know, this is exactly why it shouldn't surprise me that you're in love with a *houseplant*. You've become so soft, it's like you're faded. You're not an angel—you're a *ghost*, James. You need to find your edge."

He shook his head. "And you need to find your heart —but I guess after all these hundreds of years, I won't hold my breath."

She frowned and tossed her hair over her shoulder.

"I'm not interested in your judgment. I'm interested in what we're going to do up here, in order to defeat our enemies."

Luke sat down next to Eden. He faced his mother. "Does Dad know you're here?" he asked.

"Of course he does. You two still haven't got his number—he acts like he's evolved, but he nevertheless sends me to do his dirty work. Don't be surprised when he calls you and authorizes my plan. Now tell me more about these wolves. I want to know everything, so that I recognize who to decimate."

Luke cleared his throat. "James and I have established that there's a legitimate pack here. They're all at the property on Spruce, the one I told you about. It's a ramshackle house and a farm. It should be an easy fight, but I don't think we can go over there and slaughter them—at least, not yet."

Marietta blinked at him. "Why not?"

Luke shrugged. "Because there isn't provocation. They haven't attacked us."

James leaned forward. "They've just been gathering information."

"You don't know that. *I* think they've already shown us what their endgame is; you just don't want to face it. I've been paying closer attention than you might realize." Marietta pointed at me. "Their leader has been courting the human's stepmother. That was happening over the summer. Which is how the newest vampire joined our coven."

"You mean me?" Eden's eyes glittered with excitement. "I'm part of your *coven*? That's so cool!"

Marietta silenced her with a look, then turned back to James. "The point is, they've been targeting us for months. You've just been too fixated to see it."

My face burned. I knew she meant that he'd been too fixated on *me*.

James leaned forward. "It's more complicated than that—"

Marietta held up her hand to stop him. "Your father's told me everything. About the balance, about the acceleration, all of it. I understand what you think has been going on up here."

"And?" James waited, his jaw set.

"*And* I don't believe that's the issue. It might be *an* issue, but it's not the predominant one."

Marietta straightened her spine and continued, "The wolves have been lying low for decades, regathering their strength. Their kind has adapted, becoming more skilled at concealing themselves. But they're still after the same thing: to exact revenge on our kind, to seek reparations for what they feel we took from them. And now these Mount Desert shifters think they've found our weakness."

"What's that?" Luke asked, but I already knew the answer.

"Your human." Marietta nodded toward me. "That's why they've been targeting her family. It's easy pickings. Through her, the shifters have had access to everything. They've been using her stepmother for months to get to you, James, and you didn't even realize it."

"What's happening with Becky isn't just because of the werewolves," James said. "It *is* because of the balance. I can feel it. Things are shifting—the energy is changing all around us."

"That energy you feel is the wolves gathering their strength." Marietta pursed her lips. "That's what's shifted: their potency is reawakening. You thought the changes you saw taking place were all about *love*. Which is very romantic, but which also misses the point. It's about power. Remember darling, it's always about power."

The muscle in James's jaw bulged. "That's enough, Mother."

"Oh, I'm just getting started. Luke, can you bring some wine? Being here makes me…" Her gaze swept over me. "Parched."

"Fine," James said. "Luke, get her some wine. I'm

taking Taylor home." He squeezed my hand and pulled me to my feet.

"Are you sure you want to do that?" Marietta called. "She has a part to play in all this."

"No, she doesn't." James didn't look back, and he didn't look at me as he ushered me outside. "I need to get you out of here."

Patrick and Josie sat at the opposite end of the deck. They saw us facing off against each other, then quickly pretended to be busy with their phones.

I yanked my hand away. "James, *no*. You heard her— she thinks this is my fault."

His face was pale but determined. "That's not what she said."

"Actually, *yeah* it is."

"She doesn't know what she's talking about." He headed for the truck, and I had no choice but to follow.

I turned and waved goodbye to my friends. Josie looked worried. Patrick frowned, shaking his head.

"Didn't you hear her? She thinks they've been targeting you for months through Becky, through *me*. I thought… I thought…" I paced back and forth in front of the pickup. I didn't know what I thought.

"Get in the truck, Taylor."

I gave him an exasperated look, but he didn't see it. He was staring past me, at the house. His expression was impassive, unreadable. Which was the only reason I gave up and got in the cab: I wanted to hear what he was thinking.

But he drove me home in stony silence. He pulled into the driveway and just sat there, truck idling.

I turned to face him. "James. Don't let your mother do this to you."

"What?" he asked sharply.

"Drive us apart." I put my hand on top of his.

He shook his head. "My mother doesn't have that sort of power over me."

"Okay." I took a deep breath. "Then don't pull away from me. Don't shut me out."

"Taylor." He slid his hand out from under mine. "You know that's not what I want."

He wouldn't look at me.

"But?"

"*But* look at what's happening. My mother's here, threatening to drown puppies and slaughter a local family in the middle of the night. I can't have you anywhere near that. You need to stay away from her, away from *this*."

"Okay." Nervous energy bubbled inside my chest. "I won't come near her while she's here. It's not a problem." Frankly, it would be a relief.

"It's not just that." His voice was gravelly. "Ever since

I met you… Just look at what's happened. What if my mother's right, huh? Think about it. What if Mali befriended you to get closer to me and Luke? I thought I was being paranoid, but now I doubt it."

"But she hasn't gotten that close." I shook my head. "She hasn't done anything."

"Okay—but what if Bryant Pierce is only with Becky so he can get to you…and get to *me*? What if she's been his puppet this whole time, and we didn't even know it?"

"If that's true, I-I'm sorry," I babbled.

"You don't need to apologize to *me*. But what about the danger I've exposed *you* to? How am I ever supposed to forgive myself for that?" He sounded anguished.

Panic seized my chest. I'd seen myself as the weakest link in our relationship because of my physical human frailty; I'd never imagined my emotional weakness would be the crux of my inferiority. I'd trusted that Mali liked me for me. I believed that Becky and Bryant were having a torrid affair on their own terms.

I never imagined that *I* might be the target, that my weakness deemed me entry-level access to the vampire I loved.

James scrubbed a hand over his face. "I thought everything that happened since we met—Adam, Becky going crazy, even the werewolves showing up—was happening because of us, because of our love."

I wrung my hands together. "I don't understand where you're going with this." My gut told me it was someplace bad.

He sighed. "I believed that this all occurred naturally, or *super*naturally, however you want to say it. But I never guessed that someone was doing it *to* us—especially not to settle ancient grudges. My mother was right about one thing: I didn't see the werewolves coming. I've lost my edge."

He raised his gaze to meet mine. "I've failed you again."

The desolation in his voice gutted me. "I won't ever talk to Mali again," I quickly, shakily promised. "I'll scare Becky away from Bryant. I'll threaten to tell my dad, or something. Then she won't see him anymore, and he won't have any connection to my family. We'll be free of them."

"I think she's under his spell, Taylor. I don't think it's the sort of thing she can just walk away from."

"She has a choice. She chose to have an affair in the first place—"

"Who knows how much of that is free will?" James shook his head. "Maybe he tricked her, somehow. Shifters are crafty. They're master manipulators."

"He didn't manipulate her out of her pants and her

marriage vows." My blood pressure was rising. "She shouldn't get a pass for *adultery*."

"True, but that doesn't change things. She's already involved with him. There's no going back." He shook his head. "No, there's no going back from any of it."

"What do you mean?"

"If Bryant Pierce wanted Becky because of you, it's *my* fault. You've been in danger since the day you met me."

I shook my head. "That's not true."

"Sure it is. The werewolves, Becky…Eden. Both what I did to her, and what she did to you. Not to mention that she's lost to her family now. And look at what happened to Amelia yesterday. She shouldn't have to see her mother like that, beholden to a werewolf."

I struggled to stay calm. "Let's stay focused on what we have to deal with, okay? Your mother's waiting back at the house with a sack full of wolf pups."

"That's what *I* have to deal with," he corrected me. "*You* are going to go inside and keep yourself safe. Stay in your room, stay away from Becky. I'll go deal with my mother. I'll make sure we watch your house tonight."

"I'm supposed to go hiking with my family tomorrow." I felt miserable. He was leaving me again, and on bad terms. There didn't seem to be anything I could do about it.

He sighed. "We'll be watching you—you'll be safe."

"Why can't you just come with me?"

He shook his head. "It might not be the best idea right now."

I winced. When he remained silent, I ached.

"So what is this? Goodnight?" I peered at his face, but he kept his eyes downcast. "Good*bye*?"

"Don't be silly." But he still wouldn't look at me. "You keep yourself safe inside the house, I'll make sure you're safe outside."

"Gee, thanks." I didn't mean to slam the truck door so hard, but the cab rattled.

I went inside and shut the door tight behind me. My hands were shaking. I ran to my room, seeking refuge, but I knew I couldn't hide from my thoughts.

I CREPT DOWNSTAIRS a few hours later to check on Amelia. She was on the couch, scowling at her phone, taking selfies, and browsing luxury-brand websites. She was fine—no signs of a memory relapse. Becky and my dad were having a drink in the kitchen. I heard their voices drifting out, normal talk about remodeling a bathroom, it sounded like.

I climbed the stairs to my room. I stared out the

window at the darkness, wondering if James was out there, watching. Why wouldn't he come to me? My phone was empty, silent. Why was he pushing me away? The pit in my stomach was familiar, which somehow made the ache more acute.

I might never convince him it was safe to love me.

What Marietta said was true: the wolves had targeted my family. I hadn't seen it coming, and neither had he. But I didn't see that as a colossal failure the way James did. Now that we knew better, we could do better.

Marietta had *also* said that I had a role to play in all this.

Eyes wide open, and deep into the night, I pondered what that might mean.

33

PEEPERS

I ROLLED OVER JUST as my alarm went off. I checked my phone—still no texts from James. I felt cheated by another night without him, and I continued to ache over our last conversation. *You've been in danger since the day you met me.* I didn't care. But how could I convince *him* to let it go?

I groaned, staring out at the brightening sky. I had to hike with my family in the park and I wouldn't see him *again.*

Is everything ok? I texted.

He responded right away. *We've been out here all night. All clear.*

Thanks, I texted back. *I love you.*

His response was instant. *I love you, too.*

But that was it. I wanted to call him—better yet, to

run into the woods and find him—but if I didn't hurry, get dressed and go downstairs, I'd make us late for the water taxi. Wary of poking Becky's massive bad side, I hustled to the shower.

Awkward wasn't a good enough word for how I felt as I joined my dad, Becky, and a scowling Amelia a few minutes later. It appeared we were all actors playing roles. Later, after our masks were off, we'd get back to business—shaking uncontrollably, visiting secret apartments, spending time with supernatural lovers, vaping THC.

I wondered if my dad had any secrets. I truly hoped not.

The mist hung heavy as we traipsed down to the dock. "Why are you guys making us *do* this?" Amelia whined. "My hair's already getting soaked!"

"We're going to hike Bubble and see the foliage." Becky frowned at her daughter. "And we are going to enjoy every minute."

"*Bubble?* No freaking way! We're going to die!" Amelia started complaining further, but Big Kyle held up his hand.

"We're hiking South Bubble—the easier one—and you're welcome." He winked at his daughter. "You girls can handle it fine, especially since both of you are officially high-school athletes."

"Is it a hard hike?" I asked him. I was still sore from stupid cross-country.

"Nah." He patted my shoulder. "My long-distance runner will crush it."

The *Breathless* appeared out of the mist and collected us from the dock. Captain Bud navigated through the thick fog that hung over Hart Sound, easily maneuvering toward Pine Harbor. I wrapped my sweatshirt around me, chilled. I knew by the end of the day I'd be hot, but for now, I was damp and miserable.

I tried to ignore my stepmother and failed. My gaze kept trailing back to her, a moth to a toxic flame. Becky wore her hair in a high ponytail, her fake lashes framing her ice-blue eyes. A teal rain jacket and thick black running tights encased her lithe body.

I wondered how she could sit there with us, with her daughter and her husband, when she'd been with someone else so recently. I was jealous that Amelia couldn't remember what happened—she was lucky.

Becky asked Amelia about her upcoming golf match, and I tuned them out.

Big Kyle leaned closer to me. "Are we going to talk about your college applications, or do you intend to keep blowing me off?"

I sighed. College was the last thing on my mind. "I

don't know where I want to apply yet. Everything's kind of up in the air."

"You mean you don't know where James is going to be next year." Dad frowned. "That's not a reason to hold off on making plans for your future. You need to get an education, Taylor. You need to take care of yourself."

"I know—and I will—but it's kind of overwhelming," I admitted. As recent as last spring, I'd planned to attend community college. That way I could take classes, keep working at the sub shop, and continue to look after my mom.

"UMaine's got a campus in Orono." Dad looked at me hopefully. "That's only about an hour from MDI. You could live at the dorms there, maybe come home on the weekends."

I patted his arm. "That sounds nice. I'll look at it, okay? I definitely think a state school is the way to go. I don't want to get into a ton of debt."

"I have a college fund for you, pumpkin. You don't have to worry. Make a list of the schools you're interested in—we'll figure it out."

"Thanks Dad." My eyes pricked with tears. He was such a good guy. Becky didn't know what she was throwing away.

I tried to get ahold of myself. Feeling sorry for my dad wouldn't accomplish anything besides making me rude to Becky, and that had *not* worked out well for me yesterday. I vowed to compartmentalize my thoughts for the rest of the morning. There were the matters I wouldn't consider—Becky, Bryant Pierce, Marietta Champlain, werewolves, and college. The subjects I *would* think about were the pretty fall colors and making things right with James.

Becky drove us to Acadia in her spotless SUV. We stopped at the One-Stop for coffee and protein bars. I'd hoped for donuts, but of course Becky didn't allow them. I drank my French roast in silence, amusing myself by glaring daggers into the back of Becky's stupid blond head as she drove.

Acadia National Park was mobbed. Leaf peepers from all over the world visited the park in the fall. They hiked the trails, snapping pictures of the glorious foliage. I was glad for the crowd—there was safety in numbers. The wolves wouldn't show themselves, and Becky wouldn't dare go off in front of a hundred tourists.

My stepmother exhibited no signs of strangeness. She zipped her cellphone into her pocket and carried her expensive water bottle up the trail. Occasionally she stopped to take pictures of the stunning views. She took a selfie with Amelia, and one with my father. I didn't hold my breath waiting for her to ask for one with me.

The panoramas of the park were breathtaking—we could see Jordan Pond below, remarkable in its blue-green glory. The trees were sensational; orange, red, and yellow leaves swayed in the gentle breeze. It was so beautiful it was almost impossible to believe.

The foliage wasn't the only thing that was unbelievable. I stared at Becky as we climbed higher, my head pounding with a mixture of distaste and mounting dread. Who was the real Becky? The one hiking in front of me? Or the one who'd been lost in Bryant Pierce's embrace? An image of her face, contorted in ecstasy, flashed in my mind. Was having sex with her lover really so great, it was worth throwing away her family?

I thought about James. I loved him, and I would do *anything* for him. But sex wasn't love. Was Becky in *love* with the werewolf? Did he have genuine feelings for her, or was getting close to the Champlains his only endgame?

While the questions churned, I considered Bryant Pierce. Was he really the same being as the wolf I'd seen in my backyard? My gut told me yes. The way his eyes had looked, that burning amber, was exactly the same. The growling and the snarling were familiar—the wolf had sounded the same the night it growled outside of our house.

Now it made sense that he'd sat, in his beast form,

staring at the bedroom window: he hadn't wanted Becky to be with my father. That's what he'd been growling at.

He wasn't looking for *me.*

I'd said as much to James, but I considered it further. The wolf's full attention had been on the bedroom. On *Becky.* If he'd needed to get to me, why hadn't he just done so? I wasn't exactly a match for the big, bad wolf.

I turned down this avenue of thinking in my mind. James was certain that Bryant was involved with Becky in order to get closer to us. But what if that wasn't true —or rather, what if that was only *part* of the truth?

I considered that as we hiked higher up the dirt trail. And there were so many other moving pieces. Luke had told his mother there was a werewolf *pack* living on Spruce Island. So... What about Mali? Bryant was her uncle. Did she *know*? If yes, what did that mean for my pretty friend?

Was she a shifter, too?

As if my thoughts had conjured her out of thin air, Mali stood on the trail ahead of us. I stopped walking and gaped—then I rubbed my eyes, convinced I was seeing things.

But there she was, taking a selfie in front of the Bubble, the famous round rock that they had named the hiking trail for. Thousands of years before, a glacier deposited the boulder on the edge of a drop-off; all the tourists wanted a picture with it.

"Is that Mali?" Amelia asked. "What a coincidence."

"Huh. Yeah." But I no longer had the luxury of believing in coincidences.

My friend didn't appear to see us as she snapped another selfie, grinning. Her hair was a mess, her skin glowed with sweat, and her glasses were foggy. She must've been making good time on the trail.

"Mali," Amelia called, "hey!"

Mali looked up, surprised. "No way!" She came over and hugged me, then grinned at my family. "I didn't know you guys were hiking up here today! It's gorgeous, isn't it?"

Becky smiled at her tightly. My dad appeared friendly and clueless. Amelia checked out Mali's cute flannel, which she wore open over a tank top.

"Yeah, it's so pretty." I looked her up and down. Upon closer inspection, Mali's hair was frizzy, her tank was spotted with sweat, and dirt and twigs clung to her flannel. "You must've really hustled up here early, huh?"

"I did." She wiped her brow. "My grandmother said it gets crazy crowded on the weekends, so I wanted to beat the rush. Do you guys want me to take a picture of you by the bubble?"

"Sure, that'd be great." Big Kyle handed her his

phone, then gathered me, Amelia and Becky into his arms. We all smiled at Mali, our faces frozen, as she snapped a bunch of pictures.

Out of the corner of my eye, I saw another hiker coming up the path. *No way.* Tall and lithe, I recognized him immediately.

"Luke?" I called.

"Hey Taylor." He gave me a friendly wave as he made his way toward us.

"Weird that we're bumping into so many people, isn't it?" Kyle said to Becky. He chuckled. "Popular trail."

"I guess so." Becky didn't sound as though she found it amusing.

Luke got closer, and I was eager to hear what he was doing there. But out of the corner of my eye, something else drew my attention. Mali was watching Luke, too, and smiling. But as I observed, Mali's appearance…*shifted*. Her hair de-frizzed, becoming smooth and sleek. Her complexion brightened, the sweat evaporating. Her glasses cleared and both her flannel and tank top straightened out, the dirt and twigs flying as though they'd been brushed off.

But Mali hadn't moved.

It took only a second. My friend looked perfect, and I was pretty sure I'd gone completely off the deep end.

"Hey Luke." She flashed a megawatt smile as he reached us.

"Hi Mali." He gave her an appraising, flirty grin back. "Fancy meeting you here."

"Right? It's a busy route, I guess." She flicked her glossy hair for good measure.

He tore his gaze away long enough to nod at me. "Hey Taylor."

"H-Hey."

Luke went and said hello to my family. Then we continued, as an awkward, newly formed group, up the trail. I waited until my father ensconced Mali in conversation to corner Luke. "What're you doing here?"

"I'm following you, of course." He smirked. "Did you think Lover Boy would let you hike a big bad mountain all by yourself?"

"So why didn't he just come?" I whispered.

"He was talking to our father—not exactly a conversation I'm privy to. Also, he wanted to make sure that my mother didn't get loose. He doesn't trust me to babysit her. Go figure." He frowned. "So I volunteered. I also had a feeling Mali might be watching you today."

"Why?" I glimpsed at my friend. She laughed at whatever my dad said.

"Because she's keeping tabs on you. And maybe Becky, too." He shrugged.

"Mali did something... When she saw you, she *changed...*" I didn't know how to describe what I'd just witnessed.

He glanced at me. "You caught that, huh? I think it means she likes me."

I grimaced. "That's not exactly what's important right now."

"True." Luke nodded. "And I shouldn't go there, anyway. It's taboo to play with your food."

"Please tell me that's a joke." I groaned. "You're not helping my state of mind."

He chuckled. "You're the one dating an immortal. If you wanted peace, you should've fallen for the soccer captain. Or maybe someone on the crew team. My kind comes with our own brand of excitement."

Amelia slowed, dropping back toward us. We wouldn't be able to talk more. I sighed. "I don't know how much more excitement I can take."

"Funny. That's exactly what James said."

But my half-sister joined us, and I couldn't ask him what he meant.

TOP DOG

By the time we made it back to the base, I was sweating and sore. While Big Kyle and Becky went to buy more water, we said goodbye to our friends in the parking lot.

"There's another bonfire tonight," Amelia offered, fake-casual. "You know, since there's no school tomorrow."

"What?" Mali and I asked simultaneously.

"It's a teacher in-service day—we have them once a month. You guys didn't know?" Amelia looked at us as though we had three heads each.

"No." Mali shrugged. "But I haven't exactly been staring at my academic calendar. But cool, I'd love to go to another bonfire! Just so long as nobody pukes near me this time."

"Yeah, that was bad." Amelia wrinkled her nose.

Mali smiled at Luke. "What about you—want to hang out with some under-aged partiers again?"

He waggled his eyebrows. "Barely legal's just my type."

"Ha! Great." She turned to me. "See you tonight too, Taylor?"

"Um, I guess. Sure."

"Perfect, I'll text you." Her black ponytail flying behind her, Mali headed to her car.

"So, awesome." Amelia tried to bring Luke's attention back to her. "I'll see you tonight?"

"Absolutely." He gave her a killer smile, then nodded at me. "I'll be in touch, Taylor."

I believed that was vampire-code for *Don't worry, I'm still stalking you*.

We got back to the island later than expected, almost time for dinner. Dad was grilling tuna, Becky was making an arugula salad, Amelia was flat-ironing her hair for the bonfire, and I kept checking my phone. There had only been one text from James that afternoon: *Talking to my dad, will call soon.*

I stared at my cell, willing it to ring. When it didn't, I texted Josie. *How's it going down there?*

She wrote back immediately. *Patrick and I evacuated to his house. The Red Queen booted us.*

I called her. "So Eden's been alone at the Tower all day?"

"Oh, no." Josie snorted. "Eden's been up Marietta's *behind* all day. James barricaded himself in his office, and the two redheads were in the living room making all sorts of plans. I tried to eavesdrop, and that's when Marietta kicked us out. We came down to Patrick's a couple hours ago."

I struggled to picture Marietta and Eden together. "What were they planning?" I asked, my panic rising.

"I don't know, because Marietta asked us to leave. I texted James to warn him. But he didn't come out, so." She sounded pissed.

"Ugh, I'm sorry. I'll talk to him."

"Taylor, about that." Josie took a deep breath. "James and *I* had a long conversation last night."

"Okay..." I sank down onto the edge of my bed. "About what?"

"He's worried about you."

I laughed without humor. "He's always worried about me."

"I think it's getting to him." Josie sighed. "Don't go all crazy in your head, because you know he loves you. We *all* know he loves you. But this thing with Becky—it's hard. It's like it's the final straw. He told me he can't stand to think about it. Every time he looks at Eden, he thinks about Becky. And then he thinks about what *he* did to Eden, and how Eden tried to bite you the other night."

"I already talked to him about that." I tried to keep my voice light. "Nothing happened. He's overreacting, as usual."

"C'mon, Taylor. He's not overreacting. There are *shifters* involved now. Not to mention the shaking, and the stuff about Becky getting freaky with the Alpha…"

I clutched the phone. "Woah, hang on. What do you mean, Alpha?"

She sighed. "We think Bryant Pierce is the Alpha of the MDI pack. James's dad has been doing some research."

"But what does that mean?"

"You know, sometimes I forget you're a regular human, and you don't have experience with all this," Josie said. "Sorry about that. An Alpha's the leader of a shifter pack. They're stronger, bigger, tougher than the other shifters. They dominate. The other wolves *have* to follow the Alpha's orders, it's like some supernatural law. If they don't, they're cast out of the pack. And shifters are like normal wolves in that respect—they can only survive as a group."

"So what the Alpha wants, the Alpha gets." I got up and started pacing. "Is that right?"

"Yeah."

"But what about Becky?" I asked, lowering my voice even though I was up in my own wing. "How does that power work with a human?"

"Hmm, Becky isn't part of the pack, so she doesn't *have* to follow his rules. But like I told you, a physical relationship between a supe and a mortal can be very, very intense. I would think you'd know that by now." She chuckled.

"James and I haven't exactly gotten that far."

"But you still understand the attraction part," Josie said.

"Sure, but that's what I'm curious about. Is it… Is it *just* physical? I know with me and James, that's not the case. I'm obviously very attracted to him, but it's more than that." I hesitated, unsure of how to phrase what I wanted to ask. "But let's take Bryant and Becky—if James is correct, he pursued *her*. But could Becky have refused him? Is it difficult to resist the Alpha?"

"Not for everybody," Josie said quickly. "If Bryant Pierce propositioned *you*, you'd say no. But Becky's different. Let me think about how to explain this."

She was quiet for a minute. "I think although she *couldn't* know what he was, she would still be massively attracted to him. I bet even in his human form, he's powerful. Muscled, handsome, dominating. Am I right?"

"Yep." I nodded. "He definitely has an air about him."

"As the Alpha," Josie continued, "he would have a particular power that I think someone like Becky would find irresistible—he thinks he's the *best*. Actually, Alphas *are* the best. To their packs, they are gods. Their word rules. Their desires impact the entire group."

"Huh." I thought about that for a second. "My friend Mali—his niece—said that she and her dad *had* to move up here. So did her other relatives. They all came to MDI at the same time. So I guess that makes sense— Bryant must have ordered them here."

"That sounds right," Josie agreed. "From what I know about the packs, sometimes they go their own ways for a while. But when the Alpha calls, they have to come running."

"It also adds up that Becky would fall for someone like that. She has a pretty high opinion of herself," I said.

"*And* she was pissed at your father for moving you up here. The timing was perfect. I hate to say it, but it's true," Josie said. "I've been thinking about it: the big, bad wolf might've come knocking at exactly the right time."

"About that." I frowned. "Do *you* think he's trying to get at James through me—through Becky?"

"Yes," she said immediately. "It was a safe way to gather more information without putting a shifter directly into the mix. She was a surrogate for him."

"What about the shaking, then?" I sure was glad I'd called Josie.

She sighed. "I guess it's a blend of things. Becky was gutted by the fact that you and James—the island's resident billionaire—had such a powerful connection. Again, no offense, but she thinks you're trailer trash."

"*Taylor*-trash," I corrected her. "She thinks I'm Taylor-trash."

"Right." Josie groaned. "No matter *who* Becky was involved with, your relationship would've rattled her. I think the shaking comes from that, from an upset in the natural order of things. Like that other guy who attacked you—the tourist—it was a reaction to the shifting of the balance."

"Okay…" I pondered that. "But do you think Bryant's doing something to her, too?"

"I think all the hot werewolf sex is making Becky unstable. She's playing with a force she can't begin to understand. When I called her his surrogate, I meant it. He might control her more than we know, like a puppet master."

"It's a lot to think about…" I shivered. "One more thing. The other night when the werewolf was in our yard—he was staring up at Becky's bedroom window. I think… I think my father and Becky might've been having sex." My face heated. "The wolf didn't seem to like it. He was growling."

She chuckled. "Yeah, his favorite chew toy was getting gnawed on by somebody else."

"*Ew*, Josie. Gross."

"Sorry, I know we're talking about your dad." She took a deep breath. "But the thing about the Alpha is, they're *very* territorial. Once they mark something, it's *theirs*. And it sounds like Bryant and Becky have been very, um, *active* in the bedroom. They're into each other. I told you sex with a supe is addictive, but that goes both ways. The supes love their human playthings—they can get very possessive of them. So I am certain he doesn't like the fact that Becky is still with your dad."

My mind was whirling. "So why is she? Is it because Bryant *wants* her here—to spy on me and James? Or is it because she still loves my dad?"

"Maybe Becky doesn't even know. It could be both. But…" Josie went quiet for a minute. "You know I never liked her. That Becky—she always has an angle. I wouldn't be surprised if she had an agenda all her own. Sorry, I have to go. Dinner's ready."

"Okay, Josie, thanks, really. You just helped me a lot. So—there's a bonfire later. Can you guys come?"

"Maybe." She snorted. "Nothing I love more than a

bunch of drunk island kids binge-drinking their parent's liquor."

"Please?"

"I'll think about it."

We hung up, and I stopped pacing. *That Becky.* Maybe she did have an agenda all her own. But what was it?

I headed downstairs, vowing to find out.

SPLASH

LUKE TEXTED me before I reached the kitchen. *I might not see you at the bonfire.*

I stalled on the stairs. *Where's James?* I wrote back quickly.

He went rogue. Three dots appeared. *Stay out of trouble, okay? He told me to watch you, but Mom summoned me. Do not die or he'll kill me.*

Okay, I answered. But what I wanted to know was— rogue what the *what*? Was James safe? And what did it mean that Luke had been summoned by his mother?

I texted James. *Where are you?* But there was no answer.

I was tired of so many questions. I wanted answers. Who was with me, and who was against me? And more importantly, *why*? It was time to find out. I had an idea—

maybe it was more of an instinct, but still. Since it was *all* I had, I intended to go with it.

"Can Amelia and I go to the bonfire tonight?" I asked my dad at dinner.

Becky stiffened. "Is Brynn going, Amelia? Or is it all older kids?"

"Brynn will be there." Amelia shrugged like it was no big deal. "Taylor will probably be the only senior. She thinks she needs to babysit me."

"She's just looking out for you, like I asked her to," my dad said quickly.

"Taylor doesn't need to babysit her." Becky picked up her wineglass. "Amelia's been on her best behavior for a long time now. Haven't you, honey?"

"Yep." Amelia's cheeks at least had the decency to burn pink.

"I know Amelia doesn't need me. But I want to go, if it's all right." I had a sip of water. "I don't feel like staying home alone again."

"Is James going tonight?" Dad asked.

I shrugged. "I'm not sure."

I didn't miss the look exchanged between Dad and Becky. "Is everything okay with you two?" Dad asked.

I shrugged again. "I don't think so."

Becky put down her glass. "What's the matter, Taylor?"

I shook my head. "I'm not sure. We're just taking some time, I guess. He's busy hanging out with Eden and working for his father. I've been busy with school and practice. So we're just...taking a break. It's no big deal. I'm fine."

Amelia appeared scandalized. "You didn't say anything about it."

"It just happened." To prove that I was okay, I fake-smiled. "We're still friends and everything."

"Huh." Becky looked more troubled than she should. "But Luke hiked with us today..."

"Like I said, we're still friends. All of us."

I went back to eating as silent shock settled over the table. I guess no one had seen my fake breakup coming. Since I was flying by the seat of my pants, neither had I. It felt almost sacrilegious to lie about my relationship, but weren't all gambles a little risky?

The three of them took turns staring at me. Becky's brow furrowed as she ignored her food and concentrated on her wine. She seemed as though she might be worried about something.

I had an inkling I knew what it was.

I finished dinner quickly and excused myself. Ten minutes later, Amelia and I headed out the door in jeans and lightweight puffer coats. She didn't try to wear her tiny shorts and tank top again; not only would my father have had a coronary, it was already turning too cold.

"I can't believe you and James broke up." Her eyes were wide as we walked down the dirt road. "What happened?"

"It was like I said at dinner. We both just have a lot going on."

"Luke didn't seem like he knew." Amelia glanced at me. "Did you tell him? Or Mali?"

"I don't know if James told Luke, but I haven't said anything to Mali yet."

"So I'm the first to know." To her credit, she only seemed to gloat for a moment. "Wow. I can't believe it. I thought you guys were, like, going to get married."

"Yeah well." I ducked my head. "Maybe not." Again, I felt blasphemous. I still wasn't sure exactly where I was heading with this, but I was following my gut. There was nothing to be done about it now.

We reached the same beach as last time. The bonfire blazed, flames rising into the sky. The sun was setting; it was already getting darker. The kids near the fire had their faces illuminated by the glow, their backs gloomy with shadow. It almost looked as though they were having some sort of pagan ritual...

But then I noticed the keg, and the red cups they were all drinking from. The island was mysterious, but this was more of a frat party than anything else. I nudged Amelia. "Don't you *dare* try to drink or smoke tonight. Dad and Becky are going to be up when we get home."

"I won't—*sheesh*. I know you're in a bad mood and all, but you shouldn't take it out on me. Hey, there's Brynn. I'm gonna go say hi." Amelia took off toward the group, but I stood back a bit. I didn't recognize anyone aside from Amelia's friends; Mali wasn't there yet.

"If it isn't my old pal, the hall monitor." An unfamiliar—and unfriendly—voice said in my ear. I turned to find Chris very close, scowling at me. He swayed a little on his feet.

I smiled cheerfully. "I thought you were grounded."

"My parents went to dinner. It's not like they can lock me up." He pulled a bottle out from his coat pocket and had a swig.

"Maybe not, but they're going to be able to tell that you're trashed."

"So?" He got in my face, his whiskey breath washing over me. "I shouldn't be in trouble, anyway. It's your fault—I know you left that note on my step."

I focused on him, but in the back of my mind I thought: *James would never let this douche get so close to me. He must not be anywhere near the beach.* I wondered where the hell he *was*, but Chris was still breathing noxious fumes in my direction.

"Yeah, I left the note. And all your vaping crap." It was pleasant to be rude—and honest—to his face. I'd been doing *way* too much pretending lately.

Chris glowered. "You had no right—"

"Your parents should know what you're up to." I straightened my spine. "By the way, don't ever pressure my sister into letting you use the apartment again. I'll blow up your life."

"What I do isn't any of your *freaking business*." He shook his head, his face twisting in anger. "You know what? I'm gonna to show you. Just wait and see."

I tensed, preparing for him to advance on me—he was a solid-six drunk, after all. But instead, he stalked down the beach, directly to Amelia's side. I couldn't hear what he said to her, but his tipsy, flirty smile flashed in the firelight. He turned to make sure I was watching, a triumphant smirk on his face.

I curled my hands into fists. Luckily Amelia declined the booze Chris offered her. But she still smiled back at him. I wanted to ask her to leave with me right then, but I knew she'd have a fit.

I went closer to the fire, determined not to let them out of my sight.

Mali showed up a few minutes later by boat. A man,

driving a slim silver skiff, dropped her off at the dock. He was older, handsome, with big shoulders and a dark, full beard. He surveyed the crowd, his eyebrows knit together, as Mali hustled down the berth toward the beach. She saw me and waved.

The man stared at us for a moment, then turned the boat around and headed back toward Spruce.

"Can you believe I got my father to bring me to a party?" She laughed. "I told him there wouldn't be any drinking, but I'm pretty sure he noticed the keg."

"It's kind of hard to miss." The keg was right next to the bonfire, its aluminum hull reflecting the light from the flames. "Is he coming back to pick you up?"

"Yep, I have until nine. Me and my wild life." She giggled. "Is James coming tonight?" She surveyed the crowd. "And where's Luke?"

"You seem awfully interested in him." It didn't come out sounding very nice.

"Yeah, he's super cute." She nudged me. "I hope it doesn't bother you that I like him. I'm not trying to ride on your coattails or anything."

"It's fine." I shrugged. "James and I aren't together anymore, anyway. Which leaves me without coattails."

Her eyes widened in shock. For a moment, her brows knit together, as if she was thinking something through.

"Oh. Wow," she said, after an awkward silence. "I'm so sorry—I didn't see that one coming."

I frowned. "Me neither." At least that was the truth.

"Does that mean Luke won't be here, either?" She tried, and failed, to hide her disappointment.

"I have no idea. I'm out of the loop at the moment."

She scrutinized me. "Are you okay?"

"Sort of."

"Why didn't you mention anything earlier?" Her tone was a little sharp.

"Um…because I didn't want to talk about it?"

Mali shook her head. "I feel bad—I was with you all day, and I had no clue. When did it happen?"

"What's with all the questions?" I arched my eyebrows. "Why do you care so much?"

"Because I'm your friend." She looked genuinely hurt, but there was a glimmer of something else underneath.

"I know you are." Although I meant that, I also knew there was more to it. "But Mali…c'mon. If we're really friends, isn't there anything you want to tell me?"

She tilted her head. "Like what?"

I sighed. "I was thinking along the lines of your deep, dark secrets."

"I'm pretty sure you don't want to hear them." She smiled, but I caught that glimmer beneath the surface again. "Trust me on that."

Mali leaned closer and picked up my pendant. "You're still wearing the necklace James gave you, huh? That's sweet. Who knows, maybe you two will figure things out. I hope so."

"I guess I'm not ready to take it off yet." I stared hard at my friend. "Wait, did I *tell* you James gave me this necklace? I don't remember—"

"What the hell? There's somebody in the water!" One of the kids further down on the beach yelled. "Who *is* that?"

"Look!" Another girl called. "Someone's swimming!"

"What's he, crazy?" The boy named Keith asked. "That water can't be warmer than fifty degrees."

Mali and I joined them at the edge of the surf. I stared out at the ocean, at first not seeing what the others pointed to. But then—a flash of pale, muscled arms cut through the waves. The swimmer's head rose above the surface, and I glimpsed his handsome face and his dark, wet curls. He went underwater again, disappearing from sight. *Luke.*

My jaw gaped as I watched my friend swim across the channel. He was heading toward Spruce.

The kids kept talking excitedly. "He must be training for the ironman," I said, a little loud. "Those people are *crazy.*"

"Yeah, my uncle did that," Keith said.

"Ew, my mom knows a guy who *pees* himself so he can keep running and get a good time," another girl said.

I felt the tide of the conversation shifting away from the nearby swimmer and breathed a sigh of relief.

But Mali backed away from the group, eyes still on water. She had a distressed expression on her face. "Taylor. Is there anything you want to tell *me?*"

"Like what?"

Her gaze flicked to me. "Any deep, dark secrets?"

"N-No. Nothing I can think of."

Mali looked stricken. "You know what? I have to get going."

I clutched her wrist. "Why? What's wrong? It's just someone doing a night swim. They're probably training for a triathlon. There's so many hardcore athletes up here," I babbled.

"Oh, it's not about that." Mali shook her arm free. "I'm not... I don't feel so good, okay?"

"Want a ride back to Spruce? My father can bring you over."

She headed up the beach toward the road. "No, I'm all set. I'll have my dad grab me, no big deal!"

"I'm sorry you don't feel well." I followed her. "Do you want to go to my house? It's right around the corner."

Mali shook her head quickly. Suddenly, she did look

a little sick. "Uh-uh. I need to be alone. *Now.*" She hustled down the street and out of sight.

Crap, crap, crap.

I headed back to the party, making sure Amelia and Chris were in my direct line of vision as I whipped out my phone. I called James, but it just rang and rang.

Perfect. Just perfect. I remembered the last time he hadn't answered my calls—he'd been out of range.

He'd also been swimming.

"Amelia." I went to her side. "We have to go. *Now.*"

Chris ignored me; he was busy staring down her shirt.

She hesitated. "I'm not ready. We just got here," she whined.

"I said *now*." I didn't have time to placate her.

"Hey Hall Monitor—the lady said she's not ready." Chris tore his gaze away from Amelia's boobs long enough to protectively put his hands on her hips.

I grimaced. "You get *away* from her."

He pulled her against him, so he pressed up against her backside. Amelia squirmed uncomfortably, and something in me snapped. I literally didn't have time for vindictive, groping, rich-kid deadbeats—I had were-wolves and vampires to deal with.

"Grab a vape, not my sister." I picked up a nearby empty beer bottle and whipped it at his head.

Chris dropped like a rock. "What the actual *fuck?*" he screeched.

"My family's *my* freaking business! So hands off, loser."

I grabbed Amelia's arm and hustled her away. Together, we ran from the bonfire.

DID SO

"Why did you do that?" Amelia asked. She stopped running and leaned against a tree to catch her breath. "I had it handled."

"You are fourteen years old. You shouldn't *have* to handle things like that."

"He *did* get a little grabby. But you went off." She surprised me by giggling. "Where'd you learn to throw like that?"

"My mom dated some real losers." I shrugged. "We should get home, okay? I have some stuff I need to take care off."

"Like what?" She eyed me warily. "Target practice?"

"Ha ha. Let's go."

My mind raced as we headed for the house. What

had Luke been up to? I had a bad feeling I knew what it was...

I checked my phone again. There was nothing. My stomach became heavy with dread. Was James in the ocean, too—or was he already on Spruce? Not knowing was making my head pound. I called Josie but it went to straight to voicemail.

"Are you trying to call James?" Amelia asked. "Because maybe you should try playing hard to get. Let him come to you, you know?"

"Huh. You know, maybe that's good advice." I clutched the necklace he'd given me and picked up the pace. All the lights were on at the house; I could see the flicker from the television. "I'm not coming in just yet," I told her. "I need to do something."

Amelia hesitated. "Are you okay?"

"Oh, yeah—I need to call Josie. She's back on the island for a couple of days, I want to see if she can hang out."

Amelia nodded. "Thanks for helping me with Chris."

"Sure thing." I grinned. "Honestly, it was my pleasure."

I sent a quick text to Josie, so someone knew what I was up to: *Going to look for James.*

Text sent, Amelia safely inside, I ran to Becky's pickup. As with all island cars, the key was in the ignition. I pulled out of the driveway quickly, before anyone could ask me what the hell I thought I was doing.

Becky had never exactly offered to let me drive her truck before.

I flew down the road, gravel spraying, toward the boathouse. If James and Luke were headed to Spruce—or if they were already there—there was only one way to find them. I needed a boat. But I cursed when I pulled up to the dark building. The Hinckley wasn't at the dock. There was the *Mia*, James's sailboat, but as I had zero experience sailing, and it was getting seriously dark, I decided against it.

I went into the silent boathouse, giving thanks that no one ever locked anything on the island. James kept a small aluminum rowboat inside, along with oars. We'd never taken it out, but there was a first time for everything.

It must've weighed about a hundred pounds. I groaned as I dragged the boat out the side door and down the beach. I was breathing hard once I finally made it to the water's edge.

Spruce Island was located northwest from Dawnhaven; I knew that from watching the dials on the Hinckley as we drove. But how did I get there in the dark? I wasn't even sure if it was safe to row out onto the ocean, let alone in the middle of the night...

"What do you think you're doing?" A familiar, and most unwelcome, voice called down from the dock above me.

"Becky?" I could barely make her out, hands on her hips.

"Did you just *steal* my truck?"

"No," I lied.

"Are you planning on going out in a *rowboat* right now?"

I nudged the boat out further. "Maybe?"

"You get up here this instant, young lady."

"I don't think so." The last thing I wanted was for Becky to start shaking, then toss me into the water from the high dock.

"Fine, I'm coming down," she huffed. All too soon, she made it to the sand. Up close, it was easier to see her expression. Instead of royally pissed, which was what I'd been expecting, she looked concerned. "Are you okay?"

"I'm great." I took a step back from her. I'd learned the hard way that I could never trust her. "I'm just going out to get a better view of the stars."

Becky wrapped her coat more tightly around her. "I came down here to talk some sense into you."

"W-Where's Dad? Does he know you're here?"

"Of course he knows. We're *concerned about* you, Taylor. Even me." Becky blinked. "Your dad seemed happy when I volunteered to come down and look for you—he said it was a nice gesture."

That's because he's clueless. I licked my lips. "Are you worried about me because of James?"

"Absolutely! You know that I care about him—and *you*," she added as an afterthought. "I'm just surprised at how casually you announced the breakup. You two seem pretty into each other—I feel like you need to give it more of a chance."

Relationship advice from Becky? Really? "I think that's for me to decide."

She shook her head, ponytail swinging. "Trust me. James isn't exactly the kind of person you just walk away from. You don't know what you're giving up, here. You can't just quit."

"Why do you care?"

"What I *don't* care for is that tone." She arched an eyebrow. "Listen—at my age, you see things more clearly. You're too young to know what you're throwing away. You need to give this more of a chance."

That Becky had a vested interest in my love life didn't surprise me, but the fact that she had more ulterior motives than I could keep track of rankled. "I'm so sorry for your loss," I said.

"What?"

"I said *sorry*, because I can tell you're upset. It was

convenient for you for me to be with James. You might not have liked it at first, but Becky being Becky, you found a way to make it work for you."

She shook her head. "I have no idea what you're talking about. Are you *drunk?*"

"No. I'm talking about the fact that you want me with James because it's convenient for *you*. First, it was the gala. Now, it's because it gives you an inside advantage. You said you were coming out on top, and oh boy, you meant it."

"I don't know what you're talking about—"

"If I'm not with James, you've lost your edge. What're you going to report back now, huh? You've got nothing. He might not even want you anymore."

"He? He *who?*" Fine actress that she was, she looked genuinely incredulous. "Are you *accusing* me of something?"

"I'm not accusing you. I already know the truth."

"I'm calling your father—you sound like you need immediate clinical assistance. Probably doing drugs, just like your junkie mother." She whipped out her phone, but I swatted it from her hands. It landed on the wet, rocky beach. "You did *not* just do that."

"Yeah, I did." I felt a pressure building inside me, going straight to my head. I'd wanted to let Becky have it for a *long* time.

She quivered as she regarded me. The edges of her body blurred, as though she were a mirage. It happened so quickly, I might've imagined it—but I knew better. *Oh crap.*

She stepped closer, trembling. "I d-d-d-don't know what you think you k-k-k-k-know."

Becky petrified me, but I held my ground. "I know about your apartment. I know about Bryant Pierce." I practically spit the words out. "I know you've been spying for them."

"Y-Y-Y-You s-s-s-shut your m-m-m-mouth." Becky reached for me, her small, pale hand clasping my jacket surprisingly hard. She shook as she jerked me forward, almost pulling me off-balance.

No. That was all I could think. *No no no.* I was *not* going out like this.

She yanked me again. "C-C-Come h-h-h-here."

I looked around wildly, then spotted the oars. Just as she grabbed me with her other hand, I lunged for it. I brought the oar up and slapped Becky full across the face with the paddle.

She went down hard, crumpling into a heap on the beach.

I held the oar above her. My hands were shaking. For one moment, I considered whacking her with it again. Repeatedly. Hard. In the head.

Instead, I tossed down the oar and considered my options. I could leave her on the shore and row away, try to get her into the boat with me, or plan "c."

It was getting darker by the second. The day had officially turned into night. I wasn't sure what plan "c" was, but that seemed like my strongest option—the likelihood of me ever reaching Spruce with no daylight was small at best. I didn't even know for sure that James was out there…

Becky couldn't weigh much more than the rowboat. I took a deep breath, then dragged my step-monster up the beach toward the truck.

I was coated with sweat by the time I got there. I lifted her up under her shoulders, like I'd seen people do on tv, and tried to stuff her into the cab. It was impossible to move her dead weight.

In the end, I got her in the pickup by shoving her little by little. I even pushed her bony butt. For the first time, I was glad Becky was such a freak about watching her weight and exercising. It made it *so* much easier to drag her up the beach and attempt to kidnap her, if that was in fact what I was doing.

I tried not to think about it as I threw the truck into drive and took off, speeding toward the Tower.

READY, AIM...

WITH ONE EYE on Becky and one eye on the road, I couldn't manage my cell phone. I wanted to call James again, or Luke, Josie, Eden, anyone. But more than that, I wanted to find a friend before Becky woke up.

I drove too fast, passing by the mini-golf course, the store and the school in a blur. The gravel spewed out from underneath my tires as we flew down the drive to the Tower, the rose bushes screeching against the sides of Becky's truck.

She hadn't moved. I didn't *think* I'd hit her hard enough to kill her... I reached over and searched her neck for a pulse. She moaned and swatted me off—good enough. But I frowned... I'd left the oar down on the beach. If she woke up, I needed to be able to handle her.

I finally made it to the house. It was completely dark

except for one light on up in the Tower itself. I checked my cell—there was a text from Josie, only seconds before. *Where are you? We are freaking out.*

Becky moaned again and I cursed. I texted quickly, hoping it was coherent: *Tower—where is James*

My phone buzzed, and at the same time, Becky blearily opened her eyes. "What are you... What happened... *Ow.*" She rubbed her head.

I glanced at my screen. *Get out of there*, Josie had just responded.

Becky struggled to sit up and I hopped out of the cab. If she went crazy and started shaking again, I needed to be able to run away from her. "What're you doing?" Her voice was slurred.

"Um." I looked around the dark yard. "Freaking out?" Why had Josie warned me to leave the Tower?

There was a long, rough growl behind me. *Uh-oh.*

I turned slowly. A huge, dark form came forward from the woods. Its eyes burned a bright, eerie blue. It slunk out from between the trees and stopped. There in the moonlight, I could see it more clearly: it was a large, black wolf. Another low growl escaped its throat.

"O-O-Okay. Easy." I swallowed hard as it approached.

"What the *fuck?*" Becky gasped from inside the pickup. She locked the door behind me.

The wolf took another step closer, its large teeth visible. It definitely wasn't the same wolf I'd seen before —this one was slightly smaller, more lithe. Then there were its eyes: a bright, azure blue. They looked familiar…

It came closer to the truck, circling it. I stood pressed against the bed, heart pounding, as the beast came even with me.

But it didn't snarl again. It just stared.

"W-What?" I asked stupidly. "What do you want?" I glanced toward the house, but no more lights had come on. But *was* someone up in the Tower? It looked as though a figure cast a shadow up there…

The wolf woofed—once.

I turned to face it, bracing myself for an attack. But it just kept staring at me and then woofed again.

It seemed to be trying to tell me something. "I-I don't know what you *want*."

It sneezed and then went to the door of the truck. Then it looked inside and whined.

"You want *her*? Oh, you can have her."

Becky peered out the cab. "If you think I'm coming out there, you're crazy!"

Suddenly, there was noise coming from the Tower. The lights came on in the kitchen. Through the window, I saw a flash of red.

"You choose, Becky: vampires or werewolves."

"What the hell are you talking about?" she cried.

The wolf blinked at me, and I prepared to make a run for it. "Time's up. Make a choice."

"Myself—I choose myself!" Becky babbled.

"Of course you freaking do."

The wolf shook a little, a trembling that at first seemed all too familiar. Then, as I watched, it *shifted*: fur became pale flesh. The creature elongated in front of me, stretching into something taller—something *human*. It happened slowly, and then all at once.

Mali stood naked before me.

"Oh, my god!" I put my face in my hands. "What the… You just… *You*…? I can't…"

"Taylor, *please*, don't freak out. I know it's a big ask— but we've got to get her out of here. *Now*." Mali rapped on the truck's window. "Becky, let's go. Uncle Bryant sent me to take care of you."

"I don't know what you're talking about." Becky slid to the opposite side of the cab.

"Becky, come *on*! Taylor already knows!"

"Knows what?" Becky asked, fake-innocently.

"About you and Uncle Bryant. She's knows every-thing—she probably knows more than you." Mali cursed under her breath. "So stop pretending—and stop being a conniving bitch for once in your life! Let's *go*!"

There were more signs of activity from inside the Tower. The living room lights came on. Through the window, I caught another flash of red. I felt, deep in my gut, that James wasn't home. If he'd been anywhere near, he'd have already been protecting me.

"Seriously, open the door!" Mali sounded panicked. "If I don't get you out of here, they'll kill you, and then he'll kill *me*. I mean it! He told me your safe word—"

"All right, right!" Becky unlocked the truck and Mali grabbed her.

I thought they would run. Instead, Mali held Becky perfectly still for a moment and stared at her. Mali's eyes glowed bright-blue again. "You're going to come with me now," she said, in a monotone, "and you aren't going to cause any trouble."

Becky nodded, entranced. "I won't cause any trouble. I'm coming with you." Becky seemed oblivious to the fact that Mali was naked. She stood beside her, waiting, ignoring that we were down at the Tower in the middle of the night.

Mali breathed a sigh of relief. "Taylor, c'mon."

They started toward the woods, but I stayed at the truck. "I can't—"

"I know you're probably pissed at me right now, but I'd like it if I could avoid dying tonight." Mali stopped at the edge of the forest. "They're coming for us. If you don't protect me, they'll kill me and Becky both."

I shook my head. "No, they won't. I'll talk to them."

"You don' have that kind of power," she said quickly. She ushered Becky into the cover of the darkness. "Come *on*, Taylor! It's safest in the woods."

"How can I trust you?" I asked hoarsely.

She glimpsed over her shoulder. "You can't—but I promise I won't hurt you. I can't say the same for the Queen Vampire, though. Last I heard, you weren't her favorite."

Mali wasn't wrong about that. I followed them to the edge of the woods. If Marietta came outside and found me with a shifter and the human who was the Alpha's chew toy, she might not be very sympathetic. She wasn't exactly my champion.

James, where are you?

The floodlights came on in the yard, and Mali gripped Becky by the jacket. "It's now or never, Taylor —we're making a run for it. I understand if you can't trust me, but I'm telling you the truth: I won't hurt you."

Voices boomed out from the deck, an argument rising above the sound of the crashing tide. "I told you— if you don't get out of my way, I'm going to sharpen a stake and *finally* be rid of you!"

"Marietta," a man's voice said, "*enough.* Absolutely not."

"I'm going to slay them all," she said, her voice fierce. "Just as soon as you get the *hell out of my way!*"

"Taylor!" Mali hiss-whispered from beneath the firs. "*Please* come with me. I'm sorry I'm a shifter. I'm sorry I couldn't tell you. But if that vamp gets her hands on me, I'm dead meat. Becky, too. I need your help—I'm *begging you.*"

Edgar cawed from above, and though I didn't speak crow, it seemed like he was urging me to run.

"Fine. Let's go—I'll do my best to keep up." I followed her into the pitch-black forest, heart pounding.

I didn't know what awaited me in the woods. But I knew Marietta was up at the Tower. It seemed as though I was choosing the lesser of two evils—I prayed that was right.

As we ducked from tree to tree, my mind raced. What had I *done?* I was out in the woods with a shifter and my step-monster. Marietta was chomping at the bit to come out and annihilate the pack. It sounded like someone was holding her back, but for how long?

And James…where the *hell* was James?

Heart thudding, I followed Mali deeper into the forest. I was likely making an enormous mistake, but what could I do? If Mali was killed, I'd never forgive myself. If Becky was… How could I explain that to my dad? *I knocked her out with an oar, and then James's vampire mom drained her dry. By the way, she was cheating on you with the werewolf Alpha!* It wasn't exactly a conversation I needed in my near future.

We ran for what seemed like a long time. My cross-country lungs told me it was at least a mile. For such a small island, Dawnhaven had a deep, intricate forest. Finally, we made it to a narrow clearing and Mali stopped for a second. Cardio junkie that she was, Becky was hardly winded, but I was almost hyperventilating.

"You l-lied." I could barely catch my breath. "You faked being out of shape at practice."

"That was real." But Mali wasn't struggling at the moment. "I shifted into a normal eighteen-year-old girl for school. It wasn't an act—I was suffering, too."

"I don't understand."

"It's a lot to take in." Mali shrugged. "This probably isn't the right time for Shifter 101 class."

"Shifters…" Becky frowned. "Why does that sound familiar?"

Mali scowled at her. "Um, because you're having an affair with one?"

"Huh. I don't know why I get so confused some-times…" Becky shook her head as if to clear it. She suddenly seemed more animated, more herself. "What was it you were saying before? About a *vampire*? Are we in danger? Why are you naked? Where's Bryant? He promised to protect me at all costs. Do you think you could call him? Because I don't really feel like running around in the woods all ni—"

"Oh, shut *up*." Mali groaned. "You are so much more trouble than you're worth."

Becky arched an eyebrow. "I beg your *pardon?*"

Mali leaned toward her, eyes glowing again. "Be *quiet*. And forget that I was rude to you, okay?"

"Okay." Becky sounded more agreeable than I'd ever heard her. *Note to self: ask Mali how to do that.*

Mali glanced back at me. "My uncle's a sucker for a cougar, but *jeez*. He could do better. She can only remember about the supes when she's with him, in the love-zone. The rest of the time, she just makes demands. She's *such* a pain in the ass. Seriously, how do you deal with her?"

"Not very well." I'd caught my breath enough to talk. "But if you think she's a pain too, why are you out looking for her?"

Mali bit her lip. "I'm going to tell you the truth, but only because I'm naked, you already saw me go through the change, and you obviously know about my world. But we have to keep moving. Stay close."

"Okay." I crept alongside her in the darkness. It was

quiet, except for the breeze; even the crickets had abandoned their posts for the night. We were deep in the island woods, the treetops swaying as the stars stretched out above them.

Mali sighed. "At the bonfire, when I saw Luke in the ocean, I knew where he was going—to my family's compound on Spruce. And as soon as I knew it, so did Uncle Bryant."

"That's because he's the best," Becky boasted.

Mali jerked Becky to a halt and stared into her eyes. "You are required to keep your mouth shut. Also, you will forget everything that I tell Taylor tonight."

Becky blinked at her and didn't make a peep.

"That's what I thought." Mali started hustling her through the woods again.

I almost tripped over a root, but caught my balance at the last second. "What do you mean, Bryant knew about Luke as soon as you did?"

"When one of our pack senses a threat, a notification gets automatically transmitted to the group."

"Like an alert?"

She nodded. "But not on your cellphone. You feel it in your gut."

"Huh. Wow."

"That's why I had to leave the party so fast," Mali

continued. "Once he knew Luke was taking action, the Alpha commanded that I shift."

"And then what happened?" I asked.

Mali glanced at Becky. "Uncle Bryant wanted me to make sure *she* was okay. But at that point, she was still home safe and sound. So I went down to check out the Tower, to take a head count of what vamps were still on the island. That's when I ran into you guys."

"And what about Luke?" I asked. I wanted to ask about James, but somehow keeping his name out of the conversation seemed safer.

Mali shook her head. "I have no idea what's happening. The fact that I haven't gotten a pack warning is probably good, though—for *us*. I don't know what that means for you."

My heart sank. "Would you know if they hurt him? Luke? Or…"

She shook her head again. "Not necessarily."

We continued through the dark forest. "Where are we going?" I asked.

"We should get Becky back to the house. Uncle Bryant wants to make sure she stays out of this."

This. The business between the vampires and the werewolves. I still didn't know where Mali really stood, or what she wanted…

"Why did you come to the bonfire tonight, Mali?" If

we were having this conversation, we might as well get it all out.

"The same reason I was hiking South Bubble today," Mali said. "I was keeping an eye on you."

"But *why*? There are plenty of supernaturals to keep you busy."

"True," she said. She slowed again as we reached the edge of another clearing. "But you're the one who they'll do anything to protect. You're at the center, Taylor."

"The center of *what*?" I stared at my friend as we headed into the clearing. In the moonlight, I saw her pretty face twist, her lips curl into a frown.

"Picture a target, one of the circular ones with the red center." Mali pulled Becky close to her side. "That's you. You're the one we've been aiming for."

SEEING RED

You're the one we've been aiming for.

"But I don't understand *why*." I shook my head. "I'm nothing—a normal human. I can't help you."

"You *have* helped us. We've learned a lot about the Champlain vampires from you—what their current plans are, the number in their coven, their…predilections." Mali tilted her chin and scrutinized me. "That's why my uncle targeted Becky in the first place—to get closer to you. But then I guess it turned into something more…"

She wrinkled her nose as she inspected the petite blonde next to her. "He literally has the *worst* taste in women."

"Why didn't you just spy on the Champlains yourself?"

Mali arched an eyebrow. "Seriously? The deadliest vampire clan that ever walked the earth? They're ancient, wealthy, powerful beyond any other supernatural family in existence. They're *legends*. *Myths.* They've been impossible to get close to—until now."

She shook her head. "You made it so easy, Taylor. You live in the real world, and because he's in love with you, James has been less secluded these past few months than I imagine he's *ever* been before. A Champlain hosting a party at their house for the humans? A Champlain *grocery shopping* with his human girlfriend in the middle of the day? Getting coffee? *Hiking?* James offered me a ride on his boat without ever suspecting I was anything other than just a normal girl. That's literally unheard of."

My stomach dropped. My naivety had exposed James to the wolves, to extraordinary danger, without my knowledge. I'd never even had an inkling. I thought he was being paranoid about Mali, when instead, he'd been exactly right.

"Why do you want to hurt them?" I asked, genuinely curious.

"I mean, *I* don't. But there's a lot of history between our kinds," she explained. "Things that can't ever be forgotten or forgiven. They came to MDI and stole from us, when all we wanted was to help them. You shouldn't let them fool you, Taylor. Vampires are parasites."

"Not all of them are." I shook my head. "James is *good*. Even Luke—he has his moments, but he's not all bad."

"I get what you're saying. Sometimes the stuff my uncle rages about doesn't make sense. It was, like, a thousand years ago. You're right—not *all* vampires are bad. We should move on."

She shrugged. "But we haven't done anything to the Champlains—not yet. We were just trying to find out more, at least for now. That's where you came in handy."

"Well, I can't help you with James anymore. Like I told you, we're on a break," I said.

"You know, I believed that for about one second. Interesting timing, that his brother was swimming out to my family's land at the same time you were lying to my face about your broken heart." Mali shook her head. "It's a good thing I rescued Becky tonight. Otherwise, I might've been in trouble with my uncle for wasting time. Luke bailed on the party, and so did James. You were covering for them."

I swallowed hard. "I wasn't."

She stepped closer. "Maybe that doesn't matter."

"H-Hey—stay back. You promised you wouldn't hurt me."

She raised her right hand. "And I will keep that

promise. But that doesn't mean that the others are bound by the same oath."

"Others?" But suddenly, there was growling coming from the trees all around us.

Five giant wolves crept out onto the edge of the clearing, surrounding us. All of them had burning, glowing eyes. They snarled as they circled us. The largest one, with black fur, and bright, familiar amber eyes, went directly to Becky's side. It put its snout against her. Becky beamed at the wolf and gently stroked its fur. It sneezed once, then protectively nosed her behind it.

Then the giant beast bared its teeth and snarled at Mali.

"Hey, I did what you asked," she told it.

"What did it ask?" I wailed.

When it snarled again, she glanced at me. "I'm sorry, Taylor. For what it's worth, I really do like you. Is it weird that I started thinking of you as my friend?"

"It's only weird if you're totally selling me out right now!"

Mali watched as the largest werewolf with the amber eyes—the Alpha—advanced. She took a step closer to me. "Don't hurt her, okay? She hasn't done anything."

The wolf bared its teeth, then gnashed them together.

"I mean it. If you want to take her back to the compound, fine. But you can't torture her, and you can't wound her. I won't let you—I gave her my word."

The werewolf growled, shouldered its way past Mali and headed directly toward me.

"H-Hey." I eyed the creature. "Please don't hurt me. I haven't done anything, and James doesn't even care about me anymore. We're through. So if you're trying to get to him by hurting me, it's not going to happen," I babbled.

The wolf snapped at me, and Mali cursed. "Uncle Bryant, please—"

Just then, a streak of red tore through the clearing. It moved so fast I couldn't see more than a blur, but I *felt* it. My hair whipped in its wake.

The wolves—plus Mali in her human form—all crouched, ready to spring out and attack.

But Becky was...gone.

"Becky?" I cried. "Where the hell is she?"

"Oh, *crap*." Mali whirled, wildly searching the forest. "I don't see her anywhere!"

The Alpha roared.

Another flash of red streaked into the glade, but this time, it stopped directly next to me.

Eden appeared, grinning, with Becky at her side. Eden's arm was tight across Becky's windpipe.

My stepmother's eyes were bulging. She clutched at Eden's forearm, but Eden didn't give her any relief. Eden nodded toward the giant werewolf with the amber eyes. "Seems like I have something that might interest you."

The Alpha snarled at her, hackles quivering in the moonlight.

"Down boy." Eden tightened her hold and Becky's arms started flailing—she clearly couldn't breathe.

I stepped forward. "Eden, *no*—"

"Aw, she's got a few more seconds until she blacks out. And maybe a full minute until she asphyxiates."

Eden leaned down and stage-whispered in Becky's ear. "I kind of owe you, anyway. A life for a life, right? This is karmic—it's a dark night, we're out in the forest again… Only this time, I'm not the weak one."

The Alpha ran forward, snapping. Eden used Becky as a shield. "You have to get through her first, Chomper."

"Let her go!" Mali cried. "She's going to die. Stop it!"

"Give me Taylor, then." Eden jerked her chin at me. "Or I'll drain Blondie dry right in front of the big bad wolf. And trust me, I won't even feel sorry about it. And then I'll *still* kill all of you."

Becky clutched at Eden's arm, then went limp. Her eyes rolled back in her head. Eden laughed, her fangs springing out.

"Eden, *stop!*" I ran at her, and at the same time, the Alpha ran at me.

Bluish-white light burst through the trees. "Taylor, get *down!*" James yelled.

I threw myself onto the ground as a blinding brightness illuminated the glade, turning nighttime briefly into day. It was like lightning, sudden and surprising. The Alpha yipped as though he'd been shocked.

"Eden, let her go!" James roared as he and Luke tore into the clearing.

Eden dropped Becky to the ground, and I crawled to my stepmother. This time I found her pulse—it was weak, but she was still alive.

Fighting broke out all around us. James landed directly in front of me. He faced the Alpha and crouched protectively, shielding me from the beast. Eden took off, chasing the nearest werewolf. Another battle waged on the opposite side of the clearing—fangs bared, Luke sprung at a large gray wolf.

A rumble issued from deep inside James's chest. "Don't you *ever* come near her again. Oh, wait—you won't. Because I am going to *end* you right now!"

He roared and leapt at the Alpha, who snarled and snapped at him. "James, no!" I jumped to my feet.

At the same time, Mali struggled to get in between Eden and the wolf she fought. Eden's fangs were bared, her eyes crazed and blazing. The wolf snarled and snapped at her, trying to grab onto flesh. "Stop it!" Mali hollered. "Both of you, stop it!"

The wolf sank its teeth into Eden's side, and she screamed in pain.

James and the Alpha were a blaze of light and fur. Then they suddenly stopped—James was on top of the wolf, his hands pressing against its giant neck. James's fangs were bared, his eyes wild. "James—*James!* You'll kill him!"

"You *really* want a piece of me?" Luke called merrily from his side of the clearing. Two wolves circled him, snarling, as he held a smaller third wolf against his chest. It thrashed beneath his grasp. "C'mon—are you going to fight or what? Or do you just want to watch me have a midnight snack?"

Luke was about to crush the wolf. Eden's side was caught between her wolf's razor-sharp teeth. And James appeared to be on the verge of draining the Alpha dry.

Mali and I glanced at each other. The look on her face matched the feeling in my heart. We had to stop them. If we didn't, both sides were going to lose.

We moved at the same time—I dove at James and the Alpha, just as Mali tried to pry Eden from the wolf's deadly grasp.

I threw myself on top of the giant wolf, inserting

myself between him and James. I almost didn't recognize the love of my life—his face was so contorted with rage and bloodlust. His eyes blazed, and his fangs flashed. He grabbed me to throw me off of the wolf.

"James, look at me—*look at me!*" I screamed. "You don't want to do this! You need to stop!"

He seemed shocked into stillness for a second. "Taylor." His voice was hoarse. "*You* need to get out of here."

"Not without you. *Please.*" The beast struggled and snapped beneath me. I elbowed it in the head. "Stop it! I'm trying to help you!"

The battle raged on all around us. "Let go of her!" Mali roared at the wolf who was fighting Eden. She was still in human form, but she seemed an even match for the beast that had Eden trapped in between its jaws.

"James, please." I gazed up at him. He was shaking, his eyes wild. "This isn't you—you don't want this. Look, Mali's trying to help. *Please.* There has to be another way." I gripped his hands.

James took a deep breath. In that instant, his fangs retracted. He shuddered. "Get behind me."

When I hesitated, he commanded, "*Now.* I won't kill him." I obeyed, and he pressed me against his back.

He leaned over the Alpha. "Call off your dogs. Do it now and I'll let you go, at least for tonight."

They stared at each other as screams of both pleasure and pain erupted in the surrounding clearing. Luke plunged his fangs into the werewolf he'd captured. He sounded as though he were laughing as he guzzled its blood. It shuddered beneath him, and the other wolves circling him kept snapping and retreating. Eden wailed as Mali tried to pry her from the wolf's bite. Eden's fangs were bared, her eyes blazing and wild, but she couldn't fight back as the wolf shook her between its teeth.

The Alpha's amber eyes blazed. It snarled at James, foam dripping from its mouth.

"Do it *now*." James raised his hands, bluish-white light pulsating through them. "Or I'll end you all."

The Alpha suddenly howled. Its cry pierced the night. As if he had flipped a switch, the other wolves stopped fighting and joined him. The sound was mind-bending, overwhelming. I had to cover my ears.

"Luke—release it!" James yelled over the cacophony.

Luke immediately let the wolf he'd been drinking from drop to the ground. It got up, shakily, and limped to the other two wolves nearby. It lifted its snout and joined in the howling, although it seemed weak.

The wolf that had Eden in its grasp released her. It also raised its face toward the night sky. Its eerie howl joined the others, reverberating. Eden watched, scowling at it. I was happy to see her expression—if she was feeling good enough to glare, she was probably going to be okay.

At the edge of the clearing, Mali stood apart, trembling. She shifted again, but this time flesh became fur. She seemed to drop *in* on herself as she transformed, going from pale and curvy to broad, furry and powerful. Once she was back in wolf form, she raised her glossy black snout and howled at the sky for all she was worth.

Suddenly, the howling ceased. All at once—and as if somehow orchestrated—the wolves shot off into the dark forest. Except for the Alpha. He went to Becky's side and sniffed her. Her eyes fluttered open. "Hey, handsome." Her voice was gravelly, but she smiled at him.

The wolf bent his head, seeming to bow to her. Then he backed away into the tree line.

Luke rushed to Eden's side, but she swatted him off. I heard her complaining as James quickly turned to me. "Are you okay?"

"I'm better now that you're here, you're *you* again, and I know that you're alive."

He pressed his forehead against mine. "I'm sorry I couldn't call you. I was—"

"Out of range," I finished for him. "Yeah. Do me a favor, okay? Never do that again."

He nodded, his forehead still pressed against mine. "I

love you. Thank you for…getting me back to myself just now. I would've regretted killing him. I mean, I would have *eventually*."

"I know." In spite of everything, I smiled. "And I love you, too."

I didn't think it was possible for Becky to annoy me any further, but then she tried to get to her feet, and I had to leave James's warm embrace.

"Easy." I went to her side and helped her up.

"Taylor?" She looked at me confused. "Aren't you out past your curfew?"

I took a deep breath. "I think we both are, Becky."

A HEART OF HEARTS

EDEN SEEMED embarrassed when Luke asked if she was okay. "It was a *werewolf.*" She snorted. "I was totally letting it think it had the advantage. I was just about to crush it when James had to go and spoil all our fun."

James helped guide Becky back through the woods. She leaned on him but said nothing. I wondered if she was still somehow under Mali's trance.

Then I wondered if there was some way to make it permanent.

"What are we going to tell my dad?" I asked, as we slowly wound our way through the trees to the truck.

"I'm thinking." James kept his arm protectively, firmly, around me. But he didn't say another word until we reached the grounds.

Josie waited by Becky's pickup. "There you are—

thank God!" She rushed and hugged me. "When you texted me that you were down here, I almost lost it! Rogue werewolves and Queen Vampires are a bad combination."

"James." Marietta called to him from the deck. "Come up here right now. Your father and I expect a full report."

"I have to deal with something first," he told her. "Eden and Luke are on their way—make sure she's okay. She got injured, fighting your battle for you."

I didn't hear exactly what Marietta said, but it definitely sounded like a curse.

James turned back to Josie. "Can you make sure she's okay to go home?"

"I'm not going home!" I objected. "You can't make me!"

He surprised me by laughing. "If you think I'm letting you out of my sight anytime soon, you're crazy. I'm talking about Becky."

"Oh."

At the mention of her name, Becky seemed to snap to attention. "What's going on, now?"

Josie went closer and examined her, looking into her eyes and feeling her throat. "She seems pretty out of it to me. Do you remember what happened tonight, Becky?"

Becky blinked at her. *"Josie?* When did you come

back on the island? And did you ever talk to your agent about my daughter? Amelia would be a great model. She's got the perfect measurements, not to mention the *perfect* look. I was thinking she could start with L.L. Bean, seeing as they're local…"

Josie turned back to James. "She's fine. Get her out of here."

He helped Becky into the truck, and together, the three of us drove home in silence.

When we pulled up to the house, all the lights were on. Big Kyle paced in front of the window.

"Uh-oh." Becky pursed her lips. "He doesn't look too happy with me. Again."

"Can you blame him?" I frowned at her.

She shrugged. "That's between your father and me."

I took a deep breath, then we followed her into the living room.

"It's about goddamn time," my dad roared. "I've been worried sick! Where have you two been?"

I glanced at the clock. Only a few hours had passed, but it felt more like a year. "Becky came down to find me. Then I went and talked to James for a while. She waited—she wanted to make sure that I was all right." Lying on Becky's behalf, putting her in a positive light, made me feel as though I was talking over an enormous boulder in my throat. I had to force the words out.

"And?" Dad glared at James.

"We're good." I took James's hand. "Everything's fine."

"So you're not broken up."

James held very still, but I didn't hesitate. "It was just a misunderstanding. We had an argument—I took it as more than that."

"I'm sorry if I made her upset, Mr. Hale." James gripped my hand. "It's the last thing I want in the world."

"I told her she was just being silly." Becky smiled easily. "But see? Everything's all better."

Big Kyle turned his attention to his wife. "I don't know if that's true."

"What do you mean?" Becky seemed more interested in inspecting her nails then listening to her husband.

My dad frowned. "While I was waiting to hear from you guys, I started organizing the recycling to take down to the dump tomorrow."

She rolled her eyes. "Is this about my drinking? We've been over this—I'm still in summer mode, I'll tone it down."

"Your drinking's definitely a problem, but that's not what I'm talking about. I found a couple of utility invoices. Something about a rental unit in Bar Harbor?"

"Um." Her cheeks flushed a little.

"Hey Dad?" I interrupted them. "Do you mind I head

back down to James's? I haven't seen him all week. We really need to talk."

"Go ahead." Dad didn't look at me; his gaze was still trained on Becky, who'd returned to looking at her nails. "It's already late—you can stay out past curfew tonight, but I expect you home at some point. You understand?"

"Sure, Dad."

"James? Will you bring her home safe?" Dad's voice was strained. He still stared at his wife.

"Yes, sir."

We left them in the living room. Through the window, we could see them facing each other, both of them tense. "I don't think Becky will mind if we take her truck," James said.

"I don't really care if she does." I climbed in and shut the door, but then I hesitated. "Do you think it's safe to leave them alone?"

James nodded. "The wolves won't come back tonight. Becky's never gotten the shakes around your father. And that"—James jerked this thumb toward them—"has been a long time coming. We should let them figure it out."

I sank back against the seat. "You're probably right."

"Taylor." He put his hand on my thigh. "Are you sure you're up for coming down to the Tower after all this? My parents are there. Both of them."

"When did you father show up?"

He sighed. "After I called him and told him I'd drop Luke off on his doorstep if he didn't come help me with mom. He was already in Boston—I think he figured he needed to be nearby just in case she went off. Which, of course, she did."

"So that's who kept her from coming out to slay all the werewolves. I should've known."

He nodded. "She and Eden were planning to attack the pack. That's why I had to bring my father up, and also, why I had to intervene with the wolves."

"Can you tell me everything?" I asked. "I saw Luke swimming to Spruce... What happened?"

He stopped at the end of the driveway. "I'll tell you everything, but you have to promise me you're really up for it. You've been through a lot today—too much."

"I *am* tired." Weariness washed over me, but it was mingled with a deep, satisfying relief. To be back with James, to be safe—even with all the craziness that had occurred—was to feel whole. "But I want to be with you more than anything. I also want to know what happened tonight. Okay?"

"Okay. But you have to promise to tell me everything, too."

"I promise." I put my hand on top of his, and for the first time in a long time, all was right in the world.

James slowly maneuvered the truck down the road.

We passed the mini-golf course, the school, the store. "I spent the afternoon on the phone with my father, like I told you. Also, I was eavesdropping on my mom and Eden. When I heard what they had planned—a bloody attack on the wolves—I insisted my father come to the island. I also knew I had to get out in front of what she wanted. She and Eden were plotting to slaughter the entire pack."

I shivered and he tightened his grip on my thigh. "I couldn't let that happen," he continued, "so I made a pact with Luke. He was supposed to watch over you and make sure you didn't get into any trouble. I would sneak out without my mother knowing and go over to Spruce by myself. I wanted to see if it was possible to…influence…the shifters."

I wrinkled my nose. "Influence, as in *erase*? With your light—like you did the other day with Amelia?"

"Something like that." He shrugged. "I hoped that maybe I could at least soften their interest in us—make the details about my family fuzzy, I don't know. I didn't know if it would work, but I had to try."

"And?" I asked, genuinely curious. "What happened?"

James sighed. "Not much. It was a fluid situation—some of the family was inside the house, some outside. I never had a chance to try my light on enough of them to make it worth alerting *all* of them. Then Luke showed up on the property. I think that tipped them off, somehow, because all of a sudden, they left. And they were sneaky about it. We didn't realize that they'd fled into the water until too late. They were already on their way to you at that point."

James shook his head. "I'm so glad you're okay. I'm so *angry* that you almost weren't."

"James, I'm *fine*. But I don't understand why Luke went to Spruce—he texted me, saying he was doing something for your mother."

"That's because my father showed up. That's when my mother realized that I'd snuck out to see the wolves. She was so angry, she sent Luke to bring me back."

I nodded. "We saw him, you know. From the bonfire. Right after that, Mali said she had to leave. Now I know why—she shifted."

James winced. "I can't believe I wasn't there to protect you."

I leaned over and kissed his cheek. "You were trying to protect me by saving us all from a fight with the wolves."

"I came as soon as I could. It wasn't soon enough…"

"Yes, it *was*." I nestled against him. "You saved me. You saved us *all*. Everything is okay."

He sighed, put his arm around me and pulled me even closer. "You're giving me a lot of credit."

"It's nothing you don't deserve." I smiled up at him. "Eden helped too, you know. Maybe you could…forgive her?"

He laughed and shook his head. "How am I supposed to say no to you?"

I grinned. "Don't."

"I'm so lucky I found you. What would I do without you, huh?" He kissed the top of my head. "You're my reason, my everything."

I snuggled against him. "You don't ever have to find out what you'd do without me. I'm not going anywhere —you're *my* everything."

"Speaking of everything." James chuckled. "It's your turn to tell *me* every single thing that happened tonight. Don't leave any details out."

I shook my head. "It's so crazy. First of all, I had a feeling something was up with Mali earlier today. I didn't have a chance to tell you, but she bumped into us when we were hiking South Bubble."

James nodded. "Luke mentioned it."

"She did something weird when she saw him on the trail—she fixed her hair and cleaned herself up."

James glanced at me. "How is that weird? I mean, aside from the fact that she did it for my brother."

"Ha ha." I shook my head. "Sorry, I didn't explain it well. Her appearance just *shifted*. She didn't touch herself. When we first bumped into her, she looked kind of wild—her hair was a mess and she was all sweaty. Her shirt was dirty. Now that I know she's a shifter, I wonder if that's because she ran up the trail in wolf form, and maybe carried her clothes in her mouth… But anyway—once she saw Luke, her hair smoothed out all on its own. Her complexion instantly became less red, and then the dirt and sweat just kind of evaporated from her clothes like *that*." I snapped my fingers.

"Remember when I told you some of them can change their human appearance?" James asked.

"Yeah."

"That's a perfect example of their talent. They can make themselves more attractive. They can also completely morph their presentation, but I don't know if Mali has that particular talent. She might. I think these MDI wolves aren't the hicks my mother believes. I think they're a high-ranking squad."

"Woah. There are levels?"

He nodded.

"Well, I saw her *shift* shift tonight, too. After we saw Luke swimming, she left the party like I told you. I walked Amelia home, then I took Becky's truck and drove it down to the boathouse. I found your rowboat—I was going to take it out and try to row to Spruce, or something."

"What?"

"I didn't know what to do! All I wanted was to talk to you and see if you were okay. But you didn't answer your phone, and Josie wasn't picking up either. I didn't know where you were, or what to do."

James's eyes got huge in his face. "I am *very* glad you didn't try to row across the channel to Spruce. What were you thinking, Taylor? The currents can get wild. That's so dangerous."

"I just wanted to make sure you were okay."

He arched his eyebrows. "By drifting out to sea in the middle of the night? Great plan."

I groaned. "It ended up okay, didn't it?" When I thought about how the rest of the night had gone, it made sense to maybe not pursue that line of reasoning. "Anyway, that's when Becky showed up. She said she wanted to talk some sense into me."

"About what?" He frowned. "Is that what your dad meant when he asked if we were back together?"

I nodded. "I told them at dinner that we'd broken up. I wanted to see if that would push Becky's buttons somehow. I had a theory."

"Can we hit pause on that for one second?" We were only halfway down the Tower's drive, but he stopped the truck and put it in park.

"Sure...?"

He frowned. "Out of all the times something has scared me tonight, hearing you say that we'd broken up is right up there with the worst of them."

"What do you mean?"

"I don't...I don't know what I'd do without you, Taylor. I love you so much. I meant it when I said it before—it's a blessing that you came into my life." He brushed the hair back from my face. "You have a heart of hearts."

"So do you. I love you so much."

"Good." He grinned then kissed the top of my head. "Then don't ever say that we broke up again. It makes me feel sick. It makes me want to crush something."

"It's *fake*." I giggled. "But if it makes you feel any better, it makes me feel sick to say it."

He laughed, too. "Really?"

"Really. Although crushing something doesn't come to mind. Hmm, except for maybe my lips against your lips." I leaned up and kissed him slowly. He moaned, and I enjoyed the sensation of him melting beneath my touch.

I knew the feeling.

When I pulled back, I continued, "I *said* it because I wanted to see how Becky took it, and also, Mali. I was trying to force their hand."

"I like it—even though I hate it. That was very

cunning of you." He grinned and nudged me. "How'd it work out?"

"Um, I think you know. I was out in the woods surrounded by a bunch of werewolves until my big, bad guardian-angel protector came and saved me." I shook my head. "Anyway, where was I? Oh yeah— Becky. Down at the boathouse, I accidentally mentioned what I knew about Bryant Pierce and the apartment."

"Accidentally? Or accidentally on purpose?"

"Well, she pissed me off and then I accidentally blurted out that I knew the truth. Then I knocked her cellphone out of her hands. She started shaking again— she grabbed me, and I don't know, I panicked. I whacked her in the head with one of your oars."

"Nice." James sounded genuinely impressed.

"I carried her up the beach and stuffed her into the truck. That's when I ran into Mali. I was looking for you, so I drove down to the Tower. I was hoping you'd come back. But instead, there was a werewolf waiting at the edge of the woods. She tried to get Becky from me, but I didn't understand. So Mali shifted back into her human form and talked me into going into the forest with her and Becky."

We'd made it to the Tower. James turned the truck off, but he still clutched the steering wheel. "How did she convince you to do that?" I could tell he was trying to sound patient.

"She said that if I didn't go with her, the vampires would find her and kill her and Becky. She said if I stayed behind, Marietta might hurt me…" I shrugged. "I wasn't sure about that last part, but I knew they'd be in trouble if your mother found them out in the woods."

"Question." James scrubbed a hand across his face. "Why didn't you guys just take the truck and drive away?"

"Well, I didn't think it through at the time, but now I know." I frowned. "She said the forest was safer. But she was trying to lead me out to the middle of the island so that the others could ambush us."

"Mali better watch her back." James's voice was completely flat, lethal.

"James—no. She promised me she wouldn't hurt me, and she kept that promise. I think they were just going to kidnap me or something." I shrugged. "Maybe use me as bait to get to you. Even though I told them we'd broken up."

"They didn't believe you, huh?"

"No, they didn't." I leaned against his side. "Please don't hurt Mali. She told me a lot tonight. If you should be mad at anyone, it probably should be me."

"Taylor, *please*."

"No, I mean it. She told me that she'd been targeting me since she came to MDI. You were right about her—she didn't want to be my friend. She wanted to get to *you*."

He held me close. "She fought for you tonight. I might've been right that she had ulterior motives, but you're wrong: she definitely cares about you."

"Which is why you can't hurt her."

James sighed. "Which is the *only* reason I won't hurt her."

"Deal." I snuggled closer to him. "I guess we have to go inside, huh?"

He frowned as he looked at the house. All the lights were on.

"Let's just get it over with. C'mon." I nudged him. "The sooner we go in there, the sooner we're done."

"Fine." James looked sour. "But I'm putting everyone on notice: they can have a few minutes of our time, but then we're going to bed. *Alone.*"

"I'm not going to argue with you on that."

Hand in hand, we headed toward the Tower.

TERMS OF ENDEARMENT

IT WAS A GLORIOUS NIGHT, but I couldn't be dazzled by the moonlight on the water, or the stars stretching above our heads. I had to face the Marietta Champlain, who was probably none too happy that the houseplant her son was dating had survived yet another round of supernatural fighting.

I peered into the living room. Luke, Eden and Josie were on the couch. Marietta was seated in one of the armchairs, and Nelson paced the Oriental rug. "Where's Patrick?" I asked.

"I think he's still at his mom's. He's upset about Eden and, you know." James shrugged. "How she seems to like my brother."

"I don't blame him."

"Me either." James gave me a long look. "You ready for this?"

"Not at all." But I took a deep breath, then followed him inside anyway.

"There she is." Luke hopped up from the couch and embraced me. "I'm glad you're safe, Taylor."

"I-I'm fine." Luke released me, and I searched my friends' faces. "Are you okay, Luke? And Eden, are you better?"

"I'm fine—I was *always* fine." Eden seemed to pout a bit. "Like I told you guys, I *had* that wolf. I was just letting it bite me, so it thought it had the advantage."

Marietta snorted. "They outmatched you, dear. It happens. You'll do better next time."

"There isn't going to be a next time, Mother." James faced her. "We don't have to turn a battle into a war. There are other ways to handle this. We can talk to the pack. They have to know that we're not here to take over their land, or to fight them for position."

"No, that's exactly why *they're* here." Marietta straightened herself in her chair. "They want to destroy us, son. The sooner you open your eyes to that, the sooner we can act."

James sighed and looked at his father, beseeching him. "Will you talk some sense into her, Dad?"

Nelson Champlain threw up his hands. "I've only been trying to do that for the last century."

"Limit your drama, Nelson," Marietta sniffed. "It's so self-serving."

Nelson pointed at his wife. "I had to hold her back tonight. She wanted to go out and rain hellfire on the pack."

He turned to face Marietta. "Do you understand that we can't do that? We're the end game, darling. We're two of the oldest vampires in existence. If you and I go fight the local wolves, it'll spike a global war between the races. Do you want to report *that* to the council? Don't we have enough going on right now?" His gaze flicked to Luke, then away.

"I listened to you, didn't I?" Marietta didn't look happy about it.

"But you still sent your minions out to battle on your behalf."

"Um, Dad?" Luke adjusted the collar of his shirt. "I don't really appreciate the term 'minion.' It's a little emasculating, don't you think?"

Nelson just shook his head.

"There's something else we need to discuss. This is an inquiry directed to James," Marietta announced. "I need to know what your intentions are toward Taylor. They targeted her tonight. She's been marked for months by these wolves, just like I told you. I need to know how you're planning on incorporating her into your future plans."

"First of all, you make it sound like she's an item on a Champlain Enterprises agenda. She's not. She's the woman that I love." James pulled me close against his side. "Second of all, our future plans are none of your business."

Nelson's shoulder sagged. "Son, if Taylor's going to be in your life, we need to identify what steps we all should take to protect her. She's human—that automatically makes her a liability. No offense, Taylor. But if we can't determine where she fits into our family picture, it becomes a chronic problem."

"You know what, Dad?" James shook his head. "I am so sick of you. You pretend like mom's the bad guy, but you're just as guilty of overstepping and looking out for your own interests."

"Our interests, James." Nelson crossed his arms against his chest. "*Our* interests."

"I think what Mom and Dad are asking," Luke said, "is—are you planning on making her immortal? Or is she going to be a vulnerable piece of meat for the rest of her existence?"

"Really, Luke?" James laughed, but he looked pissed. "I thought you were finally coming around."

"I am. I *did*. I'm totally Team Taylor." He nodded toward me, an earnest expression on his face. "I love the girl, and I happen to think she's the best thing that ever happened to you. That's why I want to protect her. So long as she's human, she's fragile. I don't want to see you lose her, bro. That's all I meant."

They exchanged a brief look, then James turned back to his parents. "I am not prepared to end Taylor's mortal life. But so long as she'll have me, I will stand by her. I'm going to keep trying to be the man she deserves. And part of that means keeping her safe at all costs. Including being safe from *me*."

Marietta rolled her eyes. "That isn't a plan. That is a collection of earnest sentiments, which will only serve to get the girl killed."

"What Taylor and I choose for our future is exactly that—*our* choice." James eyed his parents. "As for the wolves, Luke and I will handle them. You two go back to the west coast, get things in order with the council. We can manage the MDI pack. Can't we, brother?"

Luke nodded immediately. "I know we can. I'm staying for as long as you'll have me—I want to help. We'll figure it out together."

"Exactly." James turned back to his parents. "Now if you'll excuse us, Taylor and I need some space. Thank you to everyone for the help tonight. Mother, feel free to be gone by the time I come back downstairs."

He hesitated. "Wait a minute—what happened to the wolf pups?" James asked.

When his mother frowned, he said, "Please don't tell me you drowned them."

"No," she said, "I did something worse than that. I got bored, so I started feeding them your raw steak. And then Eden set them up in one of the guest rooms—they've quite torn it apart."

"So we have pets." Eden smiled hopefully. "I hope that's okay!"

James didn't answer. Instead, he grabbed my hand and stalked upstairs.

We stopped at one of the guest rooms—we heard growling and barking inside. James opened the door a crack. Like errant rock stars in a hotel room, the puppies had trashed the place. The lamp was smashed, and they had torn apart all the pillows. There was a pile of shoes in the middle of the carpet.

"Eden," James bellowed, "you need to clean this place up and walk them!"

"Okay, James," she called back, her voice eager. "I'll do whatever you want! No problem at all."

James glowered, muttering to himself, until he pulled

me into his bedroom. Once he'd locked the door behind us, though, he seemed cheered.

"There. That's better."

I threw my arms around his neck. "It sure is."

He didn't hesitate. He kissed me deeply, pressing himself against me. I reveled in being so close to him, to feel the heat that came from his body mingling with mine.

We tumbled onto his gigantic bed and he sank his hands deep into my hair. He sighed happily as we broke apart. "I've missed you *so* much."

"Let's make a deal, okay?" I asked. "Let's not be separated again. Not *ever*."

He loomed over me, gazing into my eyes. "That's all I want."

"Me too."

He lowered his lips to mine again. They were soft and firm all at once. He deepened the kiss, his tongue searching for mine.

When they connected, I felt it all the way down to my core.

He pulled me on top of him and I relished the sensation of being above him, in control. I ran my hands down his solid chest, then kissed him deeply. Sparks shot through me. Just to be with him, to be held by him and to hold him, was the best thing I'd ever experienced.

I lost myself in the moment, in James. I was breathing hard when we finally broke apart. "I love you."

"I love you more, babe."

I sighed happily as he ran his hands over my hair and down my back. He didn't say anything for a minute. His brow furrowed and his blue-gray eyes seemed far away.

"What are you thinking about?" I asked softly.

He sighed. "That I *don't* ever want to be apart from you. I want to be closer. I want more."

"O-Okay." My heart thudded in my chest. I wasn't exactly sure what he meant, but I recognized the feeling: I couldn't seem to get enough of him. I hesitated. Then I asked, "Does that mean you're considering what your parents said? About…making me immortal?"

I held my breath as I waited for his answer. I didn't know what I wanted to hear.

"No," he said eventually. Then, "Yes."

James frowned. "I don't know. I don't ever want to turn you—I don't want you to go through the change, I don't want to subject you to this life, and I don't want you to have to distance yourself from your family the way Eden's had to. You deserve better."

He brushed the hair back from my face and stared.

"But?" I asked.

"*But* I don't want to ever have to live without you. I don't think I could bear it."

My heart lifted. I hadn't been sure what I'd wanted him to say, but that was it—the words I didn't know I craved.

"I don't ever want to live without you, either," I whispered.

He waggled his eyebrows at me. "Maybe we should start with a proper date night, huh? Or maybe a vacation somewhere warm, where *no one* can find us, and *no one* brings puppies. And then we'll get to the heavy stuff. What do you think about that?"

"I think *yes*. Can we go now?"

"I wish. We have some errant relatives and a couple of werewolves to deal with first."

He grinned, then kissed me again. Then he gently and deftly flipped me onto my back, propping himself up above me. He kissed me and then kissed me again. I ran my hands down his biceps, dizzy from all the kissing and his bulging muscles.

I moaned when he finally pulled away. "I want more," I whined. "I want more *now*."

"I know the feeling." His eyes glittered. "And I have plans for that—big plans. But not tonight, my love. Tonight you have to sleep."

"Not yet." I pulled him closer. "I'm not done—not even close."

He grinned down at me. And then he kissed me again.

I WASN'T sure what the status was at home: Becky went off-island, and Dad headed down to the co-op early. Amelia had plans with Brynn to make dance videos of themselves all morning.

"I heard you and James are good," she said.

"Yeah, we're fine."

"I knew it! You're like an old married couple." She winked at me on her way out the door. "Tell that hot brother of his I said *hi*."

"Sure thing, Amelia." I was so glad to be back with James, and rid of the werewolves for the moment, I couldn't even be annoyed with her.

The day was sunny, warm and bright. I went outside and smiled. Edgar cawed from a nearby tree. "Hey buddy." I still owed him some loot for saving me from Eden.

James came and picked me up in his truck. I couldn't wipe the smile from my face as we drove down to the Tower.

Josie, Luke, and Eden lounged on the deck. Nelson and Marietta had left earlier. We planned to spend the entire day out there, cranking music and enjoying the view. Josie confided that she was going to stay on the island for a while—Dylan was busy with school, and she didn't want to be stuck in the city when there was so much fresh air and excitement on Dawnhaven.

She gave Luke a wide berth. As he worked his way through several bottles of red wine, punctuated with flirting with Eden, he didn't seem too bothered.

Patrick didn't join us. He sent a text to James before lunch: *I'm still watching my mom. No signs of a change.* I vowed to ask James about it, but he kept kissing me, and I kept forgetting.

"You two are romantic today." Eden winked at us as she flounced to Luke's side. She grinned at him adoringly. "Would His Highness like some more wine?"

"He would." Luke smiled at her lazily. "And bring out the chocolates my mother left, I'm going to show you that eating can still be *fun*."

He checked her out as strutted into the house. I imagined she was sticking her chest out for his benefit.

"You haven't changed at all," Josie tsked.

"Have too." He grinned at her, but then his phone buzzed. It was sitting on the table in between us, and I glanced at it.

A picture of Mali appeared on the screen. I raised my eyebrows. "Seriously? She's *calling* you?"

Luke looked pleased as he picked up his cell and saw who it was. "You know the saying—*feels so good being bad*. Somehow it's more fun when it's taboo."

"You're unbelievable."

"True, true." He winked at me. "But if you'll excuse me, I have to take this."

He sauntered off to answer the dark-haired shifter's call, while the redheaded vampire fetched his drink.

And I just sat there, wondering what in the world would happen next.

A NOTE FROM THE AUTHOR

I TRULY HOPE you loved reading PROMISED! I love these characters and this world so much.

Coming next is Book 3, FAITH!

SIGN up for my emails at www.leighwalkerbooks.com so you get all my new notification releases!

DEAR READER

Thank you so much for reading this book! It means everything to me!

If you enjoyed *Promised*, please consider leaving a review or rating online. **Short or long, ratings and reviews help other readers find books they'll enjoy. Your opinion means a lot!**

Thank you again. It is THRILLING for me to have you read my book. I'm currently writing Book 3, *Faith*. There's lots more to come. Please sign up for my newsletter and continue with James and Taylor's romantic adventure!

xxoo

Leigh Walker

The Vampire Kingdom Trilogy

The Trade (Book #1)

The Pact (Book #2)

The Claim (Book #3)

ABOUT THE AUTHOR

Leigh Walker lives in New Hampshire with her husband and their three children.

Leigh has degrees from Suffolk University School of Law and the University of New Hampshire. Right now she's doing what she loves most—being a full-time writer and sports-mom!

Outside of writing and family, her priorities include maintaining a sense of humor, picking up her children's tube socks, and a busy Netflix schedule that includes Grey's Anatomy, Emily in Paris, and Chris Rock's "Tamborine."

She loves to hear from readers! Email her at leigh@leighwalkerbooks.com and sign up for her mailing list at www.leighwalkerbooks.com.

www.leighwalkerbooks.com
leigh@leighwalkerbooks.com

ACKNOWLEDGMENTS

First of all, thank YOU for reading this book! I hope you enjoyed the story. I truly loved writing it and I can't wait to share the next book, *Faith*, with you. I am so blessed to have people who read my stories. Thank you from the bottom of my heart.

I have to thank my mother, who has always supported my dreams and my writing. She's my number-one fan! How lucky am I? Love you, Mom!

Finally, thank you to my ride-or-dies: my husband, Bob, and our children, Carter, Max and Graham. Love makes you humble, and in this case, love keeps you in the kitchen, cooking and cleaning, so that you are forced to take breaks from your writing. (My writing. You get what I mean.) What's more humbling than living with a bunch of dudes who don't want to talk about your swoon-worthy angel-reformed-vampire hero and your obsession with crows? Nothing I can think of. Thanks for keeping it real, guys. Maybe someday one of you will make dinner. Maybe. Either way, I love you all. Thanks for being my reason.

Printed in Great Britain
by Amazon